absolutely fan...

'I absolutely loved everything about this book'

'Rebecca Raisin has a way of writing that is so evocative, it
brings each and every scene to life'

'Romantic, emotional, hilarious in places, but most of all
beautiful'

'Full of anticipation, a real page-turner. Loved it!'

'A good holiday read'

'Be whisked away on a beautiful adventure and pick up a copy
today!'

REBECCA RAISIN is a true bibliophile. This love of book morphed into the desire to write them. She's been widely published in various short story anthologies, and in fiction magazines, and is now focusing on writing romance. The only downfall about writing about gorgeous men who have brains as well as brawn, is falling in love with them – just as well they're fictional! Rebecca aims to write characters you can see yourself being friends with. People with big hearts who care about relationships, and most importantly, believe in true, once-in-a-lifetime love.

Also by Rebecca Raisin

Christmas at the Gingerbread Café
Chocolate Dreams at the Gingerbread Café
The Bookshop on the Corner
Christmas Wedding at the Gingerbread Café
Secrets at Maple Syrup Farm
The Little Bookshop on the Seine
The Little Antique Shop under the Eiffel Tower
The Little Perfume shop off the Champs-Élysées
Celebrations and Confetti at Cedarwood Lodge
Brides and Bouquets at Cedarwood Lodge
Midnight and Mistletoe at Cedarwood Lodge
Christmas at Cedarwood Lodge
Rosie's Travelling Tea Shop
Aria's Travelling Book Shop

Escape to Honeysuckle Hall

REBECCA RAISIN

ONE PLACE. MANY STORIES

HQ
An imprint of HarperCollins*Publishers* Ltd
1 London Bridge Street
London SE1 9GF

www.harpercollins.co.uk

HarperCollins*Publishers*
1st Floor, Watermarque Building, Ringsend Road
Dublin 4, Ireland

This paperback edition 2021

1
First published in Great Britain by
HQ, an imprint of HarperCollins*Publishers* Ltd 2021

Copyright © Rebecca Raisin 2021

Rebecca Raisin asserts the moral right to be
identified as the author of this work.
A catalogue record for this book is
available from the British Library.

ISBN: 9780008456986

MIX
Paper from
responsible sources
FSC™ C007454

This book is produced from independently certified FSC™ paper
to ensure responsible forest management.

For more information visit: www.harpercollins.co.uk/green

Printed and bound in Great Britain by
CPI Group (UK) Ltd, Melksham, SN12 6TR

This one is for you, Dad.
And Lily Marcon-Perez.

Chapter 1

Moonlight casts a pall of grey over London as late spring rain hits the office windows sideways, reminding me we should all still be tucked up in our warm beds, not here at work at such an ungodly hour. I rouse myself and try to jolly the team, even though I feel anything but jolly myself. The marriage proposal of the millennium is about to happen and we've all had to forgo sleep in order to be here because the surprise event is taking place in Tinseltown, no less.

It'll be livestreamed to cater to the happy couple's friends and fans alike. Celebrities, eh? They don't do anything by halves, which is where we come in: luxury concierge to the stars. Got a wish? We can grant it – as long as money is no object.

Excès curates exclusive, bespoke experiences for the super wealthy. Ever dreamed of having private access to the Temple of the Sun at Machu Picchu to propose to your paramour? Need front-row tickets to the Oscars but you're not in the movie biz? A wedding renewal with the Pope? Dinner for two at the Tower of London under the stars? Birthday flash mobs? The unimaginable is available for a hefty price tag. I bought a share of the luxury concierge club four years ago. Along with the other investors, we built our empire from the ground up and are still trying hard to expand the business and become the biggest name in the biz.

This darkened pre-dawn, the team gather around the table, stifling yawns, mainlining caffeine or eating their feelings with the smorgasbord of food I had delivered to bribe them all to be in attendance so bloody early. Sometimes I think the only 'refined' thing about me is my sugar habit, as I take another cinnamon doughnut and top up coffee cups. My bestie told me all about the clean-eating diet – but I lost interest when I found out it's not about consuming a family-size block of chocolate in the bath.

'It's nearly time!' I say, and dazzle everyone with one of my 'work rocks!' smiles. They're not fooled. They're just bloody tired and no amount of caffeine is going to shock them into faking it for my benefit. 'Are you ready for the proposal—'

'*Of the millennium!*' they all chorus robotically. OK, so they might have heard that one too many times. Aren't people down-right *prickly* when they lose sleep?

As far as proposals go, this one is fun and flamboyant and will be the envy of many a would-be bride. It's quite the coup for Excès because the couple themselves are famous and daily fodder for the tabloids.

Our groom-to-be, John Jones better known as JoJo, is one of the world's most bankable movie stars and, despite his advancing years, is still very much hot property. After a swift divorce from his loyal wife of twenty-five years, he hired Excès to mark this new stage with all the bells and whistles.

I'm a hopeless romantic and adore seeing love bloom for my clients, but, in this instance, part of me cringes that his ex-wife is bound to see the new lovers flaunting their romance to all and sundry. I guess I'm not the moral police; I'm just a luxury concierge doing her job as best she can. It's not my place to judge.

Still, I secretly grieve for the forgotten first wife. Will she flick on her telly later and relive her heartache once more? I shouldn't be worrying about that. But what happened to good old-fashioned romance, and making marriages go the distance? I'd probably be out of a job, that's what, so I grin and bear it, even though it nags at me from time to time.

'Is Harry going to tune in?' my assistant Victoria asks, taking the seat beside me.

My fiancé Harry is tucked away on some tropical island with music sensation Carly C. She's a new client of ours, a reality TV personality turned global superstar. A touch of pride runs through me as I remember when I announced I'd managed to get her to sign up with Excès – but she chose Harry to help with her album launch because he's so well connected in the music industry.

Carly C is a magnet for the tabloids for all the wrong reasons: boozy nights out, online spats with other celebs. You name it, Carly C has done it, although part of me admires her sassy attitude. She is a breath of fresh air in a world full of faux personalities. What you see is what you get and she doesn't pretend for anyone. That being said, we'd thought it'd be safer with her stashed away on an island to launch her album and shoot a behind-the-scenes documentary.

Trouble is less likely to find Carly C there because she can't exactly fight with other celebrities when the internet is unreliable! Her reputation has taken a battering in the press, so having her show her softer side and capturing the 'real' Carly had been a brainwave of Harry's. And he sold the streaming rights for the documentary for a bomb …!

I lift a shoulder. 'Harry'll try and tune in I guess, but the Wi-Fi on the island is patchy at best.' It feels so strange not to be able to check in with him, especially now with all this going on. 'It only works when it wants to.'

'A bit like Harry,' Victoria says and then quickly covers her mouth. 'Sorry.'

I smile. 'It's OK.' It's a running joke around the office that Harry swans in and out without doing a lot of work. But his job is to make people more *pliable*. He's our chief schmoozer and

3

client wrangler and sadly the office staff don't really see that side. They hear about him jetting off to exotic locations almost daily to meet with managers, owners or a board of directors, to wine and dine them and grease the wheels so the impossible becomes possible. I can see why people envy him, but deep down he's lovely and I thank my lucky stars he chose me. Although he can be a bit of a diva himself, if I'm honest …

I'm more of a homebody when I'm not working. I hate wearing high heels and fussing over fashion. My idea of a fun day out is scouring vintage shops for my philatelic collection (stamps and postage material) then finding a cheap greasy spoon to eat at. Harry, on the other hand, prefers the finer things in life: designer labels, micro food at macro prices and being seen at all the latest hot spots. I guess the old adage is true that opposites attract. I sometimes find myself staring at him as though he's speaking another language that I can't quite decipher. I'm a small-town gal, and he's this larger than life big-city go-getter. We're like the perfect rom-com couple brought to life.

Tonight's epic proposal is Harry's baby. He was the one to secure JoJo and sell him the dream, including peddling all the rights to the media for an obscene amount of money. La-La Land, eh?

Harry vowed this would be the proposal of the *millennium*, emphasising the word until everyone obviously tired of hearing it. Soon after, he flew off to a remote island with Carly C leaving me to do the rest of his job while he's away. I'm *always* doing someone else's job; I can't seem to set myself any boundaries or say no. I suppose it's because I want Excès to be a success and if I don't take up the load, who will?

More staff rush into the room and snatch seats, mugs of coffee and buttery croissants. Their excited chatter eases the tension. Everyone is eager to see what Harry's magicked up for our celebrity couple.

'Here we go!' Louisa from marketing says.

Our movie star JoJo appears on screen, new girlfriend in tow. She's a few decades younger than him, and I can't help but notice he's dyed his salt and pepper locks jet-black. Hand in hand they stroll down Hollywood Boulevard. Stars twinkle overhead, while the moon dips low. They're the epitome of superstardom, dressed to impress, not a hair out of place and their toned, tanned bodies glow even under moonlight. They look a million bucks and my heart just about explodes when I think of the surprises about to unfold.

When they arrive at Grauman's Chinese Theatre, JoJo stops to point out the stars lining the Hollywood walk of fame. I hold my breath, knowing what's coming is quite the achievement for a B-grade actress whose greatest claim to fame is a long-running sitcom where she plays the cliché ditzy blonde. To give her credit, the show has longevity, coming into its tenth season and she can act; in fact, I think she holds the show together. I admit I binge-watch it on occasion and am always left in stitches afterwards – she's got great comic timing and I hope JoJo with his connections will help catapult her onto the next rung of superstardom.

Hidden cameras pan in on our actress as JoJo points to the latest pink terrazzo and brass star bearing her name: *Chastity Cocker*. How on earth Harry managed such a feat is beyond me, but I'd hazard a guess a lot of money greased palms. The pink stars are supposed to be sacrosanct – but that's Harry for you. He could buy Warner Brothers itself before anyone was any the wiser.

Chastity's hands fly to her face and with a squeal she jumps up and down, which concerns me when she's wearing five-inch stilettos with an ice-pick heel. How don't they snap? If it were me, I know they'd break clean off and I'd topple into the only puddle around for miles, screaming like a banshee and making a fool of myself. Some people have all the luck.

She flings her lithe frame into JoJo's loving arms and lands a kiss on his lips. Before it can deepen, a troupe of showgirls with big feather headdresses prance down the steps of the theatre and onto the boulevard singing Etta James' 'At Last' as theatrically as it deserves.

Chastity has love hearts for eyes, and I heave a sigh of relief. As far as magical marriage proposals go, this is hitting the mark. A crowd has formed, recognising the celebs. They hold phones aloft as they follow the lovebirds down the boulevard. It strikes me they must be used to people tagging along, as if they're a tourist attraction. They don't even blink as the crowd around them thickens. I guess it's all part of being in the spotlight, but it'd be my worst nightmare. There's a lot to be said for being invisible.

JoJo eventually stops in front of the Dolby Theatre where the Academy Awards are hosted every year. The red carpet has been rolled out and he moves Chastity along it, as paparazzi scream into view and snap their pictures as if the awards *are* truly happening. It's all a farce, of course, but Chastity is lapping up all the attention as if she's won an Oscar and is about to thank the Academy itself.

'This is so sweet!' Victoria chimes. It really is, and makes me wonder if my very own fiancé is a little more romantic than I had him pegged for. I'd expected grand gestures, but I hadn't expected quite this level of starry-eyed expression of love drama, which is exactly the type of thing these cashed-up stars thrive on.

'Right?'

'He's done a great job appealing to all the things Chastity loves,' Victoria continues in awe. 'And pulled out all the stops to make sure this goes off without a hitch.'

'I didn't think he had it in him to be honest.' We laugh good-naturedly at Harry's foibles. He's usually more into the adrenaline junkie side of things – if you want to jump out of a perfectly good plane over the Grand Canyon, or zip line across Tokyo, Harry is your go-to guy.

He doesn't usually take on marriage proposals. Even ours had been very low key. He'd dropped to one knee over an Indian takeaway in our apartment. A nice surprise, but very simple, right down to the plain gold band that he said suited me since I'm not flashy and didn't need diamonds to know my worth. But a girl wants a diamond at least once in her life, right? And if not at her engagement, then when? Anyway, I'd just laughed it off and said yes, thrilled to marry him, and that was that. We're engaged three years later and still haven't had time to sort our own wedding out.

The paps take their shots and then disappear to beat the pack and sell their pictures. A guy wearing a bright neon ensemble approaches, and asks Chastity the time. She takes out her phone to check, not knowing it's a cue for the flash mob who start singing and dancing to Bruno Mars' 'Marry You'.

'If that's not a clue, I don't know what is!' Victoria says, her eyes ablaze at the theatrics of it all. Flash mobs are kind of passé now, but JoJo insisted, claiming Chastity would adore it. And what's not to love about flash mobs? Passé or not, I think they're fun.

Dancers circle Chastity and she soon joins in, while JoJo stands on, smiling wide like all his Christmases have come at once. When the number is over, a limo appears and the two are whizzed away to the Hollywood sign on Mount Lee. A drone flies overhead filming their journey so we can only guess what they're talking about in the limo.

'OK,' I say, while I nervously eat a handful of sugared almonds. 'This is the big finale.' The limo pulls up and the driver helps Chastity from the car, as she sips on champagne and looks up at the bright sign that so many dreams are made of.

A close-up of their faces reveals wide eyes and beaming smiles. Chastity will die when she sees what's coming next! I only hope JoJo has remembered the ring – a huge pink diamond that cost more than a small island and was just as hard to procure.

On the lawn sits a Persian rug, Louis XVI chairs and Queen Anne tables as if they're in their own little chateau and not on the side of the Hollywood Hills. The limo driver returns with an ice bucket and obligatory bottle of Cristal and tops up their flutes before disappearing.

Camera people now close in, and Chastity laughs. 'Is this being livestreamed or something?'

'For posterity,' JoJo agrees and clinks his flute against hers. 'Pretend they're not here.'

She leans in and kisses him in such a way that I'm sure it's going to be blurred on the replay. *Holy guacamole.*

'Jeez,' Victoria says. 'She looks like she's about to eat him!'

'She does!'

They finally break apart. 'I want to find a man who looks at me the way JoJo looks at Chastity, like she's a soft juicy bao bun,' Victoria says, her voice wistful.

There are a few titters around the table and we hold our breath once more as fireworks explode from the top of the Hollywood sign. 'How did he get permission for *that*?' Bailey from HR asks.

'He's a great negotiator.' *Money, money, money.*

I hold my breath as the big reveal creeps closer. JoJo turns to Chastity and bends on one knee, before whispering, 'Look up,' just as a plane flies across the sky above the Hollywood sign. Light grid mantles under its wings illuminate the night sky and spelled out in lights is the pièce de résistance:

Will you marry me, Sarah?

It's the most beautiful thing ev— Wait.

Sarah.

SARAH!

Nooooooo!

The breath leaves my body in a whoosh. No, no, no! I close my eyes – maybe I've imagined it in my fatigued state. When I wrench my eyes open to check, I see confusion dash across Chastity's face, which is swiftly replaced by a dark cloud of anger.

Her eyes flare with a rage that makes me shrink down in my seat.

'Is this some kind of sick joke?' she says in a menacingly low voice. JoJo has gone white with shock. What do I do?!

'Melanie!' I screech to our media guru and slam my hands on the table, making cupcakes launch upwards in surprise. 'Make it stop! Turn off the livestream, get those cameras out of there. Shut it down. *Shut it down now!*' Melanie hurries from the room, the others from her department follow close behind, barking orders to each other.

Onscreen, JoJo is chasing Chastity, trying to explain and letting out an expletive or two about Harry and the whole 'damn gang at Excès' – oh dear – 'who are clearly incompetent!' But she doesn't listen. Instead, she throws herself into the limo and tells the driver to make haste, but not in so many nice words. The limo skids out of the park leaving a bereft JoJo standing alone with just his long face for company. And then, praise the Lord, the screen goes black.

Chapter 2

This is a PR disaster! 'Sarah is JoJo's *ex-wife's* name! Do you think Harry just got them muddled up?' Wild thoughts swirl as I wonder how to contain this. I stand and pace around the room. 'How could this have happened?'

Victoria shakes her head. 'Harry's royally stuffed up, he has.'

'How could he make such a careless mistake …?' My former sugar high is now a distinctive low.

Victoria grimaces. 'Can you imagine how Chastity feels? This epic marriage proposal, dancing girls, walk of fame star, flash mob and fireworks, with his ex-wife's name up in lights while it's being *livestreamed!*'

'None of that is good.' Faces around the table are downcast. No one knows quite how to react. It's not a good sign, not a good sign at all. 'Can you check online? See what's being reported and then we can work out how best to spin this?'

She swipes at her iPad and gets to work. 'It's *everywhere* already.'

I rub my face; this is not a good start to the day. 'OK, how can we play it? What can we do to minimise the embarrassment for JoJo and Chastity?'

Tapping her chin with a pen, she says, 'What about showing

close-ups of the walk of fame star, the smile on her face, how happy she was dancing?'

'Yes,' I say. 'Tie that in with some stories about how she came from nothing and is set to be one of the world's most-loved actresses? Let's highlight her philanthropy work. If we can drown out today with all the good Chastity has done, we might swing this back around. Didn't she give a season's salary to a women's shelter last Christmas? Let's remind everyone about that.'

'This error is dynamite for every news outlet, Orly, but I'll do my best.'

'I know, the vultures!' I groan. 'Get onto to every reporter we're friendly with and let's get them sharing. Other celebs too. Who's she close to? Find out and start sending gifts and get them to tweet about how beautiful the proposal was, send them the first part of the video, minus the ending and let's get that online and boosted as much as we can.'

'Good idea.'

There's no time to ruminate; I need to start damage control with the couple themselves. I'll send flowers, I'll send money, I'll send a private jet! No, I'll send a posse of rescue pups for them to play with and make an obscenely large donation to their favourite animal shelter! I'll do whatever it takes to fix this while I wait for Harry to return from his island adventure and start the grovelling process himself. It irks me he's absent at such a crucial time. It's a pattern with Harry and the other business partners. They presume I'll fix their mistakes because I always do.

I call Harry and leave a voicemail: 'Harry I need to speak to you urgently—'

The voicemail cuts out and a recorded message tells me his mailbox is full. My head is about to explode – just what is he doing? Surely there's a Wi-Fi signal *somewhere* on the bloody island! Today of all days I'd thought he'd find a way to tune in.

The remaining staff leave the boardroom on pretences of having a busy day, and work to do. Victoria pats my shoulder and says, 'Let's move to our office.'

We spend the entire day attempting to make amends. I send exotic fruit and expensive champagne. I hire them a suite at the Chateau Marmont and fill it with luxury gifts. But it's no good, they've gone into hiding. I call Harry and his phone is still infuriatingly off. The story is reported throughout the day on television and social media.

Reporters gleefully discuss the disaster, the juicy livestreamed *'Cocker Love Cock-up'* a ratings win and a play on poor Chastity's surname – yikes. Memes start circulating. Gifs are next. I want to cup my head and cry. Nothing we do stems the tide.

Day turns into night and I field calls from JoJo's lawyers threatening to sue. I beg, cajole and bargain for more time, insisting that it was a gross error and that we're investigating it. All steps will be taken to punish the person responsible. Who knows, maybe it wasn't Harry? Maybe it was someone who has it in for JoJo or Chastity? It's too late to fix it, but I make all the enquires I can and alarmingly everything circles back to Harry.

When the airport emails me a copy the sign-off form with Harry's signature in thick cursive, I slump on my desk. It's right there in black and white: *Will you marry me, Sarah?* with Harry's approval.

It's a mistake anyone can make, of course, but it's not acceptable in our line of work. We have staff who double and triple check everything, yet Harry insists on going rogue and doing it all himself. And now look!

'You've done everything you can to mitigate the mess,' Victoria says, giving me a look usually reserved for lost puppies. 'Why don't you head out and meet Maya for dinner like you're meant to? They can still call and threaten you as you're walking, you know.'

Somehow, I laugh. 'Yes. Yes, they can.' I let out a world-weary sigh. 'I don't think there's anything else I can do now anyway. I've tried everything. It'll be up to Harry now. He's probably sunning himself on that bloody tropical island, blissfully unaware that this place is falling like a house of cards.'

'That's Harry for you.' She gives me a long look.

'Yeah.' I don't even have the energy to think of an excuse for him. 'I'm *so* late to meet Maya.' She's my best friend and we meet for dinner religiously at the same time every week.

'Go,' she says more forcefully. 'Maya won't mind. You're always late.'

'True.' I nod. 'OK, see you tomorrow?'

'It's Saturday tomorrow.'

'Right, sorry.' Suddenly, I envy her being able to have two days – forty-eight blissful hours – away from work.

'Have the weekend off, Orly. Seriously. Switch your phone off for once. Harry wouldn't think twice about ignoring calls if something like this happened to him. Why don't you try it?'

'I wish. What *does* my schedule look like for the weekend?' Everything else has quite flown out of my mind.

She sighs. 'It's bloody busy.' Swiping through her iPad she says, 'Tomorrow you're emcee for the charity luncheon at the Ritz.' Oh bollocks, I'd forgotten about that. Usually Harry emcees but I had to agree on account of him going away. Public speaking isn't my forte; I'm more of a behind-the-scenes kind of gal. 'And then you've got the industry cocktail party at Bars on Barges. The end-of-month reports are due, and Harry chalked you up for those.'

Of course he bloody well did! 'How can I hide, with all that going on?' I groan. 'The industry party will be a nightmare!' A room full of industry experts with this juicy gossip swirling about the room and still no Harry to face up to it. 'Is anyone else from Excès going?' I hope and pray.

'No, just you.'

'Waaah.'

'Don't go, Orly. You're busy with other things anyway. Just don't do it.'

'I have to go or it'll look bad for Excès.' When I give my word, I don't ever renege on it – something drilled into me by my father who said the one thing we can never break is our word. If you commit to something, you follow through. Dad died relatively young, when I was only ten, so those little adages have stayed with me. And I'd feel like I was letting my dad down if I started breaking my promises. That's something I won't do.

'See you on Monday.' I air-kiss Victoria and take my bag, then dash outside into the balmy evening air. Always running late, late, late!

I glance at my watch and continue down Brompton Road, past Harrods whose concertinaed green awnings resemble eyes half-closed for slumber in the inky night.

I walk then hobble, ruing the fact a cab would crawl even slower in this traffic. It gives me plenty of time to consider the fact my career isn't quite as gratifying as I'd once imagined it would be. In fact, it's a great big migraine-inducing nightmare.

Eventually I see the bright lights of the West End. Bars and restaurants heave. The streets of Soho are packed with late-night revellers. People clutch cigarettes and spill from pubs into alley-ways, their laughter punctuating the chilly night. Music blares from unseen speakers as I dodge tipsy executives who give me slow lazy smiles.

I turn down a cobblestoned lane and slip past a trio of friends wearing kilts who dance and sing as if all the world is a stage. Gosh, I love London. It's a melting pot and anything goes. But tonight, all I want to do is eat spicy dumplings with Maya and decompress.

'Sorry, excuse me, can I just … sorry.' Ever the apologetic Londoner, I slink through, imagining my first sip of wine after a very long week.

Maya is a cardiothoracic surgeon. We met by chance at a charity fundraiser a million years ago and we've been firm friends ever since. She's always around when life gets impossible or when I just need to sink a few gins and forget about the world.

As I stumble on my heels, wishing I'd changed into trainers, I finally see the little yellow lantern of the hole-in-the-wall Chinese restaurant we've been meeting at on Fridays since forever. They make the best mapo tofu dish in London. Owners Huan and Bai took us under their wing and are like surrogate parents. They always insist we eat more, fuss over us and are sweet and protective. They have a gaggle of their own children, now grown, who work at the restaurant and one who works as a neurosurgeon in the same hospital as Maya.

Bai sees me and commits to a launch hug. For a diminutive woman she packs a punch when she envelops me in her arms and squashes the air from my lungs. I make a sound like 'Ooomphfzwark …' before she frees me and I drag sweet precious oxygen back to its rightful organs. 'Hey, Bai, how are you?' I say, gasping.

Her eyes are wide with worry. 'Maya is crying – you have to hurry.'

'Crying?'

'Quick, quick. She needs you.'

Bai points to our usual table in the back. The flickering candle highlights Maya's face: mascara trails track down her cheeks and her exotic dark eyes are sunken. What on earth? Her earlier confirmation text message hadn't given any of this away. I flick my mobile on silent so the barrage of incoming calls buzzing away won't disturb us and then I rush over.

'Darling!' I drop my bag and move to hug her. 'What's wrong?'

She sobs, the kind of can't-catch-your-breath tears that imply she's been at this for some time. I hastily sit opposite and take Maya's hand, unsure of what to do. I can count on one hand the number of times she's cried like this and usually it revolves around losing a patient. She's more of the stiff upper lip variety, essential in her job.

'Did something happen at work?'

'He's gone.'

I rack my brain about who she could be referring to and then I realise. *Oh no!* 'Ernest?'

She gives me a trembling smile with the barest of nods.

'Oh, darling, I'm so sorry. What happened?'

She lifts a shoulder as if it's just one of those things. 'His daughter just called me to let me know … It was actually quite peaceful in the end. He drifted off in his sleep at home surrounded by his cats and that little barky dog of his.'

Poor Maya. 'Without you, he wouldn't have had all that extra time, but he *did* because of the excellent way you mended his broken heart.'

'I just did my job, but I love the way you romanticise heart surgery. He was the best. A true gentleman.'

Maya had been treating Ernest off and on for years. His ticker gave him trouble, then he had a stroke, but he had an indomitable spirit and never gave up in all of his ninety-plus years. They'd grown close as Maya had moved up the ranks and he'd been in and out of her care. While Maya tried to maintain a professional distance with her patients, some managed to creep into her heart, and jovial old man Ernest was one of them. Every Friday Maya regaled me with Ernest stories and I knew I would miss hearing about the incredible man.

'It's hit me so hard. I can't imagine not seeing his dashingly suited self, propped up by his cane wandering the corridors, asking if it wasn't too much trouble for a pot of tea.'

'He was lucky to have you.' I don't know many surgeons who'd scoot off and make a patient a pot of tea. In the end, Ernest would often pop in to visit Maya, making some excuse or other when he just liked having a mug of tea and some sugary biscuits with his pretty doctor who carved out a slice of time in her busy day and gave it to him.

'I was the lucky one.'

'You both were.'

She balls the napkin and averts her eyes. 'I hate that I didn't get to say goodbye.'

I squeeze her hand. 'But that's the sweetest part, darling. He didn't die after an emergency visit to hospital; he wasn't hooked up to machines and heart monitors. The last time you saw each other you shared a slice of cake and waxed lyrical about your day. And rather sweetly, he slipped off peacefully surrounded by his menagerie of fluffy critters … As far as deaths go, that's a pretty good one.'

'You always know what to say.' She takes a deep breath, her sobs slowly abating. 'Work will be that little bit less shiny without Ernest popping in to visit.' Maya exhales long and loud as if releasing some of her grief. 'Sometimes I wonder whether all the heartache is worth it.'

I stare her down in a maternal way and say softly, 'Darling, you're fighting the good fight. Look at how many *lives* you've saved! Your work matters.' Despite feeling low tonight, Maya loves her job. She thrives in the pressurised environment and always goes the extra mile for her patients. While days like today are impossible, she always bounces back.

'So does yours, Orly.' Maya knows I've been struggling with work lately and the lack of meaning I find in it.

It's not comparable to saving lives. Not even close.

I fidget with the paper napkin. 'Sometimes I feel I'd like to do something more meaningful. But then I think of how hard I've worked to get to where I am and I wonder if I'm having some sort of mid-life crisis. Shouldn't I be grateful? I dreamed of this high-flying London life but it all seems so … different to how I imagined.' I feel ridiculous moaning about such a thing after Maya's day, but here we are and I wonder if the distraction about my crazy life will help her bruised heart.

Maya nods. 'You're *right*. I can't even remember when I last enjoyed the view from my apartment. Or when I caught a show at the theatre. When I walked just for the hell of it, not because I was racing to get back to the hospital. There's never time.'

I cluck my tongue. 'We're burnt out at the ripe old age of thirty-five.'

'Looks like it. How will I ever have a baby when I'm already too tired?!' Her boyfriend Preston isn't exactly dad material either, so part of me is relieved that there's no time for making babies. He's openly bigamous and doesn't care a jot if Maya dislikes that or not. She deserves so much better than him. Conversely Maya's dream has always been to have a houseful of babies, which she's been saving for since forever. I only hope she'll move on from Preston to someone who deserves her. But then again, when would she have *time* to meet someone new? Like me, Maya works crazy long hours.

'Right?' Deep down I recognise this as a huge problem. We've spent so long striving for these lofty goals and lost ourselves along the way. We should be enjoying our youth, soaking up every ounce of pleasure in one of the most amazing cities on the planet, but there's never enough energy for all that.

'Today I went to work with two different shoes on! I had to pretend it was all a ploy to distract my patients, then I spent the rest of the day acting like some jokester so they didn't think I was losing my marbles and take my scalpel away from me!'

'Oh, Maya! You need some downtime!'

'We both do.'

'Right? Give me a bubble bath and a good book and I might last a chapter before I sink into oblivion or my phone inevitably rings and startles me back to consciousness.' For Maya, it's even more hectic. Double shifts and long surgeries in a world where time is of the essence and there's just not enough doctors to go around.

Maya flicks her glossy mane of curly black hair. 'What *would*

18

you do though if you didn't have a share in Excès? If you could just forget everything and do what you wanted to do?'

'Retire ...?'

She laughs. 'At thirty-five?'

I toy with the empty wine glass in front of me. 'No, I'd be bored. But seriously, I have these wild thoughts of escaping. Throwing it all in and going back to a small town and doing something that actually *helps* people. But how? Doing what exactly? And what if I hated it?' I shrug. 'Maybe I'm just well overdue for a holiday.' But I know it's more than that. Some days I feel like I can't catch my breath and anxiety makes me dizzy.

'What does Harry think? Is he feeling the same?'

I think of my curly-haired fiancé, with his dark broody eyes. I'm still shocked he proposed; part of me always thought we'd have this fleeting passionate romance that would burn out because Harry is so fickle – always on the hunt for the next shiny bauble. But then he surprised me by proposing and making grand life plans that we've never quite got around to.

'Harry has no idea. You know what he's like; he thrives on his high-octane life. Flying here, there and everywhere, barely taking a breath. I haven't seen him for ten days now, actually. He's been on a private island with Carly C, helping meet her every whim while she's launching her album and filming a behind-the-scenes-of-fame documentary thing, sort of like Beyoncé did.'

'Celebrities.' She rolls her eyes. 'Let's hope he's not meeting her *every* whim.'

I giggle. 'She's engaged to some YouTuber, isn't she?' You'd think I'd follow the tabloids in order to keep one step ahead, but very rarely do they get it right. I've learned it's much like every-thing in the shallow world of celebs – a big, fat lie. Usually a marketing ploy.

'I have no clue about Carly C.' Maya laughs. 'But you should talk to Harry, tell him how you're feeling about things at work. That you feel like something is missing.'

I lift a shoulder. 'Maybe. He'll just tell me I'm being dramatic.'

'Which is ironic since he panders to people who only eat the blue M&M's.'

'Right?!'

'How are you going with your plans to buy a property in the country? Is he still keen on that idea?' Harry and I sat down a while back and had a heart-to-heart about our dreams for the future and where we saw ourselves in five, ten, fifteen years. Our plan had been to save for a sprawling country property, a place that could become a sanctuary; a wonderland where we could safely raise children and have a nest to commute from. Once again, it was all just words. Promises like vapour, diaphanous and fleeting.

You can't help who you love though, and I adore him despite our differences. It's those differences that leave me enthralled; the way Harry takes charge of a room, charms everyone – men and women alike. His utter confidence that things will always go his way. It's quite blinding being in love with such a guy, almost like staring at the sun at times.

'Time has marched on and we're still no closer to buying a place. He never commits to any viewings, and definitely never has the time to spend a weekend attending open houses …'

I don't tell Maya I still spend every Saturday morning scouring the internet for my dream home even though Harry's got cold feet about it. 'It's hard to explain but I can *see* myself in that new lifestyle. A big old house with high ceilings, a roaring fire, Vinnie the little rescue pup at my ankles, maybe some adorable fluffy chickens so I could forage for eggs for Sunday brunch. Time to pickle vegetables from my garden, make chutneys for grazing plates when friends from town visit, that kind of thing. A simple life, where our children can climb trees, play chase and breathe fresh country air. Wouldn't that be the perfect tonic for burnout?' But am I dreaming? Is it pure fantasy when Harry won't even attend viewings?

'It would and it sounds bloody lovely, Orly. Who wouldn't want that?'

'Maybe Harry ...?' I consider the day from hell, his absence. It feels as though something has shifted between us and my love for him has dimmed a little. Like staring at the sun doesn't so much blind me but instead burns. I change the subject because talking about my would-be country house causes an ache in my heart – it's like I can *feel* it's the right move and yet I can't convince Harry. 'Have you heard the latest celebrity gossip around the hospital today?' I ask, knowing she probably hasn't. Maya is old-school when it comes to technology – she rarely uses social media and spends her downtime exercising, of all things. If there's a juicy story in the press about one of our clients she'll usually hear it via the nurses who fill her in on life outside of the wards.

'No, I haven't, darling. Did something happen?' So I tell her all about the so-called proposal of the millennium and everything that followed. Her jaw drops. 'It was livestreamed? Oh God, Orly, he *didn't*!'

'He did.'

'How could he get Sarah and Chastity mixed up? That's taking distracted to a whole new level.'

I nod. 'And now he's nowhere to be found.'

She clucks her tongue. 'Just like bloody always. Darling, it's not fair that he scarpers when he sees fit and coincidentally it's always when he's made some huge cock-up. Why didn't *you* go with Carly C?'

I shrug. 'She chose him. He's such a magnet for celebs – he can talk the talk whereas I'm better in front of the computer sorting out all the headaches. I don't actually mind that though,' I say truthfully. 'I can't parade around with their entourages and take it seriously. It makes me feel all sorts of awkward; I'd feel like this gangling bird tottering behind these glamorous over-the-top characters. Harry loves that side, so it's best left to him.

Anyway, let's not ruin the evening with any more talk about boring old work.'

'Darling, we can park that conversation if you want, but it sounds like you had a really stressful day. I'm worried that you're always left to fix things with very little support. I know you all have your own clients, but you all share in the successes and it's like they ride your coat-tails when it suits them and you're on your own when it doesn't.'

Bai's son pops a plate of prawn crackers down and I take one, crunching it into a million pieces over myself, while Maya delicately eats hers without a crumb in sight. 'I know, I need to get harder, tougher, but when I'm in the thick of it I'm just in problem-solving mode, you know?' What else is there to do except fix it as best I can?

She tilts her head. 'You don't need to change, Orly. They do. Especially Harry, who should be by your side when things like this happen.'

I take a bottle of wine from my bag, a freebie from the office. 'Red?' I ask, knowing Maya is right but not knowing what to do about it all.

'I'll stick with Chinese tea. I'm not feeling one hundred per cent and a wine headache will only keep me up. But I've heard—' she peers at the label '—*Congratulations Mr and Mrs Deely* is a great vintage.' She gives me a megawatt smile. Maya is one of those health-conscious types and doesn't usually partake in a lot of alcohol. Her way to deal with worry is to run, a much healthier stress reliever but not one I'd subscribe to.

'The best! Perks of planning fancy weddings at Claridge's, eh?' I laugh as I fill my glass with the exotic red, which is actually a pricey little quaffer, and top up Maya's tea. 'Here's to Ernest, one of the finest gentlemen to walk this earth.'

Maya clinks her cup alongside my glass. Her eyes fill with tears. 'May he rest in eternal peace back with his beloved Betty.' I think about the man I never met, but feel I know. He cherished his wife and talked about her every single day, even decades after she died. That's the kind of love affair I want, one that lasts a lifetime.

'Why don't we start planning *your* wedding?' Maya asks gently. 'That'll give us something fun to do, something to drag us out of this rut we're in.'

'Maybe …' I say, when I really mean no. The thought of my own wedding just seems so abstract; I can't picture it for some reason. I don't have time to ponder why as tiny Bai's thundering footsteps echo behind me.

Our favourite tofu dish is presented to us and I smile. Bai determines what we need to eat and we duly comply by hoovering up every last delicious morsel. Usually, she'll feed us something *to put colour in our cheeks*, or *meat on our bones*. Wordlessly she continues placing steaming dishes in the middle of the table and then hugs Maya whose eyes pop out of her head from the pressure. 'Now eat, girls, eat, eat; you need to put some colour in your cheeks and some meat on your bones.'

Chapter 3

The interminable weekend finally comes to a close. I'd fielded calls from reporters around the globe until my phone went into heat-saving mode and switched off. The charity fundraiser had been a disaster when a drunk guest stormed the stage to speak, knocking me from the podium hard enough to hurt my pride and my derriere. Then of course the Bars on Barges industry party went off with a bang, the smell of fireworks and muddling down the Thames too much for my constitution, so I spent most of it in the loo with seasickness. Or maybe it was embarrassment – who knows. When the barge moored, I'd been the first off, and zoomed down that gangplank with about eleventy billion industry vultures in my wake asking whether the 'Love Cock-Up' was all a publicity stunt.

Maya had popped in for a visit late Sunday evening. I'd finished the weekend over a few too many G&Ts, while clever Maya stuck to sparkling water. Always the voice of reason, she let me vent away as I sucked down gin like *that* would help matters.

Today, I head into the office regretting my life choices. Why, oh why didn't I choose sleep over drinks? Water, yoga, vitamins, even. I'm not just burning the candle at both ends, I've doused it in petrol and set fire to the whole bloody thing. Mondayitis is here with a vengeance, just like always.

As I bump along in the taxi, I make all the right sounds to my client on the phone: 'Gerald *is* our number one client, *of course* he is,' while only half listening as I scroll through social media on my iPad looking for news on JoJo and Chastity.

The paps have managed to get some snaps of Chastity in the loving arms of someone *other* than JoJo. I slap a hand to my face. What looks to be drone footage has caught them overhead next to a glittering blue swimming pool. Chastity wears a skimpy bikini bottom and not much else. Her version of damage control, I guess, proving she's lovable in the eyes of another. Poor JoJo. He is besotted by her and now she's done a runner to salvage her pride.

As the taxi creeps through the heavy traffic of London, I check my emails. Still radio silence from Harry. As my street comes into view I pop everything into my bag, all the while murmuring, 'Yes, yes, *of course* I can, yes,' to my client.

With my mobile phone pressed hard to my ear, I mouth my thanks to the driver, tap my credit card to pay and dash from the taxi, as always running late, late, late. I hurry past the designer boutiques of Mayfair before stopping out the front of the Excès office to catch my breath. It feels like I've given *decades* of my life to the cause. I'm bone-weary of the bloody place.

'Are you still there, Orly?' a shrill voice admonishes me down the phone.

'Yes, yes, Sylvia, I'm here.' Shivering through a cool summer morning, I gaze up at our swanky office. The sight used to leave me enthralled – *we made this thing* – now it just leaves me feeling weighed upon. I should be grateful, but instead I'm exhausted. Perhaps I need a vitamin injection or flat shoes or a weekend of reordering my stamp collection or … something.

'Gerald really wants to impress Coco, and I mean *really* impress. Do you think you can top your previous efforts?'

Sylvia's tone suggests I cannot.

'Yes, I know I can,' I say, oozing confidence. 'We will exceed every expectation he has.' I cross my fingers it's true. Each experience seems to get more outlandish; soon I'll be taking bookings for luxury trips to Mars. But that's my job, right? Say YES and reach for the stars!

Being a people pleaser has its disadvantages but it's crucial in my line of work. I put out fires, cajole personal assistants, butter up glum celebs, and dance around the office with a big cheese-eating grin trying to rally the troops. 'Let's make today our best yet!' Lately though, it seems that I'm getting lumped with all the problems while the partners swan off early with flimsy excuses.

Maybe I need to toy with the word *no* more often.

'He deserves only the best. And forgive me for saying this but we're not sure if *you're* the person to provide that. Are you?' Sylvia brings me back to earth with a thud. 'It's all over the news here about your disaster with JoJo.'

Really, it's a miracle we have any clients left so I do my best to get through this.

'Oh, JoJo sees the funny side,' I lie with a chuckle as if we're all in on the joke. 'Plus that wasn't *my* proposal.' I firmly throw Harry under the bus for the sake of the business and pull the phone away from my ear and suck air deep into my lungs. 'JoJo isn't one of *my* clients.' *Fix this, Orly.* 'I do hope you'll give me a chance to prove I'm capable again.' The words roll off my tongue sweet as sugar but inside they feel hard as marbles.

Gerald is a multi-millionaire techy on the cusp of billion-airedom, who uses our services every time he has a new girlfriend he wants to propose to. Which is at least twice a year. The guy just can't settle with one woman and is always extravagantly asking for their hand in marriage before the relationship stales and he's alone again.

Word is, Gerald is a bit of a control freak, a tough-talking belligerent type, but I wouldn't know. I've never spoken to the man. I deal directly with his PA Sylvia, who isn't all that saccharine herself. Being one of the elite mega-rich means he's also never happy. Nothing ever quite lives up to expectation. God could drop from the heavens and walk on water and he'd complain about the view, but my job is to pander to his every whim and grin and bear it.

'Well, let's see how well you put together a proposal for the getaway and we'll go from there.'

'Sure. What did he have in mind?' I ask as I walk towards the double doors and am welcomed in by Jorges the doorman who gives me a toothy grin. I pretend to doff a hat as I slide past and make a mental note to review Jorges' contract. He's been with us since inception and always has a smile for our clients. He's probably overdue for another raise.

'A private jet to Paris, all the bells and whistles. Caviar, Strottarga Bianco, unless there's something more luxe that you know of?'

I roll my eyes, grateful we're not on a video call. Gerald doesn't even *like* caviar. He buys the most expensive brand and to date no one on any of his proposal jaunts has ever eaten it. The staff report back and tell me how delicious it was, a little perk for them for working so hard at making our experiences go off without a hitch.

'Caviar, check. I'll look into what's trending.'

'Champagne, a crate, Dom Pérignon.'

'Perfect choice.' I stifle a yawn. I'd only snatched a few hours of sleep in the end because there'd been a problem with a booking in the States that I had to fix with my fuzzy gin head and all. Luckily it had only taken me the better part of two hours to resolve so our client, one of the most famous retired basketball players on the planet, could surprise his second wife with a week at the Bellagio and private access to his very own high roller room. My eyes water thinking of the cost and all the extras his

PA ordered for their week. *Just do it*, I'd been told, spare no expense. And so when there was a miscommunication and our sports star was left waiting, I had to fix it and fix it fast even if it was the witching hour for me – no rest for the wicked!

It's funny because I used to dream of having these luxury experiences for myself; now I dream of a full uninterrupted eight hours of sleep.

Sylvia continues, 'They'll dine in Paris itself, I'll come to that in a moment, but gourmet finger food on the plane would be ideal. Nothing messy. He *doesn't* want a repeat of last time. You won't drop the ball again will you, Orly?'

As if it's my fault that last proposal Gerald dropped the contents of a Chinese soup spoon directly onto his white Versace shirt. It wasn't even soup, but hoisin roast duck and salad, made in delicate mouthful-sized portions presented on elegant porcelain Chinese soup spoons.

'No, you can trust me, Sylvia, I won't make that mistake again.' I try hard to sound contrite. It's all part of the job. We all know it's not my fault but I accept responsibility because, in their eyes, I'm at the bottom of the ladder in this equation. *Le sigh*.

'He wasn't very happy, you know ...'

I hold in a groan. I know. He briefly tried to sue me over it before Harry schmoozed him into a more malleable mood. Note to my future children: law is where it's at these days.

'I regret that every day and I can assure you it won't happen again.' I'll pay for someone to hand-feed the damn man if I have to. At my desk I mouth *Sylvia* to Victoria, who grimaces and takes my bag from my shoulder.

'Well, as long you know, he's giving you a second chance here.' She speaks to me as if I'm an unruly child who needs taking into line.

Kill me. 'I won't let Gerald down, I promise. And I'm *so* grateful for another chance.'

'*Last* chance.'

'Yes, I completely understand.' I count slowly to ten and focus on breathing so my head doesn't explode.

Victoria presses a coffee into my hand and I shoot her a grateful look.

'I'll email you everything else he needs for the plane: flowers, masseuse, string quartet, the usual, but for the proposal itself he insists on having the Eiffel Tower closed to visitors – and he'd like to propose to Coco at the very top, perhaps in the Le Jules Verne restaurant – also to be closed to others. A luxe degustation of the chef's signature dishes afterwards, perhaps? *Can* you make all of that happen, Orly?'

Oh bollocks. Usually my clients' wildest dreams are possible, simply by throwing a fat stack of cash at the powers that be, but the Eiffel Tower is a prickly one. We've been rebuffed there before. Closing the entire structure down for hours on end is usually impossible unless it's booked years in advance. But if I don't make this happen for Gerald, we'll lose him, and as fussy as he is, he's not really different to any other of our high-flying, mega-wealthy clients. They assume that they'll get what they want, because they usually do. I wish for my bed. I don't seem to have the energy for this today – I suck down caffeine hoping it'll shock me back to life.

'Orly? You're not exactly convincing me with all these long silences.'

'Sorry, there's … a lag on the phone line. Yes, I can definitely make it happen,' I say and hope to golly Harry flies back in today and I can lump him with these gargantuan problems so I can go and eat my body weight in gelato.

'Gerald requires the best suite at the Ritz, with a spa experience in the Chanel au Ritz, front-row tickets to Opéra de Paris. Coco would like a haute couture experience with a designer, maybe Christian Dior himself if you can arrange that?'

I shake my head at that. 'Christian might be hard but I can definitely find—'

'Hard? I *thought* you made the impossible happen?'

'You're right, but even *I* can't magic him back to life, Sylvia. He died back in the Fifties.' I grin to Victoria, who smothers her laughter. 'But let me find someone of equal stature if not *better* for Coco.'

'I feel like you're already letting Gerald down, Orly.'

'I'm sorry, truly I am.' I bite down on my bottom lip to stop laughter swelling. Sometimes the ridiculousness of these situations just astounds me. So Christian Dior died sixty-something years ago and now I'm letting Gerald down?!

'Very well. Make a proposal with anything else you can think of, leaving a two-hour gap twice a day so they might wander Paris itself *organically*.'

Code word for: get sozzled in their suite. 'Great idea. I'll get back to you ASAP.'

'*Sooner* please.'

'Of course.' How did I end up here? These experiences don't spark joy anymore, they start a regular run-of-the-mill migraine.

We ring off and before I can blink an email comes through from Sylvia stipulating Gerald's every whim for a weekend in Paris, right down to the type of glassware he deigns to drink from.

This is going to prematurely age me.

He wants bouquets of Gold of Kinabalu orchids which are extremely rare and sell for around four thousand pounds a stem. A stem! With all my might I try not to think of where that money could be better spent – like feeding children in developing countries, building wells for water in war-torn cities, supporting refugees. I let out a long scream-like sigh. 'Eughhh*hhhhh*!'

'Was she a total harridan about soup spoon gate?' Victoria asks, her blonde locks falling over a shoulder.

'It was mentioned.'

Victoria grimaces. 'And pray tell, where is the proposal to take place this time?'

with too and I only wish our rich clients practised more philan-thropy rather than just taking selfies in their Gulfstream. But who am I to talk? I help them achieve this!

Victoria makes a note and continues down the list.

We spend the next few hours going back and forth about our clients' needs before we're ready to start on Gerald's proposal. I glance at the clock and wonder where Harry is.

'We need more coffee,' Victoria says, eyeing her to-do list.

'And keep them coming ...' As she swishes off to the coffee machine, I dial Harry's number but it goes straight to voicemail again. It doesn't say his mailbox is full, so at some point he must have emptied it.

I leave a message: 'Where are you? Call me please. Now I'm starting to worry you've been kidnapped and held for ransom and at this stage there's not a chance I'll be exchanging my hard-earned money for you.' I laugh, part of the anger defusing at the thought of his return. 'See you soon. Bring me a bagel if you know what's good for you.'

He's probably lost his charger again, or stopped at home and fallen into a deep sleep. Something doesn't feel quite right, but I remind myself that Harry isn't the most reliable person in the world, and his way of dealing with stress is ignoring it until it all blows over ...

There's work to be done with the JoJo fiasco, so I take a deep breath and prepare to eat humble pie, which definitely won't taste as good as the bagel I've been craving, and dial JoJo's lawyer's direct line once more ...

'Hello, Mr Kingston, it's Orly from—'

'I know who it is. We're filing a suit against Excès for breach of ...' Mr Kingston then goes into a long monologue about everything he plans on suing us over and I eventually give up trying to interrupt, especially when I don't understand the compli-cated legalese.

When he finally takes a moment I say, 'OK, I understand. If

you've informed our legal team then there's not much else I can do except to apologise once again and let you know none of this was done maliciously. I'd love to tell JoJo myself if he'd consider taking my call?'

'No.' His voice is gruff. 'You've done enough damage. Any communication can be done through me.'

'Right, thanks for your time.'

He hangs up without another word.

'No luck?' Victoria says.

'Just a whole heap of *bad* luck. Can you email our legal team and ask them what they've heard and what they suggest my next course of action should be? I probably should leave it to the lawyers now but part of me wants to personally get hold of JoJo and plead our case. Ask them if they think that's wise.'

'Sure, I'll do that now.'

Chapter 4

The day flies by and turns too quickly into evening and still no sign of Harry. My forgiving mood soon dissolves.

I'm weary right down to my bones but figure he's not going to come into the office this late anyway. I ponder it all, fatigue making me doubt myself. 'You don't think he's fallen in love with some impossibly gorgeous back-up dancer, do you?' I'm half joking but it's the longest we've been out of touch and it's unusual not to hear from him.

She guffaws. 'When he's got an impossibly gorgeous English rose? I think not.'

I'm sure I'm anything but, with bags under my eyes so big I'll probably have to pay an excess baggage fee next time I fly, but I appreciate the confidence boost. Despite Harry's man-about-town persona I've always trusted him around other women. He says things like: *it's us against the world*, which makes me feel like we're a team and can flit off here and there but know our hearts belong with each other. He's not the type of guy to keep secrets – he's too spontaneous for that. He loves the thrill of the chase, instant gratification, but he gets that through work, securing big stars and making their dreams come true.

I've always thought one of the reasons he loves me is because

I'm so different to the people he rubs shoulders with every day. I'm not an attention seeker; I prefer to stick to the periphery, and that's why we gel. I'm the place he goes for calm, and he's the place I go to feel alive.

'You're a gem, Victoria. Thanks for today.'

'You're welcome, now scoot and go get some rest.'

We hug goodbye and I grab my bag and head out into the darkness to hail a cab. 'Paddington, please.' I fall inside, making small talk with the cabbie about the state of the world, politics and the dubious summer weather.

When I get home Harry's nowhere to be found. His mobile goes to voicemail again so I pour myself a glass of red big enough to fit my head inside and run a steaming-hot bath, sure that he'll walk in at any moment with that rueful grin of his and a million excuses.

In the bath, I guzzle my wine, which has an almost anaesthetic affect. My limbs grow heavy and my knotted shoulders slowly loosen. I take a minute to figure out where it's all gone wrong lately. Why do I dread work when once it buoyed me up? From the other room my phone bleats. *Bloody Harry.* I should know by now every time I throw myself into the bath, like clockwork he'll call. Reluctantly I leave the perfumed water, wrap my robe tight and race to the kitchen to answer.

'Harry, I was—'

'It's Maya.'

'Hello, darling,' I say. I go back to the bathroom to rescue my steamy glass of wine and take another swill, but am surprised to be met with silence.

'Maya, are you there?'

I can hear her quick breaths down the line.

'Is Harry home?' she asks.

'No,' I glance around the still apartment. 'Not yet, why?'

I hear an audible intake of breath. 'It's probably nothing.'

'Spit it out, Maya. When someone says it's probably nothing that means it's a giant drama of epic proportions. He's upset *another* client and they've gone to the press?' Then another more worrying thought hits. 'He's OK, isn't he? He's not hurt or anything? Has he been admitted to hospital?' Maybe Maya recognised his name on an admission?

A bitter laugh escapes Maya. 'No, no I don't think anything could *ever* hurt Harry. I'm at your apartment; buzz me up.' There's a strange tone to Maya's voice and I wonder why she's here. She usually works late on Mondays, catching up on weekend admissions.

I press the buzzer so Maya can catch the lift to the tenth floor while I dash into the bedroom to throw on some clothes. Just as I pull my hair into a ponytail, the doorbell chimes.

'Hey,' I say, frowning at Maya's ashen face. 'What's wrong?'

She bustles past me. 'There's no easy way to go about this, so I'm just going to rip the plaster off, OK?'

'O-K.'

She grimaces then pulls her mobile phone from her handbag and fiddles with it. She then takes out a bottle of wine from the Mary Poppins-style oversized tote; a very fancy vintage she usually reserves for celebrations. But by the look on her face this does not feel anything like a celebration. Not even close.

'This is the *Daily Sun* online edition. I'll give you a minute.' She pushes her phone towards me like it's contagious and looks everywhere but me.

Flummoxed, I stare at it and within seconds my world implodes. 'NO!'

'It might be nothing, right?' She wrings her hands. 'It might just be a shoot thing; he could be an *extra* … He could be a *place holder*.'

In a perfectly filtered candid photograph is my Harry locking lips with none other than Carly C herself. 'An extra? A place holder?' My voice rises hysterically.

She screws up her nose. 'Like you see in the movies. You know, someone to replace the actual actor until they're ready to shoot. He might be a stand-in, a—'

I close my eyes and hold up a hand. 'Darling, thank you for trying to spare me, but we can clearly see—' the vision of them pressed against each other is burned into my retinas '—that Harry is a bloody lying, schmoozing pig of epic proportions! He's got his hand up her top for crying out loud! What's he looking for – his bloody CAR KEYS? The meaning of life?'

I flick through the article and it gets worse – ten-page spread worse. My gut roils as I realise this will be available on newsstands as well as online soon enough. 'Oh my good God.' My hand flies to my mouth. 'It says the *Daily Sun* reached out to me and I responded with no comment! I didn't know it was about *me*, I presumed it was about JoJo and Chastity! Urgh, I'm a fool!'

Desperation dashes across Maya's face and I sense she has no idea what to say – I wouldn't either if our roles were reversed. 'Maybe it's …'

I continue reading:

Carly C's 'hands-on' romp with mystery man!

Reality starlet turned pop sensation Carly C was spotted getting a thorough frisking from a mystery man who turns out to be none other than Harry Highland from luxury concierge club Excès. 'We're in love,' the raunchy performer announced to pals holidaying with her on a remote tropical island. 'He tells me it's us against the world.' Another source close to the star says, 'They can't keep their hands off each other.' Carly C is currently producing a music video and documentary and it's thought that Harry Highland is there to help with his very demonstrative hands-on approach! Harry was formerly linked with joint owner of Excès, Orly Taylor, who recently made headlines for 'cocking up' movie star JoJo's proposal to actress Chastity Cocker. A close friend of Carly C told the Daily Sun *this PR disaster is what drove Harry into the arms of Carly C. The* Daily Sun *contacted Ms Taylor for comment but she declined.*

For all that is holy – not only has the damn man cheated on me but somehow I've got the blame for the JoJo disaster? I fall onto the sofa in a screaming heap and flick through the many, many, *many* online pages of Harry and Carly C's brand-new 'Smokin' Hot Island Tryst' love affair. I can tell the very moment my heart shatters. It feels like it's splintering my insides. Will this kill me?

'He told her it's *us against the world!* Is that a line he used with all of us? I trusted him!' I can't get air into my lungs. 'I'm *dying*, Maya! Get the … paddles!'

'What?' She looks alarmed.

'GET THE PADDLES!'

'Do you mean the defib? I don't carry a *defib* around! Are you really in pain?' She goes into doctor mode and pushes me flat, taking my pulse or something. I don't know because I've briefly left my body and am floating just above, while below the pale-faced me thrashes and bucks as if Maya is *actually* shooting electrical currents through my body. Dramatic or what?

'Call it, Maya,' I say groggily. 'Code red, it's a damned code red!'

Maya stands and shakes her head. 'This isn't a code red, Orly! This is your standard bastardy code break-up.'

'Right. I didn't know there was a code for that.'

'There isn't.'

I slowly return to my physical body as the shock wears off. It's soon replaced with white-hot fury. 'How *could* he?'

Maya opens the wine and tops up my glass and pulls me to a sitting position. 'Here, I can assure you this is purely medicinal. Drink.'

I slug it down; Maya *is* a medical professional after all. She sits beside me. 'What's your game plan?'

'My game plan? How many steps ahead am I required to think? I don't know, maybe we could start by cutting out the crotch of his Armani pants, then move on to …'

She nudges me. 'He'll just buy more.'

'Probably with my credit card.' I mentally berate myself for trusting the flirty philanderer! 'Didn't people warn me off him? Like Lisa the barista, who makes his unicorn latte with micro foam every bloody day, even though she despises him! Baristas always know – they're like hairdressers. She told me to be wary of him, that he'd left a trail of broken hearts in his wake.'

'That should have been your first clue, Orly: a man who orders a unicorn latte has clearly got secrets!'

'Right? And remember my ex-client, Sasha? The one with the fancy car?'

'The girl who pours herself into those tight-fitting plastic dresses?'

'Yes, the rich one. She warned me off him too. Told me he was after her money, but of course I didn't believe her, because how can you take a person seriously with teeth that blinding white?'

'Harry's teeth are blinding white.'

'*Exactly!* They're so phony – just like the rest of his body parts!'

'What?'

'His hair, dyed by the way, his nose has been fixed, his cheeks, his jawline, his butt!'

'NO! Really? How did I not know this?'

I shrug. 'I didn't know either until I found a stack of photos of him with his parents and asked if he wasn't an only child like he'd always said. I thought maybe he had a brother who died, or something tragic, and the sad thing is he let me believe that for a while, until I came across a school picture with his bloody name on it and let me tell you overbite is not the word. Let's just say his orthodontist probably paid off his mortgage with the amount of work Harry needed. How did I manage to ignore this?'

'*Love-drunk* is a thing and you were clearly *blotto*. Happens to the best of us.'

I sigh. 'I always thought he was faithful, because he promised me. Told me all these stories about how he'd never felt this way before, how the women in his past were flings, all the rumours were just gossip-mongering because he hadn't felt a real connection with them, like he felt with me. He spun that yarn so well I believed every word.' Tears spill over. What an idiot. He used the same lines on all of us. 'Do you think he's been having it off with our clients the whole time? Other women when he's been away?' He's such a flirt, but did he take that to the next level every time he was away from me?

She shudders. 'Surely it would've got back to you if he did?'

'Would it though? I feel sick.' I clutch my stomach. Do you ever really know anyone? 'I don't want to see him, ever again after this. Ever. Again.'

'You need to think ahead when you're dealing with a snake like Harry.' Maya has never liked Harry, but she's never denigrated him in front of me before. I guess all bets are off now he's broken my heart.

My mobile rings and I freeze. Maya picks it up. 'Private number.'

'Answer it.'

'Hello, this is erm ... Orly's assistant.' She scowls. 'No comment.' Maya swiftly ends the call.

I groan. 'It's started already?' The press will want my side of the story. Little ol' nobody me. 'I'm never going to live this down. How will I show my face at the office? I'll be a laughing stock, a fool, a—'

'Stop right there. *He's* the laughing stock, the fool, a complete and utter cockwomble who only thinks of himself. Really, Orly, you're better off without him. And tomorrow you're going to march into Excès, shoulders back, head high and you're going to take charge, just like you always do.'

'I can't.' I groan and hold my head in my hands. First JoJo and Chastity and now this!

'You can and you will.'

'I hate him.'

'We all hate him.'

Despite my poor ravaged, splintered heart, I smile. 'Thanks.'

'You're welcome.'

'Do you think it's real? It can't be real. It's a holiday fling at best.' But what does it matter? He can't just go around having holiday flings now, can he?

Her lips are a tight line before she says, 'I know you love Harry ...'

'Loved.' But I can't switch it off just like that, as much as I want to. When I think of him my heart seizes just like it does on the rare occasions Maya drags me to one of her boxing classes.

'Right, loved, but I honestly think as horrible as this is, it's so much better you found out what sort of man he is before you exchanged vows and had a brood of chubby-cheeked children and a mortgage up to your eyeballs. You guys are so utterly different. You can't take him back after this, surely?'

'No, I couldn't. But what if there's an explanation? Could there be an innocent reason for this?' As soon as the words slip out I regret them. How can he explain away their faces being glued together, his bloody roving hands ...

Harry's the cad, the man about town, and I'm the homebody who likes binge-watching Netflix and drinking too much tea. He's the swarthy, well-manicured, designer-label-wearing metrosexual, whereas I'd be happy to live in my yoga pants if I could get away with it. While I have to look a certain way at industry events and when I meet with clients, I don't enjoy that side of things. High heels are the work of the devil and I only wish everyone else would get the memo so we could all wear flip-flops or wellies and be done with it.

No wonder Harry's left me for the ultra-glamorous Carly C! I've never fit in with the London circuit because I'm two shades too quirky but it's never really bothered me because I only cared about my job, not the social circles I'm not admitted to. If being friends with someone in society hinges on what type of holiday home I own (none) then I know they're not the right kind of friend for me, but people like Harry crave that kind of acceptance. Really, the writing has been on the wall since I moved here; I just didn't translate it.

'You mustn't let this destroy your self-esteem, Orly. Let this be the catalyst for change.'

'Yeah,' I say, still feeling utterly dazed. I'm reminded of my earlier hesitancy about arranging our wedding. Maybe deep down I always knew this would eventuate.

She falls beside me on the sofa. 'You need to make a plan and move forward with your life. And the first thing I suggest is finding a replacement. A bookworm, one of those cute spectacle-wearing corduroy-trouser types who smells a bit like fresh washed linen and coffee. Update your social media with lots of hot broody photos of him.'

'What? No.'

'Yes, straight back on the bike.' She nods. 'You're such a gentle soul. You're the one who always makes sure everyone is all right; it's time you found someone who does that for you. You need an arty type, a creative soul, a deep thinker.'

'Wow, is that *it*? You don't have any other specifics?' I laugh in spite of it all. 'I'm never trusting a man again as long as I live!'

'Not even a poetic, sultry-lipped, long-haired, nice-smelling *bibliophile*?'

'Not unless he's fictional. That's about my limit.'

'What about if he collects stamps?'

'If I ever find a man who collects stamps, I'll know he's the one. But so far, all my philatelist friends are eighty or ninety … Trust me, as far as hobbies go it's waning in popularity.'

'I can't think why. I do love your eccentricities though, you philatelic, you.'

'You know the nerd words, which by default makes you one of us.'

'Only by association.'

'That's close enough for me.' My life as a philatelic, a collector of stamps and other postal material, started when I received my first postcard in the mail at ten years old. It struck me as magical that it'd winged its way to me all the way from India. How did it not get lost, that tiny little rectangle amidst all the other mail? Paying its way, the even tinier rectangle, the statue of King Rajaraja Chola. It spoke of other worlds, far-flung places, exotic lives that were being lived and it all seemed so foreign and exciting from my little patch on earth. My dad had recently died and I think part of me imagined these letters coming from him – maybe he was still alive on another plane, another realm, anywhere as long as I could still hear from him. Of course he wasn't, but that's how my love of collecting was born.

My mum had moved on with another man quite quickly and those little squares were a tenuous link to my dad, the man I loved and missed so much.

Whenever I have bad days, you'll find me in front of my collection because it has the ability to remind me that the world is a big place, and it will keep on spinning whether a client yelled at me or not. It reminds me there's always an escape. I don't have to stay in one place forever – I can transport myself like a stamp, across vast oceans, over sunburnt plains and start anew. Like now, I remind myself. I'm not *affixed*, if I don't want to be …

I take a glug of wine and then another as I think of showing up at Excès tomorrow. It's not just the shame that bothers me, it's the job too. 'Really, Maya. What am I *doing* with my life? It's all a sham. A great big exotic sham. It's got so bad I started to believe in my very own lies, that I've been living this wondrous life, when really it's as empty as one of Harry's promises.'

'You're just …'

I don't wait for platitudes. 'I snatch a few hours here and there and guzzle alcohol to "relax" and then get back on the merry-go-round of big-city living and for what? I can't think of the last time I had a lie-in, or took a Pilates class. Looked after my body

44

and soul. Instead, I'm pandering to the most self-absorbed of society, hating every minute of it, when I could be doing something meaningful. Something that sparks joy instead of migraines. Even choosing Harry, really, what was I thinking? Practically all the inhabitants of London have dated him and I didn't think that might be a *sign*?' A big, fat flashing neon sign saying run. RUN! 'But of course, my answer to everything: Yes, sir, three bags full, sir. Urgh.'

'You're upset.'

'I'm *furious*. But I think this has happened for a reason, Maya. Don't you? I'm so over Excès, the *excess* of it all! Ordering an orchid stem that could pay for a well in a developing country. Having iPads coated in 24K gold for celebrity babies, when some children have no access to *books* to read! Pimping out private jets so they match their owners' moods when we're in the middle of an environmental catastrophe. *I'm an enabler*. Maybe this is a sign from the universe to change my life before I get stuck for good in the rut I made.'

'Change it how?' A deep frown forms and I know Maya thinks I've lost my mind.

'Dramatically. You shocked me back to life when you used the paddles, Maya, and this is going to be my rebirth …' I grin, believing every word, even if I don't know *exactly* what it means just yet.

Panic flares in her eyes. 'But I didn't use the paddles …'

I smile. 'I'm not going to be the *yes* person anymore. I'm not going to pander to rich people with bad manners. I'm not going to put up with a fiancé who cheats. I'm going to start saying no to people!' I think of our dream, a rambling country property that we'd do up in stages, bring back to life. Could my dreams come true as a singleton? Why the hell not!

The phone rings and I snatch it up.

'Is this Orly?'

'NO!' I say and hang up, realising I have zero idea what I'm going to do with my life but knowing deep in my heart I'm making the right decision.

It's time to be the curator of my *own* life!

A few hours later Maya leaves and I take out the delicate folders that house my philatelic collection. I find such solace in it. It's proof of the passing of time. How things inevitably change. That these little squares have been ferried all over the world, have their own mysterious provenance and I'll never know just what that is.

Did this Penny Black Queen Victoria stamp carry a love letter from a husband to his wife? What about this envelope addressed in perfect curlicue calligraphy to *Agnes Merriweather* – did it deliver good news or bad? What happened to the letter that was inside the envelope – does it still exist?

These are the treasures I hunt high and low for, knowing one day that I'll reunite letter to envelope, or postcard to owner, and the world will be a little brighter because these mementos matter. Love can be shown in many ways, and these relics from the past prove it. People die and life moves on, but they're not forgotten if we have their treasures.

Chapter 5

The next day, pictures of Carly C and Harry are everywhere. There are salacious articles about me, with wildly inaccurate stories. If I wasn't so devastated, I'd be howling with laughter. I've been accused of everything from selling secrets to gossip mags, to having affairs with celebs I've never even heard of – it looks as though Carly C's PR team are doing their utmost to discredit me, so none of this sticks to her and damages her launch.

They've managed to find old photos of me that are hugely unflattering – I look demented. I wonder how I'm ever going to get through this as I swipe the article away and hope it's obliterated forever.

But there's plenty more just like it all over the internet. And of course, there's a stack of flattering photographs of the new lovebirds themselves. I guess Harry and Carly weren't too concerned about having an audience every time they canoodled, which by the look of all the pictures popping up over social media, was all the damn time. His betrayal feels like a kick in the gut made worse by the attention from the media.

My phone rings and I brace myself until I recognise the number.

'*Guten Morgen*, Orly. I hope I haven't caught you at a, erm … bad time but I was wondering if Hans' dinner meeting was all sorted?' Gretel's heavily accented voice is more hesitant than usual.

She knows! And she's a PA to a German diplomat working out of the US. *I will never live this down.*

'Good morning. Yes, yes, it's all organised,' I say sweetly to Gretel. 'I'll email you the itinerary, and all Hans has to do is arrive promptly at 8 p.m. at the Museum of Modern Art in New York. They'll have staff to greet Hans and his partner on arrival, with champagne of course.'

'Lovely, Orly. And the dinner will be in front of the painting?'

'Yes, a romantic tête-à-tête in front of Vincent Van Gogh's *Starry Night*, including a bespoke degustation menu prepared by a celebrity chef so they can take their time and enjoy the evening, which is exclusive to the two of them.'

The proposal is simple as far as they go and I always enjoy working with Gretel.

'Sounds divine. Thanks again. I'll wait for your email and invoice and get that paid immediately.'

'You're welcome.' We ring off and I send the details to Victoria and ask her to forward all the relevant information to Gretel before I finish getting dressed and head out to grab a taxi. I haven't even heard from Harry but word is he's shacked up with Carly C in her mansion – just his style. What kind of person doesn't even call to talk?

My phone bleeps with a text and I swipe to find one from Maya: *Remember your worth. You're not running away, let him do that. Love you xxx*

The morning feels surreal, as though I'm living slightly outside of myself. Despite my own catastrophic love life, I still need to sort out JoJo too.

Inside the warmth of the cab I text Maya back: *Thanks darling xxx*

Soon enough I'm delivered to the usual corner. I thank the driver and take in a deep breath, centring myself before I make the walk into Excès.

Jorges blushes as he holds open the door. 'Morning, Orly. I just wanted to say ...'

Here we go ...

'Thanks for the raise. It's much appreciated with the new grandchild on the way and all.'

I let out a breath. 'You're so welcome, Jorges. It was well overdue.' Maybe not everyone knows ... small mercies and all that.

Victoria sees me, her face sombre. She rushes up with a mug of coffee and gives me an awkward hug with the other arm. 'Good morning,' I say, and take the coffee as if it's just any other day.

'Orly.' She rubs the back of her neck. 'I saw the ten-page spread in that sleazy rag ...'

OK, scratch that, the entire world knows and I'll just have to live with it.

I do what I always do and throw myself into work. The day lasts forever but I manage to hide in my office for the most part and Victoria keeps the press at bay. I'm humbled by the number of emails from clients, who all wish me well and tell me the same thing along the lines of this too shall pass and that they've all been there themselves in one way or another.

For the first time ever, I leave the office at a regular time while the sun is still shining and the traffic is chaotic. I don't say any goodbyes, I just sneak out when no one is looking and I hate myself for it.

Later that night I make a platter of tacos with extra jalapeño to add some spice into an otherwise dreary day. My philosophy in life is to live like it's *always* Taco Tuesday. And what goes best with Taco Tuesday? Tequila, of course. I crank up the music and proceed to gorge, promising myself I'll stop after two or three or four or five fiery delectables. At this point does it even matter?

The tequila goes down well, too well. It tastes like liquid happiness and I wonder if that's all a girl needs in order to be whole? A plate of tacos, some salt, lemon and tequila? Could it be so simple? I down another shot and all my problems melt away.

There's a knock at the door and I stumble over the coffee table. 'Who put that there!' I right myself as the room tilts and I swing open the door just as my favourite song comes on, 'Tequila' by The Champs. It makes me swing my hips and really feel the vibe of Taco Tuesday!

My hips soon stop. 'YOU!' Smarmy Harry himself stands there as if he's dropped in for a quick visit with a friend.

He takes a step back. 'You're drunk.'

'Well, you're ... *promiscuous!*' I go to slam the door in his face but he steps inside. I can't seem to make my hands move as fast as my head.

'Comfort eating?' he says, hands in his stupid pockets as he surveys the remnants of my taco fiesta. He picks up the half-empty tequila bottle and raises a brow. 'You should lay off this stuff, you know. It's not good for you.'

'Tequila may not be the answer but it's worth a shot.' I giggle at my own sense of impeccable comic timing. 'Get it, worth a *shot*. A shot of tequila!'

'You're really sozzled.'

'I don't want to taco about it.'

'Oh God.'

'Lettuce pray you've come here to apologise? To tell me you've made a mistake? You're sorry. You won't do it again?' I squeeze one eye shut so I can hear him better.

'Actually, I'm here for my clothing, especially my Armani suits, my collection of luxury watches ...'

My heart stops dead. Surely it can't keep stopping suddenly like this. I don't have access to the paddles! 'What?' Where's his guilt-racked regret? His promises to make it up to me? His utter devastation at making such a massive error of judgement?

'You're here for your Armani suits? Your collection of luxury watches?' How was I ever fooled by this shallow man? It beggars belief! Even the tequila doesn't blur the edges of this light-bulb moment.

What kind of man cares more about his clothing than the damage he's done? 'Yes, I'm here for those and you can send the rest of my things to CC's house in Chelsea.'

CC?! 'So you've moved in together already?'

'Yeah. It was the next logical step.'

'For what?'

'For us.'

'And what about us?'

'We've been drifting for a while. Surely you sensed that too? All's well that ends well, eh? Let's not make this harder than it has to be.'

He cannot be for real. I must be in a food coma and dreaming. I shake myself and find I'm still here, gripping on to the dining table to help keep me upright. 'I see. Sadly I needed some confetti for a client's wedding, something sustainable, so I used the first thing that came to hand, which just so happened to be your Armani suits.'

'You didn't!'

'I did!' I laugh and take another shot of tequila. 'And like you said, all's well that ends well so it's time for you to leave. These tacos aren't going to eat themselves.'

'I'm going to find my suits, or what's left of them.'

I shake my head. He can't just march in here like this, not after what he's done. 'No, I'll send you your things, Harry. It's time for you to leave.' I push him in the back towards the door.

'Orly, wait.'

'No! I'm not waiting for you ever again!' With one final shove I push him over the threshold and slam the door with a satisfying bang.

My hands quake as I fall onto the sofa, berating myself for being so blind! I take out my mobile phone and go to delete Harry from Facebook, and to unfollow Carly C for good measure too, but not before I stalk their pages and see they've already amassed plenty of support from the public. Well-wishers the world over post gushy messages to Carly C.

Emma says: You're such a role model, strong, empowering and inspirational! Your new album is the kind of anthem we need right now! And the new man is hotter than HOT!

I scroll down her page and see hundreds of messages in the same ilk. Like Carly C is some kind of saviour and her 'new man' only adds to her appeal!

I swipe them out of sight, as my heart silently shreds itself inside my body. I scream out to the ether: 'I need a new life! A new beginning! A new direction!'

I can't be this person anymore. This pushover, this workaholic, this mundane half-version of myself. Notifications pop up on Facebook, probably 'friends' tagging me in more posts about the lovebirds. I don't look, instead I flick down wondering what normal people are posting about, what normal people are doing with their lives tonight.

An ad pops up for a real estate broker and I pause, suddenly stone-cold sober. It's as though the universe heard my plea. In the thumbnail is a picture of a grand hall with a heading that says: *Escape to Honeysuckle Hall, your new life awaits!* Goose bumps break out over my skin – this is a sure-fire sign. I've been looking at properties for years and none of them have been quite right, but I know, *I know*, instinctively this is the one.

I click on the link and read about the place:

Honeysuckle Hall, situated in the picturesque town of Eden Hills, has had a rich and illustrious history and now needs a new owner to bring it back to its former glory. Whilst the grand hall has been vacant for years, it has been maintained and only needs some cosmetic work to make it shine once more. There's also a gatekeeper's cottage attached so if you're more business-minded there's the possibility of making the hall into accommodation or a venue for weddings. Wander the lush green grounds and delight in the sweet fruity aroma of honeysuckles that grow wild and free. Swim in the adjoining lake. A dream lifestyle is right here waiting for you. All you need to do is take the plunge!

I click though the pictures, and after each one my pulse speeds up. This is it! This is the place! The price seems quite reasonable but I still wonder how I can make it happen … Before sense prevails and ruins my buzz, I type a message saying: *I'll take it! As long as I can move in as quickly as possible.* I press send and fall back on the sofa with a belly laugh. I don't make rash decisions, but this somehow feels right.

Escape to Honeysuckle Hall, indeed!

*

My head throbs as I survey the mess of the previous evening. Crushed-up tacos litter the table and the sweet earthy agave smell of tequila hangs in the air. The memory of Harry's visit surfaces. Did I really tell him I'd made confetti of his suits? I didn't actually do that but I can't deny tequila me is someone I aspire to be sometimes. Someone braver who speaks her mind.

In the kitchen I flick on the kettle, throw back some paracetamol and find my phone to check my emails. I grin when I see an Etsy order I made for colourful sombreros. *Bloody hell, Orly.* Then there's another email:

Dear Orly,

Thank you for your interest in Honeysuckle Hall. It's a magnificent property and really only needs cosmetic work and someone to realise its full potential and make use of it accordingly. Motivated sellers mean we could close within about six weeks if that's soon enough for you? If you'd like to take a tour first, let me know.

I look forward to hearing from you.

All the best,

Dinesh

The previous night comes crashing back. Did I really say I'd buy a grand hall, sight unseen? I've lost my mind – I rage against the anaesthetic effects of tequila! *Curse you, Taco Tuesdays and tequila! Look what you made me do!* The head throb gets so loud it's almost like a recrimination.

I hold the kitchen bench for support and think things through. I'll tell them it was a mistake. I'll tell them heartbreak made me do it. I'll tell them it was done under the influence of tequila. I'll tell them I'm sorry. I'll tell them …

Yes.

Why wouldn't I trust tequila me? Tequila me is brave and bold and knows what she wants! I click open the email and scan the pictures and the description of the hall and know it's the sort of property I've been searching for all these years!

Hastily, I type a reply to the agent and then get ready for work.

An hour later, I stand in front of the Excès office. I glance up at our elegant signage and I know I've made a decision that will change the course of my life – for the better.

I can do this and I *will* do this and I'll do it my way for a change. Instead of scurrying inside like some little mouse, I strut in like a supermodel, and feel full of confidence.

Victoria sees me and gives me a forlorn look. 'I saw the latest in the *Daily Sun*. I'm so sorry, Orly.'

'Never mind all that,' I say with a firm smile. 'Can you call an urgent meeting with the other business partners?'

She nods solemnly. 'I'll do it now.'

While I wait, I get to work finishing off tasks and readying myself.

Victoria pops her head in my office. 'They're ready for you now, but ah … Harry hasn't made it in today.'

'He's probably shopping for more Armani suits.'

She shoots me a confused look. 'It's OK, perhaps you can take notes and email him a briefing of the meeting?' I swipe on a coat of ruby-red lipstick and I channel darling, confident Maya with my shoulders back, head held high while I head to the boardroom.

My other two partners, Angela and Dean, stare back at me. Their faces shine with a sort of empathy but I'm sure soon enough they'll understand I don't need anyone's pity.

'Thanks for joining me at such short notice,' I say and proceed to outline my plan. I stop them when they try to interrupt. I stop them when they tell me they need me. I stop them when they argue that I'm an asset. I don't say yes, not once. I say no after no after no and it feels *good!*

Dean holds up a hand. 'If this is about money, I'm sure Angela and I, and even Harry, can commit to giving you more of a share. We understand you do a lot of the heavy lifting while we … ah work on other projects.' *Translated: have long lunches that turn into weekends away.*

'It's not about the money.' I gear up to finish. 'I'm no longer passionate about Excès. I see my future elsewhere. If we agree on a payout figure today, I can pursue my new dream … and I'd really like that to happen as soon as possible. I'm finished here, and I've done all I can to bolster the business but my time at Excès has come to an end.'

Angela's eyes light up. 'What's this new dream, Orly? We'd love to be involved. Of course, we don't need to include Harry if you'd prefer not to. We know your work ethic is second to none and you'll make a success of whatever you put your hand to.' Her face is hopeful but I'm reminded of all the Friday nights I was left to do the reports, all the weekends I worked while she sunbathed on clients' yachts, greedily procuring all the perks of the job while I crunched numbers and filed paperwork. Well, not anymore.

The pushover, yes-person version of me is gone for good.

'I'm going to run a wellness camp for people suffering burnout. People mending broken hearts. People who just need to find their way. People just like me.'

If multi-millionaires can take weekends at private islands, surely the rest of us can take long weekends in the countryside when it comes to resetting the scales of work-life balance? The conversation Maya and I had back at Bai's really highlighted the fact that us everyday people need time out too. I continue, 'Thanks for your confidence in me Angela, but this time, it's best if I work alone.'

The duo sit in stunned silence. This sparkly new idea must seem like lightyears away from Excès, and that's exactly what I'm aiming for. Eventually we agree on a buyout figure, pending Harry's approval too, and an end date. I won't leave them with a pile of problems – it's not my style. They say their goodbyes and Angela says, 'We'd be silent partners, Orly. Just investors. Think on it, won't you?'

'Thanks but no thanks.' I know in my heart this new step has to be taken by myself.

*

With the buzz of liberation flowing through my veins, I phone Maya and tell her everything.

'A wellness camp? Oh, Orly, I knew you'd reinvent yourself but I didn't expect you to be this inspired, this quickly. It's genius! So tell me more about the idea.'

I fiddle with a pen as I think of how to explain the notion

that came to me as soon as I saw the photos of the hall. 'I found the most amazing hall in a little town called Eden Hills, Kent. So I'm thinking an adventure camp for adults. I see a high ropes course, kayaks, campfires, a wonderland for adults who want to switch off from high-pressure lives. Life starts outside your comfort zone, right?'

'Right!'

'I just hope I'm not having a mid-life crisis.' Am I crazy to think grown people would entertain such an idea? Sing-alongs and card nights. Apple-picking and pie-making …

'If you are then I want to have one just the same! Mid-life crisis might be the new black. How will you know until you try? But seriously—' she sighs '—how the hell am I going to survive London without you? My BFF, my confidante, my plus-one when Preston is MIA. It's going to be so strange without you. I can't even imagine what Fridays will be like …'

'At least you'll still have Bai launch-hugging you. I'll probably have to throw myself at a tree for some affection, while you parade around London with a new BFF, a shiner, happier version who'll probably be vegan, love exercising and—'

'Stop right there. No one can replace my BFF and especially not someone who won't share half my pork dumplings. Where's the fun in that?'

'True. You do love a good dumpling.'

'Dumplings are life!' She laughs. 'And even though I'm going to pine for you, I know you're finally following your heart, so I'll keep reminding myself of that and you probably should too when doubt comes a-knocking. Change is hard, but if you give it everything you've got I know you'll make a success of it, just like always.'

'Thanks, Maya. Please tell me you're going to take time off and reset at the camp.'

'You just try keeping me away.'

I tell Maya all about the tequila, the tacos, Harry's surprise visit and then the way the hall appeared as if by magic and even my befuddled brain recognised it as a sign.

'Golly, Orly, all that happened in *one* night! I'm so happy you found a place. Send me the link so I can see what's it like and feel wildly jealous. But truly, I'm so happy for you and all that your shiny new future holds.'

'The possibilities are endless!' For the first time in forever, butterflies flutter in a *good* way, and I know, no matter what, this is a risk worth taking. Our dream of a sprawling country property will still happen, but on my own, and that's OK. Instead of pandering to celebrities, I'll help regular people who are just as important, if not more so. I feel it in my gut that this is the right step for me but I know it won't be easy – nothing worth it ever is.

'I'll pop around tonight, yeah? What do you fancy for dinner, as long as it's Thai? I'll grab it on the way?'

I smile. 'I guess … Thai then?'

'I love how we're always on the same wavelength. Thai it is. I've had a hankering for tom yum goong for weeks now. But now we've talked about dumplings, I'm torn. Might have to get both since we're celebrating!'

We say our goodbyes and I look forward to the night ahead with Maya.

Chapter 6

Six (very fast) weeks later, my life – my whole life – is packed into a removal van and the rest in Maya's beat-up Toyota. She insists she's not getting a new car until this one gives up in a screaming, belching heap, which seems imminent after a very slow drive with 'Rita' backfiring and hiccoughing as if warning the end is nigh. Poor delusional Maya puts it down to all the extra weight from my boxes. She's attached to her little bomb of a car and won't hear a bad word about 'her'.

But secretly, this is another reason Maya is one of my people. She doesn't care about owning a fancy new BMW, she doesn't feel the need to be showy, even though she can afford it. Instead, she saves her money, only splurging on good meals, holidays in the sun, and time spent connecting with her circle – all things I hold dear.

'Is this the turn-off?' Maya asks, her voice laced with doubt, pointing to an overgrown laneway with a rickety fence that looks like it'll blow down in a strong wind.

'Yes, that's the one.' There's a rusted-out sign announcing: *Mrs Cully-Jones' Finishing School for Girls*. 'The hall has had a rich and illustrious history; privately owned by a noble family, and then a home for wayward children, before it was requisitioned in WWI, then becoming a prestigious finishing school for London's elite to help their daughters acquire social graces in order to find suitable husbands.'

'Thank God feminism arrived,' Maya mutters.

'Aww come on, it's an important skill, being taught the socially acceptable way to eat a banana, don't you think …?' I tease. Finishing schools were a product of the times, and I can't help but feel awe at owning a place such as this (well, I might own the front door and the bank owns the rest, but hey, it's a start).

She laughs. 'I can only imagine the teacher trying to keep a straight face with that lesson!' The car rocks and rollicks down the bumpy lane until we come to the front of the property. It's even more magnificent in the fading summer twilight.

'Oh, Orly, it's beautiful.' The hall stands sombrely as if waiting these long, lonely years for another chance at life. In front of the hall is the little gatekeeper's cottage that will be my home. It looks positively tiny in comparison and shrinks under the gaze of Honeysuckle Hall as if it is an afterthought, like an unwanted baby sister. I suppose once upon a time someone manned the front gate, which has long since gone. Goose bumps break out over my skin. There's so much history here and I can't wait to unearth it. I'd got the hall 'for a steal', the real estate agent reckoned. Surely there'd been interest in such a place? I presume upkeep of a property like this was enough to scare the savviest of buyers away.

Maya pulls up and kills the engine. 'It's haunted, isn't it?'

'Of course not!' I say bravely. If it is, then I'll be bloody hightailing it back to London. But I don't believe in all that mumbo jumbo. I mean, it's going to *sound* haunted like these old halls do when wind whips through and windows rattle but I am already mentally prepared for that. Plus, I'll be safely tucked away in the tiny cottage, not in the cavernous hall on my lonesome.

The lawn is overgrown and prickly as we make our way to the front door of the gatekeeper's cottage, carting stuff from the car.

I had the most detailed survey possible done on the property before I purchased it and it was reported that most of the repairs are cosmetic, not structural, so I'm hoping that means it's not a big ol' money pit, and just needs some gentle coaxing back to life – more of a little nip and tuck than a fully-fledged renovation.

The previous owners of the hall looked after it, and despite it being empty for half a century they still paid for it to be maintained up until the last few years, when I'm presuming the owner must've died and the executor let the upkeep lapse. All maintenance stopped and the hall went up for sale without anyone taking the plunge and putting an offer in until I came along.

'Let's get these boxes inside – my arms are about to drop off,' Maya says.

I find the key, a brass antique barrel type, and open the cottage door. I'm immediately assailed by a fusty scent of times gone by, a musty dustiness like the smell of old books. That is until we get closer to the kitchen, where the smell becomes pungent as if something curled up and died here. Well you can't have everything! Still, it's enchanting, like opening the proverbial Pandora's box – what will I find here? – but I can see by the scrunched-up look on Maya's face she doesn't feel the same.

She puts the box on the floor, making dust motes dance. 'Wow, Orly, when you said rustic I didn't think you meant quite like this ...' She coughs as if suddenly allergic to change. 'There's a stench that implies there's a dead body hidden somewhere.' She grimaces. I'm hoping it's just the dirty carpet that's soaked up years' worth of stench and not an *actual* dead body. Surely the property report would have mentioned a bonus cadaver ...?

I laugh at the shock in Maya's eyes and gaze around the damp, squat cottage but only see potential. Sure, it's not quite the London luxury apartment I've come from – on first glance, the mould needs urgent attention, the fireplace mantle needs replacing, there's cracks in the walls and the plaster needs to be redone – but it's exactly what I wanted. A fresh start. A blank canvas.

'You said it needed slight cosmetic work! It's like we've gone back in time.' Mouth puckered, Maya goes from room to room in the small box of a cottage. There's detritus of squatters: empty cans of food, beer bottles, and also flattened pillows, rugs and piles of clothing as if they were moved on quickly and didn't have time to collect their booty. 'There's no walk-in wardrobe?'

I'll have to get myself an armoire, and cull some more clothes. 'You're such a Londoner!'

'So are *you*, Orly! I'm worried. You're walking around with this big dazzling smile on your face like you've just stepped into an abandoned mansion or palace or something with a bag full of money for renovations, when in reality this little cottage is a disaster. I don't want to even think about the hall. And then there's setting up a brand-new business all by yourself, in the middle of nowhere—' Maya's positivity flies out the window because of the state of the cottage, but I know, I *know*, it's not going to be a huge job to fix it. It's going to be a dirty job, but that I can handle.

'It's Kent – that's not exactly Timbuktu.' And that's exactly what I'm going for – change!

She scrutinises me with her doctor face on. 'You said it only needed a lick of paint, some new décor ...?'

'It's all structurally sound, despite how it looks. Trust me, I've had it well checked over. You need to see the bigger picture – look past the mess and the dust, the god-awful smell, and see what I see.'

There's a confidence running through me that I can't explain. And I want to reassure her but I can't wipe the grin off my face, which does sort of make me look demented. I don't care there's no walk-in wardrobe; I don't care about the size of the cottage or the fact that it's not plush. 'There's hard work to be done, stuff I have no idea about, but I'm a fast learner, Maya, and this is all part of the dream.' If the hall and cottage had been immaculate, it would have been well out of my budget. If this is the only way I can have my grand property in the country, then so be it.

But maybe I won't shock her with a tour of the outside just yet. The grounds are wild after being abandoned by the gardener. But with some lawnmowing, rubbish removal, and a general tidy-up it won't take long to bring it back to life. While gardening is a world away from my previous work, I can't wait to get started. The only greenery I had in London was my bonsai tree, and I killed that with kindness and a little overzealous pruning, but I have faith I can improve.

She stares at me like I've got bananas for brains, so I continue to woo her with my vision. 'Fixing it up will be a labour of love. And so what if I live in a dingy squat for a while? There's open space here, green grass, hikes to take, water to swim in. A different outlook while I make a business plan and sort out the next stage of my life. My exciting *new* life!'

She takes a deep breath like she wants to believe me.

I give her a loose hug. 'I'm not having a breakdown, promise. I'm restructuring the best way I know how. And I know it looks bad, but once I dump the junk, fill up those cracks and flick some paint on the walls, this place will be a cosy little haven. Just you wait and see.'

I have YouTube tutorials and enthusiasm!

I see myself being cocooned here, and for the first time in ages, not having to answer to *anyone* except myself. There's such a freedom in that, I don't think Maya quite understands.

She raises a brow. 'Your optimism is scary.'

'Thank you. Are you going to stay for dinner?'

With a glance to the kitchen that needs a good degreasing and possibly updated cabinets, she says, 'I'll take a rain check. Salmonella is not my style.'

'How do you know if you haven't tried?'

Her eyes go wide.

'I'm *joking*. Joking.'

'It's just a big leap, Orly. From high-flying executive, to ... this.'

'Hush your mouth. You'll see – when you next visit this will be spick and span and you'll eat off the floor.' I can't help feeling a little rankled Maya isn't being supportive. I know it's only because she's concerned, but I'd hope she knows me well enough to trust my judgement. Unless I really am losing the plot and I'm the only one who doesn't see it ...

'I bloody well hope you'll spring for plates, but let's take one day at a time, eh?'

I grin as Maya rubs her hands on her skirt and looks for an exit. 'Thanks for helping me move, but you better get back. Beat the traffic and all.' I want to put the poor girl out of her misery.

'Quite right. I'll be ... back when I can.'

I swallow a lump in my throat. It's really real now. 'I'm looking forward to your next visit already.'

'Aww, Orly.' She envelops me in a hug. 'It's going to be great. Even though I think you're a little bit crazy. I know that you have the unique ability to see the good when others can't. And if you see this place as a rough diamond then I know it'll sparkle very soon.' There's the Maya I know.

'Thanks darling.' I hug her tight and walk her to the car. Waving, she takes off leaving nothing but a trail of gravel dust behind her and a belch or two from Rita for good measure.

I ignore the shake in my legs as I walk back into the little damp cottage. I ignore the panic as I survey the griminess inside. I'm going to have to get used to these waves of emotions, the ups and downs of starting over. Maya's right about one thing: I don't have buckets of money if something goes wrong.

By the time I sold my share in Excès and paid my bills and taxes, there wasn't quite as much left in the coffers as I'd hoped, hence the need to buy a property with an eye-watering mortgage that's a little beaten down by life – just like me. We both just need a bit of time, attention and TLC to get back on track. The pressure is on to get this place up and running, or I'll lose everything.

The removals team arrive and I ask them to put only my bed, the sofa, and a couple of boxes marked 'kitchen' and 'clothing' in the cottage, the rest of my things I send to the hall. Firstly, the cottage is too grimy and secondly, I'm just not sure the furniture from London quite suits this new life.

As daylight fades and the distance between me and Maya lengthens, a sort of panic starts. The *what ifs* bombard me. What if this is a huge mistake? What if my adventure camp fails? What if the cottage is haunted? What if …?

Wine time.

I hunt through a box and find a bottle and a glass and head to the kitchen to open it. The bench is in need of a good clean and declutter. There's a notepad open so I take a look to see what the last occupant wrote; that's my jam, long-lost letters that speak of other lives and times.

Take your business elsewhere.

Wow. Not the kind of thing I usually find, that's for sure. My mind spins with possibilities. Did the squatters leave it for the realtor because they didn't want to lose their free home? Maybe the realtor left it for the squatters? Or perhaps someone wrote it for me? What a ridiculous thought. I really am losing it!

But suddenly, I have a full crisis of confidence and flee from the kitchen back to the living room.

I trip over my handbag strap that dangles from one of the boxes and it flies onto the rotting wood of the floor, contents spilling while I stumble forward and land hard against the wood cladding of the wall, leaving a human-sized print in the grime.

Maya should have had me sectioned before letting me ruin my life in such a spectacular way! I'm going to be one of those old ladies who live in a derelict cottage with an overrun garden that children run past in fear, believing the occupant to be a witch! I'm doomed, I'm—

'No, no, no!' a shrill voice admonishes and I turn, startled that someone's wandered into my home uninvited. A small sixty-something woman with grey-black hair stares back me her eyes wide. 'Don't put your purse on the floor, or you'll be poor!'

'I'm *already* poor!' I'm the queen of making poor choices all of a sudden. This is why it's easier to be a *yes* person. My earlier confidence has vanished just as fast as Maya did, screaming off down the A2 with nary a glance behind …

'Didn't your mother teach you anything?' The woman seems actually offended by the fact I've knocked my purse on the floor. I'm not thrilled either; it's an exquisite, hand-sewn, vintage little number and the carpet here is of dubious cleanliness, but hey, I'm not going to lose my head over it.

'Well …?' she prompts and shakes her head while I stand frozen to the spot.

'Who are you?' *And why are you in my house!*

'Esterlita, your neighbour. They call me the Firecracker.' She gives me a proud smile.

'Erm … nice to meet you, Esterlita.' I can't even have a private panic attack – so much for all the space to roam in the country!

'Are you going to pick up your purse?' She folds her arms and waits.

'OK.' There's something about the woman that makes me duly comply. I pick up my purse and dust it off. 'Happy?' The heck does she care so much for?

She rolls her eyes dramatically as if I'm the densest person on the planet and then flings herself on my sofa with its pristine *whiteness* that suddenly looks so out of place in the run-down cottage. 'The damage may still be done, but hey, it's your life.'

'The damage? My purse is fine.'

'It's not the purse itself, it's a Filipino thing … never mind.' She waves me away. 'What brings you to Eden Hills?'

'A change of scene.' I busy myself with the box in front of me, making a show of dragging it close to the bench as if I'm about to unpack and clearly don't have time for a visitor. Actually, I'm doing no such thing until this place is spick and span. I huff and puff like the big, bad wolf and when I sneak a glance, my new neighbour is still sitting there regally, placid as anything.

'Marriage break-up?' she probes, pulling a pair of specs on as if she's about to knuckle down to an interrogation. I'm waiting for a spotlight to blind me, which will force me to confess or something. Really, who is this pocket-sized woman and why am I allowing her to sit on my sofa as if I'm visiting *her*?

'No, no, nothing like that.' Sweat beads. 'Look, if you don't mind I've got a lot of unpacking to do and I better crack on.'

'Oh, no problem. Let me help.' She bounds up and starts rummaging in the box in front of her. The box that just so happens to house my underwear. 'Ooh, pretty. You will definitely find a new man wearing this! Ooh la la.' Esterlita holds the teddy against her body and sashays around the small room. It's so outlandish I can't help but laugh. Perhaps she's just a lonely old lady whose boredom drives this kind of behaviour? I'm used to Londoners who don't show emotion easily and usually have a healthy-sized wall up so we don't have to have strange encounters like this. Maybe it's a country thing?

I gently prise the lacy garment from her hands. It had been a present from Harry, and one I've never worn. Give me flannelette PJs any day. I guess I'm built for comfort not style.

'I don't need a man, but thank you.'

'Bosh! Of course you do! You can stay home and have the babies!'

The babies. 'Not going to happen, Esterlita.' I gulp at my wine and look for a clean spot to place my glass.

Cue yet another dramatic eye roll from the Firecracker. 'Girly,' she tuts. 'Have you ever thought you might be doing life wrong? What's the point of living if you don't have a man?'

I cross my arms in a very British fashion to convey I'm absolutely livid at her intruding into my life like this.

For some reason Esterlita doesn't seem to pick up on this and continues, unabashed. 'For lovemaking, foot massages, and washing your hair, eh? If you find the right one, they can be very artistic when it comes to painting your nails; they have steadier hands, don't you know, eh? My Edward, God rest his soul, used to do this thing with his—'

Visions flash of her Edward and I cut her off before she says something that I can't unhear. 'Actually, Esterlita, I'm on a sabbatical from men at present so I can focus on my career.' My career?! More like my hastily made escape …

'Oh?' she lifts brow. 'What do you do?'

I double blink. 'I … I … I'm restructuring my life, I'm realigning …'

'You're unemployed?'

Blimey. 'Yes, yes, I am.'

She claps her hands. 'Perfect! That frees us up to find you a man. You want a rich one? Older maybe? Not as spirited …' She waggles her brows and it's all I can do not to laugh. I have no idea what to say and how to extricate myself from this whole slapstick scenario. She can't be for real, surely?

'I don't want any man, truly. I have a plan and I'm working through the steps to achieve it. And nowhere on that plan is there room for a relationship.' *Who has the energy for such things?* My poor heart hurts just thinking about it. Harry's off gallivanting around all the posh establishments in London with Carly C and I'm … here. Hoping to maybe eat cold beans from a can, if I actually packed any.

It's kind of impossible not to know their whereabouts since they're snapped by the paps every day, their faces splashed across tabloids and social media. Knowing Harry, he tips them off himself! It does make moving on hard when you see your former fiancé locking lips in a very public display of affection, and yet the cold fish was never quite as amorous with me in public, saying we had *our reputations to consider*, like we were in a Jane Austen novel or something.

'Ah.' She continues rummaging through my underwear as if she's searching for something in her size. 'So he broke your heart and you're running away and now you're just going to give up on life and become a recluse? Take up bird-watching? Start collecting stamps, eh? Sink into the sofa and watch reality TV marathons? Go on long hikes to nowhere and never return?'

'There's nothing wrong with collecting stamps.' I bristle.

Laughter barrels out of her. 'Let's get you unpacked and you can tell me all about the swine and what he did to you.'

For some inexplicable reason, the eccentric Firecracker somehow puts me at ease, even as she's going through my things as if they're hers and giving me advice based on the fact she's known me for all of five minutes.

We bond. It could be the fact she's the only one brave enough to hang out in my decaying cottage. I tell her the whole sorry story including the fact that Harry and Carly C are now perceived as the darlings of the London social scene and I'm just a footnote. I'm not usually so open, but somehow this feels right.

'Carly C's album launch propelled her further into the stratosphere, and her metaphorical "call to arms" for women to join together and stamp out oppression worked. Somehow stealing someone else's man doesn't apply to her, although he's the one who was engaged, so really, it's on him, but still …'

'Oh, my darling girl. What you need is revenge. And I don't mean paying for a hitman – unless that's what you want …?' There's a sparkle in her eye that slightly worries me, as if she hopes I'll say yes. I hastily shake my head no. 'OK, well in that case, if a hitman is off the cards, I guess you also won't want him roughed up?'

I double blink. 'No, no roughing up.'

'Of course you don't. And no hate mail?' She looks under her lashes at me.

I frown. 'No hate mail.'

'No break and entry, no graffiti, no smashing of plates and crockery?' She stares me down and I let out a nervous laugh and look for the exit. 'OK, I'm not suggesting any of that if that's what you're thinking. The best revenge is taking charge of the next chapter and showing the world you don't need him; that you've *never* needed him.'

'I don't think I ever even had him, Esterlita. It must've been all in my imagination.' When I left London, I felt on fire, inspired, ready to take on the world, but now I'm here, away from all I know, I'm a little more doubtful. Maya's reaction worries me. What if I've made a mistake? 'I managed to wrap up my entire life in about six weeks and it's only now I'm wondering if I acted on impulse. Usually, I'm the problem-solver, and I'm good with contingency plans, so how could I have upset my whole life like this without thinking it through?'

I'm going to be alone and bankrupt – what a combo.

'You've been here a few hours and you're giving up. Already?' She shakes her head. 'No, not on my watch. You're going to throw on some of those barely-there excuses for underwear, pull out the sequins, slip on the stilettos and start living for the moment, not for the past.'

'Yeah, sounds good, Esterlita,' I laugh, imagining myself in sequins and cringe. 'Or we could eat a few litres of ice cream and catch up on a season of *The Real Housewives*?' I can't remember when I had time to just be. To watch trashy TV and not be interrupted by phone calls. To stay up as late as I like because I can also lie in as long as I need! I don't *need* to do anything on schedule, and the idea appeals to me in a big way. My mobile phone has been glued to my ear for the last four years and I am relishing the fact it's not ringing anymore – not like it used to at any rate.

'*The Real Housewives*? OK, why not. You could learn a thing or two from those ladies. That's what you need, a good plastic surgeon …'

I touch the bridge of my nose. 'Let's not get too carried away. We don't all need ski jump noses for crying out loud.'

She guffaws. 'I meant as a *husband*, darling!'

'Oh.' I figure it's time to tell Esterlita about my plans to host an adventure camp for adults, so she stops hounding me about finding a man and having the babies. When I explain my still somewhat murky idea her brow knits.

'There were whispers in town about this adventure camp proposal. No, no, no this is not a good idea,' she says with disdain in her voice. 'This place should be full of children, not adults! Why can't you just focus on finding a man, eh? Why complicate things?'

'Oh, Esterlita, really! Haven't you been listening? A man is the reason for all the complications in my life. This is the first time I've had my own home, my own business, without having to consult anyone else. And no way am I going to muddy waters by adding a man into the mix. Never again.'

'This place is a cash drain! You'll lose everything!' Why the sudden change in the Firecracker? Does she really think a man will be the answer to all my problems? She can't be that last century!

My eyebrows pull together. 'Yeah, well that's the risk I have to take. Let's forget about all that tonight, eh? I've got some comfort eating to do.'

We set up my laptop because the TV is out in the hall somewhere, clean up the living room as best we can and settle down to watch *The Real Housewives*. I don't actually have any ice cream so we make do with a block of chocolate, some popcorn and the rest of the bottle of red.

'I'm going to grow into the size of a house, living off chocolate and popcorn,' I promise myself. The plant-based yoghurt, matcha-drinking me seems a thing of the past after just one day. And what a relief. If I have to slurp down one more celery juice – the much-lauded toxin-removing, blood-pressure-stabilising magic elixir of choice in L-Town – I'll scream. Though, I suppose those kind of health trends only work when they're not followed up by bingeing on a box of petit fours. Why can't we just admit that drinking our food is a punishment and be done with it? Fads are horrific when you're trying to fit in.

'You shouldn't go to sleep hungry, anyway,' Esterlita says an hour into our marathon TV sesh. 'Or your spirit will go to a place where there's no food and you'll be trapped there. Didn't your mother ever teach you anything?'

I think of my spirit going to a foodless place and being stuck for all eternity. Not ideal. Especially now I plan to eat my feelings, and I have *a lot* of feelings right now. 'No, she must have missed the memo on that one, Esterlita.'

We spend hours watching glamorous women argue with each other, drink too much wine and backstab their friends. It's quite honestly the most fun I've had in ages.

I mean to ask her about the hall and what she knows about its history but my eyelids grow heavy and Esterlita makes excuses to leave. 'So same time tomorrow,' she says more as a statement than a question. 'I'll make you some Filipino snacks.'

'OK, sure,' I say. 'Sounds lovely.'

We say about a bazillion goodbyes. Esterlita seems to pause as she takes a step and we repeat the process of farewell all over again. It's the kind of long, drawn-out departure you'd give if the other person was leaving for somewhere like Antarctica …!

I wonder what I've got myself in for as Esterlita waves yet again then stops on the front porch and turns for one more hug.

I bet I wake up tomorrow and this is all a dream. The type of whimsical dream where I magicked myself a zany neighbour to keep the panic at bay. I go to the window, and rub a hand through the dust. Esterlita ambles to an immaculate little cottage across the green.

There's no traffic, no noise. Just a bunch of stars in the sky that sparkle as if saying goodnight and I'm left with a silence that's just a little unnerving after living so long in a bustling, loud city.

I make up my bed and settle in for a good night's sleep but it doesn't quite pan out that way. Around the witching hour there's an almighty bang, and I creep deeper under the covers, until I remember I left the ladder (a present from Maya of all things) on the back deck and it's probably blown over in the wind. As I lie awake, comparing my old life to the new, the cottage creaks and groans as if trying to lull me back to sleep. It must work because soon sunlight streams in and I yawn and stretch, wondering what this new day will bring.

I brew a big pot of coffee, make some toast laden with marmalade and head to the deck to enjoy the morning before the day gets underway. When I open the back door of the cottage I see an envelope placed under the mat. I go back inside and get my letter opener, so I can preserve the envelope for my collection, even though there's no stamp and it's only addressed to: *The homeowner.*

Inside is a grainy old picture of Honeysuckle Hall. There's nothing else, no markings on the photograph, no note. Perhaps a local thought I'd like to see the hall as it looked back in its glory days? I think back to the loud bang the night before – surely they didn't come then? No, of course not. No one would be out walking at that time. The ladder simply fell over in the blustery winds.

I snatch a glance and see that it *is* lying prostrate on the gravel and remind myself I'll have to be more careful in the future, especially when campers arrive. It won't do to leave things around that they can trip over or hurt themselves on. I take a big sip of coffee and go back to the picture of the hall. While the hall itself looks remarkably the same, the grounds were well manicured compared to now, and there was a large fountain out front that is no longer working. It conjures up bygone times, different lives. Who stayed at the hall? What were their stories? There's so much history here, it's like I can feel the air pulse with it.

Chapter 7

A week later the full humidity of summer hits, which makes every task a little more arduous. The cottage doesn't have a fan, so I put that on the must-have list. It's a dense sweltering heat, like travelling on the tube in London at summertime, and I'm reminded that I'm free of all that. I think of all my friends, stuck underground, pressed against strangers in peak hour as they make their way to work, dreaming of being anywhere but there.

I open all the windows, hoping there'll be a breeze from the lake, and inhale the scent of the climbing roses that creep up the side of the cottage in wild abandon. I'll have to prune them, but part of me wants to leave them – they're so pretty escaping the trellis as if they have somewhere to be. Paintbrush in hand, I cut in under the cornice when there's a knock at the door. My progress is slow when there's always someone popping over to quote on repairs or introduce themselves, but it's a nice distraction and I'm enjoying it.

I open the door to a sprightly looking fifty-something wearing overalls. 'You must be Malcolm?'

He nods. 'That's me. Here to sweep the chimneys.'

'Lovely. You can start with this one if you like, before I paint the walls in the living room in case it's a dusty business?'

'Good idea.'

'Come in. Would you like a cup of tea or coffee?'

He gives me a wide smile. 'No thanks, I'll get started, so I don't hold you up with the painting before I move on to the fireplaces in the hall. Haven't swept them in must be five or six years now.'

Ooh, finally someone who has had some connection with the hall. 'So you swept the chimneys, even though they weren't in use?' That's a good sign.

'Sure did. Every year until the owner died. The fella never came here though. Probably had a barrage of country houses, and left the running of them to his staff. I was always paid like clockwork as soon as the job was done.'

'So you don't know who the owner was?'

'No, it all went through the name of a trust. Sad really that the place was left empty for so long, but now you're here, eh? Making the grand old dame shine once more. Rumour has it you're setting up some kind of camp for adults, eh?'

'That's the plan.' I smile. 'I hope to make my business thrive and bring some tourists to town, which will hopefully help out the community too.'

He smiles. 'Lord knows we need it. I'm sure you're going to make a success of it, lovey. Who wouldn't want to stay in such a place? It's been locked up tight for too long.'

We chat for a bit longer before Malcolm works his magic, and then heads to the hall to sort the two chimneys there. Before long he returns, face black with soot, like something out of *Mary Poppins*. 'Found this by the fireplace. Looks like someone left it for you, lovey.'

He hands me a dusty envelope bearing the inscription: *for you*. I thank him and he says his goodbyes, promising to visit once the hall is up and running. I take the envelope outside with a glass of iced tea, enjoying the chance to sit down for a bit and rest. My body aches in new places, muscles long dormant suddenly revived from all the physical work.

As birds sing to one another from trees surrounding the hall, I open the envelope, noticing on closer inspection the same small block handwriting as the note I'd found in the kitchen that very first night. *Stop your plans now before it's too late.*

I'm intrigued, and the philatelic in me senses a mystery to be solved. So I go back, and piece the clues together. A black and white photograph of the hall, the note in the kitchen on a pad, and now this one. Could they be from former occupants, young girls from the finishing school arguing with each other? Or did local teens hang out here and leave missives for their friends? Could they be more recent? I study the handwriting, the paper and the envelopes themselves, and get the distinct impression they're not very old. The notebook, for example is a run-of-the-mill cheapie you'd find in any newsagent. It's a mystery for another day, as painting calls. I finish my tea and head back inside.

After an hour or so of cutting in and sweating buckets, a local woman with ruddy cheeks arrives to quote me on fixing the fireplace mantle. She introduces herself as Celeste. 'It's better to do things right first go,' she says with an apologetic shrug at the price, as if it's exorbitant. I can't help but feel relieved as it's much lower than I accounted for.

'I agree,' I reassure her. 'Let's get that mantle replaced and I won't have to worry about it.'

'Great. I'll come by in a few days to fit it.'

'Perfect.' I am a little in awe of Celeste with her strong physique that suggests a lot of time lifting heavy things. 'That will tie in quite nicely with the painting being finished.' I hope. How long can a small cottage take?

'You're the envy of many of the townsfolk,' she says with a grin.

'Oh, yeah? I'm surprised no one snapped this place up sooner.'

She's suddenly shifty-eyed and I wonder if there's something she's not telling me. 'Yeah, you know what small towns are like. It's hard to make a living at the best of times. Don't think many around here had that kind of cash spare. And it's far too big for a regular-sized family. We're not royals, are we?' She lets out a bellow and I grin. She's a salt-of-the-earth type and I feel a real warmth for her. Maybe she's just nervous around new people?

'No, I'm not royal, that's for sure. That's why I'm so happy this cottage came with the property. Suits me to the ground, and I can run my business and still have my own cosy little haven.'

We talk about the camp for a while, which she'd already heard about, just like Esterlita and Malcolm had. Celeste grills me in that usual small-town way, which I've come to realise is some kind of test to make sure I'm not here to renovate and sell and make a buck; that I'm here for the right reasons. And I get that. I don't take offence.

By the time she says farewell, the morning has escaped and the paint has a film over it. I'm so used to the hectic pace of London life, meetings held on Zoom over lunch, phone pressed to ear while typing reports, always working on three things at once. This laid-back meandering and talking instead of working will take some getting used to.

I stir the paint, hoping it's salvageable, and get back to cutting in. I've chosen a soft white to brighten the place up and make it appear bigger. It will make a nice contrast to the wooden ceiling beams that are almost as old as the hills around here, probably taken from the woodland behind the hall once upon a time.

After a late lunch Esterlita pops over. 'Ooh, you're doing it wrong. Why paint first? Shouldn't you remove all the junk?'

I harrumph. 'I have moved the junk, Esterlita. These are boxes of my things.'

'OK, then why have them in here?'

With hands on hips I say, 'Are you going to help or hinder?'

'Can't I do both?'

It takes all my willpower not to flick her with paint but I know if I do that we'll have an all-out paint fight and I don't have the energy for cleaning up! I give her a brush. 'Cut in, if you know what's good for you.'

She laughs. 'I'm a very busy person, I'll have you know.' But she takes the brush.

'Oh, yeah? What do you do, Es?'

'I have a small catering business – it suits me. I can choose my own hours and work when I need to.'

'Filipino food?' I squat down to cut in above the skirting, my thighs burning after about three seconds.

'Yes, the best kind of food. It's not just cooking, it's pouring passion into what you love that makes it so great. You can taste my love in every bite.'

'Sounds amazing, Es. If there's one thing I like doing, it's eating.'

'And yet here you are about to take on this crazy idea of a camp. Why not just find a rich husband? I'll never understand the youth of today,' she grumbles as if I'm living on the edge by wanting to make my own way in life without a man's money! A rich one at that.

When I frown, at a loss for how to answer such an idea, she says, 'You won't find a man if you keep frowning like that!'

I shake my head, laughing. 'Why?'

She shoots me a look that says I'm dense. 'The wrinkles, of course!' I wonder if Esterlita pitches in just so she can continue to harangue me as we work.

'Did you always do catering?'

She shakes her head. 'Not for a long time. I let Edward do the work while I made our home a haven. He wasn't rich, but he didn't need to be. We had enough to get by and I liked everything being ready for him at home after a long day in the workshop. He always came home to a hot meal, and the bath drawn. It might seem too old-fashioned to you, but that's what I was taught by my mother, to make my husband feel like a king as long as he treated me like a queen, and Edward surely did.'

I consider the little pocket rocket of a woman in front of

me, who seems so much younger than her sixty-six years. While her once-black hair is peppered with white, she has this uncontained energy about her, coupled with a largely unlined face that makes her seem youthful, but when she talks about Edward it's like she shrinks into herself. Becomes so sad and lost and she loses a bit of her zest for life. I'm not quite sure what to say to comfort her, and whether words are enough anyway. But I have to acknowledge her story. 'He sounds like one of the good guys, Es.'

She gives me a half-smile, rather than the full constellation that is the usual for Esterlita. 'He really was. I know everyone says that about people they've lost, but it was really true of Edward. I remember meeting him on a beach in Cebu and knowing instantly he was the one. He looked so lost and uncertain as if he'd walked onto another planet. Love at first sight – for me, at any rate.'

'I'm sure he loved you on sight too.'

She laughs, loud and startling. 'He thought I was trying to sell him mango juice and kept saying no, since he already had two in his hand. Back then sellers up and down the beach sold cups of juice to foreigners, following them until they gave in and paid the small amount of pesos. He said something like if only I had three hands, and of course, I made a bawdy joke about what a man with three hands could do and it went from there.'

'Oh, Es! I can imagine. You and your saucy sense of humour even back then. How old were you?'

'Twenty. Old enough to know better!' She cackles at the memory. 'We were married fairly quickly and I applied to return to the UK with him. The only dampener was the weather, such a shock to the system. The first few winters I thought I'd freeze to death. Even in the so-called summer, I wore two pairs of trousers, but eventually I acclimatised.'

'From tropical paradise to drizzly cold Britain.'

'Lucky I had Edward to warm me up.' She cackles again.

'And there's our cue to paint!' I say, laughing.

We joke around as we work before we finally get to rolling the paint on the walls. For a small cottage, it seems to take forever to get one room done. It's all the drop-ins, the drink breaks and the relentless heat and hearing the gossip about everyone from Esterlita.

'Orly, if you listen to only one thing I say today, let it be this. Avoid the town busybody Freya, if you know what's good for you.'

'Oh, is she really that bad, Es?'

Esterlita widens her eyes. 'Acid-tongued and bored out of her wits. Never had a man, you see?'

And I do see. It's Esterlita's way of alerting me to the fact I need a man again! Freya's probably a sweet innocent lady who bakes cookies for her neighbours and helps at the local community garden. 'Rightio, Es. I'll keep my eyes peeled for such a menace.'

'You do that.'

Somehow I manage to contain my smile and we get back to work.

At the end of a long day, the windows sparkle after numerous attempts at cleaning the filmy residue off them. With all the squatters' junk carted away and the putrid carpet in the skip bin, the cottage begins to take shape and become a home. My neck will never be the same from being crooked at such an angle to wield the bloody pole but it's all part of the fun and I feel a sense of accomplishment when we finish the living room and get ready to move on to the next.

Hands on hips, Esterlita surveys the walls. 'Why would you choose these colours? Everything is off-white, sterile like a hospital. Sends me straight to sleep. I'll never understand you British people. In the Philippines we use bright, bold colours. Blood-red, sunshine-orange. It's like you don't want to be happy, do you?'

I laugh, so used to her now and the fact she's truly bamboozled that I won't give in to her ideas. Already, I love the fact Esterlita is unique and makes me rethink a lot of my choices, contemplating things from her perspective, which is always laced with joy. However, when it comes to decorating our ideas are wildly opposite and never the twain shall meet. 'I don't see how painting the living room walls the colour of fresh blood equates to happiness, Es.'

'Well, what about fuchsia and lime-green? Pops of colour here and there. Instead you've gone for this … what even is this?'

'It's English cottage style.' I managed to sell most of my modern furniture using a local online site because it just didn't suit and intend on finding some nice antique pieces that will fit the space better and add to the homely appeal of the cottage.

'It's like a one-hundred-year-old lives here.'

'Perfect.' I laugh. Most of the furniture *will* be a hundred years old so that's exactly the cute, quaint look I'm going for. I'm looking ahead to winter when there's a crackling fire in the hearth and lamps casting a soft orange glow around the small room. All I'll need is some comfy PJs and a good book to achieve the highest level of hygge. If that's not a remedy for burnout, I don't know what is.

She tuts. 'You're crazy.' She pulls that duck face she loves to make, and points with her lips for me to grab her a brush/biscuit/cup of tea/or something in the general vicinity. I'm now quite used to Esterlita's different ways of communicating.

'You know the duck face is actually for selfies, right?' I say. I lift each object up and am met with a shake of the head until I finally pick up the biscuit tin and she nods. Hurrah!

'The what?'

I model her look.

'That's not for selfies! Filipinos invented the duck face to express their needs without using words. It makes life easier. Didn't your mum ever teach you anything?'

I laugh. 'She didn't cover the duck face, no.'

She makes a show of looking offended by screwing up her face and shaking her head. Our Esterlita is very dramatic when I'm slow to understand her. 'You could win a BAFTA for that performance, you know.'

She lets out a wistful sigh. 'I always wanted to go into acting. I could have made it.'

'There's still time.'

She shakes her head sadly. 'No, no there's not. I'm banned for life from our local theatre, the Royal Arms.'

'What for?'

She averts her gaze and stays schtum.

'Let me guess: they underestimated your acting abilities? Didn't share the same vision as you?'

'No, it wasn't that.'

'What was it then?' I stop what I'm doing, surprised to see Esterlita blushing for the first time ever.

'I had a little fling and it didn't turn out well …'

A fling! 'And they banned you over it? How dare they!'

'Well …' She grimaces. 'At the time I was pretty upset.'

'Oh no, what did you do, Es? You didn't send him hate mail did you?' A more worrying thought hits. 'Not a hitman?'

She makes a show of acting offended. 'Of course not! I would never stoop to violence. Not unless I am extremely provoked.'

'So what did you do then?'

She groans and flings herself onto the sofa as if getting herself comfortable to share such a memory. Everything Esterlita does has a flair for the dramatic and I try my best to hide a smile while thinking everyone needs an Esterlita in their life – she's the tonic for any ailment.

'Well, Raoul and I were dating for a few months. My friends pushed me to try and date again a year or so after losing Edward. More as a social thing, you know? To get me out of the house, and back into the swing of things. But our fling was slow going.

I didn't even take my clothes off if you know what I'm saying.' She blinks and winks.

'Yes, yes, I understand,' I say quickly, lest Esterlita paints me a graphic picture.

'I was totally starstruck by him. It might be amateur theatre but he really had the goods. A method actor of the finest quality. And that should have been my first clue. Turns out Raoul liked dating *all* of the new actors at the theatre …' She shakes her head at the memory.

'All of you?'

'All of us.' She nods. 'It's a small town, you know. And words gets around pretty fast. It didn't take long for us to catch on to the deceit. Old acid-tongued Freya was the first to cotton on, and as you can imagine she was delighted to let us all know.'

'How many of you?'

'Six.'

'Golly, how did he think he'd get away with that?'

She shrugs. 'He told us all that he devoted his evenings to acting, leaving him only one night a week free. Of course we believed him. He's very debonair, very focused. I guess we all thought the same thing – that we aspired to be like him, take a little theatre show as seriously as if it were Broadway. Although for me, joining had been more of a social thing. I know I could make it if I tried but really, I'm more of a singer and I'm not really sure I'm ready for fame.'

Her total belief in her abilities makes me smile. 'So what did you do to get yourself banned?'

Her eyes twinkle. 'We staged an intervention. During the opening of the play.'

My hands fly to my mouth. 'You didn't!'

'We did and it was fabulous.' She lets out a haw so loud I'm sure the cottage shakes. For such a tiny thing she sure has a dynamism about her.

'What happened?'

'So the backdrop was a big white sheet, meant to replicate the sails of a ship. We instead projected his saucy text messages onto the sheet for the audience to see, and took it in turns of strutting on stage with T-shirts that read the days of the week – I was Thursday, as that was my given day. The other actors eventually stormed the stage and demanded we leave. We were all banned from the theatre after that. But ask anyone, they say it was one of the best performances ever held there, even if was based on heartache.'

'And what happened to Raoul?'

'Well the performance made it into the local paper, and it turns out Raoul was actually married and his wife was not best pleased. She kicked him out and took up with the theatre director. Raoul now runs his own method acting workshops in the next town over.'

'Wow.' This sleepy backwater is actually a hotbed of lust? Somehow I don't see it, but what would I know? I didn't even know my fiancé had been cheating when all the signs pointed to it.

She throws her head back and sighs. 'I'm thinking of writing to Raoul's ex-wife and asking for the ban to be lifted. I miss the camaraderie of the theatre. I miss the dramatics. And he was never the one for me. I still pine for my Edward, but I kept thinking I should at least *try* to date again, and then *that* disaster happened. Now I stick to singing, and acting out monologues in front of the mirror at home.'

'You were born to be an actress, Es. I can see that.' If all a person needed was dramatic flair, Esterlita has it in spades.

'And it's not like I hired a hitman, although Lord help me, I was tempted.'

I flop beside her. 'Well it seems like we've both been unlucky in love.'

'I had my lovely Edward. I was lucky, so lucky to have that man. No one can ever live up to him, so I've given up on finding love.' She wrinkles her nose. 'But you're young and beautiful, Orly. You can't let one man put you off.'

I don't feel young and beautiful. I feel overlooked and raggedy but hey you can't have everything. 'I won't, Es. But for now I'm focusing on my empire.' I flick the paintbrush in the direction of the overgrown yard where brambles and weeds have taken over like something out of a fairy tale and we both burst out laughing.

'Leo's coming today, isn't he?' she asks as she surveys my dusty paint-splatted yoga pants with a look I already know so well; it implies: it won't do.

'Yes, Leo the carpenter is coming to quote me to fix up the hall, and before you say anything I'm not getting changed into something "short and slippery".' Esterlita's answer for all of life's uncertainties. 'I'm just fine in these clothes.'

She scoffs big and loud. 'It's your life,' she says, meaning it's absolutely *not* your life and if it is, then you're doing it wrong so no wonder you ended up here.

'It sure is.' I grin and turn away, giving her ten seconds to begin her barrage.

'It's just how do you think you'll attract a man wearing *that*?'

'Not even five seconds. A new record!'

She shakes her head and her eyes pop as if all of her coiled energy is about to make her head explode. 'Can't you see? You're beautiful, even though you try to hide it. Why not give him the best impression, eh? Once he sees you in that lacy number he'll do the work for free!'

'Oh my God, Esterlita. Firstly, that lacy number is underwear, not outerwear …'

'Says who?'

'And secondly, I'm more than happy to pay for a good carpenter so I can get this place up and running before the end of the season. I don't want to muddle work and pleasure and what makes you think I even want to entertain the idea of a man? Especially one who I need to help me here? The only impression I want to make is—' I'm interrupted by the slam of a car door, and then we see him …

Chapter 8

The carpenter Leo is buffed and bronzed and walks with the kind of posture that suggests he's spent a lot of time working out.

'Good core strength,' Esterlita says, and it's then I realise I must've been speaking out loud. 'If you won't find a rich husband, why not Leo? He's single, well liked for being fair and honest with his work. Makes reasonable money. You'll probably never fly first class to Paris and own a wardrobe full of designer shoes but by the looks of it, that won't bother you.' She gives my sneakers a pointed glance. 'He loves camping, fishing, the outdoors. Then again, apparently he's not that interested in a relationship. Doesn't want to be tied down. Which makes you wonder, right?'

'Wonder what?'

'What he's *hiding*,' she says ominously as if this is an Agatha Christie novel, and I can't help but laugh.

I shake my head. Now I've heard it all.

'You may shake your pretty head, Orly, but the sooner you learn to look out for what people *don't* say, then the better off you'll be. You don't know small towns; everyone is always hiding something and you have to be on the lookout for it.'

I stifle more laughter. 'Maybe he likes being alone. Have you

88

ever thought of that?' In Esterlita's eyes you have to have a lover, no two ways about it. So if you're a singleton you're instantly suspicious. Except in her own case, of course, then somehow the rules don't apply.

'No one likes being alone, and if they say they do, they're lying,' she says and folds her arms, her signal that's she's prepared to battle me on the subject.

'I like being alone,' I say, wondering if it's just the novelty of it, and if that will eventually change.

'Point proven. You do *not* like being alone, but you like *pretending* you do so people don't feel sorry for you.'

My mouth opens and closes like a puffer fish as I scramble for a retort. Solitary time has been a pick-me-up, hasn't it? Aside from those few nights I've heard eerie whines that sound like ghosts trying to make contact, but are just the creaks and groans of an old cottage, I've been perfectly happy, haven't I?

I admit when the work is done, and Esterlita goes home of a night, loneliness does tend to creep in but that's totally normal, I'm sure. I'm bound to feel a little lost when it's just me, and the never-ending silence of night-time. It's all so different to my previous life, dashing to work functions after hours, swilling too much champagne, feet aching from too many hours in high heels, and then falling into bed with the sirens and sounds of London, a city that's never really quiet.

Leo is probably trying to keep people at arm's length so match-makers like Esterlita stay well away. And I don't blame the guy for that. It's like everyone in this tiny town needs to know every single thing about a person.

'He is one *fiiine* specimen of a man. I think I need some jobs done at my cottage,' Esterlita stage whispers. 'Urgent ones that will last for months, and months and years and centuries. Whoa.' She shakes her shirt as if she's overheating.

I nudge her with my hip but she's stuck in a trance-like state.

'Es …?' She's mumbling incoherently to herself. I catch words like: *take me, I'm yours* and I can't help but giggle.

'You should go for it,' I say to her. When she turns to me, her eyes are still glazed over as if she's stuck in a dream.

'Orly, this is fate! Look at that man!' One minute he's harbouring a secret, the next he's my fate? She moves so fast I get whiplash.

But I duly look. He's beautiful, heart-stoppingly lovely, but that's just the thing – I know men like that. They use their looks and leave broken hearts in their wake with a nary a care for the girl left behind. Well, no way am I doing that again. 'Yeah, he's a bit of all right, but so what? All I'm interested in is how well his hammer works …'

Her face lights up. 'Yes, finally, YES! His hammer!' She cackles like a witch.

I realise what I've said, 'Not like that, Es!' I should know by now Esterlita loves talking in euphemisms. 'You have a sick and twisted mind.'

'Freud would have a field day with you, Orly, all these phallic symbols you drop into conversation like someone who craves the company of a good bedfellow.'

'A good bedfellow?' Where does she get these words from?

With a shrug she continues, 'But that's a chat for another time. Go, go.' She pushes me hard in the back. 'Go meet him and tell him that you're in desperate need for a man with a good-sized hammer!'

'Oh my God, Es.' I go to protest but instead manage to bite my tongue and draw blood. 'Ouch.'

'What?'

'I bit my tongue. You make me tongue-tied, Es!'

'No, that's not me! When you bite your tongue it means someone is *thinking about you*! He's probably thinking about you, dreaming of his big hammer and your—'

I huff. 'Will you stop! Where do you come up with this stuff, Esterlita?'

'From my mother, from the provinces! Everyone knows these things, except you!'

With a shake of my head to let Esterlita know I'm truly befuddled, I walk out the front to greet Leo in the hopes he can get the hall in shipshape condition quickly. The camp needs to be up and running as fast as possible to bring in some money to pay my heart-stopping mortgage. Having Leo do the work will free me up to market the camps and spread the word.

'Leo, hi,' I say giving him a wave. When we lock eyes my legs buckle, probably from the uneven ground. Whew, I've never seen eyes so vividly blue before, they sparkle like precious gems. *Like precious gems! Get ahold of yourself, Orly.* I'm slowly turning into Esterlita by osmosis or something!

'Orly,' he says and holds out a hand to shake. A big man-sized hand. Golly, Esterlita is rubbing off on me in all the wrong ways. 'Nice to meet you.'

'Likewise,' I dispense with the niceties because there's something about him that makes my pulse race and I want to appear professional, dammit. It's listening to Esterlita that's sending me batty, for crying out loud. 'If you want to follow me to the hall I'll show you what I'm after.'

'Sure,' he says. When I turn to walk through the gate, out of the corner of my eye I catch Esterlita pressed hard against the window making all sorts of crude gestures. She is incorrigible! I sneak a glance to Leo and am mortified to see him staring at her with a mix of mirth and confusion. She's going to be the death of me.

'That's my neighbour, Esterlita. She's erm, cleaning the windows. Loves a shiny surface, she does.' WHAT. Oh, God. 'What I mean is, she really likes getting down to the nitty-gritty of grime.' Just stop!

'Yeah, I know, Es. She's quite the er … character.'

My toes curl. I don't dare look at him in case he's frantically searching for escape.

We come to the hall itself, an impressive sight that still leaves me enthralled no matter how much I visit it. It takes my breath away and makes me feel as though I've flung myself back a few centuries. I cough to cover my nerves and head inside the big arched door that creaks like it would in a horror movie.

'The hall needs some tender loving care. As far as I can tell, it's just some loose boards and some electrical issues. The wainscoting needs to be repaired and all the plumbing checked and everything brought up to code. I can show you the building inspection report too as that has more information.'

At the moment, inside is a big cavernous moody mess of dark wood, and dark walls, but it won't be dingy when we've finished. I plan to lighten and brighten the hall so it comes back to life. I continue to list the small but important jobs around the hall and Leo only nods.

'Let me show you the rooms,' I say, worried about why the man is so silent. Shouldn't he be making notes, taking pictures, sketching plans? 'There are ten rooms I plan to use, all in varying sizes from singles to family-size suites. They don't need much, just weather-proofing, some windows replaced. Fresh paint. The other rooms won't be for campers, not at this stage, but I'd like them to be freshened up and ready anyway, even though I won't be furnishing them yet.' The hall is a rabbit warren with so many chambers leading out of other rooms. Once upon a time it was built for a noble family with plenty of space for the court and their retinue.

Leo wanders around, and it's all I can do to stop a running commentary to make up for his silence. Maybe he's just a man of few words …

'Hello, darling!' Esterlita struts in as if all the world is a stage, and her booming voice startles us both. She holds out a hand to Leo and I notice she's somehow managed to put on mascara and a swipe of some kind of peach lipstick. The air smells suspiciously like my perfume. 'I'm sure the lovely *single and ready to mingle* Orly has told you all she needs …?'

Colour races up my cheeks and when Leo turns to her I shake my head urgently for her to stop! *Cease and desist,* I say with my eyes! Of course, my manic laser-like stare goes completely unnoticed by her.

'Hey, Esterlita. Erm, yeah, she's given me a bit of a run-down.'

'Fabulous, marvellous,' Somehow Esterlita now has a plummy English accent and I wonder if she got too close to the paint pots or something. She does have a slightly crazed look about her, but maybe this is what happens when she's in the presence of gorgeous men. 'It's so lovely to see you again, Leo. Word is, you're still resolutely single too. Don't want to waste your prime time, do you?' She flutters her lashes and makes quite the spectacle of herself.

Leo lets out nervous laughter and pastes on a wooden smile. 'No, I guess not.'

Her eyes go wide as if Leo's just invited her to delve into his love life so I hastily jump back into the conversation.

'Anyway,' I shoot her one last withering look. 'If you could draw up a quote with a price and an estimation of how long repairs would take that would be great. I'd like to have this place open by August, if I can. If we can tee up a finish time, then I can take bookings and make the first camp a reality.'

At this Leo's face dissolves into the first real smile. It transforms him somehow. 'I love the idea of an adventure camp. What sort of things will you do here?'

He seems more interested in the camp than his job but then I suppose how excited can you get about banging nails into things? 'All sorts! It's about leaving technology and work-life stress behind and reconnecting with nature while trying new things. There will be abseiling, canoeing, gorge scrambling, gardening—'

Esterlita makes a choking sound, as if the idea is abhorrent. 'Orly should just settle down with a husband. The camp idea is crazy – a huge waste of time and money. Don't you think?' She tries to get Leo onside. 'A cash drain! A pound pilferer, even. What she needs to do is find a suitable husband and fill the hall with expensive furniture and lots of babies. Now, Leo—'

I quickly interrupt. 'What do you think of the idea, Leo?'

He grins. 'I honestly think the camp idea is golden. It's something I'd do for a fun weekend away and I live here. People need this kind of downtime, and it'll be a great opportunity for them to meet others and try new things.'

I glow from the praise. Finally, someone who gets it. 'Thanks, Leo, I want to show off the local area too. I'll offer hiking—'

Esterlita interjects with a scoff. 'No one wants to hike here; be realistic, Orly. The woodlands are a labyrinth. You'll end up with a lawsuit on your hands!'

'I know some safe trails,' Leo says gently as if not wanting to oppose Esterlita but also not wanting to give in to her either. 'I can show you them.'

'Great,' I say, smiling at him.

'So what else will you offer?'

'Oh, I have so many ideas! I'm thinking about paintballing, meditation, astronomy, mountain biking. Eventually we'll expand into workshops, but for now the focus will be movement and nourishment.'

Part of me needs to right some wrongs after years of helping the mega-wealthy procure their every need with no mind about carbon footprints so large Big Foot himself would be running scared. 'Our camps will have a green component, planting trees, helping out in the community garden and living as waste-free as possible. Guests can cook hearty meals with produce from the garden and eat together and bond.' It'll take some time for all these dreams to come to fruition …

Leo's dazzling blue eyes shine as the idea of the camp takes shape. 'You're on to a winner here, Orly, seriously. I'm even happier that the hall gets to be rejuvenated and enjoyed by so many people after sitting abandoned so long. I'd love to try some yoga, take a bike ride …'

My turncoat mind pictures a shirtless Leo in the lotus position. I shake the vision away. 'You'd be most welcome to join!'

'Thanks. I'll definitely keep it in mind. That's if you don't fix it up and decide to flip the property after all. We've had a few big-city people do just that with other grand places. I guess they found it hard to leave city life behind for good.'

Do I detect a slight prickliness to Leo? As if I'm wasting his time if I decide to pack it all in and leave? 'I won't be flipping the property, Leo. You might have had other city dwellers come and go, but I'm sure they had their reasons. However, I'm here for more than just the business; I'm here for the lifestyle too.'

'Sorry, I didn't mean to sound so doubtful.'

'Not at all.'

The townspeople of Eden Hills seem to be a close bunch and they all want to see their town thrive. But I have the distinct impression I won't be let into the fold until they trust me.

Esterlita waggles her eyebrows behind the poor carpenter and I can only imagine what plans are afoot in her devious mind. She can change mood in an instant if a man is involved.

'Let me get this quote back to you within a week and we can go from there. Because time is of the essence I can hire a few extra guys and get the work done faster if you're happy with that?'

'Yes, please.'

I say goodbye to Leo and Esterlita walks him out, somehow managing to snake both her arms around him as if she's worried he'll dash off into the sunset. I dread to think what she's whispering to the poor guy. The Firecracker is next-level at the game of flirtation and I have to admire the woman. I sneak to the window to spy, pulling the dingy drapes to one side. I splutter as a century's worth of dust swirls in the air, producing a sneezing fit that I'm glad no one is around to witness. As I let the drapes go and stand away from the window, a scrunched-up piece of paper falls to the floor.

A relic from the past. Could it be a treasure map, a love poem, a letter that belongs to an envelope I might have in my collection?

As I gently unwarp the parchment I gasp as the words become clear.

You don't belong here.

Another one? It feels personal, somehow, but how can it be? It was probably hidden away decades ago and not intended for me. But the hair on my arms stands on end. Could it be because the handwriting is block letters, and not cursive like you'd expect from a finishing school? And that the paper doesn't look all that yellowed even though it's been sitting in a window? Is someone trying to scare me off?

Esterlita has openly admitted she doesn't like the idea of the camp but I doubt it's her leaving these scribbled notes. She's too open and honest for all that. Too forthright and friendly. I don't dare ask her though, knowing she'll turn my question into a monologue about why I need a husband to protect me. A big strong man to frighten away invisible enemies and concentrate on making babies instead!

That's it. I'm officially losing it. Still, I waste no time and leave the hall for the safety of the cottage. I double-check this note against the others, and confirm it's the same handwriting. I place the note in my book chest along with the others and the black and white photograph and ponder the fact someone may just want me gone from here. But why?

In the quiet of the cottage, I take out one of my collector's folders and begin reordering my stamps in the hopes it will soothe me. I've just had a few big weeks and I'm bound to be feeling out of sorts …

Chapter 9

The next day I track through the mud, the weather going from humid to stormy over the course of the morning. Good for the garden, I tell myself, as I video-call Maya hoping to catch her between patients. Her face appears on screen and gives me a boost.

'Orly, I've missed you!' she says, smiling wide. 'Let me guess, you've made friends with a ghost who has turned nasty and you want me to visit so we can perform a séance?'

'What? No! I know not to mess around with the supernatural!' But her joke has reminded me of the notes I've been finding around the place and I hesitate, wondering if I should confide in her or not. But she's already worried about me, and I don't want to make it worse.

'What is it?' she says. 'You've gone deathly white.'

'That's because I'm exercising,' I say, puffing and panting as my feet get stuck in the mud.

'Of your own accord?' She frowns as if truly perplexed by such a thing.

'Hush your mouth.'

So I'm not big on moving my body! It's just so arduous, but walking I can handle. 'This is the new and improved Orly 2.0.

'I'm taking you for a stroll through the woods, so you can see how wonderful my vast new empire is.' And to try and convince her to come and visit.

'You have signal out there? I'm impressed!'

I laugh. 'Well, I'm not going into the woods per se, just *close* to the woods so I don't lose the connection. Plus the thick dense trails creep me out.' I'm sure I'll be fine when I learn how to navigate the trails but until then I'll stick with walking the perimeter.

'Look at you go! The new Orly taking the reins of her life. I love it.'

I catch my breath before replying. 'I sure am! I've never slept so well. That's down to all the physical labour too. I crash out at night, and sleep like the dead. Anyway, let me show you around.' I change the angle on the screen so Maya can enjoy the stunning view, greenery as far as the eye can see, colourful flowers dotting the landscape. A stray chicken.

'Is that a chicken?' Maya asks.

'Aww, he must be lost!'

'You have to reunite him with his owner,' Maya says. 'Poor little mite.'

'I don't know anyone who owns chickens around here though.'

'Well, the first thing will be catching him, I suppose. Prop me up against a tree so I can watch.'

Sounds simple enough. 'He's so cute with his orange plumage!' I prop up the phone against the trunk of a felled tree. 'Operation save the chicken is underway.' I crack my knuckles in readiness to impress Maya with my newfound outdoorsy skills.

The chicken stops and stares at me with what I'm guessing is a loving look as far as chickens go. I mean, he seems to be frowning, but *can* chickens smile? He's probably starving and knows I'm his saviour come to rescue him from the evils of the woodland. From the *many* predators just a few steps away.

'Come here, little fella.' I hold out my hand like I have food, and he darts forward, nipping me with his beak. 'ARGH!'

'What happened?' Maya asks.

But there's no time to respond. The chicken goes absolutely bloody cuckoo and starts circling me, and hammering me with the point of his beak. For a little mite he sure packs a punch. I jump, I dash, I run and in the end I curl into a ball, screaming, 'Help! HELP ME!'

'Flipping heck, Orly, are you OK?'

I peek through my fingers, my heart hammering, and whisper, 'Is he gone?'

'Who, the chicken?'

'Yes, the chicken! Who else would I be talking about?'

'God, I thought someone attacked you the way you were hollering!'

'The bloody *chicken* attacked me, Maya. And I tell you what, I don't care who he belongs to, he's going to make a mighty fine roast dinner!' As though he hears the threat he flies towards me, squawking, so I drop into a ball and screech again, 'OK, OK, no roast dinner! I'm SORRY!'

And with that he disappears and I sag in relief.

'That was one crazy fowl!' Maya says laughing so hard she's crying. 'Oh, Orly, that was the funniest thing I've ever seen!'

I limp back to the phone, and snatch it up. 'I'm not in London, anymore, Toto, am I?'

'You bloody well aren't! Oh, if only I had recorded that, whenever I'm down I'd watch it and be guaranteed a laugh. Are you bleeding?'

I check my many injuries. 'Yeah, a fair bit. Maybe he hit an artery, the little devil.'

'An artery, Orly? Not that you're prone to exaggeration or anything!'

'OK, maybe it's not quite artery level bleeding but it must be *whisper* close. Plus, I really hate the sight of blood. I don't know how you work with it all day.'

She laughs. 'Well, use that first aid kit I got for you when you get back to the cottage. Make sure you clean the wounds well.'

'Yes, doctor.'

'I wonder who the chicken belongs to?'

'He's wild, I think – is there such a thing as wild chickens?'

'Golly, who knows. Maybe you should adopt him?'

'No way in the world. Once they taste blood, that's it, isn't it? They turn feral.'

'Isn't that dogs, Orly?'

'I have no idea.' I shrug as I stagger home as if I've just done ten rounds with Muhammad Ali himself.

'So aside from homicidal chickens, how's it all going there?'

'Well, apart from me bleeding from many, *many* puncture wounds, I've never felt better. Yeah, sure, I might need about a hundred plasters and a few paracetamol, but hey, look at all the fresh air I'm breathing! Look at my curvy body enjoying exercise!'

'You look fabulous, darling, and you sound like you're having the time of your life, so what aren't you telling me?'

Maya can always see straight through me. But if I tell her about the notes, she'll either say I'm losing my mind, or she will say the place is dangerous. So I think of another problem. 'Oh, it's just a little lonely in the evenings, that's all. I'm so busy during the day – there's plenty to do and see – but when night falls, it's so quiet, and it's so pitch-black, like I'm the only person on the planet. It's just different, and I guess will take some getting used to.' The inkiness of night is an oddity to me: it's like I can see for miles and see nothing at the same time. It's those few hours where I have too much time to think, and doubt creeps up on me. At first it was a novelty, but now I find it downright lonesome.

'It sounds like you need to find something to keep you occupied in those few hours of solitude,' Maya says. 'Why don't you reorder your stamps?'

'Yeah, they always calm me down.' But in truth, I've reordered them so many times, I'm sure the folders sigh when I open them as if saying: leave us be.

Maybe I should try karaoke? Esterlita dropped me off a machine a while back, claiming I'd need to practise for the annual Eden Hills singing contest, which of course I have no intention of entering.

A bleeping sound interrupts our chat. 'Go save lives,' I say as Maya's buzzer reaches the full crescendo.

'Will do and put some antiseptic on those wounds and call me if you start to feel unwell.'

'Yes, doctor.' I salute.

Later that evening, feeling down, I pull out the karaoke machine and plug it in. I shake my head when I see it comes complete with a disco ball that projects brightly coloured lights over the ceiling as if I'm in a nightclub or something.

Esterlita has it all set up with her favourite songs so I start with Celine Dion's 'My Heart Will Go On'. I belt out those lyrics as if the ship is going down, and it's my very last long song to Leo. The actor, not the carpenter but I can't help it, I can only picture my own Leo from small-town Kent, so I sing my heart out to him, knowing I'm in the safety of my own cottage and no one can see me dance and better yet, hear me sing!

There's something quite heartening about performing for oneself and I wonder if I've missed my calling as a singer or if it's the amount of wine I've consumed? All that singing and dancing zaps me so I decide to throw myself in the steaming-hot shower and wash the day away. I turn on the shower and undress before stepping into the stall. As I go to close the curtain behind me, I see a spider on the shower head that is so big it virtually blocks out the light. It's so close I can make out every one of its eight beady eyes and what I read in those are villainy plain and simple. Before it can pounce on me with the sole purpose of injecting venom, I let out a bloodcurdling scream and make a run for it.

My heart beats wildly as I replay the sight of the hairy arachnid that had been only a breath away from launching itself at me! My skin crawls, like actually crawls, and I panic about what to do. I need to remove him before he hides somewhere and jumps out when I'm least expecting it. I'm sure I saw a big bug catcher in the Honeysuckle Hall storage room so I race outside to find it. If he crawls away, I'll never be able to sleep! It's only when the cold hits me I remember I'm naked.

There's no time to concern myself with such a folly because I need to get back to the creature as fast as possible. When I run straight into a cobweb, I let out another scream and wonder if this is some elaborate prank from the universe to warn me off the place too! I run in a loop, flinging my arms all over the place to avoid any more cobwebs and let out a high-pitched wail in order to scare any other beasts away.

'Orly, what on earth are you *doing*?'

Holy mother of tarantulas! I uselessly try to cover myself with my hands. 'Oh, Es! Jeez! I was er … running under the moonlight because Mercury is in retrograde and it's the best time to do it!'

'Help me, sweet baby Jesus!' She rolls her eyes. 'Are you drunk?'

'A little.'

'Go inside before you catch your death, Mercury can't help you then.'

'I'm joking, Es. There was a huge spider in the shower at the same time as me, a very *vicious*-looking one and I came out in a bit of a panic for the bug catcher, and well, I wasn't thinking about my nakedness at that point,' I say. 'I'm no arachnologist but I'd say it was venomous, maybe even lethal.'

She stares at me like she doesn't believe me and remains silent.

'I'm going to go inside now.' I back away, slowly.

It's only later, when I'm tucked up in bed, that I realise I forgot to catch the spider. It's probably inching its way around the cottage right now …

What a day!

Chapter 10

Almost a week later, with the cottage rejuvenation nearly complete, I make a plan to head into town proper with Esterlita, who assures me the antique emporium has the most wonderful collection of furniture, even if the pieces *are* one hundred years old.

We go in her catering van, a big trusty old thing, which she drives like she stole it. My breath catches in my throat as she takes corners in a straight line. Clearly, she doesn't feel the need to brake when she can accelerate. The van swings perilously this way and that and I clutch the grab handle and send up a silent prayer that we make it to town alive.

As we zoom past other cars, I see fear reflected in the drivers' eyes. My pulse thrums so loud I can actually hear it, a cross between rattle and a moan, like I'm stuck in the death throes, halfway between here and the afterlife. I don't dare speak in case Esterlita takes her eyes off the road and we careen to our deaths.

I'm white-knuckled by the time we arrive. 'Bloody hell, Es. Were you a racing car driver in your former life?' My heart beats so loud I can barely hear myself think.

'What?' She scrunches up her face.

'Were you *trying* to beat the land speed record or something? You were *well* over the speed limit!' I open the door with shaky hands and fall to the ground, my jelly legs unable to hold me up. I kiss the mossy earth in thanks for my life.

She waves me away. 'Oh, you and all your rules, Orly!' she says as if I'm the fun police sent specifically to ruin her day.

'They're not *my* rules!'

'I'm good friends with Constable Jones – don't worry.'

'That doesn't help if you lose control and hit a tree.'

'You're so boring, you know that?' She exits the van, shaking her head and muttering.

'Only because I like being alive,' I say.

'I've driven these roads for forty-plus years. Do I look dead to you?'

I know we can go back and forth for hours when she's not going to admit defeat, so I give in. 'Right. Well, I also like walking – maybe next time we can take a nice relaxing walk into town instead?'

'Not safe. You'll probably get hit by a speeding car.'

'What?'

'Nothing. Do you want to shop or do you want to argue?' She folds her arms across her chest.

'I'd prefer to shop while I'm still of this mortal coil.'

'Good choice.'

We head into the little antique emporium and I'm assailed with the musty scent of dust and the turpentine of furniture polish. It's cosy and moody and packed wall to wall with antiques. 'Oh, Es, these are lovely.' I point to a couple of gilded bergère chairs upholstered in soft pink velvet.

'They're very … you.'

'Pink and French – I'll take that as a compliment.'

'What else do you need?'

'An armoire, a vitrine for my stamp collection, a—'

'OK, just point. I don't know what any of those are.'

I laugh and point to the pieces. 'OK, I see, very different from my house. I prefer shiny and slippery.' I can only imagine what

Esterlita's house looks like because she prefers hanging out at my cottage. I expect her décor is an assault on the eyes as she does like bright, bold, contrasting colours and patterns, although I bet somehow it works.

'I can see these would work in your cottage. I do like the gilding.'

'Me too. I need a few bits and pieces for the guest room – one of those beautiful white Hollywood beds.' Part of me is hoping Maya will come and visit soon so I intend to make the room an oasis. 'And then I guess I need some Chesterfields or similar for the hall, and ... I don't even know where to start with the hall actually.' I flick over a price tag, and sharply inhale. 'I might need to do the buying in stages.'

'Don't worry about the price so much; you have the Firecracker with you. We won't pay half of what's on the price tag, trust me.'

I grin, imagining Esterlita haggling with the poor shop assistant who'd probably give in just to get us out of the shop.

'OK, I suppose a bulk buy does warrant some negotiation. But let's just take it slowly so I don't impulse-purchase.' Esterlita has a way of badgering me to do things I don't want to do.

She clicks her fingers at a young man at the desk as if she's Carly C herself. 'These prices are highway robbery! Orly needs that, that other thing, that bigger thing over there.' She does the duck lips and the poor guy tries to follow her meaning. His complexion turns red when she gets impatient. 'No, not that one, that one!' Again she points with her pout. We'll be here all day at this rate.

'Es!'

'What?'

I lean close and whisper, 'Let me point, OK, and you can haggle.'

'Sure.' she grins. 'This young man is Sebastian. He's a good Catholic boy and I know his mother *very* well.'

He's probably about thirty years old and her words are more like a threat than an introduction as if she'll be on the phone to his mum in a flash to tell her he's not bowing to pressure.

'Hey, Sebastian, it's lovely to meet you. I'm Orly, and I've just moved into Honeysuckle Hall.'

'Oh, I've heard *all* about you!'

I narrow my eyes at Esterlita who suddenly studies her nails. 'Hope it wasn't all bad,' I half-joke.

'Nothing bad, just that you sometimes run around naked screaming.' He blushes. 'Some kind of London fad to bathe under the moonlight, or something. I wouldn't mind joining you … purely for the health benefits.'

I shoot daggers at Esterlita. How has she spread the story around this quickly? 'Thanks for the offer, but no, it's not a London fad thing. There was a very big hairy spider, you see—'

His face falls. 'You don't need to justify yourself to me.'

I'm going to kill Esterlita. 'Quite. So how about you show me around.'

'Yes, of course.'

'I'll just stay right here.' Esterlita plonks herself on a chaise longue and kicks off her heels.

'Yes, erm, make yourself comfortable,' Sebastian says.

'A cup of tea would be lovely.'

'Ah, sure, give me a minute, Orly. I'll make tea and be right back.'

'And don't forget the biscuits,' Esterlita says.

I shake my head. 'I'll take a wander around. Don't rush.'

But Sebastian duly rushes off and I turn to Esterlita. '*Bathing under the moonlight*, Esterlita! Were you short of gossip or something?'

'You said something about Mercury in retrograde, did you not?' She shrugs. 'And I had to make it scintillating, didn't I? The spider angle is so boring. Don't worry, this should get you the attention of every single man in town!'

I let out a long sigh. 'And you've got that thirty-something-year-old *boy* running scared! What are you like?'

'To me he is a boy! And it's all part of the complex rules of negotiation, darling.'

I sigh at Esterlita and her foibles. I've never known anyone like her before and I doubt I ever will again. 'Well, your majesty, if you're all set there I'll take a look around.'

She holds a hand out for me to kiss. 'As you wish.'

Her cackle follows me around the shop.

Chapter 11

I have more drop-ins from curious townsfolk and people who come to fix things at the property, but they all stay schtum about why the place never had any interest. I have that same niggle that everyone knows something I don't. Maybe it's just the way they treat newcomers? A small-town test, to see who has the mettle to stay before they're taken into the fold. And if that's the case, then I'm prepared to earn their trust slowly but surely, even though the running naked under the moonlight thing hasn't endeared me to some.

When Sophia, a young mum with kids in hand and a baby strapped to her front, drops in, I invite them to play in the garden while I make the stressed mum a pot of tea. 'Sorry for dropping in like this,' she says with a shrug. 'We were meandering and found ourselves here. These long walks help burn a bit of their endless energy and they wanted to see who the new person was they've been hearing so much about.'

They must be six and under, and they've been hearing about me? Or is it Sophia's way of explaining away her curiosity? 'No problem,' I say. 'I'm sure everyone is more interested in what's happening with the hall itself, rather than me.'

Sophia blows on her steaming-hot tea. 'No, not really. It's

mainly you everyone is interested in. Especially after Freya stirring the pot.'

'Oh?' I say. I hadn't really believed Esterlita's soliloquy about Freya.

'I don't believe a word of it, of course.' She darts a glance around the cottage as if looking for clues. 'You're not setting up a gentlemen's club, are you?'

'A what?'

She blushes. 'I don't know exactly what she meant, but she alluded to late-night debauchery, that kind of thing.'

It makes me uneasy that the local town gossip has it in for me. It can't be good for business and it's just plain mean. 'No, I can assure you I'm not starting anything of the sort! I'm going to open up a camp, a *wellness* retreat, if you will. There's nothing untoward about it! I haven't even met Freya, so I'm not sure where she's getting her information from?' And what on earth is she implying when she says gentlemen's club?!

'That's Freya, she's got spies everywhere. Knows everything there is to know about people. Gives me the creeps, she does. Told everyone that I had too many children, that I was ruining my life, popping them out one after another like that, as if I'd done something wrong by wanting a gaggle of kids!' Sophia's face falls and I can see Freya's acid tongue has caused quite a lot of damage to the young mum's confidence.

I open the biscuit tin and offer it to Sophia. Sugar helps in times like this. 'Sounds to me like Freya envies you, Sophia. Usually that's where malicious gossip stems from. As hurtful as her words are, I wouldn't let them bother you. It says more about her than it does about you. Your children are lovely and I can tell you're a fabulous mother.'

'Thanks, Orly.'

'No need to thank me, just telling it like it is.'

We watch the kids run rampant outside and finish our tea and biscuits. All the while I think of the busybody Freya, besmirching people for no good reason. I'll have to find out a little more about her and why she's trying so hard to turn people against me. Perhaps she wanted the hall? One thing I know for sure is, bullies are usually jealous of something, and what else could it be?

Sophia leaves as quickly as she arrived, the kids running backwards and waving, seemingly more energetic than when they arrived. I make a mental note to invite them back for a barbecue, so the kids can explore while Sophia puts her feet up for a bit.

I clear up the tea things and then check my emails. Leo's quote arrives. I hope to all that is holy I can afford it. I'm reminded of Esterlita's dire warnings that this place is a money pit and I'd be better off marrying a rich man …!

My finger hovers over the attachment as I freeze, unwilling to see the numbers now they're here. What if I've underestimated the costs? *You'll find a way.*

If my plans are halted before they even start then I'll buy some power tools and give it a red-hot go myself. An image of me wearing steel-capped work boots and a tool belt flashes into mind and I laugh. How hard can fixing windows be? I'll probably lose a finger in the process but I suppose I have ten to play with – or are thumbs not classed as fingers? In that case I only have eight to play with. Risky …

Just as I'm about to open the attachment a car pulls into the drive. I jump up in excitement and shock when I see it's Maya. Scouring the front room, I know she'll be surprised by the changes. She might even stay this time.

Esterlita and I have made miracles happen, even though I had to give in and agree to let her scatter some cushions in the most hideous colours ever produced. They definitely take away from the cosy cottage vibe but arguing with Esterlita over aesthetics is infinitely more stressful.

I race outside and greet Maya with a: 'Whatareyoudoing-hereohmygod!' And launch-hug her like I'm channelling Bai.

With an, 'Ummmzfphwark,' she manages to keep her balance and says, 'What a welcome!'

Holding her arms, I stand back. 'Why didn't you call and let me know you were coming?'

'I took a gamble you'd be in, unless you've already found a new love and are off for few days of debauchery?'

I cluck my tongue. You'd think I'd been a spinster my whole life the way these women talk about me! 'No, I've been very busy setting up this brand-new venture, I'll have you know. I don't have time for washing my hair, let alone men.'

She flicks one of my plaits. 'I can see that. And I thought it wise to come and check your chicken bites were healing well.'

I cup my face and groan. 'I'm bloody triggered every time I see something out the corner of my eye. He's stalking me, I know it!'

'Who knew chickens were so calculating?'

'Cluck Norris bloody well is!' I shudder, remembering his beady little eyes and the threat in them. 'How did you manage to get time off?'

'*Cluck Norris!*' She laughs and takes a small case from the back seat of the car. 'I did so many double shifts I couldn't remember what day it was. In fact, I still can't. Monday, Thursday, Wednesday? I'm due for some leave so I thought, why not? I've missed you. Like crazily, stalker-fashion missed you. I propped up a photo of you on my phone at Bai's and pretended you were there. Got a few strange looks too, I did.'

I laugh. 'I've missed you too.' And I really have, especially when Esterlita has gone home after her usual twenty-minute goodbyes and my body aches from the manual labour and sleep still manages to elude me. That's the time of night where I think about Harry, Maya, and my old life in London. Strangely, I miss the street noises and sirens that used to lull me to sleep but don't miss the hectic London life itself.

'Let me take you for a tour.' I grab her hand and lead her

inside. The entrance hall that was once a dark musty space is now a bright and airy linen-white, with golden hooks for coats and hats. A little potted fern blows in the breeze like its waving.

'Wow, this is amazing.'

'That's not all.' I lead her into the front room, and she gasps. 'You did all this?'

'I did, with the help of my neighbour Esterlita. You can thank her for those horrendously awful cushions, one of which is a close-up of a dolphin, jumping out of the water. She really loves dolphins and who am I to judge?'

'Wow, I can't believe the change! This is the prettiest little cottage I've ever seen. Before it looked like the scene of a crime. You've done wonders with it. I love the fireplace. And these gorgeous antiques, Orly, wow. All of your furniture from the apartment … is where?'

'Sold. It didn't suit here.'

'You made the right choice. It wouldn't have suited being Scandi. This is lovely, Orly, really lovely. You always had a flair for interior design.'

'Esterlita got me a criminally good deal on the antiques by threatening the poor Catholic boy on the tills that she'd tell his mother some secret.' Part of me still feels a little guilty at that until I remember Sebastian offering to join me naked under the moonlight for 'health benefits'.

'What was the secret?'

'Oh!' I lift a palm. 'Once when he was seven, Esterlita caught him peeking up ladies' skirts in church under the guise of collecting Bibles. She's never let him forget it.'

'When he was *seven*?'

'He claims it isn't true, said he was collecting Bibles and kept getting told to get out of the way of the priest, but he's terrified of Esterlita.'

'Wow, good bargaining power then.'

'Yes, poor guy. I also bought a bunch of furniture for the hall

112

but that won't be delivered until the repairs are complete. Come and see the rest.' I take her through the tiny cottage to the guest bedroom. I spent longest here, trying to get the colours and décor right, hoping Maya would visit and feel welcome.

'This is just beautiful.' The white Hollywood bed is made up with floral linen and lots of plush pillows and soft throws. There's a reading chair and a bedside with a lamp.

'I knew you'd like it. I wanted it to feel homey and cosy.'

'I don't think I'll ever want to leave, Orly. Seriously, I can't believe you've done all this in the time I've been gone. It's like I've stepped into a fairy tale. I'm just waiting for my cookies and warm milk.'

I sling an arm over her shoulder, pleased as punch she loves the cottage and that she's here for a little while at least. 'How about a pot of tea and some cake?'

'I could murder a pot of tea! So tell me everything that's happened since we spoke last.'

We head into the kitchen, which is bright and sunny now that the grimy cracked window has been replaced, and delicate lace curtains sway in the breeze. Maya props herself up on a stool at the small island bench. As I start to assemble tea things, the doorbell rings, and then promptly rings again. Esterlita's calling card. She says no one ever hears the first ring. Since the bell is more of a thirty-second melody I've assured her she only needs to do it once, but she won't be told. Besides, she doesn't wait, she wanders right on in, just like she did that very first day, so the bell is moot anyway.

Esterlita appears, holding a shopping bag. 'Who's this? Is this Maya? The pretty heart surgeon who has that on-again off-again boyfriend who's no good for her?'

I redden. 'Well, say-it-like-is Esterlita is here,' I tell Maya, hoping she forgives me for sharing that little nugget of information. 'This is the neighbour I was telling you about – what I *didn't* say was that she has a no-filter approach to life. Secrets are not safe with

113

her and she will drop you in it if there's a man within a twenty-mile radius.'

Maya grins. 'I love her already. And you're right, he's no good for me but isn't that the fun part? The obligatory bad boy! Nice to meet you, Esterlita. By the sounds of it you've taken Orly under your wing and thank goodness for that. I expected the yoga pants, but I also thought she might have adopted a bunch of rescue pets and become addicted to Etsy. It's good to see that's not the case. Although she does have Yolko Ono the adorable little chicken, so that's something.'

'Well, I'm not ruling out a rescue dog ... or cat. And that bloody psychopath chicken is *not* mine!'

'It's just misunderstood,' Maya cries.

I cross my arms. 'It's mercenary, that's what it is. Won't stop until it takes over the bloody place.'

'A teeny-weeny little chicken?' Maya says, as if he's a fluffy little chick just out of the nest.

'Well, allow me to introduce you to him, Maya, and then you can form an opinion.'

'Sure, animals love me.'

'We'll see about that!'

Esterlita chimes in, 'She does have a little problem with the decorating. I don't know if that's a new thing or not but I think it says a lot about her frame of mind. Don't you? It's like she's a hundred-year-old woman! Lace and velvet and all these fussy pastels. I just do not understand it.'

'Same,' Maya agrees, hiding a smile. The traitor.

'How can pastels be fussy?' I say, genuinely confused. They don't hear me and continue highlighting all my so-called flaws.

'And she likes hiding behind the ugliest clothes. The ugliest. Big baggy trousers and jumpers so big I think she's going to take flight in high winds. It's like she wants to be invisible.'

'Right. I thought that might get worse here. Well, we could always ditch her loungewear?'

'I'm right here, you know! And I love my loungewear, so you'll have to pry it from my cold dead body.'

'OK, it's clear she's not ready for that yet. Has she been sleeping OK? I bet she hasn't.'

Esterlita shakes her head. 'When I've gone home of a night and she thinks I'm asleep, she plays this ear-bleedingly awful music. It's like nails down a chalkboard, like cats screaming, or banshees wailing …'

I stiffen. 'Erm, that's me singing on the karaoke machine you loaned me, Es.' It's just a little goodnight ritual I've begun to enjoy before bed. I've never had time to do things like that before and now I'm finding all these moments where I can snatch a bit of me-time. I didn't realise though that Esterlita could hear me all the way across the green. I know I am a tad off-key, but I highly doubt I sound like a banshee wailing? Or a cat screaming? Can cats even scream? I make another mental note to check.

She raises a brow. 'Well, hold off on the rescue pet, eh? Your caterwauling is enough to send them off running and we don't need any more feral cats around here. Don't even get me started on what she does at midnight … Let's just say clothes are optional, no matter what the weather's doing, as she runs around the yard waving her hands in some kind of supplication to the moon dance.'

'Looks like I'm just in time.' Maya sighs.

'For what?' I ask, but again I'm ignored by the duo.

'You are.' Esterlita nods. 'I've done all I can but I know she spends a lot of time on that bleeping contraption looking up her ex, the pig. Then she searches for the celebrity who stole him away, the one with the big—'

'How do you know that? That's not true!' OK, it is true but how …? I look up to see if she's installed hidden cameras or something. So, my heart is broken and I still miss Harry, even if he is a horrible person. You can't just switch those feelings off.

It's not like I'll ever forgive him but I still wonder what he's doing and if he thinks of me.

Esterlita pretends not to hear me. 'The most *delectable* hunk of a man wandered in and she acted like some kind of disinterested robot.' She promptly mimes an impression of me with puckered lips, holding a clipboard, talking mechanically: 'Yes, Mr Carpenter, please consider the work. I can't have fun, I'm in a relationship with my paint colour charts ...' She makes a real performance of it.

'It's worse than I thought,' Maya says.

Esterlita puts her hands on her hips. 'Much worse.'

'I did not act like a disinterested robot, I was merely being professional. Now would you two stop it, or I'll have to start ... *singing.*'

Esterlita holds up her hands in surrender. 'OK, OK, I'll stop.'

Maya turns to me, her deep brown eyes twinkling with mirth but also a touch of concern. 'Have you spoken to Harry since you've been here?'

I shake my head. 'No, and I won't either. It's just some kind of self-sabotage that I like doing once I've had a few glasses of wine. You know, search their socials and then feel hideous about myself. Doesn't *everyone* do that after a break-up?'

Maya flicks her long, black curls over a shoulder. 'Yes, that's totally normal. I'm glad you haven't contacted the prig, that's all. That schmoozy charmer has a way with words and I don't trust him at all. But Esterlita says you haven't spent much time in town, haven't even tried the local pub for dinner. What's that about? The Orly of before would have already networked her way around the village. She'd have all their numbers and have invited them all for drinks already.'

I cast my gaze to the floor. 'I know, I just wanted some time to be invisible. It's not like they don't know there's a new person, but I wanted a bit of space first. I've been shopping, I've met a heap of tradespeople, every second person has dropped in to say hi – that's enough for now.'

She taps the empty stool next to her and motions for me to sit. 'But, Orly, the success of the camp will come from word of mouth. I know you need some time to heal but you also need money.'

I let out a dramatic Esterlita-like sigh. 'So?'

'So … what?'

'So what does it matter?'

'You might not be able to see it but these are the classic signs of someone who is shutting off from the world, when in fact, you need to be doing the exact opposite. Strutting down the high street and making your presence known.'

I do my best impersonation of Esterlita and roll my eyes so dramatically I can almost see my brain and am rewarded with a dizzy spell for my efforts. 'You sound like Es.'

'Who has *obviously* been giving you good, solid advice.' Maya gives me a half-smile.

OK, they might have some teeny, tiny valid concerns, but I'm still not ready to show my face at the pub in town. Local pubs are always a hotbed of gossip and I definitely don't want to give Freya or the other jaw-flappers any ammunition.

What if someone recognises me from the horrendous photos in the *Daily Sun*, taken when I'd been looking anything but my best, with headlines screaming: *The woman who drove Harry into the arms of Carly C!* Like I'd been some kind of harridan and kept him locked in a basement until he made his timely escape into the loving arms of the saucy singer herself. They'll judge yoga-pants-me on sight and I'm not ready for all that.

So far I've managed quite well here, casually seeing people who come to the hall and a few hair-raising expeditions with Esterlita to buy supplies, keeping under the radar, and all.

On the slow days it's just me and my stamp collection and all is right with the world as I flick through them, wondering who owned each sheet before me, who designed them. And the ones soaked lovingly from envelopes, and sold as singles with all this mystery surrounding the little square – where did this singleton stamp ferry the letter to? What was it about – a love letter, a break-up letter, a letter from a mum to a daughter? There's so much life in stamps, but it's all about imagination. And I can easily waste hours sitting with them and doing just that. I'm not hiding per se, I'm hibernating, two very different things.

The very last thing I want is any scrutiny; I want to be normal for a bit. But I'm surprised that Maya has picked up on any of this all the way from London, unless … 'You two have been in contact!'

Maya shrugs as if it's nothing. 'I rang one day and Esterlita answered. You were busy crying over the wild roses apparently.'

'The wild roses?' I think back. Oh, yes. 'I've never seen such a pretty flower before – they stopped me in my tracks for a bit.' Those escaped tendrils of loveliness, racing towards the sun as if they have somewhere important to be.

'She says they're her friends,' Esterlita says, folding her arms.

'Your friends. *Roses?* I'll admit they can be mesmerising, but friends? Oh dear, this is more serious than I thought.'

I huff. 'I didn't say the roses were my *friends*, I just said, if roses could talk I wonder what they'd say. And I was feeling very lonely that afternoon and I thought I'd confide in the delicate stems as I viciously deadheaded them. It was more an apology, than anything.'

They exchange a worried glance and I hurry to reassure them. 'You would have done the same. Am I right?'

Maya crinkles her nose. 'Erm, yeah, I think gardening might best be left to the professionals, don't you? Somehow I don't think you wielding a pair of razor-sharp secateurs is a good idea at this point. You're bound to cut off a pinkie or something.'

'I guess. I *did* sustain a fair bit of damage from the thorns.' I survey my hands, which now have a certain number of cuts, scratches, and an assortment of paint samples, and I feel quite proud of all I've accomplished.

'What we need is a night out!' Maya says. 'And tomorrow we can get back to work. I want to help as much as I can.'

'Can't we have a night *in*?' I grumble. 'We're up to a very important episode of *The Real Housewives* and I don't want to miss it.'

'It's on Netflix – you can watch it any time.'

Esterlita does her usual push-me-in-the-back thing and fires out, 'Come on, lady, get those glad rags on, something short and slippery should do it.'

'Do I look like I own something short and slippery?' I say, arching a brow as my heart beats a rhumba at the thought. I love my loungewear, and I can finally wear it here because I'm not Orly from Excès anymore. Every time I slip into my flat shoes, I smile.

But Esterlita shakes her head and her eyes light up as she reaches for the mysterious shopping bag, producing a tiny slash of bright red sequins. 'I'm not wearing that top.'

'It's a *dress*, darling – don't be so sarcastic.'

'It is so *not* a dress. I have tank tops longer than that.'

'And yet they haven't got you a man yet, have they?'

'This again, really?' I look to Maya to be the voice of reason as she so usually is.

'Red is your colour. With your lovely blonde locks and big blue eyes, you'll set that little number off nicely.' She hangs me out to dry, just like that.

'You can't be serious.'

'We are.' They speak in unison and I wonder just how many phone calls Esterlita has intercepted while I've been busy. And how on earth she's convinced my usually responsible friend that *this* is the answer.

Knowing two against one is futile, I snatch the pitiful excuse for a dress and head into my bathroom. As soon as they see it on, they'll realise their mistake. Untying my plaits, I wait for the bath to fill, adding half a bottle of bubbles, hoping they hide me from now to all eternity and I avoid having to go out wearing a dress more suited to an actual Barbie doll.

My ploy doesn't work and soon enough Maya knocks and enters the small bathroom, uselessly waving the steam away. 'Don't think you can hide under all those bubbles.'

'Damn it.'

She hands me a glass of real bubbles. 'Don't try and butter me up with French champagne, you traitor, you turncoat, you terrible friend.'

She goes to snatch the glass back.

I hastily bring it close. 'Well, I've had a sip now, so I may as well drink it.'

'Fine. Get that down you, and then get your make-up on. I'll curl your hair and then we're off out.'

'I can hardly wait,' I say with heavy sarcasm and take a big gulp of bubbles as Maya shuts the door behind her.

My phone pings just like bloody usual when I'm almost eyeball-deep in the bath. I ignore it but it continues so I force myself out and wrap myself in a towel, then find my phone, realising with a grin it's not going to be an Excès drama that I have to sort out. There's such a freedom in that, I'm still smiling when I swipe to see a bunch of comments on the new Honeysuckle Hall Facebook page.

I gasp when I see the comments: *You better leave Carly C alone! This is her chance at real happiness and your opinion is not wanted! Be careful or you'll have the #CarlyArmy after you!*

Sometimes I despair for the human race. I haven't contacted Carly C, nor will I, and who on God's green earth are the Carly Army?

But they get worse: *We know you're hiding out at the hall, plotting revenge! We have spies everywhere! Watch your step! #CarlyArmyInFormation*

Not only are these threats ludicrous, they're also really bad for business. I go through and delete the lot of them and only hope by not engaging with these trolls they go away.

'Are you out of the bath?' Maya yells from the living room. I shut the page down quickly and put it out of my mind for the evening.

Chapter 12

'I look like I'm on the prowl.' I'll definitely be unable to blend in when I flash and sparkle like a Christmas bauble, which is probably their plan. The minxes!

'Aren't you?' Esterlita looks genuinely confused.

I stare her down, which only makes it worse as she scrutinises me up close; before long she's directly under my chin like she's looking for more of these wrinkles I'm allegedly growing at a rate of knots.

'She needs more lipstick. Why you gotta wear that nude stuff for? Why can't she wear pink, or purple? It's your fear of bright colours again, isn't it? This is the root of all her problems, mark my words.'

'I didn't realise you'd studied cosmetology, Es?' I say with a scoff. 'And I'm not wearing pink or purple lipstick and don't start on the blue eyeshadow thing again. I'm going to freeze to death wearing this. If I don't get picked up by the police first for suspected soliciting!'

Spritzing on spicy perfume, Maya ignores me and says, 'You look ravishing!'

I roll my eyes. 'Why do *you* get to wear clothing that covers your knees?' She's got a multitude of layers on like she's trying to make up for the lack of mine.

She sighs as if I'm testing the limit of her patience. 'I have a reputation to uphold as a very serious and together surgeon.'

I don't know if it's the amount of bubbles I've consumed, or I'm just over pleading my case, but I acquiesce. 'Fine, let's get this over with. I'm hungry.'

'Let's eat somewhere first,' Maya says. 'And then we can check out the nightlife.'

Esterlita grimaces. 'There's not much nightlife. It's the Tipsy Tadpole and that's it.'

'The Tipsy Tadpole – is that the name of the pub?' Maya asks laughing.

'Yes,' Esterlita says as if it's obvious.

'Well then, let's do it.' Maya saunters outside while I flick through the coat rail, hoping to find a light jacket that's long enough to cover my derriere. And my pride.

'No, no you don't need that paint-splattered thing,' Maya says. 'Take a scarf instead.'

'Fine.'

'I'll drive,' Esterlita says.

'Oh no no no,' I panic. 'Maya is a real walking nut.' I send her a signal with my eyes alone and she catches on fast. 'Loves a bit of one foot in front of the other action, she does.'

'Yes, I'd love to walk, see a bit of the town.'

'Youth of today. Always got the devices pressed into the palm of their hands but don't like automobiles – I will never understand.'

'It's a health thing.' As in staying alive.

'Fine.'

I internally breathe a sigh of relief. Maya's life is too precious to be put in the hands of Esterlita's Formula One driving. The few times I've had to brave her van in order to pick up supplies my life has flashed before my eyes like a movie reel and I definitely don't want it to end like this, not before I've at least made a success of the camp.

We totter into town and I'm surprised to find how pretty it looks lit up at night-time. Small shopfronts are locked up; warm lights highlight display windows. There's a bakery, a café, and a bookshop. We continue on past a lolly shop, a chippy, and the antique emporium with a display of luscious ruby velvet furniture in the window. 'Ooh, look at those chairs.' I point. 'They'd go nicely in the library room of the hall.'

'We're definitely coming back here tomorrow,' Maya says.

'Want me to help negotiate?' Esterlita says.

I send her a weak smile. 'We're just going to window-shop, Es, but thank you.' What I don't say is I think poor Sebastian has suffered enough.

'OK, but just say the word. Newcomers don't always get the right prices.'

'What do we get?' I think of all the people I've commissioned to work, and so far their prices have seemed more than fair.

'New people prices, of course. Different to someone who's known their families for forty years.'

'Small towns, eh?' Maya says with a smile. 'Where's this pub then?' she asks, folding her arms against the evening breeze. I fairly freeze, with so much of my flesh showing. When my teeth start chattering, I hurry them along.

'At the end of the high street. It's cosy and warm, full of locals and gossip. I'm sure Orly's name would have been mentioned once or twice in the last few weeks.'

'Urgh,' I groan. 'I can imagine. Crazy cat lady from the big smoke buys haunted property. Last seen chasing small terrified children away.'

Esterlita's eyes widen. 'You heard?'

'What?' I say.

She clocks my expression. 'Oh … nothing.' She quickly averts her eyes.

124

Have you heard about the new woman? She wore a red sequin top instead of a dress for a quiet night at her local. Rumoured to be unhinged. Kill me.

'Here we are,' Esterlita says, gesturing to a pint-size pub that has a lean to it as if it's in constant battle with woolly weather but is just hanging on. The thatched Tudor style brings back memories of growing up in a small town that centred around visits to the local.

A ruckus floats from the open windows; the sound of so many people unwinding on a Friday night. When I peek inside, I see it's jam-packed with people clustered in groups around the bar, or at tables. As if anyone will notice us! This is the perfect setting to remain invisible.

'Let's find a table,' I say. 'My stomach is eating itself, I'm so hungry.'

Esterlita walks in and we trail behind. The noise is almost deafening. The Firecracker pushes her way to the bar and waves us over. 'Orly!' she yells and suddenly the din stops. The place goes completely silent and all eyes land on me. I freeze like a statue as panic hits. Yikes. Just as I'm willing my body to engage, to make a run for it, I make contact with those lovely blue eyes that are impossible to forget and I find comfort there. He edges past a few people and makes his way to me.

'Orly.' He holds out his hand. I take it and pull him close to me so I can hide behind his muscly chest. I rest my head against him and wonder if I'm now invisible enough. I knew this was a bad idea!

'Leo,' I muffle, wondering what he tastes like before I catch myself. *What he tastes like?* What is he … an ice cream? A taco! Get ahold of yourself, woman!

'Your dress, it's so ah … red.'

I'm going to kill Esterlita with my secateurs. 'Thanks,' I say, tugging the dress down with my free hand.

It's only then I realise Leo was probably meaning to shake my

125

hand, not have me bury my face in his chest and dream of eating him for dinner.

Note to self: don't skip lunch again. I can't think straight when I'm hungry.

I promptly let go and let out a nervous laugh as the patrons of the Tipsy Tadpole slowly resume their conversations. Without their scrutiny I slowly lower my shoulders, which are somewhere up around my ears. How I miss *The Real Housewives*!

'Well, I best be off home.'

He frowns. 'But you only just arrived.'

'Right. Erm.' The word scatterbrained comes to mind …

Maya finally finds her voice. 'Hi, I'm Maya, Orly's friend from London and you are …?'

'Hey nice to meet you. I'm Leo, the carpenter hoping to help out with the repairs for the camp.'

'Ooh, *Leo*. Yes, I've heard all about you.'

He actually blushes.

'Nothing bad!' I quickly add. 'Nothing good, either!' I reassure him. He tilts his head. 'What I mean to say is, it was all above board, all very professional.'

He laughs, his perfect pearly whites on display. How do some men have it all? It's a ruse though, all smoke and mirrors and I remind myself that behind his supreme good looks probably lies another schemer, like Harry. Just because he's from a small town doesn't make him wholesome, even though that's kind of the vibe he's got.

He blushes a deeper pink. 'That's good to hear. Did you get my quote? I hope it was OK. If you need to amend it in any way, I can go over it again with you.'

The quote! 'Maya surprised me with a visit, so I haven't had a chance, but I promise I'll take a look as soon as—'

Maya nudges me. 'Actually, it'll probably be better if you go over it together, right, Orly? You really want to nail down those figures.'

126

I elbow her in the ribs for good measure. 'I don't want you to go to any trouble.'

'No trouble,' he says. 'How about I pop over tomorrow around lunchtime?'

Before I can form words, Maya says, 'Perfect. And why not stay for lunch tomorrow after you and Orly have gone through the quote?' She elbows me back.

'If I'm not imposing?'

'The more the merrier.'

My life is being orchestrated before my very eyes and I'm not sure how to regain control. I get it, my friends want me to fall in love, or more worryingly lust, but they just don't understand. I can't move on as quickly as all that. Besides, Leo is *not* my type. Not anymore. The next man for me is going to be the sort who *doesn't* stand out. Who isn't devastatingly gorgeous. Who isn't swoon-worthy. I'm done with men like him. They're not ready to settle down and I'm not nursing any more broken hearts if I can help it. Harry was one in a long line of guys who broke my trust in one way or another. I am hopeless with men, *hopeless*. I can't seem to tell who's genuine, and while Leo gives me the impression he is, it's been proven I cannot trust my own judgement.

Leo brings me back to the now by planting a hand on my waist. 'Let me help you find a table, or you'll never get served in here,' he says, playing the chivalrous sort.

'Thanks,' I say, ignoring Maya's cheese-eating grin.

He leads us to a cosy corner, which is mercifully quieter due to a small room divider. 'Will you join us?' Maya says, as Esterlita comes barrelling in, holding several exotic blue cocktails with little umbrellas and a piece of pineapple wedged onto the glass. She's transported me back to the Eighties and I only wish I had a pair of legwarmers right about now!

'I'd love to but I've got an early job tomorrow, before I pop over to the hall. Enjoy your night.' He gives me a nod before he leaves and seems to take all the air in the room with him. All the joy too. It's not real, I remind myself. It's a ploy to weaken women's resolve. I remember Harry having this exact same effect on me, and look how that played out.

I slump over the table. 'God, that was so awkward! What was that?'

'The man is smitten, methinks!' Esterlita booms.

I scoff. 'As if, Es. And I didn't mean Leo, I meant why did the place fall silent like that? I've never felt so exposed in my entire life!'

'You're the new girl, that's why.'

'Let's hope someone else comes along soon then.' I'm only a novelty because I'm new, and I guess that's expected in a small town, right?

Esterlita waves me away. 'Of course not! Soon you'll be part of the furniture and won't get a second glance, which is why you have to act now while you've got the spotlight. You have your choice of men while you're hot property!'

'Urgh, no thanks.'

'Which eligible bachelor would you suggest then?' Maya asks, leaning her arms on the table.

'Over there, see the one with the grey hair, very debonair – that's Matthew, fifty-something, owns a distillery, from a good family, never married.'

'Fifty-something, Es? I'm thirty-five.'

She raises a brow. 'He's got a lot of money. And look, he's one of those grey wolves, isn't he?'

I laugh. 'A silver fox, you mean.'

'Whatever. Same thing. You don't like him, Orly? Is it because he's never been married? Stinks like a secret, doesn't it? Like he's hiding something? Probably into bondage, and M and S.'

I don't correct her this time and try, with all my might, to hold in laughter.

'Yeah, looks like an M and S man to me,' Maya says grinning. 'Who else?'

'OK, if she wants younger, then there's Patrick over there. Loves older women. He's only twenty-two or three. But hold on to your money, Orly. There was a bit of a scandal last year when he broke up with his thirty-eight-year-old girlfriend. Rumour has it he demanded *maintenance* from her, for services rendered if you get my drift.' She winks and blinks just in case her meaning isn't obvious.

'Wow, no, avoid him. Next?'

She shrugs. 'It's a small town. There's really only Leo left. If she wants a looker, that is. There's plenty of others, but most of them look like they've been hit in the face with a frying pan.'

The laughter I've held in check for so long bursts out and soon we're all clutching our bellies.

'This is why she has to move fast. Men don't stay single long here. Orly has the advantage of being new. Mark my words, it won't last forever.'

'From your mouth to God's ears,' I say, and Esterlita hastily crosses herself.

The sooner the new girl status is gone the better. A waitress takes our order and we settle down to dinner, drinking cocktails that taste like pure sugar.

'So, what are we going to cook for the resident town hunk tomorrow?' Maya asks.

'What's with you two? It's like all you can think about is setting me up with someone, anyone, when I've got real-life, proper scary things to worry about right now.'

Maya nods. 'That's true, you do have a lot of anxiety-inducing things to fret over, and I know you, Orly; if we don't step in, you're going to do the exact same thing you did in London, which is work yourself to the bone and miss out on living. You've moved away from all that, yet here you are working from sun up to sun down and probably until the early hours of the morning.' There's been a lot to do behind the scenes: sort insurances for campers, set up social media accounts, crunch numbers and panic, and plenty more besides.

'I'm working a lot *now*. It won't always be that way,' I reassure her, but am I repeating the same old mistakes as before? 'It's the size of the mortgage that keeps me up at night. And whatever the costs of the repairs will be.' It could all crumble before my eyes if I get too lax.

'I can't see how this can fail. Every time I mention it to someone at the hospital they're all over me wanting details. I know it's scary, but I think once word spreads, you'll be inundated. An adventure camp for adults really appeals to people. I think you're onto a winner but you also need to enjoy it. You need to schedule days off, so you can enjoy this new lifestyle.'

'I'll enjoy it when I know it's viable. Until then, I just need to work hard to make sure viable becomes a reality. And the work is so different to Excès because this is all for me, and I'm enjoying it despite being covered in paint and grime most days and getting stalked by a homicidal chicken and a deadly spider.'

'It's just such a huge risk.' Esterlita takes a slurp of her cocktail and adds, 'Why not give up on the idea and make it a place for weddings? You could print your own money with that kind of business.'

'No, no I don't want to deal with any more bridezillas. I had my fair share of them at Excès. They prematurely aged me with all of their demands.'

'What about looking for an investor?' Maya says, sucking her gums and speculating.

An investor? 'No way. I don't want to answer to anyone. I'll be OK, I just need to focus hard at the beginning.'

She shrugs. 'It'll give you a good cash injection and set the business up right from the start. Otherwise, you're going to be chasing your tail from day one.'

Esterlita tuts and makes a show of being put out. 'You girls just don't get it. Orly should hunt out a minor royal. Marry into nobility. Then the hall can become your fifth home. You'll probably use it once a year for a weekend and spend the rest of your time at your castles with your horse-faced noble lady friends who drink tea with pursed lips and pinkie fingers poked out. You can fret about the family miscreant who secretly slugs out of a hip flask, but is the only one who knows how to have fun.'

'Wow, when you paint such a tempting picture, Es, how could I refuse?'

'It's worth thinking about. I can see this kind of life for you, even though your lady-in-waiting would have to wrestle you into formal attire.' She touches her nose as if she's Mystic Meg or something.

I laugh. 'Did it come to you in a dream?'

'It might've.'

I shake my head.

'If finding a lesser royal doesn't work out and you're feeling stressed about money, an investor could take that pressure off, Orly,' Maya says. 'You'd have extra funds for marketing and an advertising budget. You'd have someone to help with the camps. I mean, you say you love fitness but you only lasted five minutes in my boxing class. Who's going to take the campers gorge scrambling or any of those other high-octane adventures you have planned?'

'I was intending on beating my fear and doing it myself. How hard can it be?'

'Hard. Very hard. And what if you get out of breath and give up like you did when I took you abseiling?'

'I won't give up.'

'Or like when I took you to dance class?'

'I wasn't feeling well that day.'

'Or when I took you to CrossFit?'

'I hadn't slept well.'

'Or pole fitness?'

131

'I was uncomfortable sliding up and down that pole. More so when that guy tried to tuck money into my active wear.'

She rolls her eyes. 'There was also the Bokwa class, aerial yoga, tai chi and salsa dancing just to name a few, and each and every time you sat on the sidelines. My point is, with a group of campers following you, their leader, you *can't* sit on the edge and catch your breath. What I'm saying is an investor might be the answer to all your problems and then you can get that shut-eye at night. You're fabulous at marketing and customer relations; there's no one better than you. An investor would free you up to build the camp numbers and organise all those other fun activities like meditation evenings under the stars and planting the community garden.'

She's right in one sense. If my life depended on exercise I would gladly wither up and die. It's just not my thing. It's the exertion I don't like, pushing my body to the limits, and for what? I'm more of a fan of incidental exercise, like running for cabs, pounding the pavement searching for rare stamp collections in long-forgotten dusty shops, building my biceps by drinking extremely large glasses wine, that kind of thing.

Although, I don't think an investor is the way to go. My dream includes me not being accountable to anyone anymore. Not being a *yes* person, not having to ask permission. I've had that kind of life up to my eyeballs. But of course, I have another plan …

'I'm glad you mention my lack of fitness prowess because my cunning plan is to hire a camp leader, someone to run the more physical side of things, while I do the behind-the-scenes stuff. The slightly *less* athletic pursuits.' Crafts. Candle making. Cookie decorating. That I can do. As long as I don't have to bake the cookies – cooking is also not my forte but I plan to work on that here. 'I know I'll eventually need more staff, but for now, I just might get away with two of us. And then when the number of campers grow, our staff can grow.'

'I'll help too,' Esterlita says. 'You can pay me in food.'

I laugh and throw an arm around her. 'I don't know about that. I've seen how much you eat. For a skinny person you sure can pack a lot away.'

'It's my Filipino metabolism. Don't hate me for it.'

The night continues and it's only when I stand to find the loo that I remember the cringe-inducing sequined red dress, but a few cocktails in I find it funny rather than mortifying – although I won't be wearing it ever again! It's going to have a rather unfortunate accident, or at least that's what I'm going to tell Esterlita when it never sees the light of day again.

When the night comes to an end, and we zigzag home laughing and joking about inane things, it strikes me I haven't felt this relaxed in ages. With my two friends by my side, I feel like I can take on the world, no matter what obstacles I may trip over along the way …

Chapter 13

Filmy sunlight streams through the sheer curtains and wakes me from a dream. Groggy, I try to snatch the memory back, but it's fleeting, just out of reach. It'd been about the camp and off in the distance there'd been someone, blond and buff and … Leo. Leo, the lion with his unruly mane of golden locks. I shake the vision away. There's work to be done.

I throw back the blankets and don my robe. In the kitchen I make a pot of tea and wait for Maya who I know will already be outside pounding the pavement, running along one of the cobble-stoned laneways, or in the woodlands, not because something is chasing her, just because she loves running. I suppose a heart surgeon has to keep in tiptop shape if she's going to dole out orders about healthy living, diet and exercise.

After I stuff my face with toast lathered in butter and marmalade, I wash and cut fruit for Maya, who tends to avoid fun things like carbs and saturated fats.

When she arrives, a sweaty panting mess, I wave from my spot on the back deck that overlooks rows of fruit trees that still need a good prune to bring them back to life. After a quick shower she joins me.

'What a beautiful day! This place is a tonic, Orly. I can't believe I doubted you.'

'Can I have that in writing?' Birds chirp and the soft sunshine lulls us into a lazy daze. Once the back garden is tended, it will be even more relaxing; like a little oasis right here in Eden Hills.

'You may not. What were you doing in the middle of the night?' Maya asks. 'Sounded as though you were scraping paint from the walls or something.'

I freeze. I'd heard a scratching, rasping sound a few nights ago as if someone was trying to heft open a window using all their might. Impossible, because everything is locked form the inside, but still, kind of creepy. I'd figured it was just my overwrought mind playing tricks on me at bedtime but now Maya has heard it too. Last night, helped by the numerous glasses of bubbles and one too many cocktails I slept like a log. I hasten to think of an excuse. The last thing I want is Maya to run off screaming because she thinks the place is haunted. 'Oh, yeah, just tidying up.'

She gives me a look that suggests I'm changing as a person. In turn, I give her a smile so stiff I assume it's what rigor mortis feels like and hastily look away. 'Oh look a butterfly,' I deftly change the subject quick as anything.

I give Maya time to enjoy her breakfast before we head into town. We take a long leisurely walk at my slow pace, not the doctor almost-a-jog that Maya prefers. We head to Rise, the bakery. The scent of freshly baked bread assails the senses before we can even see the little shop.

'You can tell it's artisan bread by that smell alone,' Maya says.

'Isn't it glorious?' Inside we make our introductions, explain about the camp and the owner Dot invites us to try some of her loaves over coffee.

'I'll give you a taste tester of the rye, the sourdough, and the cob. I also have a gluten-free bread that tastes delicious.'

'Thank you, they sound divine.'

'Take a seat and I'll be with you shortly.'

Maya and I take a booth, and sip our coffees. Locals wander in and shoot the breeze. It's not only a café cum bakery but a place to catch up on gossip by the looks of it. A couple of women sit at the booth behind us, and suddenly I hear something that makes me pay closer attention.

'Apparently she has a thing for sequins. Jerome said she walked into the Tipsy Tadpole like she was some kind of celebrity, strutting around in ridiculously high heels. Her dress was so short it left *nothing* to the imagination!'

Freya in the flesh, gossiping about me!

I glance at Maya who bites her lip to stop from laughing.

'Well, what's wrong with that? I love a woman who has confidence,' the second woman says. 'My mum used to say, if you've got it flaunt it.' I don't know who she is, but I like her already.

'Really, Mabel! That's not the only thing she's done. I heard she propositioned Sebastian from the antique emporium!'

What!

'I highly doubt it – that mama's boy has always made up rumours to make himself look good.'

'I'm telling you now that woman is going to be a danger to this town. Josie from my knitting club mentioned something about her using us *innocent* residents as a cover for her unlawful activities. She wouldn't elaborate, but I'm worried. You have to wonder how a single woman of her age can afford such a property ... The only answer is illegally, don't you think?'

My unchecked laughter soon dries up. Unlawful activities? Now I've heard it all! And who is this mysterious Josie from the knitting club? I'm sure I've never run into her and now she's on the gossip train too?

Mabel scoffs. 'Josie is a busybody and you should know better than to listen to her! The girl has probably worked her butt off before coming here and just because she's financially able to afford

136

such a lovely property, that shouldn't make her a target for those with a jealous streak.'

'She also runs around the woods naked!'

'Now you're just being wicked, Freya. Who'd do such a thing?'

'It's true! She's some kind of pagan; it's a moonlight ritual. It's not right, Mabel, and I'll be the first one to tell her so.'

'That's your cue,' Maya says.

I know I'll have to stand my ground if I want all of these scurrilous rumours to abate. So even though my legs shake, I stand up and move to their booth.

'Hey,' I say brightly. 'I'm not a pagan and it's not a moonlight ritual. There was a great big hairy spider in my shower and I raced out to find the bug catcher in the hall – I subscribe to the live and let live policy even when it comes to spiders the size of my head. While Sebastian is a lovely guy, he's not the one for me, and the only propositions that took place were for furniture. The red dress, well, I'm sorry if I offended your sensibilities but my friends gave it to me as a present, and I was brought up to accept such things gracefully. As for illegal activities, if you count my midnight karaoke as criminally bad then I'm guilty as charged. I hope I've cleared all that up for you? But you said you'd be the first to tell me, so what is it that you wanted to say, Freya?'

I squat lower to look her straight in the eye, all the while wondering if this fifty-something woman is the one leaving the mysterious notes. Her puckered-up mouth and her judgemental dark eyes certainly make me think so.

Freya blushes to the roots of her hair. 'You shouldn't be eaves-dropping.'

'You shouldn't be spreading malicious lies, but here we are.'

Mabel speaks up. 'I'm sorry you had to hear all of that, Orly. It's one of the downsides to village life. Someone new comes along and stirs up envy in those who don't know any better. I'm Mabel, and I hope we can be friends.'

'Lovely to meet you, Mabel. I'd love to be friends. Maybe you could drop past the hall for a coffee whenever you have a free moment.'

'Consider it done.'

With a nod I slip back into the booth with Maya. 'I like this new Orly. She's badass.'

'Did you just say badass in an American accent?'

She shrugs. 'So sue me.'

We laugh as Dot brings us fresh bread to taste and I tell her I'll put in a running order for the camps. After the bakery we head to the delicatessen and the butcher, where I introduce myself and explain about the camps and what I'm hoping to achieve. I find a new sense of vigour from the visit to town and I know no matter what gossip has been said about me, the only way to face it is to show myself around town more, so they know the real me, and not the one who's been whispered about. It's time to stop hiding!

We head back home with an armful of groceries for lunch with Leo. After we unpack them we make our way to the hall so I can show Maya the work Leo has quoted on and explain the repairs.

She says, 'Once it's all spruced up it'll be a fun place to stay. More of a luxury retreat than a camp. I'd expected tiny dorm rooms but these are more than adequate for guests, especially having their own bathrooms. When I think of camps, I'm taken back to school, where we had those god-awful stretcher beds lined up, and the showers were half a mile away and we were always worried the boys were peeking in. But this is nothing like that at all.'

I laugh. 'God, I remember the same kind of thing. And it seemed like it was always bloody freezing when we had to make the trek to the showers. This is infinitely more of a luxe escape and I want to it to be perfect so that everyone who stays here leaves with a new outlook on their lives.'

'You're very clever to think of all of this. I must admit my earlier doubts now seem so unfounded, I should've known that you'd make this place a destination, rather than a town people simply pass through.'

'I'm not quite there yet, Maya, but thank you. I didn't think you'd come back when you saw the cottage for the first time. I couldn't see your car for the dust you left behind when you scarpered out of here.'

She laughs. 'Yeah, you're right. It was just a shock, I guess. I'm used to clean and clinical, and it was such a huge change from your London pad. Maybe part of me had hoped you'd change your mind and come back – the selfish part. But now I see you belong here. I know you've got a way to go, and it will be a long game, but somehow you suit this place, this new life. You don't have that same harried look you had in the city, even though you're still busy, it seems like a different kind of busy and that you're relishing it, rather than getting through it like you did before.'

I'm touched she's noticed, because that's exactly how I've felt here. Like I'm home, for some inexplicable reason. That all roads led me here. And if I believe hard enough, magic might happen. What that means is still fuzzy, but the murky shape of it's there. 'I am relishing it, Maya. Especially the wearing of flat shoes, and no make-up. I always envisaged myself in this kind of life, but I guess I thought it'd be after marriage and babies when big-city living lost its appeal but I still had the safety net of savings, and a husband who could commute or work close to home. Doing it alone makes it all the sweeter. No one can take it away from me, except the bank and I won't allow that to happen.'

'It won't. Show me the rest of this magnificent hall then, before you make me buy the property next door, with this charming life you're painting for me.'

I show Maya to the long open parlour that the campers will congregate in together. It's disarmingly spacious with its high ceilings, but somehow cosy with parquetry floors and decorative leadlight windows spotted throughout. At the far end is a grand fireplace. 'This is almost royal,' she says awed. 'I see why Esterlita thinks you should hook up with the gentry.'

I laugh, remembering the previous night and Esterlita's answer to every problem being a man. 'Isn't it? And it's surprisingly well maintained. All I've asked Leo to do in here is polish the wooden wainscoting, and check the windows are sealed well enough for winter. Once the repairs are done, the antique emporium are delivering my order. I've got some beautiful Persian rugs coming and I found some wrinkly old dark leather chesterfields that will go quite nicely in front of the fire. The dining table here—' I point to a long rectory table big enough to fit twenty people that was a relic from a former owner '—he is going to sand back and stain. And the benches too.'

'I can't believe someone left that behind.'

'It was shoved up against the wall and covered with old mattresses. Let me tell you that was not the most fun I've ever had, carting those stinky things to the skip bin, so I'm happy I've been rewarded with the beautiful table.'

'This place must have a thousand stories.' She leans against the wall, and folds her arms.

'I can't wait to discover them.'

'Well, it's time we opened that quote and see what the damage is, eh?' We wipe dust from one of the benches and sit.

I take a deep breath and open the email attachment on the phone with Maya leaning over my shoulder. 'It's not too bad at all!' she exclaims.

Leo has quoted for the work to be done within a two-week timeframe including extra labour for a very reasonable price. Almost *too* reasonable. 'At this rate I can probably ask him to tidy up the garden too. At least have it neatened up ready for the first camp. What do you think?'

Maya nods. 'I think get as much done as humanly possible so you're free to focus on getting camps booked. Your survival here is going to be down to that. And I know that's your forte, but spreading the word takes time and money.'

'Yeah, so much time! Let's take some pics while we wait for Leo so I can post online.' We take some close-up arty pics of the hall. I'm careful not to show the dingy side – that will all be fixed soon enough.

An hour later we've snapped some beautiful photos that show just how pretty the property is. The dense woodland behind is a riot of colour with fragrant wildflowers, and an abundance of orange-pink honeysuckles whose sweet perfume swirls around us as we disturb their sunbaking by traipsing among them. I imagine campers striding out in small groups to hunt for floral treasures to display in their suites.

'Once the lawn area is tidied it's going to be perfect for games of bocce.' I add a note to my list to buy some sets, and look into other lawn games that we can store in the hall for campers to use on their downtime. 'Maybe cricket, a badminton set, a few footballs.'

'Sporty activities will go down a treat and give you a break from hosting.'

The community garden is overrun but the bones are there. 'We should get this going as soon as possible,' I say to Maya. 'That way campers can forage for herbs and salad ingredients when they're here.'

'Yes, let's make a start on that today.'

I add that to my list: potting mix, herbs, lettuces, chillies, tomatoes, cucumbers.

'What about an outdoor kitchen? Or at least a bigger barbecue? If you can make the campers self-sufficient that's even better for you.'

'Yeah, they'll do all their own cooking; I'll supply the ingredients. Although Es wants to cook them some Filipino specialties because she says if I'm in charge of food they'll all die, so I think that'll be a nice personal touch. They've got the shared kitchen in the hall and I have a new fridge coming.' I consult my notes, wondering just how far the budget will stretch now that Leo's quote is a lot less than I banked on. 'An outdoor kitchen is a great idea, Maya. Would it be more cost-effective for Leo to build one with an extra-long hot plate to cater to bigger groups?'

'It would be better in the long run.' We both jump at the voice. And I turn to face him, the sight of him making me tongue-tied once more.

Chapter 14

'Leo,' I say, gathering my senses. 'You're early.'

'No, we said lunchtime. It's just after.'

I glance at my watch. 'The morning has run away from me.' My heart beats staccato, probably because he snuck up behind me.

'What did you think of the quote?' Even his voice is lovely, deep and velvety. Exactly the kind of man I want to avoid. He's the type that every woman would swoon over, which puts him in the risky category. Anyway what am I even saying?! He's going to be my carpenter, *not* my boyfriend, for crying out loud! With the soft sunlight falling across him, he quite takes my breath away. No use pretending he's not mesmerising, like looking at a price of artwork that's enthralling. Yikes. I need to discuss this with the wild roses … at least they don't judge.

I cough and gather my senses, which all too often seem to fly away when I most need them these days. 'I thought your quote was very cheap. Are you sure you've covered all of your expenses?' The last thing I want to do is take advantage or have him change his mind and add a few more zeros on the invoice at the end when he realises he's quoted too little.

He grins and it lights up his beautiful face. 'I think you're used to city prices, Orly. The quote is fair for both of us.'

Maya nods. 'He's got a point. We are used to being charged the London tax,' she says with a laugh. 'Everything is triple the price!'

I'm still not convinced. I did ring around and get some prices over the phone from other carpenters and they came in a lot higher. 'Well, if you're sure? You can always crunch the numbers again before we agree on the job.'

'Trust me, Orly. I've checked and rechecked. I'm sure. So you're not going to make these amazing camps and then sell up and head for the Bahamas?'

It's not the first time Leo's implied I'm the sort to take the money and run. Why does he care? 'The Bahamas sounds nice, but I'd probably fry with my English rose skin and all.' I laugh. 'Why, Leo, will it bother you if I leave?' I don't mean it to sounds as flirty as it does but I can't snatch the words back.

A blush creeps up his neck. 'I'd like you to stay. For the benefit of all future campers.' He coughs.

'Right. I'd like to stay too. For their benefit.'

'Unless you're here to make a quick buck, and in that case the quote will be triple.' He grins.

'No, Leo, I'm not here for that, I promise. The only thing that would make me sell up would be if my business fails and believe me, I don't want that to eventuate.'

'Neither do I. There's been some speculation that you're here to develop this place and move on to the next. Not that I put much faith into what I hear in town. Still, sometimes it does make a person curious about where these stories come from.'

'Yeah, I'd like to know too. It seems these fictions are gathering momentum rather than dying down, which is a bit of a worry.'

'It'll slow down eventually.'

'I hope so.' Why are they all so untrusting? I look back at the prices Leo's quoted and know no matter what he's heard he hasn't charged me the new-person tax. Maybe there is hope.

'If you're happy with the quote I can start on Monday.'

I tilt my head. 'I'm really happy with the quote. I was hoping you'd also tidy up the fruit trees and if you can build an extra-large outdoor barbecue area that would be fabulous too. Just let me know how much I'm in for to make certain and we're good to go.'

Esterlita arrives and after much fanfare drags Leo away to show him something and Maya grabs my elbow hissing, 'Can't you see what he's doing?'

'Quoting for the hall repairs?'

She rolls her eyes. 'He's trying to work out if you're genuinely going to stay in Eden Hills.'

'Yeah, he made that abundantly clear. So?'

She slaps her forehead. 'So if you *are* staying, then maybe it's worth getting close to you. Risking his heart ...'

I shake my head. 'I don't know how you managed to join those dots, Maya. Seriously.'

She gives me a long look like she's trying to hypnotise me into thinking the same way. 'I can read between the lines.'

Our conversation is interrupted as Esterlita drags Leo back. Is he really puzzling me out like she says? For a moment I pretend it's true.

With the sun behind him, lighting up the blond of his hair, he looks like he fits here too. I imagine him as if he's just come in from tending the garden, his hands blackened with earth, his stomach growling for sustenance. I get lost in a little scenario, picturing Leo kissing the top of my head, as I sort my stamps, waiting for his return, carrying his booty: plump sun-warmed tomatoes for the salad ...

'What salad?' Maya asks alarm written on her face.

Oh, please God don't let me have spoken out loud again! 'I really do love tomatoes, which are not a vegetable but a fruit, did you know that? *And what a fruit*! More like a vegetable. It's not every day you see fruit in a salad is it? Well … unless it's a fruit salad, that is.'

'Do I need to get the paddles?' Maya leans in, whispering, '*For your brain!?* What are you on about?'

Holy guacamole. 'I have sunstroke.'

Leo grins at me, like he's in on the secret, and I don't have enough brain capacity at the moment to think what it could mean. I shake off my fugue-like state; Leo has some kind of sorcery about him that makes me leave my body and float away. It's not good, not good at all. I can't *think* when he's around.

To counter the strange feeling, I remind myself of my bank balance and that's enough to shock me back to the present. 'Right, let's continue.'

We spend the next little while going through every small detail. Leo seems intent on making sure I'm aware of the costing for each job and just what I can expect to be done, and to talk through the other work that we can leave until the following year when I hope the coffers will be a little healthier.

As we wander around the grounds more ideas come to mind. 'What about the grassed area near the lake? Do you think you could tidy that up too? I don't think it needs much but it's hard to tell while it's so overgrown.'

The lake is what attracted me to the place. It's not part of the property but it runs directly behind it next to the woodland. I'm envisaging future summer camps; kayaks whipping along the glittering blue water. Campers sunbathing on the shoreline.

'Yeah, sure,' he says. 'I'm fairly certain from hiking along here that it's flat land, so I don't think it'll take much to get that in order. What did you want to do with it?'

'Don't laugh but I'm thinking of tepees. For those who want a real camping experience but perhaps a little more luxurious than a tent.'

'Glamping?'

'Sort of, but there won't be TVs and that kind of thing. And no actual beds, just air mattresses for the foreseeable. That view needs to be enjoyed.' And just like everything it all comes down to money, money, money.

'I love that idea.'

He loves it. It's a good sign. 'Good quality tepees are a little pricey though so I'll have to ring around and see what I can get them for.'

'I can help with that. There's a guy in town who makes all sorts of camping equipment. I'll ask him if you like?'

'That would be amazing. I'd love to support local businesses as much as I can.'

'OK, leave that with me. And we'll get that area tidied up and go from there.'

We discuss various ideas and before long I realise he's been here for an hour or so and Maya is nowhere to be seen. I can't even remember when she left us. I've probably been running on autopilot again, rambling to keep the nerves at bay. 'Sorry, I've kept you chatting for so long. You must be sick of hearing about the place!'

'Not at all. I'm looking forward to starting the work. This place just needs a loving hand and it really won't take much. For its age, it has held up well. And all it needs now is to be filled with the sound of laughter, of people enjoying it for what it was always intended to be.'

'That's going to be the best part. I can't wait to see campers wandering around and soaking up the scenery. Did you know the previous owners?' The estate agent didn't have much to say about them, just that the price had been drastically reduced because it had sat on the market too long and squatters had begun to take over.

Leo shakes his head. 'It's been empty since I arrived in town over a couple of years ago. But there's always the same old rumours buzzing about.'

I cock my head. 'Like what?'

He waves me away. 'The usual gossip you get with old halls like this.'

'Let me guess, it's haunted?'

He grins. 'Of course – aren't they all? Have you seen any ghosts?' he says with a half-smile as if there's no such thing.

'No, not a thing, how disappointing is that!' I think of the strange notes but stop short of telling him for some reason. I don't want to be thought of as the nervous newcomer.

'It does make you wonder though, right? Maybe if you slept in the hall you'd have a visit.'

I shudder at the thought. 'I suppose I should test it out if I'm going to stick other people out there,' I say jokingly while I really think: *No way in hell am I sleeping out there even if you paid me.* Although I'm sure my campers will be just fine. Safety in numbers and all that. And ghosts aren't real!

'You could do ghost tours!'

I laugh, while internally I quail. 'There's an idea. I could fling a white sheet over Es and have her scare everyone with a long *boooo*.'

'Esterlita does like performing, that's for sure.'

'She sure does! Seriously though, I do wonder about the history. From the first noble family, and then a home for wayward children, which just sounds evil, and then being requisitioned in WWI. And finally becoming a finishing school. So many lives have been lived here, the grand old dame must've seen it all. And then you have the local lore … although no one is all that forthcoming about the place, like I thought they'd be.'

'They will be once you've been here a while. You'll be inundated with gossip. Once it travels up and down the grapevine these things tend to get out of hand. Like with you for—' He stops suddenly, catching himself.

'Like with me?' There's more? I can only imagine, especially

148

after the red dress fiasco. 'What do "they" say?' Little does he know I've already heard half of it at Rise.

He kicks at the ground, looking anywhere but at me.

I touch his arm. 'It's OK. You can tell me.'

He runs a hand through his hair and looks as though he wants the ground to swallow him whole. 'They say that you were friends with the A-list, whatever that means. That you brushed shoulders with royalty, billionaires, the list goes on. Some say you got them anything they wanted, from visits with celebrities to tickets to sold-out events. Others say that was a cover because you were dealing in stolen artworks and diamonds.' He grimaces. 'Sorry.'

Laughter barrels out of me. 'Wow, I'm a trafficker?'

He shrugs as if he doesn't quite know what to believe. 'Well, there's also a rumour that your fiancé ran off with some reality TV singer and apparently it was because you kept him on a very short lead. Did you have a basement in your London flat by chance?'

I smile again. 'No basement. He wasn't locked up and he was most definitely not on a short lead. But he did run off with Carly C, once a reality TV star, now world's biggest pop sensation. So "they" did get that part right.' That there's more truth than I thought to the gossip in town worries me a little. Maybe that's the way small gossip starts, from a kernel of truth. While I grew up in a tiny village, I wasn't privy to that side of things as a youngster. I'm still shocked at how much they've managed to unearth. Don't they have better things to do than dig up my past?

'Wow. I'm sorry.'

'Well … that's Harry.' It's my turn to shrug. 'I think I prefer being known as someone who sells stolen art and big fat diamonds.'

'Why did he do that?' Leo seems sincerely confused.

I sigh. 'Harry always had an eye for the finer things in life, and Carly C hit the spot. It helps she's absolutely gorgeous and talented, I suppose. I'm rather lacking in comparison.' Urgh, who wants to be this person, but I'm not fishing for pity, I'm being brutally honest. There's no point lying: Carly C is genuinely stunning, talented and hot property right now. Why wouldn't Harry jump at the chance? Trust and love mean different things to different people. 'Anyway, enough about all that. I guess I'll have to keep the town on their toes and not tell them a thing!'

Leo laughs. 'Well, then there was the pub visit … They'd been expecting a sedate sort of Kate Middleton vibe and you showed up in that very short, very red, sparkly dress and it threw everyone off.'

I groan and cover my face. 'Esterlita and Maya made me.'

'It sure got tongues wagging.'

'All publicity is good publicity, right?' I'm reminded of thinking the exact same thing about Carly C, back when I thought I could trust my fiancé, before an exposé put paid to all that. Remembering it now doesn't hurt quite so much. Is it because of Leo? Staring into his glittery blue eyes, it's hard to not to compare him to Harry but I can see that they're two totally different personality types. The only thing they have in common is they're both a little too good-looking. Why can't Leo have some fault? Why does he have to be so perfect? What am I even saying?!

'Right.'

'Let's go have some lunch so you can forget about all of this!'

'I don't think I *can* forget the dress, sorry. It's burned into my retinas.'

'That's because of the *blood*-red. Bloody Esterlita!'

'Yes?' she calls from the comfort of the porch. 'I can't stay long today, I have to help set up for a wedding at church tomorrow. But I'll pray for you. For your decorating skills, dress sense *and* the fact you're single.'

My complexion doesn't redden; I'm either getting used to Esterlita's pronouncements or she's losing her touch. 'That's very kind of you, Esterlita.'

'You're welcome. I had this vision …' *Maybe not.*

'I bet you did. Tell me later, yeah?' I give her my goggle-eyes and hope she translates my meaning for once.

The last thing I want to do is scare my ultra-cheap carpenter away with one of Esterlita's 'visions'.

Inside Maya has made a feast of summer salads and seafood. 'Hey.' She smiles. 'How'd you guys go?'

'Great. Leo says we can have this place up and running in two weeks. So that means I've got a lot of organising to do. We can start taking bookings!' My mind spins with my already massive to-do list. I still need to order new mattresses, pillows. I need kitchen crockery. From my back pocket I take my phone and add a few other things to the list. There's a bunch of notifications on Facebook and I quickly swipe to see who they're from.

We're keeping tabs on you! #CarlyArmy

I delete them and hope they'll soon get bored. The media storm about me certainly hasn't helped. I have done nothing and yet have been painted in such a bad light by Carly C's fans who have this unwarranted notion I'm all set for revenge. Little do they know I wouldn't go near Harry again if you paid me, and Carly C isn't on my hit list. I'm only disappointed the whole 'wear your crown, queens, and lift each other up' stuff is all another spin.

'You OK?' Leo asks.

'Yeah, sorry, work stuff.' I swipe out of Facebook and go back to my notes. 'I'm going to try and source as much as I can locally to help the community,' I say for Leo's benefit and hope he'll spread that little nugget of information around. They might believe that I sell stolen priceless pieces of art but hey, at least I spend the profits in town …

'First up is finding the camp leader. Leo, do you know anyone who would suit?' Maya fills Leo in on the idea.

'There might be a few people in town who'd fit the bill, but it'll be a matter of finding someone you gel with, Orly.'

'Preferably one who doesn't think I deal in stolen goods.'

'What the heck?' Maya asks.

'I'll tell you later.' I laugh. Living in a small town sure will take some getting used to. Although with Leo here, things are looking that little bit brighter. He'll sort the hall and grounds while I focus on the biz. A tingle races the length of me and I realise I haven't felt this inspired since I started Excès all those years ago. The buzz of a new challenge is a heady thing.

After lunch, Leo says a slow goodbye. I can't help but tingle at his touch when he leads me outside to show me where he thinks the old fountain in the photo used to be, and how he proposes I build a new one when the money starts coming in.

I know the girls will be peeking out the window so I try and push that from my mind and focus on him alone. He stares at me like I'm a mystery he's trying to unravel and holds my gaze until I blush and look away. What does he see when he studies me so closely? We make small talk about this and that until we eventually run out of things to say and just stare at each other. There's something so compelling about Leo and I can't quite put my finger on it.

'Well, I'd better head back inside and make sure Esterlita isn't painting the walls tangerine.'

'Yes, sorry I kept you so long. I'll see you soon, and thanks again for lunch.' He goes to shake my hand, but I lean in and give him a quick peck on the cheek, which surprises us both. Didn't I just give myself a silent pep talk about why this *wouldn't* be a good idea? What is it about him that I find so captivating? It's more than just the way he looks; it's the way he makes me feel when I'm alone with him, like we could be the last two people on the planet and that would be fine by me. I get this electric buzz, this strange sort of fire inside that makes me want to act rashly around him and it's hard to rein it in.

There's a commotion at the window. I turn and see what looks like someone getting brutally murdered by the curtains but is more likely Esterlita tangled inside them. 'You'd better go rescue her,' he says, laughing.

'Thanks, Leo, and see you soon.' I watch him drive away, taking a teeny-tiny piece of my heart with him. I don't want to have to trust a man again, but clearly my body and brain haven't got the memo. When my pulse slows to its usual rhythms, I go back inside the cottage, ready to be interrogated.

'What was *that* about?' Maya asks.

'What was what about?' I stall for time.

She stares me down. 'Did you not just yesterday spend an hour telling me how you'd sworn off men?'

Moi? 'Yes, yes I did. But Leo has some kind of pull over me and I forget who I am and what I'm doing when he's around. I don't think I can be trusted to be alone with him. If he calls tell him I've moved. Tell him I've changed my mind. I'll dye my hair red and say I'm Orly's twin sister come to fix up her bad choices.'

'Why?'

'Why what?'

'Why pretend?'

'Because I do stupid things like peck him on the cheek!'

She groans. 'Orly, you should follow your heart.'

'Look what happened last time I did that, Maya! Harry happened.'

'Leo is nothing like Harry.'

I fold my arms. 'You don't know that for sure.'

'I don't, but I'd hazard a guess Leo is a good guy. I've seen the long, lingering looks between you two. Your *heart* recognises he's a good guy; you just need your brain to catch up.'

I scoff.

'She *is* a heart doctor,' Esterlita says. 'I think she's more qualified in this department than you.'

'Yeah, well, you've got me on a technicality there. I'm just not ready for all that.' But the words are hollow, even to me. It's tempting to think of Leo in such a way, but it's too risky.

153

'What if we found out more about him?' Esterlita says.

'No,' I groan. 'Not another Esterlita intervention.'

'I think it's a great idea,' Maya says.

'What don't we know?'

'Well,' Esterlita adds, 'why has he been single this whole time? Why isn't he married? Why does he hike like he's got something to hide?'

'See what you've started?' I say to Maya and shake my head laughing. Why does he hike like he's got something to hide, for crying out loud? Esterlita just can't understand why people behave differently to her. It instantly makes her suspicious when there's absolutely nothing there.

'Let's find out what makes Leo tick,' Maya says.

The poor guy is not going to know what hit him, but I suppose it'll be one way of scaring him off.

We retreat to the hall to check the rooms and decide on colour schemes for the linen and décor. 'Before you even suggest it, Es, there's not going to be any blood-red, no fuchsia and definitely no magenta.'

She drops her bottom lip before saying. 'Orly, you're going to give yourself bad luck you know.'

'I like living on the edge.'

'One day you'll fall off,' she says ominously.

'That's something to look forward to.'

'So rugs, bed linen, towels, artwork – a print of some kind – what else are you thinking in here, Orly?' Maya asks.

'I've got small desks with chairs coming from the antique emporium. They're all different but they fit the era and will look great in the room. They're also delivering armoires for clothing so I'll need coat hangers, a notebook and pen for the desk, or do you think we should make a keepsake like a diary they can take home? The cover could be a photograph of the hall and grounds?'

'Love that idea. What about the beds? Are you getting new ones?'

I look to the wrought-iron bed frames, touched with a small amount of rust from age and disuse. Even though they've been abandoned, they're still top quality and sturdy as the hills. 'Leo reckons he can save these frames.'

'Well, they suit the look you're going for. And that will save you some money.'

'So what colour for the linen?'

'Navy blue with white piping. Practical and also lush.'

'Yes!' Maya says. 'That's very luxe.'

'Then navy towels, and navy and white pinstriped satin curtains,' I say.

'I still think this is a lot of money to sink into a place when you could just renovate and sell for a profit, Orly. Have you ever thought of that?'

'That's not what I'm after though, Es. I really want to help people, and this is the only way I know how.'

The girls wander into the next room, while I double-check the bathroom. As I'm about to close the door I see another scrunched-up note on the floor. It could just be rubbish but somehow I know it isn't. As I drop to unravel it I see that it says: *You're putting people in danger.*

It's got to be Freya, or her knitting club friend Josie. Then there's the Carly Army – but could a bunch of young adults really take their love of a celebrity so far? Or could it be someone else in town who believes the gossip? Maybe there's a whole bunch of Freyas who want me gone. Do they really believe I deal in illegal activities because a woman my age shouldn't be able to afford such a property? It's as though I've jumped back a few decades when it comes to being an independent woman here, almost as if it's a bad thing!

I pause as a new thought hits. Is it Leo doing this? He could have slipped this in as we did our tour around the hall! I talk myself down. What would he have to gain by my leaving? In fact, he'd have a lot to lose if I left, like the rejuvenation work I've hired him for. Then again, he'd probably be the one to secure the renovation work for whoever took over the hall … Part of me wonders when I remember those prickly comments he made about me potentially flipping the property for a profit and rushing back to big-city life. It's almost as though he doesn't trust my motives for buying Honeysuckle Hall …

It's something to consider before I plunge into any real friendships around here.

I can't help but shiver at the idea someone is trying to scare me off for no good reason. One or two notes I could explain away, but now it feels as though it's a genuine campaign into scaring me to leave. Again, why? What does it matter I'm here, and who does my being here affect so badly? My heart sinks, and I realise it's because I really don't want it to be Leo, but part of me suspects that it is. Is this my own trust issues coming to the fore?

Chapter 15

A few days later I'm out in the garden pruning the overgrown fruit trees when a van arrives. I do a happy dance when I see who it is. 'Maya!' I call back towards the cottage.

She comes dashing out. 'What?'

'The furniture is here! And all of our goodies!'

We race outside to meet the driver, Bob, a local guy who does deliveries and was eager to go and pick up all of our loot from the various shops in town we visited. Once again I'd been surprised at the price of things being so much more affordable outside of London.

'Hey,' he says, jumping down from the cab. 'Managed to fit everything in, might need some help unloading it though.' Even though the hall isn't finished, the storeroom is, so we have plenty of space to load all of our furniture for safekeeping. When the hall is ready we won't have to wait around to get everything in.

'Where's Leo?' Maya asks when Bob opens the back of the truck to reveal ten antique heavy-looking wardrobes.

I'm still a little suspicious of Leo. I've managed to avoid him by sending Esterlita to do my bidding. And why was he around just when I needed him? Seems suspicious to me.

Maya must see the hesitation on my face because she says, 'What's the problem? I'm sure he won't mind lending a hand.'

'We can do it,' I say. 'How heavy can they be?'

Bob pipes up, 'Hernia-inducing heavy.'

I shoot Bob a glare.

'Let me find Leo.' Maya dashes to the back of the hall where Leo and his gang are working on the electrics.

He soon comes along, wearing his lazy smile, as he and his guys happily help Bob unload the truck of all our precious cargo while Maya grabs me by the shirt and pulls me away in a very brash bossy manner that clues me up to the fact she's about to lecture me. Leo reserves his widest smile for me, and my legs almost buckle at the beauty of it. I quickly turn away.

'Don't think I haven't noticed,' she says giving me an icy stare.

'Noticed what?' I study the ground as if it's a wonder.

'You've been avoiding Leo like he's got the pox and I want to know why. What did he do? I'm guessing it's a big, fat nothing.'

I cross my arms. 'I have no idea what you're on about?' But what she doesn't know is there've been even *more* notes, and always right around the time Leo leaves for the day, coincidentally right where he's been working. I will be devastated if it's him. So I do what I do best, and hide, hoping it'll all go away.

She grunts. 'Don't try that delaying tactic with me, I can see straight through you.'

Damn it. 'What delaying tactic?'

'The one you're doing right now, and you know it!'

'I don't know what—'

'STOP!'

'OK, OK, sheesh. So, I've been avoiding him, yes, but it's not a big, fat nothing.'

'Then what is it?'

Reluctantly I tell her about the old sepia photograph I found and the scrunched-up notes. I don't dare tell her about the noises in the cottage in case she thinks A: I'm losing the plot or B: she makes her excuses to leave and never comes back. I'm sure they're just the sounds of an old place creaking and groaning ...

'OK, so let's think about this logically; maybe someone just dropped the picture off for you as a keepsake when they went past on their morning walk?'

'Yes, that's perfectly possible. But what about the notes?'

Maya considers it. 'Well, you'd think being a finishing school back in the day, those sorts of notes were passed around all the time. You'll probably unearth many a snarky note from one to another. They were stuck out here together with no means of escape; surely tensions ran high every now and then.'

'I thought that too at first, but the paper is more modern, even the handwriting is block letters, not cursive like it would have been back then. I get the feeling that it's a more recent thing; that someone has it in for me. They all say the same type of thing: you're not wanted here, you're putting others in danger, and things like that. I don't know how else to explain it, but it feels like someone has something against me, and I think that person is Leo.'

'But why would he?'

'I think he believes the rumours about me. He keeps asking if I'm going to flip the hall for a profit as if I've come to Eden Hills under false pretences or else I'm setting up a business that I can sell off for pockets full of cash, disappear into the sunset and never look back.' It sounds ridiculous saying it out loud, but who else could it be?

She shakes her head. 'He doesn't believe the rumours. No self-respecting person would. When he's quizzed you, I think it's purely to see where you're at! That you're not going to give up on small-town life and head back the bright lights of London. Look, the notes are creepy – I'll give you that – but it's not Leo. I feel it in my gut. It'll be Freya and her gang of bored desperate housewives or something. I don't think you need to worry. Look at the number of times you've called Leo after hours for one emergency after another and he's come running. Someone trying to scare you away would just say they're busy and let you deal with it yourself. His quote would have been sky-high, if he wanted you gone. He wouldn't have helped source the tepees, and all the other people he's had a quiet word with to get you a good deal, would he?'

When Maya lays it all like that I do wonder. Sometimes I think this place is getting to me and making me look for things that aren't there.

'I need to know for sure that it's not him.' And right now, I don't know that.

Maya shakes her head. 'Is this a subconscious ploy to push Leo away? I've seen the way you two snatch looks at each other, well up until you ghosted him, and I think deep down that scared you, so you've invented this mystery to hold him back.'

'I didn't invent it; it's real.'

She sighs. 'I know it's real, but you made him the scapegoat. And he's such a lovely guy, a really sweet, laid-back guy. If you don't move fast someone else will snatch him right up.'

'Urgh, that'll probably happen anyway.'

'Harry really did a number on you, didn't he?' she says gently. 'You don't have to pretend you're not still hurting.'

I lift a shoulder. 'I'm not pretending; I just don't want to dwell on it. What's the point? But the thought of moving on so fast makes me nervous.'

'You can't think like that, though, or you'll never move on.'

'It's only been a couple of months.'

'Come on let's get this furniture sorted and we can chat more later.' I still need to tell Maya about the Carly Army and see what her take on that is. Once the furniture is unloaded I ask one of Leo's guys to heft the antique vitrine into the cottage living room. I spend the next few hours displaying my philatelic collection inside the lovely piece. It has the desired effect, calming me as I work out the best way to show off my stamps and the old love letters of strangers.

*

The only way to know who is guilty is to catch them in the act. I find a tree of moderate height, okay, it's the smallest tree around because I'm not keen on climbing too high and I commit to my very first stakeout. I have water to last the duration, and binoculars so I can peer at the hall from a distance. Three minutes in, I realise I've forgotten my snacks, and wonder just how long I can last without them. Hopefully I'm not here all day, because I don't want my blood sugar dropping when I'm so far above the ground – besides I've got bloody work to do! Who knew country living would mean being so furtive and living in the shadows like this!

I'm adjusting my legs around the branch of the tree, wondering just how I can explain away splinters in my nether regions, when Leo comes into view and I freeze. He has some planks of wood in his hand, so it doesn't look quite like he's about to hide a note, but I watch him closely. I use my thigh muscles to hang on and grab the binoculars. I should have brought a rope and tied myself to the tree. My legs burn and I wonder how much longer I can hold on for. Spies really must do a lot of cardiovascular exercise in order to get the job done and I know I'm lacking that department. Still, they're also mentally tough and I have that in spades … don't I? Urgh, I wobble on the trunk as I watch Leo cart bits and pieces from the hall to the bin.

His muscles ripple (who knew muscles actually rippled?) in the sunlight as he lifts heavy things. Whoa. I don't let such a sight ruffle me, as I'm a professional and this man might be my enemy. He runs a hand through his thick, blond, too-long locks and then takes a great big guzzle of water, before pouring it over his head, letting it trickle down his lovely tanned body. *Don't get distracted, Orly! That's what he wants you to do!*

But I can't help it! For some reason all his movements appear in slow-mo and I hear some kind of tough-guy music as if I'm watching an advert on TV selling tough-guy aftershave or something. He really is too good-looking! He shakes the excess water from his skin – just like a bloody cliché – and a rush of longing races through me. It's too much for my thigh muscles and I start to wobble alarmingly on the branch of the tree that now seems rather too thin to hold my weight. The ground seems so far away, like any fall would break every single one of my bones. What was I thinking?

It's when the satanical chicken comes pecking into view that I know my days are numbered. I drop my water bottle and binoculars and let out a blood-curdling scream. Now all I need is Henry the hairy spider to come creeping along! The chicken shrieks threateningly.

'ARGH!' I shimmy and shake and end up upside down on the branch, the chicken narrowing his beady little chicken eyes and squawking at me so shrilly I know he's saying something foul (*fowl?*) in his own language. 'Help! He's after me! HELP! I don't want to die like this!'

My triceps burn, or biceps, or one of the *ep* muscles as I struggle to hold on upside down with my hands. I'm a sweating, panting mess as my vision clouds from exertion. Cluck Norris starts pecking away at my hair and I'm sure he's going to rip it clean off my scalp. 'HELP!' I hear the thunder of footsteps and then I'm suddenly liberated from the tree and in the loving arms of none other than Leo. I hastily look around for the maniacal beast but he's nowhere to be found.

'Are you OK?' Leo asks, with smiling eyes.

'No, I most certainly am not!' Just in case, I loop my legs around his waist and arms around his neck, looking this way and that for the demented fowl. 'That chicken is trying to intimidate me! He won't rest until he sees me running scared!'

'What chicken?'

I give him a 'what do you take me for' look. 'You know what chicken! The one who was just here, squawking and making a ruckus, trying to separate the skin from my bones! He's an extremist, a guerrilla! And I'm going to make chicken nuggets out of him when I catch him!'

Leo searches the ground but I don't let him go. He smells nice. How can he smell so good while doing manual labour all day? Yet he does. Like hopes and dreams and holidays in the sun and ...

'Are they your binoculars?' he asks.

Shoot.

'No, they must be his!'

'His? An extremist, guerrilla chicken who wears binoculars and chases pretty girls up trees?'

'YES!' Did he just call me a pretty girl? *Focus, Orly, focus!* 'He, erm, chased me up this very tree. I *wasn't* spying, I was running for my life!'

'I can see that.' He grins. 'I'll hold you as long as you need.'

'It might be a while. I'm fairly shaken up.'

'I've got time.'

I rest my head against his shoulder and pretend for a minute he's mine, all thoughts of chicken nuggets and secret notes gone.

Chapter 16

Friday evening rolls around and I'm weary right down to my soul. It's been a busy but fulfilling week. Maya is showering so I sit on the back deck behind the trellis with a jug of orange juice and survey the hall. Sunlight slowly turns to moonlight, the sky moving from blue to a dusky pink and then to jet-black. I can't find the energy to stand and turn the light on; there's something so peaceful about sitting in the shade of evening.

'Orly? Are you here?' Leo says, appearing from the side of the house.

'I'm here, behind the screen!' I say.

'I've missed you.'

Missed me?

'I mean, I keep missing you. I needed to get your approval on a few things that have cropped up. You like sitting in the dark?'

'Sure do. I like waiting to see the stars appear.'

Leo outlines a few issues with the plumbing that need to be fixed, and a few extra electrical problems that need to be sorted for safety purposes. I give him approval to get them all done. We lapse into silence. I don't know what to say or do – asking him outright isn't going to work. I can't even see his facial expressions with the light off.

I stand up to turn the outdoor fairy lights on when I see a figure in the distance.

'Who's that?' I whisper to Leo. 'Is it one of your guys?' It's hard to tell from here because they're wearing black clothing and a baseball cap. Whoever it is hasn't seen us behind the screening.

'Where?'

I point and watch the figure creep into the hall; Leo sees just as the door is quietly shut.

'Hey, stop right there!' He jumps up to investigate and I follow close behind, clutching on to his jacket for good measure. The notes didn't bother me so much before, but seeing someone slink around the property gives me the right heebie-jeebies.

Inside the hall, Leo flicks on the lights, and together we go from room to room searching for the intruder. Once we've done a lap of the place, I notice the door from the kitchen is open an inch. 'Look.' I point to Leo. 'Whoever it was went out that way.'

He wrenches the door open and we scan the rear garden, but I can barely see two steps ahead. It's so gloomy at night because of the woodlands behind.

'We should check all your antiques, Orly, make sure nothing has been taken.'

'It's OK, Leo.' Then I see a balled-up note. I pick it up and pocket it while he's looking the other way. As soon as I saw the figure tiptoeing into the hall I knew what I'd find. That person wasn't looking for furniture; they were looking to hide another note. 'I'm sure the antiques are fine, Leo. There was no time to take anything.' Only time to leave something.

'I don't like the idea of someone wandering in here, I don't like it at all. You're going to have to lock it up of a night-time, especially now you've got all your furniture in here. What's stopping them from wandering into your cottage? Do you have sufficient locks on the cottage doors?' I nod, finding his protectiveness quite adorable but also sensible. 'You need to alarm the place, Orly. I can get one set up for you, free of charge.' His face is full of concern and I wonder how I ever doubted the guy. 'It would help me sleep at night.'

'An alarm is a good idea.'

While my heart gallops at the thought of someone creeping onto the property, I also feel relieved that I can safely cross Leo off the suspect list ...

'I think you should report this to the police.'

Should I though? And say what – that someone ran in and straight out of the hall? Doesn't sound like the most serious of crimes. They'd probably laugh me out of the station. All I know is I need to get away from the place for a while.

'I don't know about you, but stress makes me ravenous. Would you like to go out for dinner with me?'

The concern in his eyes is replaced with happiness. 'Sure. I'll go home and freshen up. Meet you in an hour? We can go to the Italian trattoria, Basilico.'

'Perfect.'

*

Just shy of an hour later Leo arrives to pick me up for dinner. As he parks his car, I pace the small hallway, wondering if I should cancel. It seems too sudden, being alone with him. Like I'll do or say the wrong thing and end up in his arms or something crazy. It'll be better if I renege but how, since he's already here? I could come down with a swift case of food poisoning? Headache? Something contagious might be a better idea ...

Maya and Esterlita have their faces pressed against the glass, managing to steam it up while they titter away, unaware of my angst.

'Get away from the window,' I hiss, unable to think of a good excuse while they're giggling and whispering away like a couple of unruly teens.

'Ooh, would you look at that. Boy must do a lot of squats to get a butt like that. It makes you just want to slap …'

I slap a hand over her damn mouth. 'Don't do it, Es. You're banned from talking if Leo comes in. In fact, don't worry, I'm going to out! Bye!' There's nothing left to do but go through with it, even though I know it's a bad idea.

Maya laughs, noting the distraught look on Esterlita's face. I've spoiled all her fun with Leo, and I don't care one little bit.

I grab my bag and make a dash for it, slamming the door behind me and waving to Leo to stay in the car. I feel like I'm back in high school, escaping fast so my mum doesn't embarrass me!

'Hey,' I say, and clip on my seatbelt. 'Go, go, *go!*' I dart a glance behind me to make sure Esterlita hasn't bounded out behind me and attached herself to the car. I wouldn't put it past her.

He frowns. 'Are you hungry or something?'

'Ah, yeah, something like that.' The man is going to think all I care about is pizza! And to be honest, I really am partial to pizza. 'It's just—' I scramble to think of an excuse for my erratic behaviour '—that I feel a little bad leaving Maya and Esterlita, that's all.'

'Oh …' He stops the car before we've even left the driveway. 'Why don't we invite them then? I'm sure they'll love Basilico.'

'NO!'

He blanches. This is not going well. 'Just erm, keep the engine running, keep driving, that's the way. I'm sure a bit of space is good for all of us. I can bring them home a pizza.' *Stop talking, Orly!*

'OK, if you're sure.'

'I'm sure.'

We get to the trattoria ten minutes later after a silent ride. This was a bad idea. We've already run out of things to talk about and we're not even inside yet! I panic. I look for a way out. Maybe

167

I can text Maya and tell her to call me with a fake emergency? A small fire. A robbery. A spider infestation?

'Here we are. After you.' He holds the door open for me and I'm immediately assaulted with the most intoxicating smell of roasted garlic. My mouth waters. I suppose it's only good manners to eat with the damn man. Inside I see a few of the locals I know, like Bob and his wife. I go to their table as Leo waves to one of his workers and heads to their table to say hello.

'Hello, Bob.'

Ruddy-faced Bob wipes his hands on his napkin before shaking my hand. 'Hey. Orly this is my wife Iris. Iris, this is Orly from Honeysuckle Hall.'

I expect Iris to quiz me like the other locals have but instead she blushes and looks over my shoulder. I turn to see what she's looking at and make eye contact with Freya, of all people.

'Iris, you should pop over to the hall for a cup of tea sometime.'

She snaps her eyes back to mine. 'I'm so busy with … work at the moment. You know how it is.' A guilty look flashes across her face. Is she worried about being seen talking to me because of all the rumours or am I just imagining that? She appears distinctly uncomfortable whatever the reason is.

'Iris works in Josie's craft shop.' The mysterious Josie who also has it in for me …

Iris looks pointedly back at her meal.

'I understand,' I say. 'Enjoy your dinner.'

I turn to Freya and give her a big wave and smile. Kill them with kindness, don't they say?

Leo and I are shown to a table and a carafe of red wine arrives. Leo pours us two oversized glasses and I take a big gulp. 'You're a fan then?' he asks, as I wipe my red wine smile away.

'Big fan, yes. Love wine. Red, white, blue. I'm not fussy.' I take another gulp. It really is a delicious table wine and I inhale it to cover my nerves and the aftereffects of such a strange meeting with Iris.

He nods and I notice his eyes widen a little as if he's what ... regretting this? The wine soon hits the spot and I feel a sort of lethargy come over me. A sort of loosening. Let them all watch and judge me! 'So, word is you have a secret past,' I say, trying to recall the rumours about Leo or whether Esterlita made them up because she was short of something to say.

'Who says that?'

'*Everyone.*'

He grins. 'I'm not sure I can trust you. You'll probably sell my secrets to the Russian mafia or something.'

'You can trust me! Unless you own a priceless masterpiece, a van Gogh, or a Dalí. Or maybe the Hope Diamond. Then you most definitely *cannot* trust me.'

'Good to know.'

'Well, you haven't answered the question.'

'What do you want to know?'

'Why did you move here?'

'Probably the same reason as you. It's a picturesque place to live, but still has that small-town vibe where everyone knows everyone and as long as you're a good person you'll get along fine. There's plenty of work for me and I like the fact that London isn't too far away when I want a taste of the big-city buzz every now and then. Although I've been here two years, I'm still considered the new guy.'

'That's the most boring answer I've ever heard.'

He lets out surprised laughter. 'OK, fine. I'll tell you the truth but you've got to promise you won't tell a soul.'

'Pinkie swear.' We link pinkie fingers and swear on it.

'Before I came here I worked as a spy for ze Germans. You know the type, hides in plain sight as a sports teacher.'

'Really?'

He nods.

'Who were you spying on?'

'Other spies.'

'Of course. Russian ones?'

'Mainly.'

'So what happened?'

'Got tired of the game, you know how it is. Always on the run, never settling in one place too long, unable able to form attachments. So I did what any good spy would do ...' He lifts a shoulder as if I should know the answer.

'*You had a face transplant*!?' I bellow, drawing the surprised gazes of a few other patrons.

He laughs. 'Yes! It was the only way to break free. So I had this face transplant with someone much uglier than I originally was, sadly, and then I burned off my fingerprints, and went rogue. It's been two years and still they haven't managed to find me.'

'You must look over your shoulder a lot.'

'Nope, trained not to do that. Must always look forward, never backwards. Hide in plain sight, remember?'

'How could I forget. Wow, the stories you could tell.'

'But I won't as I don't want to put your safety in jeopardy.' He grins and takes a sip of wine.

'Thanks.'

'You're welcome.'

'I hope they never find you,' I whisper across the table as candlelight flickers between us.

'How can they?'

'I could talk– I bet that information is worth a lot to someone.'

He lifts a brow. 'I know where you hide your jewels.'

'Then we're at an impasse?'

'Better to just forget our pasts, and think of the future.'

'Do you know what I see in my future?'

His eyes light up. 'What?'

'Pizza!'

The night continues in a more relaxed way once we break the ice with silly stories and when it comes to an end, my jaw hurts from laughing so much.

'I'd better get you home before midnight.'

'Or my wicked stepsisters will send a search party.'

'I can imagine Esterlita peering through the window ...'

He doesn't know how right he is. Esterlita spends her life peering through windows at Leo, probably without his knowledge eighty per cent of the time! The poor fool has no idea. But to be fair, Es peers out at most men, most of the day, so it's not as though she's only focused on him. 'She's probably out there now,' I say only half joking. You never can tell with that woman.

'She's a sweetheart, despite her stalking.'

He knows?!

'She is. I don't know how I would have coped here without her.' I might have been able to cope but it definitely wouldn't have been half as much fun. 'What was her Edward like? Did you know him?'

Leo leans back on his chair, all thoughts of leaving now vanished. 'He died before I arrived in town. He was the local car mechanic, so pretty much everyone knew and liked Edward. He worked right up until he died at seventy-something apparently. One of those guys who liked to tinker away at things, an old-school sort. From what I've heard, Esterlita has never really got over losing him. There was a lot of talk at the time, churchgoers tried to coax her out of her house, locals took her plates of food. They even tried to cook some of her Filipino dishes hoping that would tempt her but she stayed inside for an entire year.'

'She stayed inside for a year?' I can't imagine vivacious Esterlita doing anything of the sort; she's such a people person. A social butterfly if ever there was one.

'Yeah, people were concerned. But I guess that's grief. She had to do things her way while she healed. Luckily she has a lot of friends in Eden Hills who all stepped up to help in one way or another.'

Goose bumps break out over my skin despite the warm room. I feel bad for not realising she'd been so grief-stricken.

'I feel like I haven't been there for Es, always going on about my own trivial problems, when she's probably wanting to share something personal with me but never getting a word in.'

Leo shakes his head. 'Don't think like that, Orly. I think you've been a bit of a saviour for Es. She's back in town a lot more – people have been chatting about it a fair bit. It's like she's got a new lease on life. Apparently she was never quite the same after, but maybe she's finding the light again …'

Finding the light again. He's so poetic at times. But it stuns me silent as I think of my new friend and the smile she hides behind.

'Shall we go?' he asks, as the staff not so subtly bang and crash in the kitchen, alerting us we've overstayed our welcome. Just how did the time flash by so fast?

'We better. I had such a great night, thank you. This one is on me.'

We wrestle with credit cards, and arms, until he reluctantly gives in and only lets me pay for my half when I remind him I can ruin him by telling everyone he was formerly a German spy who wouldn't be easily recognisable because of his face transplant.

'Fine, fine, keep your voice down,' he says, laughing, showing off those pearly whites of his.

Chapter 17

As the sun rises, so do I. My long lie-ins here are now a thing of the past. I wonder if it's because I know Leo will already be outside in the hall, hammering away at something, or if it's the fresh country air that does it. Whatever it is, I wake these days feeling full of energy, so very different to the burnt-out former me who woke up every day with leaden legs and a groggy head. I take a quick shower and slip on my work clothes. Who knew I'd be this person?

I make coffee and take it to the hall, hoping to share a cup with Leo before everyone else arrives. We've managed to steal some time together these last few days, with only the birds for company. And I've enjoyed it more than I can say. Leo is surprisingly funny when you get to know him and the more time I spend with him the more I like him. He's also kind of quirky, has a touch of the poetic about him, which is rare in a guy, and very attractive. He's well read, despite most people pegging him only for the outdoorsy, handyman kind of guy.

'Can I tempt you with some caffeine this fine summer morning?' I ask sneaking up on him as he studies something. He jumps and hides his hands behind his back. 'What have you got there?' I ask.

'It's nothing. A coffee would be great.'

'What is it, Leo?'

His face darkens. 'Look, Orly, I don't want you to be afraid, OK?'

Oh my God he *is* a German spy who's had a face transplant and he's going to kill me because I know! 'O-K,' I say as my heart races. How will he do it? A hammer to the temple? A quick slice through an artery? No something less messy – an electric shock with enough vaults to stop my heart. Where's my cardiothoracic surgeon when I need her?

'Don't look so afraid.' He laughs. 'It's like you're picturing your own demise or something.'

I let out a nervous laugh. 'What – no!' I sneak a peek in case there's a newly dug hole around, you never can tell with these carpenters. Always digging random trenches in the earth for no discernible reason.

He opens his hand, and I fight the urge to scrunch my eyes closed. It's another note. 'Oh.'

'Oh?' he asks. 'You know what this is?'

'Let me guess, it says something like: *You're putting others in danger* – that kind of thing?'

His eyes light up with surprise. 'You've found one before?'

I sigh. 'Yeah … a few.'

He frowns hard. 'Why didn't you tell me, Orly?'

'What's to tell?' Do I confide in him and risk looking like a fool? Again.

I sit him down and tell him the whole convoluted story.

'Wow, Orly, you're playing it down a fair bit if someone is trying to scare you away.' He wears that same expression, which is half anger and half worry. I secretly love that his protective instincts kick in so quickly.

'I'm not playing it down, Leo. But what else can I do? I don't want them to see me running scared, so I have to show them I'm not.' I lift my hands in the air.

'How do you know it's not someone dangerous?' Anger radiates off him and I feel whoever is trying to scare me now has him as an enemy.

'A few hastily scrawled notes aren't the work of a serial killer, I'm sure.'

He blanches. 'Do you have any idea who it is?'

'It could be Freya, or Josie. I've also been getting the worst kind of online trolling from Carly C fans. Would they go so far as this? Hard to tell. Somehow I think it's closer to home. You've heard yourself all the rumours Freya's started about me and what I intend to do at Honeysuckle Hall. From gentlemen's clubs, to secret laboratories! Bob's wife Iris couldn't even look at me the other night at Basilico as if talking to me would tarnish her reputation or something.'

'I can't see Freya sneaking in here to leaves notes like that. I know she can be nasty, but this doesn't seem to be her style. It could be anyone.' He scrubs at his face and then stops abruptly, lifting his eyes to meet mine. 'The person we saw running in here the other night – it's them, isn't it? Did they leave a note then?'

'Yes.'

His jaw works. 'Why didn't you tell me at the beginning, Orly? I could have helped.'

I stay silent.

With a groan he says, 'You thought it was me!'

I have the grace to blush.

'Orly, I promise you it's not me.'

'Yes, I know that now. German spies would have far superior methods than a few hastily scrawled notes. So do you have any ideas? If we made a list, who'd be at the top?' I still think it's Freya – she has disliked me from the get-go and has managed to make others feel bad being seen talking to me. And that's half the reason I'm not that bothered. What can she do to me except try and freak me out? We'll have the alarm set up soon and no one will be able to access the hall without a lot of noise.

He shakes his head. 'Let me have a think about it.'

'OK, I will too. Surely if we make some discreet enquiries in town we might be able to narrow it down?'

'Yeah.' He takes my hands. 'Promise me if you get any more notes you'll let me know?'

Worry flashes across his face. I've never known a man to be so caring before, and while I can handle myself it's nice to know I've got someone to call if I truly am fearful of my safety. 'I promise. But I'm sure it's all fine, Leo. Like I said, this started when I arrived, and I've managed to ignore it thus far.'

'Yeah, but the campers aren't here yet. That's what worries me.'

I go to ask why, but he leans down and kisses the bridge of my nose and all thought vanishes. What was that? Before I can think he pulls away and is gone with a backwards wave. 'Call me if you need me,' he says. 'Until then I'm just going to check a few things out.'

'Detective Leo.'

He winks at me from the cab of his truck. 'Got a nice ring to it, doesn't it? I'll be back soon.'

'I'll be here.' He drives off and I put a fingertip to the bridge of my nose that still tingles from his touch. I spend the next hour going over the kiss in slow motion and tormenting myself about whether it was the kiss of a friend or something more and then panicking about it. Just the usual, then.

Back to my to-do list. I call the web designer about the Honeysuckle Hall website. 'Hey Lorelai,' I say. 'How are you?'

'Great, Orly. How'd you like the layout of the site?'

From my desk, which is a stool at the kitchen counter, I flick through the site. 'I love it. You've nailed the brief.' Lorelai designed the Excès website and we've worked together for years on various media projects. She's the best in the biz and I'm grateful she put together the website for the camp at such short notice.

'Great. So hit me with it. What do you think could be better?'

I particularly like working with her because she takes feedback very well and listens to even the smallest changes and gets them done without fussing over it.

'I'd like the Honeysuckle Hall text to be a little bigger. When it flashes up on screen as you enter the site, can we slow that down so they have a bit more time to read it?'

'Yes that's easily done.'

'Aside from that, it's perfect. These are only interim pictures until I get a professional photographer to snap some pictures once the renovations are complete. I'll also ask for the first lot of campers to sign a media release and hopefully we'll have some action shots to add of the camp.'

'Just send them over when you're ready and I'll change them out.'

'Thanks, Lorelai. You've made magic happen.'

'Shucks, you're good for my ego.'

I laugh, knowing how lucky I am to have her. 'Any chance you can use the same sort of formula for a poster for some community newspapers?'

'Sure? When do you need it by? Let me guess, yesterday?'

'Something like that.'

It's her turn to laugh. 'I'll send you over some proofs tomorrow, yeah?'

'You're a gem.'

'I've been called worse.'

We ring off and I go online and order a big bouquet of wild honeysuckles to be delivered to her office in London as a thank you for always stepping up last-minute for me. As I'm keying in my credit card number for the order, Esterlita comes rushing in, her eyes wide.

What now? I brace myself.

'You won't believe it,' she says, her chest heaving.

'What?'

'It's Leo!' She's so hyper she paces up and down the small

kitchen; there's barely room for a few steps before she turns and repeats the process.

'What about him?'

'He's not who he says he is!'

I rub my face, not sure I have the energy for any more surprises. 'How so?'

She plonks herself on a stool next to me. 'He's got a secret past.'

That old chestnut! 'Of course he does. Big-city guy moves to small town to hide from his past. Buys an apple farm and makes cider, whilst hoping no one recognises him. It's a Hallmark movie, right?'

Confusion flashes across her face. 'He doesn't own an apple farm, does he?'

'No.'

'You think I'm joking?'

I laugh. 'It's Leo, Es. Lovely Leo who's always there when we need him.'

She shakes her head. 'You're too close to him now to see what I see.'

I lean back against the kitchen counter and sigh. 'You're the one who told me to consider him as a husband if I wouldn't consider approaching a minor royal.'

She wrings her hands. 'You're in danger, Orly, and you're making this out to be a joke!' Her voice rises an octave.

'How am I in danger?'

She shrinks down and looks over her shoulder as if Leo is about to storm the cottage to stop her from spilling all his secrets. 'He's a bad guy; he's not who he says he is!'

I suddenly clock what's happened, and reel in faux surprise. 'Let me guess, he's a former German spy?'

Fear flashes across her face. 'He *told* you? Oh, Orly, this is not good, not good at all. Now you're really *truly* in danger! German spies are well known for their torture techniques.'

'But if you know aren't you in danger too?'

She blanches. 'Oh help me, baby Jesus, YES!'

I bite down on my lip to stop smiling because poor Esterlita is truly frightened. 'OK, let's think about this for a minute. Who told you?'

'That doesn't matter.'

'It does matter, Es.' I think back to visiting Basilico. 'Freya strikes again.'

Her hands fly to her mouth. 'Yes! But there's more! He's got a different face! That beautiful man was probably hit with the ugly stick before and now he's only gorgeous because it's not his face! Why aren't you listening, Orly? The man HAS SOMEONE ELSE'S BEAUTIFUL FACE!'

Laughter bursts out of me. Poor Esterlita seriously believes Leo is a former German spy who had a face transplant. 'Oh, Es! Really!? Freya overhead Leo and I talking on our date. We were being silly, pretending to have secret pasts and obviously the town gossip latched on to that and ran with it. Poor Leo is probably going to have to explain himself to everyone in town now.'

'So he's not a spy?' Her eyes are so wide they seem huge in her small face.

'Does he look like a spy?'

She shakes her head. 'Well, of course not, he's been trained to look the very opposite, hasn't he?'

'I hate to think of how this will spiral out of control.' Even though it's hilarious.

'Well it has grown legs, and taken off,' she admits, blushing. 'I thought …'

I go to the fridge and take out the jug of iced tea and pour us two glasses. I'm tempted to top Esterlita's up with a shot of vodka to take the edge off. 'I know, you thought I was in jeopardy, I get it. It's very sweet of you to be concerned.'

'Well, it's always the ones you least suspect, isn't it?'

I nod. This place sure has the ability to make a person run

away with themselves. 'Sure is, Es. But anyway, we're all safe and I'm sure Leo only wanted a new start, just like the rest of us. You came here for love, I came here to cure burnout, and Leo came here because he wanted to be part of village life, even though *some* of those villagers need a hobby …'

'It's Freya's fault. I should know better than to listen to that woman.'

I shrug. 'She spins a good yarn.'

She exhales all the worry, long and loudly. 'Don't tell Leo about this, especially not the part where I said he was hit was the ugly stick and that's why he got someone else's beautiful face.'

'Your secret is safe with me, Es.' So the story doesn't grow any further and we have MI6 on the doorstep, I tell Esterlita about a real-life drama – the curious note leaver – and see what she makes of that. 'You've been getting threatening letters this whole time and never thought to tell the Firecracker?' Her face falls as if I've offended her.

'Sorry, Es. I didn't want to worry you, that's all. I'm sure it's nothing, but unlike the German spy story, this one is real.'

She gasps. 'Then you really might be in danger! You need to slow your plans down, rethink the idea of having strangers here who will be relying on you. I don't like this, not one little bit. How can you blithely invite campers here when it's clearly not safe?'

'I'm sure the campers will be safe. It's more a ploy to rattle me. And I'm not going to give in to it.'

She waves me away. 'Orly, are you even listening to me? I told you this place wasn't good and you never listened! What if it's the mafia? What if it's the CIA, IRA or—' she inhales sharply '—the KGB?'

I feel I've made an error in judgement telling Esterlita. 'Your overuse of acronyms aside, why would it be the CIA, IRA or KGB? That doesn't make any sense.'

She shakes her head as if I'm dense. 'Oh, Orly, you are so naïve!

This place was once requisitioned by the government, right? There's probably a bunker here with all their secret files or something! For all we know, they could still *be* here! Have you ever thought of that?'

I'm so dumbstruck I can't form words.

'I've got to go, Orly. I'll go to the library and see what I can find, but please think about this seriously!'

She bustles out as fast as she arrived, iced tea forgotten.

Chapter 18

A few days later we soak up the blazing sun outside. 'None of the interviewees are the right fit, are they?' I say to Maya as we sit on the back deck, nursing glasses of sparkling water.

She sighs. 'No, they're so wrong it's not even funny. What was with that guy who said he hates the outdoors? Why would he come for an interview for a camp leader job with a heavy focus on being outdoors?' I can't help but think we're not getting the best candidates because of all the rumours circulating around town. It seems some locals are taking a wide berth of Honeysuckle Hall and who could blame them?

I shake my head. 'Trying his luck I guess.'

Maya continues: 'And the one who wanted to treat it like a military training camp, up at 4 a.m., beds made, standing to attention! Shudder.'

'It does make you wonder just what they think an adventure camp means!'

The rejuvenation of the hall and the grounds is almost complete but we're yet to find a camp leader, despite interviewing a lot of people who just don't fit the bill. Sometimes I think they've come for an interview just to have a stickybeak. 'I might have to try an agency; we're running out of time.'

'There's always Es?' she says doubtfully.

I shake my head. 'Es is amazing, but I'm not sure she's the right person for the job.' I can't see her being the outdoorsy type either somehow. 'She's most comfortable hanging around the cottage, reminding me of my shortcomings. Plus she's got her own little catering business and I wouldn't want to pull her away from that. I think she truly does find comfort in feeding people.'

'True, true.' She sighs. 'I'm sure the perfect candidate is just around the corner. I only wish I could stay for the first camp.'

Nerves flutter at the thought of Maya leaving. She's been right beside me these last few weeks and I've come to rely on her judgement. It's not going to be the same here when she goes back to London. 'It seems unfair that you've done all this hard work and you won't get to meet our first bunch of campers.'

'Right?' She grins. 'But you'll tell me all about them and what they get up to. I'm expecting daily updates.'

'Of course.'

'How many have booked now?'

'There's six booked in, as of today.' I scroll through the list of people and the surveys they filled out. It was Maya's idea to ask them why they were coming and what they hoped to get out of the adventure camp – a brilliant plan to get to know them a bit better before they arrive and learn how we can modify the activities to suits their needs. From reading the surveys it sounds as though we've got a mixed bag of personalities who are in dire need of some time out.

'Six is a good number for the first one, so start advertising the next one, yeah? Keep those numbers ticking over.'

'Already done. I've got two people booked so far for the following week. And this Wednesday the ads go out in community newspapers across London and the city outskirts, so I'm hoping that draws a big crowd. It's going to be trial and error to see what works in terms of advertising. Social media will be our best option but it's going to take time to grow the pages. I've done a few ads online so I hope they'll get some traction too.' And if numbers don't expand, there won't be anything in the coffers to pay for such things but I don't mention that to Maya. We've gone over everything so many times, I don't want her going home with a headful of worries about me.

'This is going to be a different sort of challenge for you, Orly, but already you've created this wonderland that campers are going to love. You're going to have a lot of fun, I can tell. So make sure you put the work away sometimes, and join in too.'

I well up, hating the fact she's leaving. 'I will, I promise. I'm excited. It doesn't feel as much like work as it does chasing a dream. My main goal is for the camps to have a positive effect on people. I hope they'll leave Honeysuckle Hall refreshed and ready to tackle their busy lives once more, but know they always have a place they can return to and switch off for a while. If that happens, I'll know I've done my job right.'

'You'll make it happen.' She stands and collects our coffee mugs.

'You're leaving already?' I'd thought we'd have one more long lunch together.

'Yep, real life calls. This place has worked its magic on me, Orly. I've never slept so well. And despite all the hard work you made me do, I'm going back feeling like a million dollars.'

I cross my arms as if bracing myself for her departure. 'Well, that's a promising start. If our super-busy surgeon feels relaxed despite me working her to the bone! I'll take a picture of your herb babies so you can see them grow.'

She laughs. 'Maybe you'd better not. When the campers come and chop them up for dinner it'll be like losing my best friends.'

'Ah so you admit talking to the herbs you planted?' I'm reminded of apologising to the roses before I deadheaded them and how the girls thought I'd lost my marbles.

'It's scientifically proven that if you talk to plants they grow more heartily.'

'You big softie.'

'Guilty. You have fun now, OK? Remember this is as much for you as anyone, so enjoy it.'

'I will, I promise.'

'And no more notes have appeared? I don't have to worry some lunatic is after you? And the Carly Army? Has that died down?'

There *have* been a few more notes, but I don't tell Maya. I keep picturing Freya leaving them in order to get me riled up so they don't so much scare me as annoy me. The Carly Army have gone quiet too, praise the fickle nature of young adults. 'I think I'm all good. I've got Leo the lion to back me up.'

She waggles her brow. 'That's the spirit. You'll continue to pursue that delectable carpenter?'

I make a big show of being put out by such a question.

'Are you taking acting lessons from Es?' Maya asks.

'Maybe.'

'Have you arranged another date?' she asks.

'It wasn't a date. It was a thank you for all the work you've done dinner and also a sorry I suspected you were trying to scare me away from my own property drinks.'

'You are such a drama queen. It was a date. And usually the process is, you start with one date, then you go on another, maybe partake in a bit of kissy-wissy—'

'You did not just say kissy-wissy. Who even *are* you?'

'Well, sometimes you just gotta break it down for a girl.'

'Just stop.'

She shrugs. 'Fine, fine. But if you take too long I'll have to tell Es to step in.'

'Oh no you won't.'

'Oh yes I will.'

I glare at her.

'Is that the best you've got?'

'Yes.'

'I'm a cardiothoracic surgeon, I *know* a thing or two about hearts, would you agree?'

'Grudgingly.'

'Good. When hearts have been damaged the surest way to mend them is with love. Don't argue.' She holds up a hand. 'And you could do a lot worse than Leo. He's absolutely lovely, he's smart, clever and funny, and bloody hot to boot. So stop making excuses and at least see where it takes you. Your heart needs it, and that's free advice from a medical professional. Don't let it wither and die. I can't keep bringing the paddles with me.' She grins and I remember that fateful night when I indeed thought I was in the throes of a heart attack, so painful were the images of Harry and Carly C. They don't seem too painful now to recollect.

'Fine! I'll go on another date then, if that's your honest medical opinion. But if it turns bad, then you're responsible.'

'How will it turn bad?'

'Well, what if we date and things are lovely and then suddenly it comes to light he secretly loves wearing Armani trousers and then we break up and then I see him every damn day in the local hardware store and it's super awkward and then—'

'How have you ever had a relationship? Truly how have I missed this overwrought part of your personality?'

'I hide it well.'

'You do. OK, so in the real world, when things like that happen, and you run into your ex, you simply wave and move on. Then you call me and tell me everything and I will agree he's an idiot, and we can list all his flaws until we run out of words. Deal?'

I nod. 'Deal.'

'But it could also go the other way, and we could be planning a wedding by the lake, baby names, and the pros and cons of Montessori schools.'

'You sure can jump ahead, Maya. Sheesh.'

'It's called thinking positive.'

'Right. Speaking of, any word from Preston?'

Her mouth is a grim line. 'He's missing me terribly, I'm sure. But all I've seen is pics on his Insta of him and a gang of groupies. The usual.' Maya's on-again, off-again boyfriend is a musician who openly pursues other women and then splashes their pictures all over the place. What she sees in him is beyond me, but I guess it's the pull of the unattainable.

There have been times I've wanted to bang her head against a wall to make her see sense but she's quite aware he's no good for her and she just doesn't care. It boils down to the fact they don't place any rules or restrictions on each other, so Maya can work as much as she has to with nary a word from him, and he can go missing for days on end and she doesn't question it. It works for them and she seems happy enough with the arrangement so what can I do? Still, I do hope she moves on to someone who worships her like she so deserves.

'Well, I'm sure he'll be happy you're home. Whereas I won't be.'

We collect Maya's things and Esterlita comes over for a twenty-five-minute goodbye and then Maya's off with a fluttery wave. Back to her busy job saving lives.

'I hate goodbyes,' I say, trying not to cry. 'It's not like she's moving to Australia, is it? She's only a train ride away.'

Esterlita wraps her arm through mine. 'She'll be back. Mark my words, once this place gets under your skin there's no cure for it, except to return. Small towns have that kind of magic. And Eden Hills is that little bit more special too.'

'I hope so, Es.'

'You're lucky to have a friend like Maya.'

'She's your friend now too.'

'Then we're both lucky. Actually, we're going to have a Zoom chat about you later. Don't tell her I told you but she wants all the gossip and she knows I'll give it to her straight.'

'The way it should be.' I smile. 'Your secret is safe with me.' In truth I think having a bit of Esterlita in her life will help ground Maya on those days when she feels like she's going under. Our Esterlita has the unique ability to bring sunshine and laughter to any situation and I'm glad my two friends will be there for each other, under the guise of gossiping and worrying about me.

'Good. Ooh, who's *this* fine specimen of a man?'

I shade my eyes with a hand to see a tall, athletic guy wandering up the gravel drive. 'Did I forget an interview?' I check the appointment schedule in my phone – everyone is accounted for. 'I haven't. Maybe he's lost.'

'Can I help you?' I say as he approaches. He's got light brown hair and a ready smile but I don't recognise him.

'Hey, I'm Noah. I'm sorry to intrude without warning but I heard about the vacancy for the camp leader and I was hoping we could chat?'

Esterlita nods. 'Yes, yes, come in! Can I get you a tea, coffee, some wine perhaps?'

She is hopeless around men. Hopeless. 'Come on in,' I say. 'How'd you hear about the position?' I ask. The whole town knows, but I don't recognise him as a local. Esterlita races ahead and goes straight to the kitchen. I send up a silent prayer that she's not mixing cocktails or whipping up some delicious Filipino dish that she swears is an aphrodisiac. Please just let her bring the guy a glass of water!

We sit at the dining room table and he says, 'Mike from the Tipsy Tadpole told me. Apparently you need someone sporty and capable of leading a group of campers? I've had experience with tour groups before. I used to take groups of hikers along Hadrian's Wall. Before that I taught surf lessons in Australia. I've travelled a fair bit and worked in tourism. But I'm back home now, ready to settle down.'

Esterlita returns bearing a tray with drinks. 'Ready to settle down, eh?'

Honestly, how does she have that incredible sense of timing?

'Yeah. I've ticked off everything on the bucket list and now I'd like to make a home, somewhere I can stay for good. I've been transient for so long; it still feels strange but I love this town and I know it's as good a place as any to put roots down.'

'This is certainly the right town for that,' Esterlita says and fusses with pouring some concoction from jug to glass, clinking in cubes of ice as she goes. I'm hoping it's not juice laced with vodka – you never can tell with Esterlita.

Noah smiles. 'Yeah I think so too. It's a really cool little town and once I got to know a few locals I felt like this was the right place for me. The woodlands and lake are a big drawcard too. I can lose days hiking.'

Esterlita manages to knock into the table and the glasses crash together before shattering into a thousand tiny pieces. I sneak a glance and see she's bitten down on her lip as if trying to keep words from spilling out. Probably curse words. 'Leave it, Es,' I say, worried why she looks so upset over some cheap glassware. 'I'll sort it after we chat to Noah.'

'No, no, I'll clean it up now. I don't want anyone hurt. That's all.'

'No one will get hurt, it'll be fine.'

'But they will, they will,' she says and bustles off. Must be another Filipino superstition I don't know about where breaking glasses is bad luck or something.

When she comes back she's composed. 'Here.' She puts fresh glasses on the table. 'Let's try that again! Sorry I'm such a butter-fingers.'

'Sit down, Es, I'll pour the drinks.' I hand them each a glass and take a seat next to Esterlita. 'So, Noah, do you have any refer-ences? A CV?' He certainly looks the part of camp leader, with his athletic physique and khaki outfit, like he spends all day hiking the woodlands.

The apples of his cheeks are pink. 'I should've been more organ-ised. Sorry, I wasn't sure what you'd need and I didn't bring anything. I can give you some phone numbers, character references that you can call but I don't actually have a CV. My work has been more of the backpacker kind, picking up bits and pieces here and there. Walking tours, hikes, bikes, surfing, that sort of stuff. I taught English in Japan for a bit. I've worked in cafés and bars around the world. I guess you could say I'm a jack of all trades.'

Noah could be the perfect camp leader with qualifications such as his. He's athletic, has experience and seems easy-going, like the type of guy who'd remain unruffled under pressure. 'OK, yeah, whatever phone numbers you've got would be great. Can I ask you some you questions about how you'd handle scenarios that might crop up?'

'Sure,' he says with a smile.

'How would you handle a nervous camper, say someone who was scared to try any of the activities, or felt like an outsider?'

He taps his chin with a finger. 'I'd take them aside and remind them why they're here, which is to step outside their comfort zone and try new things, and assure them I'll be with them every step of the way.'

'Nice, I like that. And what if you needed to administer first aid? Are you up to date with that?'

'Yes, I had to take a first aid course in Australia when I was a surf instructor. I'm the full bottle on it and won't hesitate to help even if it's only a plaster they might need. I'll make sure I'm well prepared for anything.'

I quiz Noah for a while longer and am impressed with his on-the-spot answers and fill him in on the camp and what we hope to achieve now and as we grow.

'Honestly,' he says, 'it sounds like my dream job. I hope you'll consider me for the position.' With that he takes a sip of the drink and scrunches his face up. What has she put in it this time?

'I will. I'll check your references and we'll go from there. Would you be happy to start next week a few days before the first lot of campers arrive?'

'For sure.'

'We can go through my itinerary and you can tell me what you think is viable, weather permitting, and how long each activity will take and we can make up a schedule so they know exactly what they're in for.'

'Ready when you are.'

We shake on it. I catch Esterlita's eye but she's shifty-eyed as if she's still embarrassed about the water glasses. 'I'll wait for your call,' Noah says as I walk him to the door and wave him off.

Inside, Esterlita is still mute so I hurry to reassure her. 'Es, we're going to have a lot of breakages here; it's no big deal.' I smile and wait, expecting she'll have something lascivious to say about Noah, but she doesn't respond. Instead she looks to the dappled sunlight and sighs.

'I'm tired today, Orly. I'm not myself.'

I've never seen the Firecracker so dejected before. 'Aw, Es. You're doing too much around here, that's why. You need to have a break, have a few days where you sloth on your sofa and read romance novels, OK? Stop your research about the hall and it's mysterious links to … the KGB or whoever it was. I love having you here, but you have to look after yourself, too.' Guilt rushes me at Esterlita working so hard to help me and putting her own health at risk. 'Can I make you dinner for a change, Es? You can put your feet up and let me look after you.'

'You're sweet but no. I've seen your attempts at cooking and I don't need a tummy bug on top of everything else.'

'There's the Es I know!' I laugh, knowing she's probably right. Cooking is best left to the experts or the microwave. Esterlita bustles off home while I call Noah's references who assure me he's a reliable and energetic employee. I call Noah and offer him the position of camp leader and he hoots and hollers as if he's won the lottery. I think the first camp is going to be a success!

*

191

Taking Maya's advice, I schedule a day off on Sunday. After seeing Esterlita so bone-weary, I know I can't afford to get like that, either, even though there's still so much to be done. So I take a day to myself to wander around Eden Hills and explore.

Mid-morning, I stumble on a tiny little shop down the back of a laneway. I can tell by the lemony scent alone there's something magical about it. A sign swaying in the breeze says: *The Little Shop of Lost and Found*. This is the kind of place I find treasures for my collection and I didn't think such a place would exist so close to the hall. It buoys me up that I just might have somewhere to escape to when I need it, somewhere I can while away time looking for precious gems …

I push open the door and wind chimes tinkle, alerting the shopkeeper to my presence. 'Hello there,' a voice says from behind the counter. I can't see who it belongs to so I make my way through the labyrinth of curiosities until I'm rewarded with the sight of a grey-haired woman wearing a brightly coloured kaftan.

'Hello,' I say. 'I'm so happy I've stumbled across your shop!'

She gives me a wide smile. 'Thank you. I'm Lilac. Were you looking for anything in particular?'

'I'm a philatelist,' I go to explain when I see she knows exactly what the word means.

'A collector of stamp and postage memorabilia. You're not the only one in Eden Hills. It's a shame that it's not as popular a hobby these days. So many things to be discovered if only you care to spend the time looking.'

'That's exactly how I feel.'

'Come through,' Lilac says, motioning to a maze of threadbare carpet to follow. It's like following the yellow brick road, with twists and turns through precarious stacks of leather-bound books and occasional tables full of delicate trinkets like glass vases and candelabras. I realise the shop is surprisingly spacious as we make our way through, coming to a room filled with glass cabinets.

'Oh!' Inside the cabinets are all sorts of stamps and postage paraphernalia. There are stamps worth a lot of money, rare collections that I know on sight, but they're not the ones I go for. I prefer the singles, the ones with a story, the ones that have actually been affixed to an envelope and travelled somewhere before being gently soaked off and dried. They're worth less for avid collectors but not for me.

'Shall I leave you to peruse?' Lilac says, bringing me a stool. 'The cabinets aren't locked so feel free to take a closer look.'

'Thank you.' Lilac bustles back the way she came and I spend a few delightful hours agonising over what to buy. When I come across a letter with a mention of the hall my pulse quickens. And I know whatever it costs I have to have it. It reads:

Dearest George,

I miss you terribly and count the days until we can be reunited once more. Time seems interminable whilst we're apart and it is all I can do not to dwell on it lest I am miserable company and become an object of pity. The girls here are gregarious and frivolous; I do wonder if they'll ever find suitable husbands, as they don't seem to have the deportment for such things. Perhaps, I'm just missing you and it is clouding my judgement?

The hall itself is a marvellous place to stay, although rumours abound that it is haunted. I am yet to see any evidence of this myself. The gardens have been a tonic and I spent an inordinate amount of my day wandering through them, enjoying birdsong and the perfume of honeysuckles that grow abundantly along the lake.

Father has written and says he will allow you to pay him a visit. Although, you know what he is like and is likely to change his mind and tell me once again that I must marry a

*man who is my equal. I do not understand why I cannot
marry for love. However, I do have hope that he might change
his mind considering he agreed to meet with you.*

I wish you were here. Or I there.

All my love,

Elizabeth

What a relic to find! My mind spins with it all. Did Elizabeth
marry George? Did her father agree, even though it sounds like
he was in a different class to her? Did they have children? Sadly
there are no surnames on the letter so I don't even know how
I'd begin to search for them.

I take the letter and a handful of stamps and wend my way
back to the counter.

'You found it!' Lilac says. 'These things tend to have a way of
finding those who understand.'

'Do you know what happened to them?'

'No idea.' Lilac gives me a dazzling smile that says otherwise.

'I wonder if they were married, if they went against conven-
tion.'

Lilac's glasses sail down the bridge of her nose as she stares at
me. 'Do you think her father summoned the young man to a
meeting to give him their blessing?'

My heart falls. 'No, no I don't. I think he probably threatened
him to stay away from his daughter.'

'I had that feeling too.'

'I don't suppose this letter is for sale?'

Lilac's face crinkles into a smile. 'Of course it is. Somewhere
out there, there's a reply. Isn't that just the thing? Not knowing
where to find it.'

'And if it still exists.'

Lilac stays silent and I wonder if there's more to this little
mystery than meets the eye …

Chapter 19

Later in the week I find another note scrunched up by the back deck: *Your business isn't welcome in Eden Hills. This is your last warning.*

I really hope it's the last warning, because they have the ability to upset my entire day.

I'm angrily tending the veggie patch, taking my frustrations out on the weeds while confiding to the thyme and basil when a shadow falls over me. 'Leo, hi. I was just, erm …'

'Sharing secrets with the herbs, I get it.'

I smile. 'Something like that.' I don't even bother to tell Leo about the note – I don't want to give it any more of my time or energy.

He grins. 'We're all done.'

'Like done done?' *Wow, what a hold you have of the English language, Orly!* I stand and dust myself off. We've both been busy finalising the last of the renovations – Leo doing his bit here, and me doing mine inside the office – that time has once again run away from us these last few days.

'Yep, like done done.'

'Wow, I don't know who I'm going to be without the noise of … whatever it is that makes that horrendous noise and you

195

all coming and going.' I fold my arms, marvelling that we're finished, the hall has had its grand makeover, and soon people will be traipsing up and down the parquetry wearing wide smiles as they spend a week trying new things!

'You're the proud owner of a fully rejuvenated Honeysuckle Hall and soon you'll be surrounded by happy campers.'

'Yeah, new faces every week.' Which means more goodbyes too. I'm still missing Maya, like I've lost my right hand, and it aches a little.

'Do you want to come and check everything is A-OK, before we leave?'

'Sure.' I follow Leo to the front of the hall, feeling a strange sense of desolation. It strikes me that I'll be saying a lot of good-byes on this new venture, but saying goodbye to Leo is odd. I'll miss our early morning coffees, our late-night meetings, heads pressed together planning the next day. Even the happy smiles of his crew as they go about their days.

I guess some farewells will tug at the heartstrings, and others I'll be counting down the minutes until they're out of sight.

'Close your eyes,' Leo says.

I do a silly little screech-jump thing. I've been busting to see inside the hall for the last few days but Leo wouldn't hear a word of it. Told me he wanted the final reveal to be a surprise.

He laughs and covers my eyes with the palm of his hand. A shiver races the length of me. Must be excitement. It's not his proximity, but with the world suddenly blacked out all I can sense is him, the ocean scent of his aftershave. I feel his pulse quicken too.

I stumble and he rights me. 'Sorry, I can't see.'

'I've got you,' he says into my ear and it's all I can do not to fall. Am I that man-deprived I get this sensation when one is touching me in the most innocent of ways? How mortifying.

'OK, small steps. I won't let you go.'

I shuffle forward and feel the temperature drop as I enter the hall.

196

'Don't scream,' he says and removes his hand.

I blink several times before I duly scream and then clamp my hand over my mouth. I'm not usually an overexcited person but the transformation is incredible. 'Oh, Leo, I knew it would look good but I didn't expect this ...' The dark dingy hall has been transformed with big new chandeliers. The leadlight windows have been replaced and glorious kaleidoscopic sunshine streams in through the stained glass and shoots prisms of colourful light on the stone floor like some kind of immersive art experience. The panelling is polished and all of the furniture has been moved into place, including some truly gaudy dolphin cushions. Where does she get them from!? On the walls are huge framed photographs of the woodlands and the lake. Close-ups of the fruit trees ripe with apples with bubbles of early morning dew on the skins. 'Did you ...?'

'A little gift.'

'Aww, Leo, these would have cost a fortune just for the frames, let alone the photographs. Who took them?'

'I did.'

'They're beautiful and they suit this space so well. Thank you.' I'm so touched by his gift. 'I'll pay you for them.'

'Then it's not a gift.'

'You've done so much already.'

'It's nothing.' He waves me away. 'Check out the kitchen.'

The once run-down space has been transformed with white country-cottage-style kitchen cupboards and a butcher block bench. 'I don't think I want anyone to cook in here now. It's too nice for all that.' I take my phone from my jeans pocket and start taking snaps to share on social media.

'Next up, the bedrooms. All you need to do now is make up the beds and hang the towels.'

The rooms were a dusty, dirty mess but they've been fully cleaned. The windows shine and the electrics are fixed. Leo's team managed to restore the wrought-iron beds where rust had leached in, which saved me such a lot of money. To look at them now you'd never know. The new mattresses sit loftily atop, patiently waiting to be dressed.

New curtains hang jauntily by the small windows, making the room appear grand, like a suite rather than a room. The small desks each have a green banker lamp atop, and a notebook and a pen with the Honeysuckle Hall logo stamped on both.

'Wow!' I say, inspecting the notebook. 'This is beautiful!'

'They're a gift from Maya. She had pens and notebooks made and put into every room for guests. She also supplied boxes of travel-sized shampoos, conditioners, and body wash for the bathrooms with the camp logo on them. She wanted it to be a surprise.'

'Aww.' Tears well up thinking of her planning such a thoughtful gift for the campers. 'She's such a sweetheart.' I head into the tiny en suite and see the little navy-blue bottles set up on the vanity. They'll match the towels and the colour scheme we have planned perfectly.

I blink back tears. 'I'm amazed at the transformation. It doesn't look like the same place – but it's more than that, it has a totally different feel to it. It almost feels regal, somehow. Brought back to life and ready for the sound of laughter, the tinkling of cutlery, the crackle of a fire at the end of a long day spent outdoors.'

He grins and it's like sunshine on a gloomy day. I have this overwhelming feeling that for the first time ever I'm on the right track with my life – but I don't want to say goodbye to Leo. Seeing his happy, lazy smile every day has energised me and helped me forget about the past. Without him and his guys the place will feel deserted. Lonely.

Thankfully I have the Firecracker to keep me from falling into despair! I know in the coming days it'll feel empty around here without the footfall of tradesmen and visitors alike. I try hard to hide a sniffle as I realise the best part of my days have been when I've wandered outside, coffee cups in hand, and spent time with Leo, with just the tender sunrise between us.

'Did you manage to find a camp leader?' He unclips his tool belt, flashing a sneak peek of muscled abs.

The news hasn't spread around town yet? That's a first! 'Yeah, we found a nomad called Noah who seems almost too good to be true. He's had a lot of experience with similar ventures so I'm hoping it all works out. Can't be any worse than me attempting to lead them, anyway. He's been in and out a bit already. We've sorted the schedule and he's been checking out the woodlands and the lakes for suitable activities to do.'

'Noah? I haven't heard of him around town.'

I make a doubtful face. 'The gossip mill has ground to a halt?'

He gives me a half-smile. 'Is that even possible?'

'Probably not.'

We fall into silence, and I kick the floor, wondering what to say. Part of me wants to think of an excuse, another job to keep him here. Am I so desperate for friendship that I'd resort to paying for it!? But really, I know it's that Leo is an all-round good guy and we've spent the past couple of weeks working for a common goal that's made me feel closer to him. My days will feel so strange without Leo here! Where's the bloody chicken when I need it! I could innocently leap into his arms and I wouldn't need to explain why!

'I'd better go to the Tipsy Tadpole and make enquiries about Noah, then,' I say only half-jokingly.

'Make sure you do, Orly. I might even ask around about him.'

'Really?' He has a slight edge to his voice as if he doesn't like Noah already, sight unseen. 'I was joking, Leo.'

He mumbles something and then says, 'I just want to make sure he's above board. Make sure you'll be safe.'

I grin. 'My knight in shining armour, you.'

Her averts his eyes. 'I know you have Es close by, but still.'

'Well, thank you. Let me know what the rumour mill has to say, but I have a feeling he's a good sort.' His eyes flash with something I can't translate. 'I'll transfer the remaining money I owe you.'

He waves me away. 'You can pay next month.'

'No, no, I'm sure you've got bills to pay too.' We head outside and Leo stops and stares at me as if debating what to say.

The sun sinks, leaving the sky awash with lilacs and magentas. We lapse into silence and it's at that moment a small part of me falls hard for this new life. With hands dirty from being plunged into the earth, the fruity scent of honeysuckle in the air, the glorious riot of colour the sun produces as it leaves us for half a day, and this man who stands in front of me with a good heart and warm smile. Could I tempt fate and think of dating again? It seems like the universe is pointing the way, as the sun makes a halo around Leo's lovely head, as if saying: *Here's the one for you!*

He leaves me with a soft kiss on the cheek and I stand there for ages, tears rolling down my cheeks. Happy tears at the hall being complete and the idea that love is in the air if I take a chance …

Later that night I'm tucked up in bed, with freshly washed locks even though Esterlita has warned me many a time not to sleep with wet hair or I'll lose my mind. Something to look forward to. Her Pinoy beliefs amuse me so. While sad music plays in the background I call Maya.

'Darling, how's things?'

Her bright, bubbly voice is just the thing to keep me grounded. 'Good, the hall is finished and it looks fabulous. It's hard to believe we'll have six campers here tomorrow!'

'Tomorrow! How I wish I was there.'

'I'm nervous but I think that's only because it's the first one and once I get to know them all, things will click into place.'

'That's to be expected, and of course you will. You're good at people-ing.'

I laugh. 'I think I've seen the last of the notes too.'

She gasps. 'How do you know?'

'Oh, it said something about being the last warning. I'm hoping it really means it's the very last attempt. It's bloody tiring and I'd hate a camper to come across one.'

'I hope so too, darling. They were starting to get a little tedious. Quite repetitive.'

I laugh. 'Yes, as far as campaigns to frighten one away, they were really lacking in imagination.'

'So do you still suspect Freya?'

'Yeah maybe, but I'm beginning to wonder if it's not teenage kids. There's a bunch of them who smoke cigarettes along the banks of the lake. I'm guessing they had free rein of the place before I moved in. Maybe there weren't squatters here, but teenagers using it as a hangout place and now I've ruined all their fun.'

'Makes sense.'

'Yeah.' But as I say it, I wonder if I'm right. I tell her all about Esterlita's theories and how she's certain I'm sitting on a ticking time bomb.

'She thinks it's the CIA? But we're in the UK.'

'Or the KGB, FBI or IRA. I think she's watched too many spy movies to be honest.'

Maya laughs. 'How's that delectable man?'

'Bob? Haven't seen him for a while, but I can put in a good word for you if you like?'

'Oh stop, you know I'm talking about Leo!'

I fall back onto my bed. 'He's too perfect, Maya. And it's been the longest night ever, knowing tomorrow I won't wake up to him waiting for me. I won't walk outside and be greeted by that wide smile that makes my heart race. I haven't felt like this before, and I don't quite know what to do about it. I should be panicking about the campers arriving, I should be checking the hall one thousand times to make sure everything is ready, but instead I'm in the cottage listening to sad music and missing him.'

'Ooh, ho, ho, you've got the classic signs.'

I clutch my heart. 'Of what?'

'You're lovesick, my friend. And there's only one cure.'

I close my eyes. 'What's the cure?'

'Leo. Leo is the cure.'

I groan. 'I don't have time for this.'

She clucks her tongue. 'Yes, yes you do.'

I feel like I'm stuck inside a love bubble and all I can do is think about the damn man and wish he was here. 'I don't want to be lovesick. Can't you prescribe some kind of remedy? Wine, yoga, something?'

She laughs so loud I have to remove the phone from my ear. 'I'm going to google bridesmaid's dresses. Let me know what palette you prefer.'

'Wow, Maya, once again, you sure can jump ahead with these things.'

'When you know, you know.'

'You sound like Esterlita.'

'I haven't heard from her in a while actually.'

I toy with the edge of the pillowcase. 'She's not been herself. I think she did too much work around the cottage, and even though she's a Firecracker, she needs a bit more downtime than she was having. I told her to rest up for a bit.' Still, I thought she'd pop in for an episode of *The Real Housewives* but she hasn't. I put it down to the fact that she can't help herself if she's over here – she'll start rearranging my cushions, cleaning out my fridge and telling me I'll prematurely age if I keep drinking too much coffee.

'Maybe she's got some catering jobs.'

'Yeah, I have seen her van fly past a few times. It's a wonder any of her food arrives edible, the way she drives.'

'Like she's got something to hide.'

I laugh. 'You sound exactly like Esterlita, talking like that.'

Chapter 20

Car doors slam and a babble of voices ring out. I peek out of the front window to catch a glimpse of my very first campers! There's a group of four already, with two more due soon.

'The dark-haired guy, Thomas, is single!' Esterlita booms, making my soul leave my body. How does she sneak up like that?

'How did you get in?' I ask, downplaying the fact I'm thrilled to see her. Her eyes are bright and she looks refreshed as if the break worked wonders for her.

'Through the back door. I see you're suddenly security-conscious and locked me out the front way …'

'I knew it wouldn't stop you. Es. You'd climb in the window if you had to.'

With a tut she says, 'That was one time, Orly. You're never going to let me live that down, are you? I was concerned about you, and …'

I raise a brow. 'What?'

'Oh … nothing. Why are you rubbing your temples like that?'

Like always, Esterlita bamboozles me with her machine-gun voice and inklings that she's been spying on me for whatever reason. The woman is hard to keep up with. 'I've got a cracking headache. I hope I'm not coming down with something. Look, they're here – I don't have time to get sick.'

Esterlita slaps a hand to my forehead. 'Ouch.'

'Stop fussing,' she admonishes. 'Have you got a cold?'

'Maybe it's just nerves.'

She scoffs, reaches into her handbag and produces a family-size jar of Vicks VapoRub. 'Golly, who knew they made them that big.'

'Only if you know where to look,' she says and touches her nose. 'Sit down.'

'Es, I don't have time!' Another car arrives, followed by a cab, and our last two campers step from the vehicles and stand apart from the group, looking decidedly anxious. We need to sort welcome drinks, fresh fruit and give them a tour. 'Where the bloody buggery is Noah?' I've set start times for the guy but he must think they're just a suggestion because he only turns up when he wants to.

'SIT.'

I comply begrudgingly, knowing I'll only delay matters if I don't listen to her. 'Well hurry up, Es, They're all here.' I'm jittery with nerves and just want to get the day underway.

But the Firecracker has to lecture me first. 'Health is number one. If you don't have your health, you don't have anything.'

'Yeah, yeah, get on with it.'

Esterlita dips her index finger into the family-sized jar. 'Close your eyes!'

'My eyes, why? You can't …'

'They're waiting; now do as I say.'

I huff and I puff but of course I do exactly as she says.

She promptly starts swiping the thick white goo on my temples, my forehead, behind my ears, under my nose, before I push her hands away. 'What are you *doing*? I'm going to stink to high heaven!' The campers are going to take one sniff of me and bolt.

'Hush your mouth! In ten minutes you'll be cured! Don't you

want to be cured? Didn't your mother ever teach you anything? Lie down. I need to do your feet and you need to put socks on so it soaks in.'

'What? No? How can Vicks cure nerves?'

'Pssh. It cures everything! How can you not know this?'

I quickly take my shoes and socks off wondering how I get myself into these predicaments. A few minutes later we're mercifully finished and I bustle to the kitchen while Esterlita follows closely behind. We wash our hands before preparing welcome drinks.

'Alcohol-free this time, Es.'

'Bosh, you're so boring.'

I shake my head. 'I think it's called duty of care, but OK, yes, I'm boring.'

'Stop that frowning right now or you'll wrinkle like an old prune, eh. And then what? No man, no babies. A big old rattling hall with just the ghosts for company.'

'You're on fire today, Es.'

She waves me away as she assembles glassware on a tray. It's then I note she's wearing the busiest dress I've ever seen. Its motley colours are so bright it actually hurts my eyes to look at it. 'Does your dress have cats on it?'

'Yes, cats wrestling one another, a glimpse into your future if you don't listen to me.'

I laugh; only Esterlita could tie her clothing to what she envisages as the demise of my love life. I take great delight in teasing her back. 'A houseful of cats wouldn't be so bad.'

'I'm going to pretend you didn't say that and hope the spirits didn't hear.'

'OK.'

'Not OK.'

I hide a smile.

'I notice you're not stressed anymore,' she says giving me a 'take that' look. 'The Vicks worked, eh?'

205

Damn it, she's right. My headache is gone and I feel a lot more relaxed. 'Or maybe it's your sunny personality?'

'Sometimes you make me want to hurt you, Orly.'

'I aim to please. Now let's go welcome our campers.'

Outside, our campers hold their suitcase handles and look anywhere but at each other. We make our way to them, glasses clinking on the tray Esterlita holds aloft.

All eyes turn to me and I see only excitement reflected back. Noah is busy out back giving the hall a once-over and organising their first activity, thank the Lord. The guy is much more of a free spirit than I imagined, but at least he's here now. 'Welcome to Honeysuckle Hall!' I say brightly, grateful the bloody Vicks VapoRub has worked so I can enjoy this moment. 'I'm Orly and this is Esterlita. We're here to help, so if you have any questions just let us know but, for now, please help yourself to refreshments.'

On a tall table we set out fruit cups and a selection of flamboyant Filipino cakes that Esterlita assures me will be popular. They jiggle like jelly when campers bump the table.

Once everyone has helped themselves, I hand out name badges as Noah joins us carrying a big foam ball. He sniffs the air as if he finds something repulsive and then I realise the offending scent is *me* but there's nothing I can do about it now.

'This is Noah, everyone. He's our camp leader and will be in charge of most of the activities. He's your go-to guy when it comes to all the athletic pursuits, and when we take you through to the hall he'll share the timetable with you so you know what's on the cards for the next few days.'

'Welcome!' Noah says and flashes a megawatt smile. The group grin back and slug their drinks. 'I thought we'd start with an icebreaker game called "Catch the ball" so we can all get to know each other a little better,' he says. 'If you'd like to make a circle we'll start.'

We fall into a circle on the soft grass.

'When you catch the ball you have to tell us something about yourself, and then throw it to someone else. It can be anything you like: why you're here, what you do for work, what you dream of …'

There's a few nervous titters as the ball is lobbed into the sky before resting in the hands of the dark-haired guy Esterlita assures me is single. 'I'm Thomas,' he says in a broad Liverpudlian accent. 'I work in middle management for a big supermarket chain. I'd been about to call my boss and tell him where to stick his underpaid and overworked job when the ad for the camp caught my eye. Used my sick leave to be here and figured if this doesn't help with corporate burnout then nothing will. If I'm still feeling exhausted by the thought of returning to work then I'll march back in there next week and quit. There's got to be more to life than this, right? Tell me I'm right?' Half-moons darken the underside of his eyes and I notice he truly does look as exhausted as he claims. He's burnout personified and the reason I wanted to start these camps in the first place.

There are murmurs of agreement as he throws the ball to a tall blonde who I know from the completed surveys owns her own fitness club. 'I'm Teani. I dream of packing it all in and backpacking around the world. Of course, I won't do it, but a girl can dream.'

I make a mental note to ask Teani later why she feels she can't follow her dream.

The ball is swiftly passed to Jock, a Scottish gent with a roguish vibe. 'Yeah, the name's a cliché, what can I say? I'm here because a camp for adults intrigued me. Why should kids get to have all the fun? Some of my best memories growing up were school camps and sleep-outs, and a nostalgic part of me wondered if the magic would still be there as a bald, fifty-something man who's kind of set in his ways.'

Everyone laughs and I think Jock might be the type of guy everyone is drawn to for his jocular, easy-going nature.

'I'm Lulu. A harried mother of five children, one husband,

two dogs, three cats, and a goldfish named Stumpy – don't ask. I'm here, simply to get away from it all. Let them see just how much I do, how much they take for granted. I didn't stock up the freezer with ready-made meals, I didn't lay out their gym kits, I didn't even make my bloody bed. The idea of doing something just for myself appealed in a way nothing has for so long. So let's throw ourselves off a gorge, or fling ourselves up and down mountains. I want to take the reins of my life back and if that means scaring myself silly doing it, then so be it. I just want to feel alive again.'

We all let out a cheer for no-nonsense Lulu who sounds like she's going to give everything a red-hot go, no matter what.

'I'm Jo,' says a girl who hides behind a long fringe. 'I'm Teani's neighbour. She dragged me here, like she does most days to her fitness club. I'm the quiet, reserved type who's easily led – clearly – so I'll probably hate most of the activities but I'll look like I'm enjoying them and I'll leave a glowing review. It's just my way. This is probably the most you'll hear from me too, so … hey.'

We fall about laughing and I say, 'I love your honesty, and the glowing review part sounds wonderful, thanks, Jo.'

Lastly the ball is pitched to a tall guy wearing all black clothes and black eyeliner. He's got a musician vibe about him. 'My given name is Walter, but I prefer to be known as Anomaly. I'm in IT. I'm only here because my therapist thought it'd be good to open up to others. Apparently I spend too long online gaming and the like, as if that's different to any Gen Z these days,' he scoffs. 'But her main concern is she thinks I have an unhealthy attachment to alcohol – you would too if you'd walked in my shoes. She thought the camp might be the perfect launch pad into a healthy new me. The only reason I'm here is because I *really* like my therapist. But if I can be excluded from everything, that will suit me best.' He drops the ball to the grass.

Whoa. My brain goes into overdrive about just how I can get Anomaly to participate. By the looks of it, it's not going to be easy. Even though he scowls at me as though I'm the reason for all his troubles, I smile. I'm sure we can get him to enjoy himself; it'll just be a matter of peeling the layers back and finding out what makes Anomaly tick.

Already, I love the idea of these six wildly different individuals, and what they'll bring to the group.

I pick up the ball. 'I'm Orly, and this is our very first camp so I hope you'll all get something great out of it, no matter what that means for you, whether it's trying new things,' I glance at Lulu, 'or opting out.' I give Anomaly a smile. 'We simply want this to be an experience you'll never forget. If we're speaking about dreams, it was mine to do something that would help others, so I hope you find Honeysuckle Hall does just that for you.' I toss the ball to Esterlita.

'I'm the Firecracker AKA Esterlita. I lost the love of my life, my Edward, about three years ago. There wasn't much sunshine after that, until Orly moved in. Now, I've got Project Orly, I feel like life is meaningful again. We have a long way to go. She needs a lot of help with fashion, décor, and cooking, but we're getting there, slowly but surely. I don't think she needs to bother with these camps, instead she should marry a rich man, but she's proving very stubborn in that regard. I've decided to cook you a big Filipino feast as a welcome and so you don't suffer any of Orly's cooking.'

Project Orly. I smother a smile. She's so damn cute sometimes. Even when she's denigrating me. And never in a million years is she going to change my fashion sense, but it's amusing that she thinks so.

I'm about to lead the campers inside when she pipes up again, 'When I dream these days, it's for friendship and I've found that here with Orly, even though she doesn't listen or heed any advice. I hope I can find it with you too. And if you have any good-looking single friends, let me know. Orly needs to get back on the bike, if you know what I mean.'

And there she goes.

Noah quickly takes control. 'Let's head into the hall and show you your rooms so you can drop your bags off and freshen up …'

We give them time to settle in before Noah resumes his place and takes the campers away for another activity.

Esterlita starts on a nourishing dinner of pork adobo and pancit bihon for the campers, and I do my best to help. Naturally, she claims I'm a hindrance, and I probably am, as I worry about the first group of campers who are off out to do some archery. I pray no one comes back with an arrow through the head.

She gives me a pile of onions to chop. 'Why do I always get onion duty?' I'm sure she likes to watch me cry.

'Because you need to get the unshed tears out. Else you'll wind up bitter.'

'What?'

She huffs as if I'm taking up precious time while she has to explain the obvious to me. 'The unshed tears, Orly. The Harry tears. The end of your relationship tears. The cheating-no-good-lying-ex tears. The …'

'OK, OK, I get it. Harry cheated. I remember.'

She holds her razor-sharp knife into the air. 'Good. It's good to remember every now and then and even better to get all the tears out of your body.' She gesticulates with the knife, which slightly alarms me when it flashes before my very eyes, so close I can see my reflection in the silver of it. 'So they don't turn to vinegar, and make you bitter. You see?'

'No not really.'

The knife comes closer. 'When my Edward died, I cried every day for an entire year. I had to wait until there were no more tears. And that took a very long time because he was such a great man. If I didn't get them all out, they would have started to pickle me from the inside out, do you see?'

I gulp. 'I think so.'

'You want to move on; I can see you're trying, but you still have some things to work through and one of them is the unshed tears for what might have been. There's no shame in that. Let them come so you don't pickle in your own sadness.'

The thought is so wildly different that it makes sense. I've come to realise Esterlita's way of doing things might be out of the norm but at the heart of everything she's usually right. I haven't grieved for Harry, for what I lost, because it hurt too much to dwell on it. Instead, I've buried those feelings and poured my heart and soul into this place, hoping to forget, to fool myself it doesn't matter. But am I just turning my insides into something sour, like Esterlita says?

'OK, pass me the onions.'

She does and I take a deep breath before chopping them up and letting the tears fall. As I cut the onions I think of all the dreams I had with Harry, and I say goodbye to them. Goodbye to the wedding and honeymoon, goodbye to the man who made me catch my breath when he walked into a room, goodbye to the memories, the great times we shared, and the not so good, too. My tears turn into more of a bawl, and I can't wipe my face, so I continue unabashed. *Goodbye, Harry. Thanks for showing me that settling for someone who isn't right, is never the answer …*

'Keep going,' Esterlita says and dabs at my face with a tissue. 'Your tears will probably turn into rain, but they need to come out.'

Chapter 21

Day two of the camp arrives with a huge thunderstorm and sideways rain. Dammit! Esterlita predicted rain! Could my tears really have turned into this? Is rain actually the product of so many broken hearts? I add it to my ever-increasing 'things to google' list. But crying over the onions certainly has a therapeutic effect. I feel lighter somehow. Like I've left a bit of the heaviness of the past behind.

But with the sky awash with tears, I worry about my campers. Today Noah has gorge scrambling and orienteering scheduled. I peek outside again and see angry black clouds moving swiftly in our direction. Somehow I don't think it'll be safe for our campers to be scrambling over slippery gorges, no matter that Noah's attitude to having fun is in rail, hail or shine.

Dressing quickly, I go outside to see who's up and about already. It's just past seven so maybe they're still sleeping after a massive first day where Noah had them doing a high ropes course and archery, before settling down with games around the campfire.

I hurriedly pull my hoodie up as the rain feels like bullets against my face, before I make the dash over the grass into the hall. The wind slams the door behind me with a bang and I fear whoever isn't awake will be now!

Most of the campers sit silently with folded arms, around the kitchen bench. Oh dear, where's the camaraderie of yesterday gone? Their faces are long and drawn. Where're my happy campers?

'Good morning, all!' I say brightly, as I scan each person to see who's missing. Anomaly is absent. And Noah isn't here yet. Although it's still early and he had a long first day, so he's probably rushing to make an alternative schedule. Of course, we should have factored the mother of all storms in bloody *summer*! 'It's chucking it down out there, so I'll hazard a guess we won't be following usual programming today.'

Silence. Eyes cast to the floor. What on earth?

I let out a nervous giggle. 'Yeah, it's a bit grey but I'm sure Noah has a Plan B so I don't want you to worry. Can I help with the breakfast things? There's some fresh eggs in the fridge from a little farm up the road …' I peter off, unsure of what to say or do.

Do I ask outright, or just try and shimmy them along and wait for things to become a little more jovial? I send Esterlita an ESP message to get her butt over here. The Firecracker would have them talking in an instant. Maybe I don't have what it takes for this kind of thing? I'm used to throwing large stacks of cash at whatever problems I'd faced for Excès clients. Here I can't do that.

'Right, I can see you're all a little subdued this morning. If it's because of the horrid weather, don't let that get you down. There'll still be plenty on the cards today.'

Jock holds up a hand. 'It's not the weather.' He glances at Lulu who gives him a slight nod as if to continue. 'We had Walter, *sorry*, Anomaly, drunk and playing some kind of loud video game all night. It kept us up, and when we approached him about shutting it off he only got more belligerent. We did try to call your number, and Noah's and there was no answer. At around 4 a.m. we took his game console away – had to use a bit of force, I'm sorry to say – and he was none too happy about it.'

By force. Yikes. How could I have missed that call? I'd been out like a light, but usually I *always* hear the phone. Always. 'I'm so sorry I missed that call and that you guys had a bad night. Shall I go talk to Anomaly? Perhaps he can play his video games in the cottage in future?'

I didn't think of altercations like this. I presumed, everyone being adults, this sort of thing wouldn't happen. It's like I can imagine my future: one-star reviews as far as the eye can see and a whole heap of *un*happy campers.

'You can do what you like,' Jock says. 'None of us have slept, except Anomaly, and a few of us were considering packing things in.'

This is a disaster! 'No, please don't. I'll make it up to you, I swear. Anomaly can move into the guest room in the cottage.' With some very strict rules in place! 'And we'll take today slow. Maybe we can factor in some downtime this afternoon? I'll light the fire and everyone can relax and we'll see what the weather is doing, yeah?' I can't hide the desperation in my voice, but I really need this first camp to be a success. I need their feedback and reviews to send to mailing lists and social media. But more importantly, I want them to have the time of their life! This is all crumbling right before my very eyes. What was Anomaly *thinking!*

Jock looks to the group and gives them some sort of signal with his raised brows. I knew he'd be the one to hold them together. I look away, feeling like I'm intruding while they do almost imperceptible one-shoulder shrugs.

'OK,' Jock says. 'We'll take it easy today and see if things improve. We know it's not your fault, Orly, but answering the phone in the wee hours would have gone a long way to helping. What if it had been an emergency?'

I want to kick myself. 'Trust me, I've noted that, Jock, everyone. And I totally agree. It's not good enough, and as far as I'm concerned it *was* an emergency and I wasn't here, which is unacceptable. However, this is the first camp and there's bound to be teething problems, so I hope you'll all forgive me? When I get a moment, I'm going to call my carpenter, Leo, and have him install a bell that will alert me in the cottage. I'll also make some rules about noise and lights-out time in future.'

'Well, I personally think that shows leadership, Orly, and I'm satisfied with that,' Jock says. 'I won't speak for the rest of the group, but I'm happy to stay.'

There're murmurs all around and all five sets of sleep-deprived eyes land on me. 'I'm happy to stay too,' Jo says. 'I've come this far, and let's be honest, it's going to make one helluva story when we go home.'

The ice is once again broken and the group relax around the kitchen bench. 'Did you say something about fresh eggs?' Thomas says.

'I did.' I beam. 'Fridge is full of them. There's bacon, sausages, tomatoes, beans. And for the plant-based among us, there's organic veggies, avocados. Sourdough's in the bread bin. There's a juicer somewhere ...'

Esterlita struts in wearing some kind of shiny parachute suit, a throwback from the Eighties if ever I did see one. I'm so relieved to see her happy, smiley face my knees almost buckle. 'Did I hear the word *sausage*?' She waggles her eyebrows suggestively. 'Love me a big, long—'

I hastily slap a hand over her mouth to stop any double entendres spilling out. Our fragile campers don't need any more shocks today. 'I did. Can you help the gang find everything, Es? We have oranges, apples – Es, can help you juice them?'

'And here I thought I was just popping over to say hello,' Esterlita says but catches my look and thankfully lets it go. 'Allow me,' she adds, rolling up her sleeves. 'Jock, you can slice the bread;

Thomas, you can work the juicer; and girls, you relax and let them serve you. Men should be the ones in the kitchen, serving their queens, am I right?' I give her a half-smile, and go, worry sitting heavily in my belly.

I knock on Anomaly's door and am greeted with a grunt. He acts more like a petulant teenager than someone who is twenty-three years old. 'Can I come in?'

'If you must.'

I sigh and enter the room that already has the distinct smell of musty socks. 'Anomaly, I heard about last night. You kept everyone up.'

He's a skinny mass under the blankets. '*So* ...?'

'Well, this is a retreat, a place to unwind and relax. I thought it would go without saying that getting drunk and playing video games until the sun comes up isn't respectful to the others. You could have at least used headphones.'

'Perhaps you need to write some explicit instructions, Orly. How was I supposed to know? I presumed since none of us have to work that this would be a place we could all unwind and for me that means sinking a few beers and playing games.'

'OK, that makes sense. I hadn't thought of it quite like that before.' So maybe his idea of relaxation is more nocturnal; it doesn't mean he shouldn't be able to do it. But getting drunk and arguing with the others isn't on. How to meet in the middle with him and the others?

'And I paid just as much as the rest of them to be here.'

'I understand,' I say, used to talking with these kinds of people. 'But do you understand that they all nearly packed it in, and left my very first camp. They didn't come all this way to have this experience ruined. They've left jobs and businesses to come here. They've left their children. They've sacrificed to have some down-time that they rightly deserve.'

He doesn't reply, just glowers at me as I turn to leave. I have a feeling Anomaly is hiding behind a façade. 'Just think about it for me, OK? I want you all to leave here renewed. Refreshed, whatever that means for you. If you want to play games all night, then we need to figure out another solution.' And I only hope that Anomaly will be better behaved after this talk and won't actually need to move into my cottage. Making that suggestion earlier in haste seems like a potentially bad idea. There needs to be boundaries in place and I need to make sure I have my own cottage to escape to when I need a break.

Back to the group, I'm relieved to hear bacon sizzling and happier chatter punctuating the air. I go to the fire and get it started, hoping they can all have a nice day indoors, without boredom setting in. Just how can we entertain them all day? Chess, cards, cupcake making?

Anomaly lopes out and sits silently at the bench beside Jo, his hair a bird's nest, his eyeliner smudged.

He rolls his eyes at the group and says, 'Sorry,' then under his breath: '*that you're all so boring.*'

Esterlita cackles like a witch. 'Bold move, young man, calling everyone boring. But can I give you some advice? I'm not called the Firecracker for nothing, you know. If you're going to speak up, don't whisper, don't mumble, use your voice loud and proud. Yeah, sure, they might not like what they hear, but being sullen about it only makes you look weak. Let me show you …'

She sits next to him and acts as if she's him. Her acting history is really coming in handy and it's all I can do to smother a laugh, not quite sure where's she's going with this. 'SORRY!' she booms, making us jump. 'That you're all so BORING!' She exhales a pent-up breath and takes it in turn to glare at the group one by one before she relaxes into a smile. 'See? It's all about timing and voice projection.'

Anomaly's eyes widen in surprise and the rest of the group wear startled expressions. With that, I make excuses to leave and tell the group I'll be back after breakfast. Esterlita gives me a wink to let me know it's all under control.

'There's a leak!' Jo calls out as I reach the door. 'I forgot to say, the window in my room is leaking and a fair bit of rain got in. I've got a bucket set up, but at the rate it's filling, it's not going to last if we go out.'

'Leave it with me,' I say smiling, when inside I feel like going back to bed and starting the day over.

Chapter 22

I dial Leo's number and plonk on my bed, feeling the adrenaline of the morning's dramas slowly leave my body.

'Orly, how's the first camp going?'

I groan in response.

'That good?'

I laugh and fill him in on the morning's events.

'Sounds like you handled it well though. These kinds of things are bound to crop up from time to time when you've got so many different personalities in the mix.'

I can't help feel a warmth spread over me just hearing his voice. 'Right? I guess I thought as long as they were all entertained we'd have no problems, that being adults on their best behaviour, it'd all be sunshine and rainbows. A big wake-up call for me. And made worse by the fact I didn't hear any commotion and didn't hear the phone ring! Noah didn't answer his phone either so I'm not sure what's going on there.'

'You've been working all hours into the lead-up, no wonder you didn't hear. So how can I help? Do you need me to wrestle Anomaly off the property?'

'What!' I snicker. 'No, I need you to install some kind of bell, so they can contact me if they need to. In case I can't hear my phone, or I lose it or something.'

'OK, sure. That shouldn't take much. From memory there's already the electrics in place for such a thing.'

'Great. Also there's a leak in one of the bedrooms, coming from the window.'

'I'll fix that too. How's Noah shaping up?'

'He's been OK, but a tad unreliable. To be honest, I think I hired him too quickly because there weren't many suitable applicants and he was the only one who seemed to fit the bill. He comes and goes when he wants, doesn't follow the schedule we made but he did a mammoth day yesterday, so I suppose that's most important thing. And now we just have to figure out what they're going to do today since it's like the Arctic all of a sudden and no one has slept except our troublemaker. Noah's not here yet so I'm hoping that means he's sorting alternative activities. I've got Es standing in to keep the peace.'

'I asked around about Noah but no one's heard of him. Seems he's keeping a low profile.'

'Probably smart in a town like Eden Hills.' I laugh.

'Hmm,' he says as if not convinced. 'Shout if I can help. My plans have been skewed today too because of the rain. If you get stuck I can teach them how to make something? Photo frames, book boxes, that kind of thing.'

I smile big and wide even though he can't see me. 'You'd do that?'

'Of course. Keeps the boredom at bay. Chat to Noah and let me know.'

'Thanks, Leo.'

'My pleasure. But about Noah …' He pauses as if debating whether to start this line of conversation again. 'From what I can tell, no one has bumped into him yet either, which is weird, don't you think? And another reason why I'm more than happy to hang about today, to be honest. Did he say where he was staying?'

I think back to our first interview. 'No he didn't, but I'd have it on the employment contract. I'm sure he's fine though, Leo, really. I sense that Noah is the type who prefers adventure to hanging out in town. His idea of a great night out is flinging himself off the highest rock into the lake. That's probably why no one has heard of him – he's probably closer to the birdlife, than real life.' From my conversations with Noah about his exploits, he's more the type to go hunt for truffles in the woodlands than sit around drinking beer. He's probably camped out in there … I make a mental note to check his paperwork and see where he said he lived.

'OK, it's just it doesn't sit right with me for some reason. I'll come around now to install the bell and fix the leak.'

'You're the best.'

'Thanks for noticing.'

I laugh and hang up, feeling a little frisson that soon he'll be here. Leo to the rescue yet again. His concerns about Noah are valid but once he meets him I think he'll realise our camp leader is a wanderer at heart. I get the impression Noah isn't used to taking orders and prefers to do things his own way.

The phone buzzes again and I snatch it up. 'Hello?'

'Darling, it's me, how's it all going? Tell me how much fun I'm missing out on.'

'Maya, it's so good to hear your voice! You're missing out on so much fun! And when I say fun I mean fun tinged with a teeny-tiny bit of disaster.' I hurriedly tell her everything.

'This Anomaly fellow sounds like a handful! I'm surprised there wasn't bloodshed. But I'm thankful, too. Who knew adventure camps could be fraught with so much drama?! I am *kicking* myself I'm not there.'

'Right? Who knew I'd have to spell out rules about not making noise at that time of the morning? But anyway, I think it's sorted now and Leo's on his way now to fix those things, and make some picture frames with them because of this ghastly rain.'

'Ooh, he is! Why don't you tell him you need some of the picture frames hung above your bed? That way you can get an idea of what it would be like with him sitting on your mattress …'

'Oh, God, you sound like Esterlita! You sex-starved woman!'

'I am actually; I haven't seen Preston for ages.'

'What, why?'

She makes a sound like a groan and a yawn. 'It's a long story. I'll ring you later in the week when we can chat over a drink, eh?'

'OK, good plan. When the campers are gone we can have a proper Friday night debrief. You can take me to Bai's. Well, virtually.'

'Great, that'll be a cheap date since you can't actually eat through the screen.'

'True. It'll be torture missing out on those morsels.'

'Come up for a few days when you can, yeah?'

'I will, as soon as I can.'

'OK, love you, darling, now go have fun. If there's any more drama at least try and film it for me, won't you?'

I laugh. 'Yeah, right, that'll help for all the lawsuits I'll be served with. Love you too.'

Chapter 23

I dash back through the rain, which feels more like hail, to see what the new plan is. Thankfully Noah has finally arrived and has everyone lined up in the activity room playing balloon basketball. I did think he'd organise some better activities but I guess we're both new to this. It doesn't take long to hear a pop as the balloon bursts. The culprit Teani is then made to answer a question from the group.

'Who's going to start the interrogation?' Noah asks, and we all settle down to listen.

Thomas raises his hand. 'You said yesterday your dream was to throw it all in and backpack around the world, yet you'll never do it. Why? As far as dreams go that sounds pretty achievable to me.'

I'm thrilled he's asked – I've been curious about that too.

Teani taps her chin before saying, 'Well, you're right, I guess. It is a doable dream. Especially as a backpacker. But the thing is, I built my little fitness club up from one member to over a thousand. It took *so* much work, so many hours, to the point I was obsessed with the numbers in an unhealthy way. People join gyms and cancel all the time, right? But for me, if one cancelled that meant I had to find two more to replace them. It took over every facet of my life before I ended up being hospitalised for stress. My hair started falling out; I was tired all the time. To any outsider, I looked the part – fit and trim and healthy – but inside I was a mess. When I started seeing a therapist, my whole life changed. I put some boundaries in place. Made myself stick to certain work hours and I switched off when it was home time.'

'It sounds like you've come a long way,' Thomas says gently.

She smiles. 'I have. But there's still that stubborn part of me that thinks if I took a year off, trusted my baby to a manager, I might return to a gym with no clients. Everything I worked for *p-o-o-o-f* ...' She blows on her open palm. 'Gone. And then what?'

I can understand her hesitation, but if that's her dream goal why not try? 'I know it's scary taking that risk after building up your gym for so long,' I say. 'But what if you set yourself up with a fabulous manager, someone who is also driven by numbers, with the ultimate motivation, like, every time they sign up someone new they get a bonus. It might not come cheap, that year off, but nothing good ever comes easy.' It's easy to say all this, when I know I'm a lot like Teani and don't often get the work-life balance quite right either.

She stays silent for the longest time. 'What if I came home twice the size I left?'

We all laugh. Even twice the size, Teani would be smaller than the average person, but I guess if your whole life is fitness these are the things you worry about.

'Then you start a program with your clients and see who can drop the most weight in three months,' Lulu says. 'I'd join something like that,' she says. 'If only to get away from my kids.'

'You make it sound so easy!'

'What if it *is* that easy?' Jock says. 'What if the only thing stopping you is your mind?'

'Yeah.' She shrugs. 'I guess.'

'Think about it like this,' Thomas says. 'A year abroad, backpacking, no work stress, no life stress, following your heart, or your stomach if you were me. I largely travel to hunt out new food! Wouldn't that be something your doctor would recommend? So think of it less like a year off for a frivolous pursuit and more like a necessity for your health. You obviously look after your body with exercise, but do you look after your mind with as much care?'

Something changes in her eyes, as if Thomas' words ring true. A little shiver of excitement runs through me; this is exactly the kind of life-changing experience I hoped campers would have. Little did I know it wouldn't come from climbing trees or sailing down the lake, but from the support of strangers in the group.

There's a rap on the door and Leo wanders into the hall. Dang it, I forgot to tell Noah about the possibility of doing some hands-on work. Today feels a hundred hours long and it's not even lunchtime yet. Leo catches my eye and every other thought flies clean out of my head. It feels like it's been months since I've seen him. Time sure has slowed down since he left.

'Leo, hi.' I introduce Leo to the group and I notice Noah giving him some serious side-eye. What's that about? 'Leo's here to install the bell and fix the leak in your room, Jo …'

'There's also some problems with *my* room,' Anomaly says. 'The wind whips in there like I'm in the Artic. Horrible, I tell you, and part of the reason I was up all night. Couldn't sleep with that racket.'

I hold in a groan.

'There's no such problem,' Jock says. 'We were all in your room last night, Walter, and the only thing whipping around was the game controller. Why are you trying to cause more problems? Just to save face?'

All eyes land on Anomaly who sits with arms folded, mouth like he just sucked a lemon.

'Well, it was very cold in there. Maybe it was a chill I was feeling.'

'The beds have electric blankets, Anomaly,' I say. 'And all the rooms have heating …'

'He's not sleeping in here again, though, right? He's going to sleep in the cottage,' Lulu demands. 'I'm here to get away from kids, not to deal with someone else's.'

She's got a valid point. Even though he's twenty-three he sure as hell doesn't act like it. How he's successful in IT is beyond me – perhaps he's one of those genius techies who have trouble in social situations, and if that's the case then maybe the camp can help.

'Ah, well,' I say to Lulu, regretting my earlier on-the-spot offer to move Anomaly into the cottage. It's my retreat, my quiet place to go and make sense of things, so I can't have this petulant man-child invading my space. There must be another solution?

Leo gives me a worried look, like he also doesn't like the idea of Anomaly in the cottage. 'I can set up one of the tepees, Orly. They arrived yesterday.'

Anomaly's eyes light up. 'A tepee!'

'If he thinks the heated room with an electric blanket is cold, how is the fragile lad going to last in a tepee?' Jock says.

'I'm not fragile, and don't you speak about me like that. You're not the group leader, even though you think you are.'

Oh boy. 'Why don't we give the tepee a go?' I say, butting in. 'If you don't like it, you can always move to the cottage, yeah?' The tepee won't have any electrics either, so he won't be able to keep anyone up with his games. But what about the woolly weather, as if the seasons got themselves all mixed up? While it's chucking it down, it's not supposed to last.

'I'll set it up in the grassed area near the orchard, Orly,' Leo says. 'That way it's a bit more protected than by the lake where we originally planned for them to go. If the sun is shining tomorrow, we can move it near the lake. What do you say?'

'What do you think Anomaly?' I ask.

'I'd like to try it. I've always wanted to sleep in a tepee.'

'Great. Leo's also here to do some woodwork with any of you if you're keen? Since the rain has put paid to our outdoor events we thought we'd partake in some activities that will keep you dry!'

Noah frowns. Leo grins.

'No thanks,' Anomaly says. 'I'd rather just hang out in the tepee, if you could put that up first.' He folds his arms.

I look to the rest of the group but no one speaks up.

'Anyway, Leo will be busy for a bit so no rush. You can chat to Noah about the plans for the rest of the day and we'll reconvene for lunch. Esterlita is cooking up another Filipino storm for those who want to partake in her amazing cooking, or you can help yourselves to anything in the fridge.

'Sounds good,' Leo says. 'I'll get these jobs done and then I'll meet whoever is keen in the undercover area and we can bang some nails, eh?'

'Great, or you can come kayaking with me,' Noah says. 'It's only water, not poison. The lake is a lot more fun in weather like this. We can paddle to the point and check out the view over the gorges. It'll definitely give you an appetite for Esterlita's food.'

My mind goes to a camper falling overboard in the freezing water, but I guess they're adults and they'll be able to swim to safety. I hope so anyway.

'I'd prefer to be left alone,' Anomaly says. 'I'll take my lunch in the tepee.'

I clench my jaw. He's the reason everyone is a little ratty today and yet he doesn't care one iota. 'Then that's your prerogative. But I hope you'll try an activity. You never know, it might help you sleep so you don't feel the need to be playing games all night. Leo isn't going to put up the tepee until later today, anyway, so you won't be able to hang out in it for a bit. And lunch will be served in the hall, today and every day.'

'That's not fair.'

'It is fair. The itinerary was emailed to you before you paid for the camp, Anomaly, and that included specifics about eating meals as a group and lending a hand to cook and clean when asked. This isn't a restaurant.'

He gives me a dark look. 'You can say that again.'

'Why not give kayaking a go?' Noah says. 'You can go in the two-person kayak and just sit there if you want.'

'What fun,' he says with heavy sarcasm.

'What do you think you'll try?' I say to the rest of the group, not wanting to give Anomaly all the attention when he so doesn't deserve it.

Lulu pipes up first. 'Kayaking in a lightning storm sounds risky and unsafe and something a mother of five kids, one husband, two dogs, three cats, and a goldfish named Stumpy should definitely *not* do – so count me in.'

With his hands tucked into his jeans pockets, Jock says, 'A wee bit of carpentry might be just the ticket for me. It's been a while since I did anything like that.'

'I'll kayak, why not?' Teani says. 'Jo, want to join me in a two-person?'

She smiles. 'I'd love nothing more, but Esterlita roped me into helping with the food, and to be honest I'm pretty happy she did. We're making kwek-kwek and pichi-pichi. I have no idea what that entails but Thomas would probably know …?'

'Very popular street foods and super delicious. Who knew coming to camp I'd be enjoying authentic Filipino foods every day?'

'I'm enjoying the cooking the most,' Jo says. 'Do you know a woman is not allowed to sing while she cooks or she will end up a spinster? Esterlita is full of these fun little facts. I'm not much of a singer anyway, but I'm definitely not going to risk it am I? Enjoy the rain, guys.'

'I'll have to put my hand up to help tomorrow,' Thomas says, 'And I'll hold off on singing too just in case.' He laughs. 'But if you want, I'm happy to go in a two-person kayak with you, Teani.'

Teani hesitates for a second and then beams. 'Great.' He holds her look for a fraction longer than I deem normal. Is Thomas here for more than just burnout? My thoughts run away with me as I think of Cupid visiting the camps and sprinkling love dust all over the place …

'And what about you, Anomaly?' I grit my teeth waiting for another sarcastic response.

'I guess I can wield a hammer for an hour or so.'

'You never know; you might enjoy it.'

'Yeah and the rain might stop this week. Never gonna happen.'

'Don't jinx us,' Teani says, groaning.

He holds up his hands as if in surrender. 'Wouldn't dream of it.'

I clap my palms together. 'OK, well let's meet back for lunch, yeah?'

The group stand up and gather their things, looking a lot happier than they did this morning. If the activities don't energise them, Esterlita's food surely will. I hope.

*

Leo turns out to have quite the skill when it comes to teaching the unskilled how to navigate a saw. I'd been thinking we'd just hammer a few bits of wood together and *voila* done! But not on Leo's watch. We've used a saw, a plane, and a sander. I should be in the kitchen helping Esterlita, but working side by side with Leo is a lot more appealing all of a sudden.

As I run my hand along the wooden frame to make sure it's smooth, Leo comes up behind me and leans over my shoulder. He puts his hand over mine and says, 'Feel that? You need to take it back a little more.'

I gulp. All I can feel is him pressed up against me. Lest I make a fool of myself I just yelp a response and realise too late, I've indeed made a fool of myself. 'Take it back. Got it.' I thank all the stars in the universe Esterlita is not here to jump in with jokes. My face is already flaming. Why can't I move on? Harry has. My camp is set up. Leo has been paid for his work so it's not as if I'm blurring the lines. He's not married. Or in a relationship. My whole body feels like it's on fire in Leo's presence.

When I close my eyes and picture my future, one of my daydreams, I *can* see Leo here … Is that a sign or wishful thinking? He hasn't made a move, has he?

Chapter 24

Day three of the camp arrives and I dillydally over my coffee, bracing myself in case there were any more dramas overnight. The newly installed buzzer didn't ring and I haven't missed any calls, so I hope that means everything went according to plan and the campers had a good night's sleep.

Outside birds chirp and the sun shines – it's a good start.

Yesterday was only a hiccough. Bound to happen every now and then. On the back deck a note is propped up between two planters.

Without any ceremony, I read it: *You're putting people in jeopardy.*

That old chestnut. It's written on the same kind of paper, with the same block handwriting. In all the visions I had of me moving to the hall and starting up camps, never did I think I'd have to turn into some kind of modern Jessica Fletcher. I'm miffed though as I thought I'd had the last of the notes.

I go back inside and call Maya and update her on all these bizarre happenings.

'Ooh, I love a good whodunnit!'

'What?' I screech. 'You told me not to worry about it before. Should I be *worried*?'

'I have no idea who and I don't think you should be worried, darling. It's not like you've had a brick through the window, or midnight knocks at the door, or anything.'

'Well, I sort of have. No bricks through the window but a lot of activity at night.' I duly fill her in on all my night-time terrors. Again, I'm sure it's just the moans and groans of an old building, but at the witching hour these things are magnified to the point that *sometimes* I hope the big hairy spider returns so I know I'm not alone, and that's how I know I'm truly losing my grip.

'So that wasn't you, banging and crashing around the house each night?'

I squirm. 'No, it wasn't. But I didn't want to tell you the truth in case you left.'

'Bloody hell, Orly. How do you stand it, being there all by yourself? Aren't you scared?'

'Well, let's just say I don't love it, especially when it sounds like the person is outside my bedroom door, but then I figured it was ghosts, come back to get some resolution, so they can find the light – you know like in *The Sixth Sense*? So I just pretend I can't see or hear them, so they know I'm *not* like that little boy and I can't see a *bloody* thing, and they will eventually give up and try someone else, but now I'm not so sure it's ghosts.'

'Oh, Orly, have a listen to yourself! Ghosts, like in *The Sixth Sense*! Are you for real? You never said they were outside your bleeding bedroom wall!'

'Bleeding! WHAT!'

'No, no not literally bleeding, darling! As in … look, forget it. What I meant was you never told me they were inside the cottage!'

'Well, I didn't think they were real. I thought they were the undead!'

'And that makes it all right? This is a nightmare. This is … this is a case for the POLICE!'

'Can you imagine, Maya? Oh, hi, I'm the new girl in town who sees dead people, and I'm a little scared. Can you help? I have these notes and a card and I collect these things usually, but now they have a sinister edge to them …'

'YES!' Maya screeches so loud the phone pops out of my hand. 'That's it, Orly! Go and say all of that – except the seeing dead people part.'

'Maya, they will laugh me out of town.'

'Just go to the bloody pub instead, darling, and start asking the hard questions. Oh, how I wish I was there. Surgery this afternoon is going to be *torture*.'

'Blimey, don't let your patient hear you saying that.'

She giggles. 'Yeah, best not, I suppose. Ring me tomorrow and tell me what you find out.'

'I've got the campers here, though. I can't just leave them.'

'Group excursion. You're supporting the local community.'

'Good plan.'

'OK, darling, gotta dash, lives to save and all that, but quickly tell me how things with Leo are?'

'Oh, nothing to report. He's probably not even real, he's probably dead, and haunting me, knowing my luck with men. The ghosts of boyfriends past have got nothing on me.'

'Now you're just overwrought. Go have a stiff drink and get on with it.'

'At 7 a.m.?'

'I'm a medical professional, and I won't be questioned like this.'

'OK, OK, a quick vodka should settle the nerves, I suppose.'

'That's the spirit.'

'*Wooooo*,' I say, laughing as we ring off.

I fling the card in the cutlery drawer and head outside, determined I'm not going to be cowed by whoever this is. Outwardly I will not show I'm freaked out. I don't think anyone wants to harm me; I just think they want the hall back, but why? Or they want to run me out of town, and again, that makes no sense. I plan to bring extra business to the community with these camps, so I can't see why that wouldn't be appreciated. Still, it could be for lots of reasons I can't even fathom right now. First priority is my campers.

In the hall, everyone is clustered around the kitchen, pouring coffee, buttering toast, blitzing smoothies. Everyone except Anomaly that is.

'Morning all,' I say chirpily. 'I trust you had a better night?'

'Sure did, lassie. Slept like a babe, I did.'

Thomas stretches lazily. 'I think we all did. It was lights out early on; the fresh air certainly works wonders on a person. I feel ready for anything the day brings.'

Noah appears, dressed like he's ready to hike in khaki pants and an athletic tee.

'Morning, gang. Who's up for some gorge scrambling?' Noah says. It's a beautiful day for it. The sun is baking, the lake glittering and I figure the gorge will be a lot safer than the day before with its freak summer storm.

Lulu jumps up. 'I've been hanging out to try this! Just how dangerous are we talking here? Hopefully super dangerous?'

'It's not overly dangerous; it's more of an obstacle course over rocks and into pools of water. It's a lot of fun and I think you'll all love it. You can't beat the view when we get through the course and you come out the other side.'

'Count me in,' Lulu says. 'The only scrambling I do is eggs, so this is going to be a definite improvement.'

There're a few titters; everyone loves Lulu's sense of humour. Already, the change in her from being at camp is visible. She doesn't look so worn down anymore; her eyes are lit with the excitement of the upcoming challenge. I wonder if Lulu will make the camps part of an annual self-care plan. I sure hope so because I love her daredevil attitude towards everything.

'You should try bungee-jumping,' Thomas says to Lulu. 'If you want dangerous.'

'Or a slingshot,' Teani says. 'My friend went on one in Bali and the video was hilarious. But it sure looked frightening.'

'Now we're talking,' Lulu says. 'Any of that possible here?'

'Never say never, but never,' I say. My stress levels would be on overdrive if I had to watch my campers plummet down on a bungee rope or up in a slingshot. 'But we do have a surprise for you all, and if you want danger, then you shall have danger! When you return from gorge scrambling all will be revealed!' And when I say danger I mean the very opposite. The goriest injury I predict might be a stubbed toe.

'Ooh,' Jo says, adjusting her specs. 'I wonder what it is? I should be able to build quite a bit of anxiety about it while we're gone for half the day.'

Teani laughs. 'She will too, you know. Give us a clue.'

I ponder it. 'OK, let's just say there're some gold medals up for grabs, so bring your A-game. And disclaimer, when I say gold medals, I mean medals made out of cardboard and painted yellow, so also bring your imagination.'

Jock rubs his hands together. 'Aye, those medals are mine.'

'But you don't know what we're doing yet. What if it's a gold medal for knitting the longest scarf?' Lulu asks.

'Then win it, I will.'

They take stock of one another and I realise we have a competitive group on our hands. Well, except Anomaly. Which reminds me. 'I'm going to check how the tepee held up overnight and I'll see you upon your return, yeah? Save a bit of energy for the next challenge!'

I leave them musing about what the challenge will entail, smiling that they're on the wrong track, with guesses about cake decorating, and a bocce tournament.

I approach the tepee and yell out to Anomaly who does his usual grunt in response.

'The campers are having breakfast, and then they're getting ready for gorge scrambling. Are you going to join in?' I yell through the canvas.

'No.'

There's movement inside and then the flap of the tepees opens to reveal a half-asleep Anomaly who lets out a big yawn. 'Sleep well?' I ask.

'There was some kind of dog howling all night; might have been a wolf by the sounds of it.' He shrugs as if it's no big deal, and I count my lucky stars that it wasn't the homicidal chicken because then I might just have a lawsuit on my hands. 'But talk about boring. No Xbox, no TV. I fell into a dullness coma in the end. How many days of this do I have left?'

'Two nights left. So why not give something new a try today? You enjoyed making the photo frames yesterday, once you got started.'

'Not really. I just knew the quicker I got it done, the quicker he'd put up the tepee.'

'Can I put your name down the for challenges this afternoon? I'm setting up a little circuit of fun outdoor games, and I'd love for you to give them a try.'

'Fun outdoor games?' He lets the words fall, full of mockery. 'Not for me. I'm going to wander into town and find some decent food.'

'OK, well I can't stop you, but there's plenty of food in the hall.'

'If that's all?' he says, then disappears back into the tepee.

'I'll come back after lunch, and see how you're feeling then.'

'Don't bother,' comes the muffled response. I walk back to the hall, dejected. Why won't he even try? I know I should just move on and focus on the others, but it feels like failure if one camper isn't getting anything out of the experience except boredom.

By the time I return to the hall, the campers have gone, leaving only the scent of toast in the air. Esterlita is in the kitchen wiping down the benches. 'Morning, Es. You don't have to do that.'

'It's no problem. They were eager to get away so I said I'd wash up. Do you think they'll be OK today?'

'Of course. Noah has done the same route himself and says it's not too challenging. And there's only five of them to keep an eye on.'

She grimaces. 'Why can't they just participate in karaoke, eh?' Already, Esterlita is like a mother hen, fussing and fretting over her brood.

Esterlita's answer to life's troubles is to pull the microphone out and get those hips a-swinging. 'Well, we've got the karaoke competition lined up for the last night, but I think if we market the place as an adventure camp then we do need to provide some adventure.'

'Bosh. I just don't understand why flinging themselves over rocks is fun.'

'The view at the end. Pushing the body to try new things. The group dynamic.'

'Yeah, yeah, yeah. You can get all that by eating my pork adobo too.'

I laugh. 'They loved your big Filipino lunch yesterday. So did I for that matter.'

'Was there ever any doubt?' She hangs the tea towel over the rail on the oven. 'Well, we'd better get this course set up.'

'I can't wait to see their faces, especially Jock.' Jock liked the idea of a nostalgic return to the past, so that's how we came up with the plan to go back in time and hold our very own Honeysuckle Hall Olympics.

We go to the storeroom for our loot and take it outside to set up.

'I'll put orange cones at each event, and number them so we can keep track of who's done what and their scores.'

'Great idea,' I say. 'I hope they think it's fun and not super cheesy.'

'What's wrong with super cheesy anyway?'

'True. Cheesy is good, like the Eighties were good. I've made a playlist with some epic beats.'

'Did you just say epic beats?' Esterlita laughs.

'I did!'

We set up our stations: sack races, musical chairs, donuts on a string, limbo and the classic egg and spoon race. The campers will be weary after their gorge session so I'm hoping some light-hearted fun hits the spot.

Esterlita tries out the limbo and of course makes it bawdy, by pumping her hips and somehow not falling backwards. 'You look like you've done a lot of limbo-ing before, Es.'

'Cebu champion 1970 through to '71.'

I shake my head laughing. Who knows with this woman?!

We finish our course as Leo arrives, his face like thunder. 'Leo,' I say. 'What's wrong?'

'Can I speak to you privately?' His blue eyes flash and I wonder if I've done something to upset him.

'Sure.'

Esterlita will only follow us to eavesdrop but I suppose he doesn't know that.

We go into the hall and sit at the kitchen bench.

'I was at Rise, having some morning tea with my crew,' he says, running a hand through his blond locks. 'And this guy came in, a real smarmy sort, hair styled to within an inch of his life, swaggering around like the owned the place. I'm sure he was the same guy who was plastered all over those sleazy tabloids.'

Oh God, Leo's seen those tabloid articles? Not one of them painted me in a good light.

'He was asking about you. Asking about where an old finishing school was. One of the locals overheard him say he knew you *very well* from back in London. He wanted to know where this place was, who was here with you, when you were likely to be alone. I got a bad vibe from him, Orly. I think it might've been Harry come crawling back.'

'Oh no! It does sound like Harry.' Could he and Carly C be over already? My gut roils. 'Oh, Leo, I don't want him anywhere near my campers. You never know quite what he'll say. I have a bad feeling about this.'

'I'll stay with you, Orly. Don't worry, OK? If he turns up, I'll convince him to leave before the campers even notice he's there.'

Despite my shock, I smile. Leo's gone to a lot effort to inform me of Harry's surprise unwanted visit by taking time out of his busy day to come to the hall and let me know in person, when he could have just phoned. His actions and his concern make me feel like I matter. I thought I had something special before with Harry but I see now it was all smoke and mirrors, whereas Leo is all heart and honesty. 'Thanks, Leo, but you've got work to do and I don't want to hold up your job on the off chance he finds me. What did the locals tell him?'

'They said nothing, didn't know who he meant, never heard of an Orly. So he made his way up the street, from business to business, I'm assuming getting the same response. People are mostly caring here, despite their gossiping about you. You're one of us now, and his brusque manner won't help his cause.'

I hate to think what he's up to, but still none of it makes sense. 'Why wouldn't he just call me and ask me where I am?'

Leo throws his hands up. 'Would you tell him?'

I consider it. 'Not a chance. I don't want to see him ever again.'

'And I'm sure he knows that, hence why he's asking around town. He figures a surprise visit will work best. It won't take long before he stumbles onto one of the old finishing school signs though and puts two and two together, so I wanted to warn you.'

A glimmer of hope runs through me. The inhabitants of Eden Hills have already taken me under their wing, and I feel like I belong for the first time since I can remember. Leo, especially, has looked out for me, not just today but many times. 'Thanks,

Leo. I'm glad you told me. Let's hope he gets bored and goes back to London, but Harry never was the give-up sort.'

'Do you want me to stay?'

'No, no, it's OK. If he comes here, I'll soon tell him he's not welcome. But I do wonder if there's more to it. Harry doesn't easily admit his mistakes, so he's probably after something.'

'Yeah, you.'

I laugh. 'I don't think that's it somehow.'

Leo raises a brow. 'You think too little of yourself, Orly. And so did he. Just so long as you know that.'

I get a little flutter at the compliment and feel my cheeks go scarlet. I've never been good at receiving praise. 'Thanks, Leo.'

He nods. 'If you're sure you don't want me to stay I'll come back a bit later once I've finished the job I'm on. Call me if you need me.'

'I'm sure, Leo. I'll be OK.' He's so sweet, but what does he think Harry is – some kind of knife-wielding maniac? More likely Harry is after something, but what that is I don't rightly know. Now I can see behind the lies, I recall all the times Harry did what was best for Harry. And so I'll be ready to read between the lines when he appears.

*

The campers arrive back with exhilarated smiles, and big appetites. They chat away about what they saw and how they managed while I assemble lunch things for them. We had a delivery of fresh bread rolls from Rise and a range of small goods from the local Italian deli. Once Esterlita hugs them all in relief – as if they've returned from climbing Everest or something equally scary – she heads to the veggie patch to harvest the fresh elements. Just then, I see Noah wander towards the green in the direction of town. Does he only plan on doing half-days? I'll have to have a word with him. He's not taking the job seriously.

They eat ravenously, and I wonder if they'll want to crash out after lunch or if they'll get a second wind. I pour them juice and sparkling water and set up the platters so they can make their own fresh rolls.

'Did I see a sign saying Honeysuckle Hall Olympics?' Jock asks between bites.

'You sure did.' I beam. 'Do you think you have what it takes to grab the gold?' I waggle my brows.

'Aye, I do.'

'I've got my eye on the gold,' says Teani and flexes her impressively large bicep.

'I'll be happy with bronze,' Jo says. 'Bronze is always overlooked, but how grateful would you be for bronze if you were close to coming fourth?'

'Yet silver you'd feel cheated of the gold,' Thomas says. 'You're right, bronze is overlooked.'

After lunch we make our way to the grassed area. Esterlita has found a megaphone somewhere and I brace myself for it. The Firecracker doesn't need anything to help make her louder, that's for sure.

'Roll up, roll up for the very first Honeysuckle Hall Olympics,' she booms. 'May the odds …'

I butt her with my hip. 'Oops, wrong competition. First up we have the sack race, and I think you'll all agree that what happens in the sack, stays in the sack, am I right?'

I bet she's got a bawdy joke for every station. The group giggle away, used to her by now and loving her personality.

Campers jostle and bump as they step in the sacks.

'Ready, set, GO!' yells Esterlita, catching me unawares as my heart jumps into my throat.

'Do you really need that?' I ask, covering my ears before they bleed.

'YES!' she screams into the bloody thing. 'Where's Anomaly?'

'In the tepee, doesn't want to join in.'

'Bosh. Did he enjoy it out there by himself?'

'Yeah, but he reckons he heard a dog, or a wolf howling throughout the night.'

Esterlita's eye go wide. 'A dog that sounds like a wolf?'

She looks downright panicked. 'Yeah, that's what he said, but I'm sure it's fine. If we come across a stray don't worry, we'll take care of it. I'll call animal rescue or something but I'm sure he just made it up.'

She shakes her head. 'No, no, no, a dog who howls like a wolf means there's a ghost outside. It's a warning!'

'What?'

Her face pales. 'It's a Filipino superstition.'

I've grown used to Esterlita's Filipino superstitions, but they're usually funny, especially the way she takes them so seriously, but I've never seen her look … so alarmed. Almost as if she's seen a ghost herself.

'I'm sure it's not the case, Es. I know you take superstitions very seriously because your mum did too, but I think it's all good.' Surely, she knows it's OK?

The race comes to an end with Teani winning, and Jock a close second. The other campers limp over the line after tripping over in their sacks.

Esterlita shakes herself, as if she's literally shaking the angst off, and pulls up the megaphone. 'Congratulations Teani, you can come and claim your gold medal. Jock, you get silver and Lulu, you have bronze!'

The campers titter and bicker good-naturedly as they make their way to the next game; donuts on a string.

'Es, are you all right?'

She's grinning madly and back in control but I still see a sort of panic in her eyes that she can hide from everyone except me. I know how well Esterlita can act, playing her exuberant self, and I know behind the façade she's upset.

'Me? I'm just grand, Orly. Let's get this game underway.'

The campers line up along a string of doughnuts at belly-button height with their hands behind their backs.

'So I'm guessing whoever eats the most doughnuts wins?' Thomas says, with a gleam in his eye. His favourite thing to do is eat, and he and Esterlita get on like a house on fire because they've connected over their love of all things culinary.

'Yes,' says Esterlita. 'My money is on you, Thomas! Ready, set, go!'

Teani nibbles on a doughnut and then stands back forfeiting her place. 'I can't eat sugar – it makes me go crazy. Like toddler sugar-high crazy.'

'It's OK. You can catch them in the next race.'

Thomas wins by a country mile, eating eleven doughnuts in about three minutes, while Esterlita doubles over laughing, tears streaming from her eyes because of just how ridiculous they look trying to catch the doughnuts in their mouths while the sugary sweets bounce and wobble on the string line.

We play musical chairs, dancing and singing to Eighties pop music. They go low over limbo, and Jock almost puts his back out. There's a lot of screaming and bellowing for 'What's the time, Mr Wolf?'. Before we finally finish on the egg and spoon race.

'Right,' I say. 'No pressure but this is the very last race of the day and if you don't have a gold medal yet—' I look towards Jo '—then this is your last chance to secure bragging rights. And if I have to trip you all over so Jo wins this one, I will.'

They all laugh and Jo gives me a thumbs-up. I stand midway down the length of the tracks so I can indeed trip them over if they try and take the lead from Jo, who I want to win a medal, because I'm also the person who comes last in any athletic pursuit and sometimes you just want to win a damn race even if it's by cheating.

Esterlita screams into the megaphone and they take off, balancing their eggs on spoons. Thomas and Jock are neck and neck in the lead, with Teani close behind. Lulu dashes around hoping to steal first and Jo is miles behind. Because they've all bunched up it's easier to get in their way, so I quickly move past them so they have to change course. They yell good-naturedly as they all bang and crash together, except Jo who races ahead. They fall in a screaming heap taking me with them and it's only then I see broken eggshell and feel a splat of raw egg hit my face as Jo makes the finish line, yodelling and hollering like she's truly won gold for the UK.

'Es, did you not boil the eggs?' I ask as I help pull the gooey campers up one by one.

'Boil them? What for?'

I let out a howl of laughter, and everyone joins in.

'Well, it's …'

She butts in. 'If they were boiled then there's no chance you'd all get covered in raw egg. Isn't that the objective of the game? And the reason you wanted to trip them all over?'

'Umm no, the objective is to balance the egg without dropping it.'

'Ohhh … that's boring.'

'She's right,' Lulu pipes up, face covered with quickly drying egg yolk. 'This is a much better way to play. I can't wait for my kids' birthdays. I'm going to get revenge on all of them!'

As if I summoned a demon, who should walk in at this very moment, when I literally have egg on my face, but dear old Harry, wearing a suit and tie, like he's come for a business meeting.

'Who's that?' Lulu asks.

'A vacuum salesman,' I say. *Full of hot air! And proper sucks.* Noah should be here to take over! 'Es, do you want to take the gang inside the hall for some refreshments?'

Esterlita hasn't heard me; she's in one of her trance-like states. Harry has that effect on a lot of women. 'Es,' I say more forcefully. 'Can you take the campers inside to get cleaned up?'

The Firecracker must sense my unease because she wouldn't normally acquiesce so easily – not without telling the guy that

244

I'm resolutely single! 'Yes, of course. Let's go, happy campers. You can freshen up while I make us some G&Ts. How does that sound?'

'Bloody great,' Jock says.

They follow Esterlita as Harry comes to a stop in front of me. 'What do you want?'

'It's nice to see you too, Orly.'

I fold my arms, knowing I look defensive, but hell, I am defensive. Seeing him in the flesh is hard, harder than I thought it would be. The lying, cheating philanderer! It's the way he saunters in here like he didn't break my heart and have me vilified in the press.

I stare him down and give him no response. He doesn't like that. Harry likes to be fussed over, made to feel welcome. Like he's important.

'Aren't you going to invite me in for a drink?'

'No, I'm not.'

'For old times' sake …?'

'It's been a few months, Harry. Not a few decades. I don't think we're quite at the *for old times' sake* just yet. You sound like something out of a bad movie.'

'My, Orly, so easily upset.'

My blood boils. I can actually feel it percolating and bubbling. 'So *easily* upset? Are you for real?' *Don't let him get to you. This is how he turns things around.*

He gives me a rueful grin as though he knows exactly what I'm thinking. The campers return to the grassed area, carrying drinks, ice clinking as they go. Why didn't Esterlita keep them in the hall? And then I realise it's because she cannot help herself and is intent on eavesdropping. She edges closer pretending to admire the climbing roses. 'Jock,' I say, 'can you arrange the bocce for me?'

'Leave it with me,' he says, smiling. Jock is more likely to keep the gang enthralled with a hilarious story of his past. He's quite the comedian and has an ability, almost like Esterlita, of keeping everyone entertained.

'Let's go into the cottage,' I say to Harry. 'You've got five minutes to say your piece, because I'm busy.'

'I can see that. Nice little set-up you've got here. Very cute, quaint, playing children's games by the looks of it.'

'You wouldn't understand. And that's exactly the point.'

Chapter 25

Inside he wanders around, picking up picture frames and plonking them down in the wrong spot. I know he's trying to goad me, but why? What does he want? My toes curl just thinking about it.

'I'm parched after such a long drive. A G&T would go down a treat.'

'You've been in town all day, Harry. The locals weren't so receptive to you, were they? Must've have been hard for your ego, not to charm your way into getting my address so easily.'

He grins. 'Small towns, small minds. You know how it is.'

'Small towns, big hearts, more like it.'

'You always did want to fit in, be accepted.'

He knows my weak spots, but so what? So what if I craved belonging somewhere? And I do, already I feel a pull for this town, for its people. They were on my side today and I know it means I'm slowly becoming one of them. 'Sure did.' I'm not going to ask about Carly C and give him the satisfaction but I really want to know what's happened between them and why he's suddenly appeared.

'How are the camps going?'

'Great.'

'You think it's viable, this kind of business?'

'We'll see.'

'You should try making them more sophisticated. Glamorous. Make them for the A-list.'

'Why?'

'You could charge a bomb for this kind of escape, but not like this. Not with egg and spoon races, for crying out loud. Did you run out of money …? Why would you buy such a grand hall and fill it with suburban people? You have so many connections and you're wasting them on people like this.'

'You just don't get it, Harry, do you? And the sad part is, you never will. I don't want the A-list here; in fact, I'd give anything for this to remain closed off to people like that. Why should they have all the fun, and yeah, this might be too basic a set-up, with food cooked on a barbecue, and parlour games at night, and conversations around a campfire in PJs, but that's exactly what I'm going for. Time out for *real* people. A retreat for those who actually do good in their lives and need a break. A place to unwind and find your inner child by playing musical chairs, or whatever the hell they want. What's wrong with that? Why does anything good have to be associated with huge wads of cash? Because that's *not* the answer. It's so *shallow!* Here, people make friends, they share stories, and they slowly let the real world fade away. And they recover. They find the energy to go back to their busy lives with a bunch of happy memories and the knowledge that there's a place in this busy world they can go to escape if they need to.'

'Touching, Orly.'

I shake my head. 'I'll always wonder what I saw in you, Harry. Looking at you now, with your smarmy face and over-styled hair, I just don't see it. I guess we all have to kiss a few frogs so we recognise the difference when our prince comes along. So if that's all, I'll ask you to kindly leave.'

'Look, sorry. I guess I'm coming across the wrong way.' He plonks himself down on the sofa with too much force, like he intends to stay glued to the spot. 'I miss you. So much. I made a *huge* mistake and now I can't function, Orly. Even work seems so empty without you.'

Little does he know I don't believe a single word that falls from his lying lips. 'Probably because you have to do your share now that I'm gone.'

'Orly, please. I'm trying to tell you that I didn't realise how good we had it until you were gone. We *were* good, weren't we? I've never loved anyone as much as you. And I want you back. I'll do whatever it takes to make it up to you.' His delivery is too slick, like he's rehearsed those sentences, or read them in a book and memorised them.

I don't trust him and I never will again but I'm curious. 'So Carly C booted you out?'

'No, no,' he says hastily. 'I walked away.'

'Really? I might message her and ask myself.'

'Don't. It didn't end well and she's a little bitter about it.' *I bet.*

'So, what happened?'

He sighs. 'She's like a very overwrought child who always has to have her own way. She's petulant and moody and impossible to be around. She has an ensemble of yes people who do her bidding and God help you if you tell her she's being unreasonable. It was like living with a dictator.'

Sounds familiar! 'Well, you made your choice.'

'But did I? I don't think I did. I think I was lulled into it under false pretences.'

He is the limit! 'How so? What did she promise you?' Did she appeal to his avaricious nature, or is this yet another lie? Whatever it is, it doesn't mean squat as I'm never taking the guy back!

'I thought it went without saying that I'd be her new manager. The previous one was controlling and domineering and quite possibly into some less than legal accounting, knocking some extra off the top for himself. I tried to tell her so many times, but she couldn't see out of those rose-coloured glasses when it came to him.'

'Wait, you left Excès?'

He lowers his head. 'I did, because she promised me the world.' I bet Carly C did nothing of the sort – if there's one thing she isn't, it's stupid. I don't believe a word he says. Harry tried to shove his way in and take over and Carly C had the presence of mind to see scam written all over him.

Now it all makes sense. 'Oh, Harry, you stupid, stupid man. You gave it all up for a celebrity and you lost! You lost your fiancée, your business and now what? You think running back to me will solve your problems? You think you can come here and take over the camp, make it into a hotspot for the A-list? You are so deluded! But maybe this is the shake-up you needed. You need to learn there are consequences for your actions.'

'It's not a bad idea, Orly. This place could be the next big thing. We could do it together, build it up like we did with Excès. It wouldn't take me long to get the word out that we've got this prestigious exclusive camp, where we're only inviting the elite. The mega wealthy. We could have hot air balloons with champagne and caviar. We could have ...'

I shake my head. 'Harry, there's no we. And there never will be. You had your chance, and you messed it up, just like you will continue to do with other hapless souls. Thanks but no thanks. And now I'm going to get back to my campers. Real people with big hearts who are enjoying being here because it's a nice part of the world, hotdogs and hamburgers and children's games and all.'

'And when they leave and you're all alone?'

'And ...? I don't understand what you're implying.'

'You're not scared staying here alone?'

'Scared of what?'

'Being single for the rest of your life?'

I laugh. 'There are worse things, trust me.'

I see Leo loping down the driveway, his face turning grim when he sees the unfamiliar car. Oh boy. 'Maybe I won't be alone forever though …'

Leo knocks at the door. 'Come in!'

'Harry, this is Leo, Leo, Harry. Harry was just leaving.'

Harry stands, and gives Leo one of his most disarming smiles, but it doesn't work on him. Leo remains stony-faced. 'Sounds like it's time you went,' Leo says, glowering at him.

'Look, mate, give me a minute with my girl, if you wouldn't mind? We've got a bit of catching up to do,' Harry says, edging close to me.

'She's not your girl.'

Harry lets out a bitter laugh. 'She'll always be my girl.'

'Not on my watch.' Leo's clenches his jaw as if he's just holding his anger in check.

'This place reminds me of that little B&B we stayed in – remember, Orly? We didn't leave that room all weekend …'

What's he playing at? Is he trying to make Leo jealous or something?

Leo rolls his eyes, obvious to Harry's ploy, and turns to face me, his jaw clenched tight as if he's using all his powers to remain outwardly calm. 'Orly, do you want him to stay or go?'

I briefly close my eyes, unconsciously comparing the two men who stand before me. Harry would never have asked what I wanted if this situation was reversed. Despite Leo's muted animosity toward Harry, he's still stopped to ask me what I want to happen.

I clasp Leo's hand in a show of appreciation and give it a squeeze. 'See you later, Harry. I hope you get yourself together and are a little kinder to whoever enters your life next. But it won't be me.' I move closer to Leo in solidarity. Our arms brush side by side and he strokes my still-clasped hand with an index finger.

Stubborn Harry stands there, every muscle in his face working.

He's never been one to give up on a fight, and it's like I can see the cogs in his brain working. 'Look, *mate*, Orly and I have a past and while I've got some making up to do, I think she knows exactly where her heart lies. And it's not with you, so why don't you give us some time alone to sort things out.' Just like always, Harry ignores me and replies to Leo … I think that says a lot about him. He gives Leo a slow once-over as if his dusty work outfit is offensive.

'Her heart was broken because you're a selfish shallow excuse for a man.' Leo's voice is ominously quiet. 'You lost the most beautiful girl in the world because you're stupid. But guess what? Orly's not stupid. She gave you a chance, even though everyone warned her about you, and that's the thing with strong, smart women: they only give you *one* chance with their heart. You didn't know how much she meant until it was too late. So your loss is my gain.' My pulse thrums at the confrontation. I've never had a man speak up for me before, let alone display his feelings so openly. That final part of me falls hard for Leo, the part I'd been holding back for so long. 'Leave or I'll *make* you leave.'

'You can't order me out of here.'

'Watch me.' Leo takes a heavy step towards him and Harry quickly holds up his hands in surrender. For someone who can talk the talk, he's certainly not so tough in the face of any real threat. 'Fine, fine, no need for any manhandling.'

With a grunt, Harry turns to me. 'I'll always love you, Orly, as long as you know that.'

I can't help but laugh. 'You'll always love yourself, Harry. But thanks for the reminder.'

'Reminder?' He lifts a quizzical brow in my direction.

'Snakes may shed their skin, but they're still snakes underneath.' I grin triumphantly, the words a direct hit and well overdue.

'Right. Well, when this amateur business comes crashing down around you, don't say I didn't warn you.'

'See? Snake-like.'

He turns on his heel and leaves, banging the door for good measure.

I let out a long breath.

'Are you, OK?' Leo takes my other hand and we stand face to face. My heart flutters at our proximity – and because, no matter what, he's always on my side. Instead of overthinking it, I lean up on tiptoes and kiss him softly. Nothing more than a quick brush lip to lip, but it's enough to make my heart gallop and my head go hazy with desire.

'I'm great,' I say, my voice embarrassingly husky. 'And thank you.'

'You don't need to thank me.' Leo's voice is a touch husky too.

'Did you really mean his loss is your gain?'

'I really did.'

The air hums with promise and I don't quite know what to say. Outside, the sound of raucous laughter brings me back to the present and I know I need to tend to my campers, but how to tell Leo what I'm feeling when it's so new and fragile? I need to give this time, whatever it is, so it unfolds naturally like the bud of a flower about to bloom once it soaks up precious sunlight.

'So, Leo, I've been meaning to ask: would you like to go out for dinner again? It'll be me, Esterlita and a whole bunch of campers if you don't mind sharing a table with us?' I can admit to myself now that I want to be around Leo, even with a whole table of noisy campers. As long as he's there, I'll be happy.

'I'd love to. What time shall I meet you for dinner?'

'Eight o'clock tonight at the Tipsy Tadpole?'

'Deal.'

I know I need to return to the fray, but I really don't want to leave Leo. With another quick kiss he leaves, taking all the air in the room with him.

I compose myself, head to the bathroom and wash my face, hoping the lovestruck glow isn't obvious.

Still musing about Harry's visit, I shoot a message to my former assistant Victoria:

Hello darling, hope things are well with you. Loving life in Kent but just had Harry pop in for a surprise visit! Care to shed some light on what's going on? =3 Orly

If there's one thing I'm certain of, it's that Harry never tells the truth, not if it will get in the way of a good story.

Chapter 26

We're on the way to the pub, meandering down the high street. A few of the campers are just ahead peering into shop windows. Noah still hasn't appeared and his phone is off. There's something odd about him, and I can't put my finger on it. It's not just that he's unreliable, it's that sometimes he's also furtive. He's not going to last as camp leader, that's obvious, and I rack my brain thinking of another solution for the camp booked the following week. Could Noah be behind the notes? Then again, they started well before he arrived in town … although I suppose I don't quite know when he did arrive in town. While his references had all seemed genuine, I guess they could have been falsified. I'll need to do some digging on Noah and see what I can find.

I notice Thomas and Teani are a few paces behind as he tells her all about his famous blueberry cheesecake recipe, and even shares the secret ingredient … thanking the berries for giving up their berry lives. Teani is in fits of laughter for the next five minutes.

'Why don't you open a café or something?' she asks. 'You love food, so why are you stuck in middle management, which you absolutely hate, when your passion is elsewhere?'

'I'm not trained; I just love cooking and trying new food

from all cultures. I wouldn't have the first clue how to run a café.'

'But you're so passionate about cooking, and making people happy through food, it seems such a waste not to use that gift.'

'I guess. I've never really thought about making it into a career before.'

'What about a food truck? Fewer overheads, more ability to move, to not be tied down. Then you can still follow your other passion – travel. You'd have more flexibility that way.'

'I'm going to look into that, Teani. Thank you! I'd be the happiest man on the planet if I could quit my job and do something that I loved. I don't know why I never thought of it before.'

'Because you were too focused on your current job and caught up with all the things you hate about it. Trust me, I know the feeling well. But after our talk the other day, I think I'm going to look for a manager and take that year off, like we discussed. Life is too short not to take chances. I keep thinking of when my health declined so rapidly and all the regret I felt, how trapped I was. And now I've got those healthy boundaries in place, why wouldn't I follow that dream while I can? It's a no-brainer. I wish the same for you, Thomas. Maybe we'll meet under a different patch of sky on some exotic island sometime?'

'I'd love that, Teani. I really would.'

The camp is working its magic! When these two arrived they were stressed, lost and anxious about work and balance. I really hope when they leave they take this enthusiasm for change with them. I know how scary the thought of starting over is, but I also know how life-affirming it can be.

I'm grinning like a fool when my phone rings.

'Hello Orly!'

'Victoria, how are you?' Her voice makes me smile. I miss working with Victoria, and wonder if I can tempt her away from London life if the camps get busy. She'd make a great addition to Honeysuckle Hall.

'I'm good, thanks. I'm so pleased things are working out well in Kent. I miss you like crazy. The office isn't the same without you, but I'm working with Angela now, so at least there's that.'

I slow down and let Thomas and Teani go ahead. 'That's good to hear. So tell me what's been going on?'

She exhales. 'Where do I even start with Harry …?! So, Carly C dropped him like a hot potato *allegedly* because he tried to get her to fire her manager of five years, so he could take over her career! Good ol' Harry trying to muscle in, I guess! But it gets worse, and this is why I called instead of texting you. There's an internal investigation happening at Excès as we speak because while Harry was away canoodling with Carly C, accounts here noticed some discrepancies …'

'No!'

'Yes! Going back almost since the business started. Claims for all sorts of business expenses that weren't legit, but also chunks of money missing and all signs point to Harry.'

'He stole *money* from Excès?' It's one thing to claim fake business expenses, but to steal money as well? What was he thinking?

'Looks like it. And the withdrawals kept getting bigger and bigger, as his confidence grew, I guess.'

'How did they not catch it sooner?'

'It had been put down to clients squabbling over the price of things. When you look back it's so *obvious*. Remember how many times he claimed that rich people were such bad payers?'

'Gosh, yes, so many times that I actually *believed* it. How could I have not seen any of this?' Guilt plagues me as I think of the rest of the staff at Excès being stuck with Harry's debt. 'Are they pressing charges?'

She lowers her voice. 'Depends on whether he returns the money. They're thinking it'd be best to keep it out of the press, and if he repays it and forfeits his stake in the company then they won't. It wouldn't look good for Excès if this all came out.'

'No, it wouldn't. Well, I guess that explains why I suddenly had him on my doorstep.'

'He has some nerve but I can't say I'm surprised. Tell me you kicked him out?'

I laugh, feeling the freedom of not being mired down by any more Harrys of this world. 'Kicked him out – but not before I doled out some home truths, and boy did that feel good.'

'Bloody brilliant, Orly. So proud of you for the way you handled the whole fiasco. It takes a lot of courage to do what you did and pack it all in like that.'

I think back to how scared I was at making such a huge change but I'm so proud I did it too. 'If it wasn't for that snake, I think I'd still be stuck in a rut, so there's that to consider. This place is just what I needed, and I hope you'll come and visit whenever you can get away.'

'You can count on it. Oh, by the way, I saw your ads in my local paper! Someone at book club mentioned it and suggested we book a camp! I was delighted to tell them I knew you personally.'

'Really? That's so cool!'

'Onwards and upwards,' she says. A few minutes later we ring off and I'm left with a fuzzy head at all that's happened since I've been gone. And how lucky I am to have seen through Harry's ploys.

I catch up to the group. 'I don't know about you, but I am ravenous,' I say.

'Me too,' says Thomas and sneaks a glance at Teani who turns and smiles at that exact moment. Could love be on the menu …?

*

The pub is as busy as it was the first time I went. We have booked a table around the back, which gives me a good view of the bar and the locals. Just who can I ask about the notes? A detective I will not make. But I need this last piece of the puzzle solved before I can truly settle in at Honeysuckle Hall. When Maya told me to go get the answers at the pub she didn't mention who I should approach. Sadly no one is wearing a neon yellow sign that says: *Ask me!*

The campers all order dinner and laugh and chat about the day while I make my way to the bar on the premise of ordering a few bottles of wine for the table. I spot Bob, and figure I'll start my queries with him. His wife Iris clearly didn't want to be seen talking to me, so maybe he knows exactly who's behind it.

'Bob, hey!' I say, grinning, trying to look cool as anything because I'm nervous about asking him in case it makes for more gossip. I must appear anything *but* cool as he frowns.

'Are you OK?'

Golly. OK, duly noted: don't try and act cool when you are not cool.

'Just grand. Fabulous, in fact. I wanted to thank you again for delivering the furniture to the hall.'

His frown deepens. 'Well, it's my job.'

'Yes, a fabulous *fabulous* job.' My sunny personality isn't winning him over. What am I doing wrong?

'Look, I don't want to tell anyone how to live their life, but if you're in charge of a hall full of people don't you think you should lay off the booze for a bit?'

Mortification colours me scarlet. He thinks I'm drunk?! I haven't even had a sip of wine yet! And of course, that's when the waitress arrives to take my order. 'Three bottles of sav blanc please.' I cough.

'Don't worry, Bob. I haven't succumbed just yet. I'm actually interested in picking your brains.' The poor man looks fearful, as if I'm literally going to get an ice pick and start chopping away at his grey matter. This is not going well.

'Oh, yeah?'

'Yeah. I'm just wondering if you know if someone perhaps

259

isn't my biggest fan? Someone's been leaving notes around the hall warning me to take my business elsewhere, saying that I'm putting people in danger – that kind of thing. Seems like I'm not welcome, by at least one person in town.'

His shrewd eyes shine with a sort of awareness before the shutters come down. 'Can't help you, love. But a word of advice. Sometimes it's better to leave these things alone, eh? Let the past stay in the past.' With that he turns abruptly and leaves me with only the back of his shirt for company.

OK, so that didn't go as planned. Bob is a funny one who seems to run hot and cold with me, or is it that he knows and doesn't want to tell me? I head back to the tables with the wine when Lulu asks, 'Where's Noah? I thought he said he'd be right along?'

I gaze around the Tipsy Tadpole, but there's still no sign of our intrepid camp leader … 'Taking an early finish today.' I don't want the campers to know the guy I've hired is so undependable. Somehow I knew Noah was never going to stay. Either he is a fickle nomad who doesn't like being told what to do or he is the culprit behind the notes. Either way, it's not good being a camp leader down. I pour myself a big glass of wine and catch Bob's eye at the same bloody time. There's nothing else to do; I raise my glass in salute to him and then take a big slug knowing I'll be called Orly the lush, soon enough!

Chapter 27

'He didn't!' Maya gasps so loud I think she's at risk of passing out.

'He did!'

'And he came to you with that bollocks of a story?'

'Yep.'

Maya stares back at me through the screen, shaking her head back and forth as shock stuns her quiet. Bai bustles over and waves. 'We miss you, Orly! Come back soon. Maya is eating your share now, and I'm worried she's going to turn into a dumpling.'

I laugh. 'That's not fair that she's eating my share! I bet she's eating all the chilli sauce too?'

Bai shakes her head. 'No, she says it gives her indigestion.'

'What? You love the chilli sauce.'

Maya makes a face. 'About that …' she says, and rummages in her bag for something. 'So, remember I said I needed to explain about Preston?'

'Yes?'

'Well, we broke up.'

'Oh, Maya, I'm sorry!'

'No, you're not. You'll do cartwheels in celebration when I end the call.'

It's my turn to laugh. 'True. OK, I'm not sorry he's gone, but I'm sorry if you're sad about it. I know you liked the obligatory bad boy for whatever reason I cannot fathom, but hey, who am I to talk? I've been going out with a thief!'

'So maybe the next lot of boyfriends will be our princes?'

'Maybe.'

'But to answer your question, no I'm not sad about breaking up with Preston. It was my choice. I can feel time marching on, Orly, so I made a decision a while back and it's come to fruition.'

She holds the little grainy black and white picture in front of the camera.

'Maya, is that what I think it is?'

She grins. 'It is! It's little baby Martinez! We are five months along already.'

Bai stands behind her, hands over her mouth, before jumping up and down and shrieking. The air in my lungs leaves with a whoosh. It takes me a minute to pull enough oxygen back to talk.

Bai hugs Maya from behind and speaks in rapid-fire Chinese, gesturing to staff to bring something to Maya. Probably dumplings for the baby!

It hits me. 'Five months along, so you were pregnant when you came here, but I saw you drink, you had that blue cocktail …'

'Mocktail. Esterlita knows. She said she saw it in a dream.' Maya shrugs as if this is totally normal. 'And I kept topping up your glass with bubbles so you never noticed mine was fizzy water.'

God, I'm so dense sometimes. 'How, what … who?'

She takes a deep breath. 'I went to a clinic and found myself a donor. He's a student at university studying to be an engineer. I know, I know, how dull, but his passion is art. So I think he might use both sides of his brain, and then you have my genes: the medical side should come in handy but also my love for music. I should have a well-rounded little poppet.'

'Wow, Maya. Just. Wow.' Tears spring to my eyes, imagining Maya as a mum, the one thing she has yearned for, for such a long time.

'I know, it's a big shock. It was so hard hiding it from you when I came to the hall, wearing those voluminous clothes and not eating the stinky cheeses. But I didn't want to distract you while you had all those nerves about the first camp.'

'Oh, Maya, no it wouldn't have distracted me! Not at all. We would have had cause for a great celebration. I still can't believe this is happening. What will you do about work?'

'I've given a month's notice; I'm going to come back in a year or … two. I've got enough saved to tide me over for a bit. I've been planning this for quite some time and I can't believe it's finally happened.'

'Please tell me you're coming to stay at Honeysuckle Hall?'

She waggles her brow. 'I was hoping you'd say that!'

'Really? You are?' My tears become torrents.

'Yes, although I'll probably rent a little cottage up the road or something. I don't want to be in your way and you know how messy I am and how much you hate that. I can only imagine having a baby will produce even more mess. All those toys and whatnot.'

'For a someone with such a precise job you really are very messy.'

'Organised mind, steady hands.'

'And an absolute disgrace at picking things up.'

'Eh, you can't have everything.'

'OK, get down here as soon as possible and at least stay at the hall while you're growing little baby Martinez.'

'I will. I've got a month to go and I'll be there.'

'Four whole long weeks away!' I think of the guest room and how I can make it even more of an oasis for my best friend, so she can rest and put her feet up when her ankles swell. She'll need books about pregnancy, about parenting, maybe some rom coms for relaxation. Then there's some extra-wide pillows so she can get into a comfortable position when her belly grows to the size of a watermelon. There's so much to do!

We end the call and I sit at my little kitchen amazed at the bravery of my friend, going out and getting what she most wants in the world. Soon we'll have a brand-new baby to love!

*

The phone wakes me and I panic as I search for it in the dark. Is it the campers? Another problem with Anomaly? Eventually I find the blasted phone and answer it.

'Orly speaking,' I feel for the bedside lamp switch.

'Darling, it's me, Maya.'

Glancing at the time, I see it's just gone midnight. 'Are you OK?' Please God not the baby!

'Fine, fine. It's just …'

'Is baby Martinez OK?'

'All good, darling. Sorry to worry you. It's just I was online when I came across a *Daily Sun* article …'

'Unusual for you to be online.'

'Baby Martinez loves keeping me awake.'

'OK, give it to me straight,' I say propping up my pillow. The *Daily Sun* have done a number on me too many times to count and I wonder what they've written this time.

'Your old nemesis Noel from the *Daily Sun*, has some pretty pictures of you and a bold clickbait headline about a mole in your camp.'

'A mole?'

'Yes, I'll send it to you, but it goes on to say you've moved on, set up a wildly successful camp and you had none other than Carly C's boyfriend arrive and beg forgiveness!'

'What? But how?' How could they know about Harry's visit? Unless … 'Noah? Is Noah the mole they're referring to?' I go on to explain to Maya all about Noah and his disappearing act, right before Harry turned up, almost as if Noah knew he'd be there! Did he go back to retrieve his camera and take some sneaky photographs?

'I think so, darling. Who else could it be?'

'It has to be him.'

'Now you know why he's been a terrible camp leader! But really the article paints Harry in a bad light. You come out smelling sweet as a rose. There's pictures of the hall and the grounds, the lake and the woodlands, and the copy is all about how it's the perfect remedy for burnout, or those like yourself, who were running away because of a broken heart. The photos of you are breathtaking too.'

I grin. That makes a nice change. 'You can't beat that sort of advertising!'

'So while Noah must've been a mole – and you're down a camp leader – you've just got the word spread about the camp for free all over the *Daily Sun* site! Let me send it to you.'

'Wonders will never cease.'

'You do lead a very exciting life, Orly. I thought people moved to the country to settle down …'

'So did I, Maya, so did I, but that's not quite the case, is it?' We burst out laughing. 'So I guess we can rule out Noah as the note leaver?'

'Yes, I doubt he'd have any reason to do that.'

Back to square one then.

Just before I snuggle back under the covers my phone beeps with a text.

Hey Orly, sorry about the whole Harry fiasco. He told me things were over between you guys, but I've since found out that wasn't the case – and I'm guessing everything else he said about you was a lie too. I'd never intention-ally do that to another queen, so I hope you accept my apology? Also, I've seen the Carly Army posts and I'm so sorry! I posted online about it a while ago, so I hope it has all stopped – let me know if they start on you again. They're just misguided in their love of me. Who can blame them, eh? Joke. Take care, Carly C xxx

I go to Carly C's Facebook page and see a post pinned to the top of her page:

Queens,

It's come to my attention that Orly Taylor has been the victim of a lot of cyber bullying from some of my fans AKA the #CarlyArmy. Let me put it to you straight: Orly has never done anything that the press have blamed her for. In fact, she's the innocent party in this whole mess and her life has been turned upside down over it. I know you queens only want to protect me, but remember words still hurt even when they're on Facebook so think before you type, always. Much love, Carly C

I always knew Carly C was cool in her own unique way. And this explains why the Carly Army posts on the Honeysuckle Hall page stopped as quickly as they started …

Chapter 28

Early the next morning, I leave Jock in charge of making break-fast for the campers and I race over to Esterlita's cottage to bask with her about Maya's baby news, even though the cunning minx has kept it from me all this time.

I bang on her front door and Esterlita answers, eyes wide. 'What is it? Orly, is something on fire?'

'You didn't tell me!'

'You know?'

'And you kept it from me this whole time! Why the long face? This is great news! And I'm only joking about you keeping it from me. Are you OK?' Esterlita looks stunned as if she can't quite keep up with me. Maybe I'm talking too fast.

She double blinks before her eyes clear. 'You mean Maya?'

I nod. 'Yes! What else would I mean? I'm so excited I could burst. She's going to come and stay and find a little cottage near us. Can I come in?'

Esterlita stands sideways in the doorway, so I edge past, wondering why I've never seen inside her cottage before. I guess it's because she's never invited me and she's always at my place, as though I conjured her bustling after me with her Pinoy advice.

'Oh, wow, Es I love your place.' As expected she has a

lime-green sofa and a pink footstool. Her walls are egg-yolk yellow, and somehow it works. It's bold and bright like Esterlita herself. 'Is your sofa new?' Everything is covered with plastic. Either she hasn't unwrapped the packaging or she's planning on committing a gruesome bloody murder.

'What do you mean is it new? Of course it's not new.' She harrumphs.

Oh. 'The plastic is to protect it?'

'What else would it be for?'

'I'm an idiot.' I deflate a little, wondering why Esterlita isn't her usual bubbly self, especially since we have such joyful news to celebrate together.

'Sometimes you *are* an idiot.'

'Thanks, Es.'

'You're welcome.'

'Is this Edward?' I say pointing to a portrait of a smiling, bald man with kind eyes.

'My beloved.' She motions to the kitchen. 'Let's go in there.'

I ignore her, wanting to see the picture up close. 'He looks like a nice guy.' Around the frame, Esterlita has set up a little shrine to her beloved.

'What's this?' I point to a framed letter.

She sighs. 'It's a love letter to Edward.' She turns the frame around so I can't read it, which I suppose is fair since it's a private letter – but it's so out of character for Esterlita, who is usually such an over-sharer. There's something about it that pulls at my mind though. 'Never mind all that,' she continues brusquely. 'What can I help you with?'

I ignore Esterlita and her sudden coldness and stand with my back to her, still facing the shrine. There's a crucifix, a bouquet of fake red roses, candles that flicker in the dim room casting shadows over the wall. There's a statue of a religious figure, with a plate announcing him as Anthony of Padua, the patron saint of missing persons and lost things. There's also a stash of relics that must have belonged to her husband, Edward. Binoculars, specs, a gold wedding band.

I turn the love letter back to face me, the letter with its neat block handwriting that I recognise, and my heart constricts so tightly that I can't catch my breath. It's an intense pain. Time stops and all I can hear is the rush of my own pulse.

'The notes?' Never in a million years …

I face her, and see her eyes are bright with tears.

We don't speak; it's as if all we have between us is secrets.

How *could* she?

'I'm so sorry, Orly.'

'Why? Why would you do this to me?' Hurt and confusion pulse inside of me.

'It's not what you think.'

'Right.' I shake my head. 'What is it then?'

'I wanted to scare you away from the idea of the camps. They're so dangerous, Orly, and you have no idea. I didn't mean …' I take care to stay very still while my heart gallops, making me feel dizzy with the realisation it was Esterlita all along. My cheery, OTT neighbour has been behind this campaign and I just cannot understand how she could *do* such a thing and face me every day in the meantime! 'I didn't mean to hurt you.'

'Well you have, Esterlita.'

'Edward went missing in the woodlands,' she says, her voice breaking.

She wipes at her eyes, and drops her head. Larger than life Esterlita suddenly appears so old and fail in the flickering candle-light, but I'm so shocked I don't comfort her. I don't quite know what to do.

She continues. 'He was a hiker, he liked birdwatching.' The binoculars at the shrine. I'm reminded of when I first arrived and she asked if I was going to give up on life and start collecting stamps and birdwatching. Go on long hikes and never return.

Goose bumps break out over my skin. 'What happened, Es?'

She shuffles slowly to the sofa and plonks down as if all the energy has drained from her. 'He loved hiking in those horrible woodlands, trying to find his way back out with only the call of birds to go by. He wouldn't take a compass, no point taking a phone as there's no reception once you're in there, wanted to rely on his senses, nature around him. He'd been walking those tracks forever so I figured if anyone knew how to navigate them, he did.' She grabs a tissue from a sequin-covered box. 'He always went alone and camped out. Once a month or so. He left on the Friday evening as usual, but didn't return on the Sunday. I didn't panic, not at first. Sometimes, he did that, stayed an extra day or two.'

A cold shiver runs down the length of me.

'By Monday I just had this feeling that he was in trouble. But trying to convince the locals was almost impossible. They knew Edward liked to wander, and no one knew where to even start looking for him. Those who helped did so half-heartedly, believing he'd be camped somewhere and annoyed at their intruding, annoyed I was panicking over nothing. But I knew. I could feel it *here*.' She pats her heart.

My eyes well up as I think of Esterlita trying to get someone, *anyone*, to listen and help her search in the dense woodlands. The hard part of me softens as I begin to realise what she's done and why.

With a shuddery breath, she continues: 'Eventually I convinced a couple of Edward's friends to help search. They knew I sometimes had these sorts of premonitions, and while we usually joked about them, they took it seriously enough that day, because I was utterly beside myself with worry. They told me to wait at my cottage in case he returned and they set out to look.'

'That must've been so horrible for you, sitting here waiting like that. Was anyone with you?' I think of how comforting and maternal she is, and I hope someone returned the favour when she most needed it.

'No, I didn't want anyone here. I just lit my candles, held my rosary and prayed. I prayed as hard as any woman ever has. But somehow I still knew it was too late. I have a very strong faith, but if it's His will then who am I to argue?'

I sit next to Esterlita and stick to the plastic on the sofa.

'They came back a day later, their faces grey, unable to meet my eye. Until that point I never really knew what heartbreak felt like. They didn't have to tell me; I knew, but I felt so devastated for them, finding him like that, and for me. Suddenly adrift in this world, with no Edward. My beloved gone to a better place.'

'What happened to him out there, Es?'

Her shoulders shake as she fights tears. When she's composed she speaks: 'He fell and hit his head on a rock, just like that, gone. He was on a steep part of the track and it was unseasonably wet that day but he must've thought he could handle it. He'd hiked that track many times before. They say he wouldn't have suffered for long, but really, how can they know that? How can they know the passage of time? I know my Edward would have suffered; even a minute would have felt like a lifetime knowing he wasn't going to come back to me. I thanked the men and then I shut my door and I went straight to bed. I didn't want to be in the world without him, but my faith helped me stay.'

I put an arm around pocket-sized Es and marvel at how tough she's had to be. 'I'm so sorry, Es. I wish I'd known; I wish I'd asked you more about Edward and had been there for you so I could understand why campers heading off into the woodlands worried you so much.'

She shrugs. 'I wouldn't have told you. I thought I'd scare you from the idea of an adventure camp pretty fast and that would be that. I don't want anyone else to lose someone they love. I didn't want your campers to have an accident. It would break my heart all over again.'

271

'That's why you kept suggesting I find a rich husband? So I wouldn't need to host the camps?'

She laughs. 'Who doesn't want a rich husband?'

I remember all her ideas: the hall as a wedding venue instead, marrying a lesser royal, so many zany ploys to stop me from having people who'd head into the woods and possibly not come out again. And it's why she's helped out since, to keep an eye on the campers and make sure they're safe. 'So you left the photo and the notes?'

She has the grace to redden. 'Yes, I tried everything I could think of to make you think that someone had it in for you, that you were putting people at risk. I'm so sorry, Orly. I never want anyone to go through what I went through. Those woodlands are not safe. And with Noah, I knew he had no idea what he was talking about when he mentioned all the activities he had planned – he was going to put innocent people's lives in danger. He said he could lose days hiking and that scared me, coming from someone who doesn't know this area and that the woodlands are not right for amateur hikers.'

Part of me is relieved it's Esterlita behind the fearmongering campaign and not someone who is truly out to get me. It all makes sense, locals not wanting to tell me any history of the hall, in case it slipped out what happened in the woodlands behind. Why they kept saying things like leave the past in the past – they were all trying to protect Esterlita. It went on the market just after he died, so no wonder the locals didn't want to buy it – they wouldn't do that to her.

'When Anomaly said there was a dog who sounded like a wolf, it confirmed to me that Edward's spirit is still here, in limbo.'

'You think his ghost is out there, unable to find peace? Wandering up and down the woodlands trying to find his way home? So you don't want anyone else out there getting lost?' I think back to all the times she tried to get me to keep the campers inside the hall, do less active pursuits so they wouldn't be in harm's way. Wouldn't end up like her Edward. It's never been a spiteful thing – it's been about keeping people safe, because of what happened to Edward.

'It means there's unfinished business.'

'Like what, Es?'

'Like this. I knew I'd have to admit what I'd done to you. Scaring you off from hosting camps wasn't the right thing to do. I need to beg for your forgiveness and make amends somehow. I'd hate my Edward to think less of me for what I've done. And if I've lost you as a friend over it I'll be heartbroken, Orly, but I will understand.'

'You'll never lose me, Es.' I hug her tight and feel all the worry and confusion leach from my body. I could never hold this against her, never in a million years. 'All is forgiven, and there's no need to make amends.' How can I stay mad at this tiny woman in my arms?

I shake my head at the tumultuous time I've had here. But I know Esterlita and I will have a lot to work through so she knows everyone will be safe. I want her to enjoy meeting campers every week, not worry they're going to suffer the same fate as her Edward. She weeps in my arms and I hug her tight.

*

As I'm crossing the road, the postie waves and hands me a stack of mail. We shoot the breeze for a bit, before he continues on. I flick through the envelopes in case there's anything urgent, and come across one that doesn't look like a bill of some sort. I open it up and inside I find yet another envelope, one yellowed and musty with age addressed to Elizabeth.

It can't be the same Elizabeth?

I dash inside and gently take the enclosed letter out.

Dearest Elizabeth,

I hope this letter finds you well. I miss you terribly too. I yearn for the days afore where we had all the time in the world to meander in the parklands, under the watchful eye of your chaperone, whereas now, I can't even see you from a distance.

Things did not go well with your father. In fact, they went frightfully badly. He recommends that I distance myself from you, and if I did truly love you, then I would see that as someone far below your station, that I should do the manly thing and walk away. Allow you to find a gentleman who will have the ability to care for you in the manner to which you are accustomed.

Of course, the thought of such a thing hurts more than I can bear; however, I do wonder if he might be correct. I can never provide for you in the way Mr Collins with his grand estate can. You father told me Collins has asked for your hand and that he was going to acquiesce, if only you would see sense in the matter. What can a poor farmer like me do?

So, it is with much regret that I say goodbye, my love, and only hope your life is as grand and happy as I hope it will be. I know I will pine for you until the day I die; however, I will take great delight in imagining you living a life of luxury as you so deserve and that, my dear, is the only reason I say goodbye today.

Ever yours,
George

No! They didn't stay together? Poor George who loved her so. I need to know more, so I call Lilac from the Little Shop of Lost and Found.

I don't bother with niceties. 'Are there any more letters?'

'Letters?'

'Yes, letters! This is Orly from Honeysuckle Hall.'

'What *are* you talking about, dear?'

'George and Elizabeth! You sent me the reply from George. Was there—'

'I didn't send you anything, Orly. Sorry.'

'But then who?'

'It's a mystery,' Lilac says laughing and hangs up. *Another* one.

Chapter 29

It's the campers' last evening and I'm setting up the karaoke machine when Esterlita comes along bearing platters of food and calling out to them all to help her fetch more from her cottage. The woman sure knows how to feed people. Esterlita has been a lifesaver, even though she tried to run me out of town at the same time.

Thomas helps Esterlita, so I take this as my cue to talk to Jo, the quiet one among the group.

'Hey, are you going to perform tonight?' I ask her, gesturing to the karaoke machine.

She laughs. 'Do you know what, five days ago I would have said no, without even considering it, no way would I embarrass myself like that. But now, I don't care what I look like, what I sound like. I'm going to get up there and sing like I'm Mariah Carey, and I'm going to enjoy it.'

'What's changed?'

She tilts her head as she contemplates the question. 'It's all that cooking with Es. She made me chop like five million bulbs of garlic, and she said the garlic would infuse with my skin and give me strength. That I just needed to think of all the times I regretted being in the shadows, regretted not taking centre stage

276

out of fear. When she explained it like that, it hit me, just how many experiences I've missed out on because I worried about silly things like being judged by others. Do you know once upon a time I wanted to act in commercials? I've always loved the idea of being the face of a business for some reason. But the thought of having the spotlight trained directly on me was enough to put paid to that idea. So I didn't even try. Well not anymore. Tonight I'm going to blow your socks off and that's all because of Es. She's taught me so much about myself, I think I'll still be processing it all when I get home.'

Esterlita to the rescue again. She's a magician with people.

'Our Es is pretty special. I can't wait to hear you sing!'

'Well, let's hope it sounds as good as it does in my mind.' She laughs and wanders off to help Jock set up the party lights over the stage.

Can garlic give a person strength? I don't know if these are indeed Filipino superstitions or just Esterlita's way of bolstering up a person. Whatever it is, it seems to have the desired effect and I smile, thinking of the Firecracker leaving a group of happy campers in her wake, sprinkling their lives with magic dust as she goes.

*

'Ladies and gentlemen,' Esterlita booms into the inky night. 'It's the last evening at Honeysuckle Hall and the annual karaoke championship! You'll be judged on your singing, your dancing and your overall performance. Give it your all and leave everything on the stage! The winner will receive this amazing prize and I know how much competition there's going to be for it!' She holds up a blank disc and is met with blank stares. 'Oh, it's my very own album of cover songs. There's a bit of everything on there, like Heart, Celine Dion, Mariah, all the best songs.' She's flushed and boisterous and everyone claps.

277

I bracket my mouth with my hands and yell, 'Give us a demo, Es!'

With her glittery elephant tee and black mini skirt and stockings, Esterlita certainly draws the eye. I love this beautiful lady with all of my heart. 'OK!' She motions for Jock to start the machine and soon the opening bars of 'My Heart Will Go On' by Celine Dion begin. Filipinos love Celine, especially this song. You'd think Esterlita was Kate Winslet herself on the bow of the boat, arms stretched out, wind in her hair, before she begins the song in earnest.

The campers go wild as Esterlita awes them with her performance, and I don't know if they truly think she's talented or they just adore her like I do, but they clap, cheer and encourage her. When the song finishes, Esterlita takes a bow and says, 'So now you see why the CD is so valuable? It's a limited edition, only so many were made and one of you, my new friends, will be lucky enough to take it home.'

I grin. Gotta love confidence like that.

Leo wanders in and the night gets a whole lot better. I run over to him and then realise I might look too eager, and then I think sod it, I am eager! I clasp his hand and pull him into the fold.

'I want that CD, Es!' Anomaly calls out and I almost faint with shock. What the bloody buggery is going on here? It's the first time ever his voice is not laced with sarcasm and I stare at him for an age, waiting for the punch line.

'Only one way to win it, Mister! Get your butt up here and prepare to be judged by your peers!'

Anomaly bounds on the stage – he actually bounds. I've never seen him smile, yet here he is looking like he's found his happy place. What have I missed here? 'What song would you like?' Jock asks.

'"Bohemian Rhapsody". For all the bohemians out there, this is for you!'

I'm still so shocked I can barely form rational thought, but when Anomaly opens his mouth to sing, I duly buckle at the knee. His range is Freddie Mercury worthy, if not better, and he performs as if he's channelling Freddie himself. I *knew* he had a musician vibe about him when he first arrived!

The campers stare at the stage, mouths agape, eyes wide. All except Esterlita, who dances around swinging her hips and singing along. Eventually shock wears off and is replaced by utter awe as we realise we're in the presence of someone amazingly talented. Someone with a gift so rare it blows my mind. That obstinate man-child has morphed into a singer who could take over the world. Whose talent *needs* to be shared!

It gives me an idea and I quickly snap a video then hastily send off a text.

When the song comes to an end we scream and yell for Anomaly, whose eyes shine with pride and thanks. Who knew that powerful voice could come from that body!

Lulu dashes over and gives Anomaly a hug. 'Wow, how did you manage to hide that talent behind that gloomy attitude for so long? Please tell me you're looking into this as career?'

Anomaly laughs. 'No, I don't exactly have the pop star look now, do I?'

'Are you kidding?' I say. 'When you walked into Honeysuckle Hall my immediate thought was that you were a musician. You have the look, trust me, and even better you have the most extraordinary voice! Freddie would be jealous of that range. Why don't you do something with it?'

He bites his lip. 'I don't know where to start.'

I raise a brow. 'I might be able to help with that.'

Lulu rubs her hands together. 'Oh, do keep me informed. I want to be there for your very first concert at The O2 arena!'

Lulu and Anomaly move to the seats and bend their heads to talk about his future. She's a mum, no two ways about it, and she chats to Anomaly just like he's her own son, encouraging him and assuaging any doubts he brings up. I know she needed a break from her family, but I can tell she's ready to hug them again. She's filled her own cup enough that she's ready to return and fill theirs once more. And I bet they're all a little bit more grateful when she returns home; maybe they've understood just how much she does for them that they take for granted. Maybe they'll help out more or even just hug her more, and tell her she's loved, and encourage her to try new things so she can escape the drudgery of everyday life and feel that spark of adrenaline when she needs it.

Stars sparkle overhead as Teani and Thomas do a duet and by the end they're holding hands and gazing into one another's eyes. Love has blossomed and I wonder if we might get a postcard from the lovebirds if they put their plans in place and backpack around the globe: Teani breaking free, and Thomas researching food for the food truck he's now intent on starting ...

And then I come to Jock who looks like he's in his element, manning the karaoke machine and organising the campers' next song requests. An idea forms, and I wander over to Jock and wait for him to play another song for the lovebirds who don't seem to want to give up the stage just yet.

'What do you think of the camp, Jock? Did you find that nostalgia you were looking for?'

'Aye, I did. I don't want to leave tomorrow, to be honest.'

'So why go?'

He turns to me. 'What do you mean?'

'I need a new camp leader, and I think you're it.'

'I'm not as active as Noah, I'm not—'

'You're exactly what Honeysuckle Hall needs. And if you're keen, I'm keen. You can stay in the hall. I'll get Leo to rejuvenate one of the larger suites for you, so you'll have privacy and also a bit more room. What do you say?'

'I say yes.'

I grin. 'We'll have to put some Scottish games on the itinerary ...'

He laughs. 'Aye, hammer throw, tug o' war, curling.'

'Sounds like fun.'

My phone beeps with a text and I make my excuses and leave.

Hey Orly, thanks for being so gracious and accepting my apology. Many a queen wouldn't, so I thank you for that. Your friend Anomaly is AMAZEBALLS and I can definitely help. Send him my number and I'll introduce him to my manager (who for the record is not a control freak as Harry would have everyone believe), who can wangle a trial with a producer and then it's up to him. It'll be my way of righting the wrongs against you, Orly. Stay cool, Carly C xx

I smile. This could be just the push Anomaly needs to leave his lair and the digital world and see what the real one is like …

Chapter 30

I bite my lip to stem the tears that threaten to spill as the campers pack up their rooms and hunt around the hall for phone chargers, hats and various personal accoutrements. I'm seriously going to have to get more of a stiff upper lip when it comes to goodbyes. But I feel like these six people have transformed their lives in the five days they've been here, and by default have changed mine too. So much has happened over that short time, my head is still reeling but in a good way.

I know not every camp will be as wondrous as this, but it gives me hope for the future. If there are those seeking change, seeking rejuvenation, then they'll find it here if they're open to it. Otherwise it's just going to be a really fun place to kill some time and be adventurous. Not everyone needs to adjust their sails and chart a new course …

Lulu comes and gives me a hug. 'Chin up, Orly. We'll be back – you can count on that.'

'Thanks, Lulu. I really can't wait. I'm going to miss you all so much.'

'The feeling is mutual.' She takes her bag and heads outside to bid farewell to the others before jumping into a cab.

Teani, Thomas and Jo are next to go. Esterlita weeps – she's making quite the spectacle of herself and I feel like doing the same. But of course I don't. There can only be one Esterlita.

The trio make promises to keep in touch and soon they're off too, leaving only Jock and Anomaly.

With hands in his jean pockets, Anomaly flicks his rock-star hair back from his eyes and says, 'Thanks for putting up with me. I promise I won't be such a fool when I come back.'

I grin, 'About that.' I pull out my phone and explain about Carly C's offer of help.

'Wow, you did that for me?' Shock rockets across his face.

'Why not? You spent so long hiding behind hostility, which isn't the real you, Anomaly. Is it?'

He double blinks. 'No, but not many people know that.'

'What happened to make you hide like that?'

He swallows hard. 'I don't really talk about it … but my mum remarried, and I felt like she cast me away. She suddenly was all Nigel this and Nigel that. I acted out for attention, but the only attention that elicits is the wrong kind. I kept waiting for her to see I needed her. See that she should put me first. But the woman has the patience of a saint and she just let me get away with bloody murder, until one day, she didn't. I pushed her until she broke. Nigel left. And she sent me packing. I'm not sure if they'll get back together, but I'm going to do everything in my power to make that happen. I'm twenty-three not twelve, but sometimes it's impossible to remember that when you see your mum staring at someone with love hearts in her eyes, someone who isn't you, isn't your father, you know?'

'I get it. My mum did the same thing when I was younger before my dad died. Soon enough I was gone, moved to London and never looked back and yet I tried to interfere with her relationship. But then I wasn't going to be there for her when I was onto my bright shiny new life and I realised my mistake in trying to stop her from loving someone new.'

'Right? Like why wouldn't that be a good thing? But I am only

283

just seeing that now too. My mum deserves to be happy and I think I've been the one thing that's made her *unhappy* by trying to get her attention like a little lost puppy.'

'Well, I think she's going to be happy when she sees the new you come home.'

He grins and it lights up his whole face. 'I hope so. I've got a lot of making up to do and I've got find Nigel and mend those bridges. Once I've sorted all of that out, I'll give Carly C a call. God, that sounds so unreal. *Give Carly C a call.* How did you swing that, Orly?'

'Let's just say she owed me a favour.' But when I think about what eventuated, maybe I owe her a favour for setting things in motion that made me change the direction of my life.

'Can I hug you or is that weird?'

I laugh. 'Bring it in.'

We hug and Jock shakes his hand and ruffles his hair. 'Come back soon, before you get too famous, laddie.'

'Will do.'

It's Esterlita's turn to say goodbye to our last camper – and I think maybe her favourite. 'Don't forget to show those record producers my CD, will you?' she says seriously and I can only imagine the scene.

'Erm, yes of course, Es. Anything for you.'

'My boy, the world is opening up to you, so you have to open up to it. Don't forget our talk, will you?'

'I'll never forget, Es.'

He bends to hug her and I wonder what their talk involved. Soon his mum is there to pick him up. She's smiling like she's missed him and I think she's going to be very proud of the change in her boy who'd just lost his way for a bit.

'Can I get a pic with you and Orly?' Anomaly asks.

'Sure. Jock, can you take it?' Esterlita asks.

We stand as a trio with Esterlita in the middle before she yells,

'No! I cannot. The middle person in the picture always dies first. Swap with me Orly.'

'But I don't want to die first!' I might laugh at her Pinoy superstitions but I'm also not risking it going against them.

'Let's take two pictures, then. As couples we should be safe.'

We take numerous pics, Esterlita finally doing the duck face for a photo rather than for communicating something she needs me to reach for.

'What was your talk about?' I ask Esterlita.

She shrugs as if it's nothing. 'I told him that I've seen his future and it's a good one but he's not going to get a girlfriend if he never leaves his room. Simple, eh?'

'That's it?' Like everyone, he most wants to be loved. So simple.

'That's it.' She chuckles. 'Come on, Jock, let me feed you. We'll leave Orly to it.'

They wander off to the hall and I take a minute to just be and appreciate how well the first camp went, and I think of all the ways we can improve on the next one.

Soon enough the sun begins to sink and so do my shoulders. I miss them already. The place is so silent without them cooking by the barbecue or playing bocce on the grass. Still, I hear Esterlita's machine-gun cackle every now and then and am comforted that, no matter what, she will always remain.

Inside the cottage, I check my emails and am delighted to find I have ten people booked for the next camp. I decide it's going to be another cracking group when I read their surveys and see what they want from the experience.

On the Honeysuckle Hall social media pages, I'm thrilled a couple of campers have already left reviews. Lulu's touches me right down to my soul.

Well, I originally went to camp to teach my family a lesson. That beds didn't make themselves, food didn't magic its way into the fridge and onto plates, and that the rubbish didn't walk itself out to the bin. Never mind the washing fairy, the tooth fairy and every other bloody fairy. Mum's taxi ran out of petrol in a big way, so I escaped, only thinking of having a full night's sleep and not having to referee sibling rivalry, not having to look for anyone's shoes except my own, and not having to remind people to bathe.

What I didn't expect was an experience to catapult me out of my comfort zone and into a perpetual state of excitement. Who knew that tumbling out of a kayak and being swept down a lake could produce such feelings of euphoria? That an egg and spoon race could remind you of all the wild abandon of youth? That cooking up a Filipino feast with the Firecracker herself would also translate into an education about 'me time' centred around chilli of all things. (You've got to spice things up in order to feel alive!)

Mostly, I didn't expect to find friendship with a motley crew of people who I'd never normally come across in my real, everyday (sort of mundane) life. We had our ups and downs and we lived about three months' worth of life in five days, I kid you not. So what are you waiting for? Pack your bags, and escape to Honeysuckle Hall. They're waiting for you, don't you know, with big hearts and smiles and, for the lucky ones, transformation awaits …

Thanks for making me realise sometimes you just need to grab life by the collar and shake it a little. Love, Lulu

There's a knock at the door and once again I'm scrubbing at my eyes. 'Oh hey, Leo. Sorry, it must be dusty in here. Allergies.'

He pulls his lips to one side. 'Must be. How did the goodbyes go?'

'Oh fine. They tugged at the heart a little, not going to lie. I wonder if they'll all feel so wretched or if I'll become immune to them. I hope I don't. But this, being the first one, feels extra special.'

He nods. 'They were a great group of people. I made you a little gift to commemorate the very first camp. I've also got a copy for each of the campers.'

'Oh, Leo, that's so lovely of you.' He hands me the box and I open it.

I blink and blink and blink but it's no use. 'Sod it.' The tears run in rivulets down my face. I'm probably a red-eyed puffy mess by now anyway. 'I didn't even notice that you took this …' It's a picture of the campers, Esterlita and I – taken last night as we all jumped and whooped for Anomaly who stands centre stage, microphone stand held aloft, back bent, belting out the song. Esterlita's face shines with pure joy.

'How did you time it so well?'

'By taking a lot of them!'

'They're going to love this. This really sums up the group so well.' On Lulu's face is a maternal pride. Jo grins as if she always knew Anomaly had it in him. Jock is wiping away a tear. And Esterlita is mid hip thrust. Of course. Thomas and Teani are holding hands and jumping into the air, like they're about to jump into their new life together.

'You keep giving me all these gifts and yet I've given you none.'

'I wouldn't say that.'

'Why?'

'You're here. That's gift enough for me.'

'I figured you didn't date because of your past history as a spy.'

'I'm going to make allowances for you.'

'I'm so lucky. May I ask why?' I grin.

'You didn't baulk when I told you about my face transplant, even though I'm left with this ugly mug.'

'Beauty is in the eye of the beholder.'

287

'Right.'

'And …?'

'And, I like a girl who can eat pizza and snort-laugh at the same time.'

'That's a real skill you know.'

'I know. I'm in awe.'

Oh my God, note to self: stop drinking wine *before* going on dates. 'Well, I don't mind the fact you're a spy; in fact, it could come in quite handy. Plus, I like your face. Even if it's not your original face. It's a still a very lovely face as far as faces go.'

'Shucks.'

'No, no, I'm just being honest.'

'I like your face too.'

'I'm thrilled.'

'So you should be. I very rarely break these solemn spy oaths not to get too close to anyone.'

'And if the bad guys come after me?'

'They won't,' he says.

'But if they do?'

'We'll run.'

'I'm not much of a runner,' I grimace.

'Then we'll hide.'

'Deal. But I'm presuming at the moment the coast is clear and we can just live as normal?'

'Totally.'

'In that case,' I say, 'would you like to go on a date with me?'

'I'd love nothing more.'

'Same.' And in the spirit of transformation, of throwing caution to the wind, and living for the moment, I leap into his arms and kiss him hard on the mouth. He tastes like fresh starts and new possibilities. He holds me tight and makes me feel like I'm home. I'm finally where I belong and that's right here at Honeysuckle Hall, in the comfort of his embrace.

As we break apart, Esterlita's voice booms out from wherever she's been hiding. If anyone could make it as a bloody spy, she could! 'He collects stamps, you know!'

I take a step back. So Esterlita finally unearthed something about Leo! 'You do?'

He shrugs. 'I find it satisfying, wondering about where they've been. Crossing oceans, flying over exotic countries. What important document or postcard they transported to another place in another time. One tiny piece of paper has been responsible for so many great things. Blows my mind.'

Mine too! 'I knew you were a nerd, deep, deep down.'

'A massive nerd.'

'I collect stamps too.'

'What are the chances?' He grins, knowing full well I collect stamps, as my collection is displayed for everyone to admire.

'Slim to none!' Esterlita bellows. 'You two must be the lamest people on the planet!'

Then it dawns on me. 'You sent me George's letter! How did you know I found Elizabeth's?'

'I walked into the shop that day, but you were lost in a daydream. I found George's letter a few weeks earlier and I'd been searching for hers when I came upon you that day.'

'So they never got together?' My heart sinks, thinking of the lovers over half a century ago.

He grins. 'Who says?'

'Well it doesn't sound like …'

'When you have a few days off maybe we can go on a road trip? There's this little apple orchard run by an elderly couple called Elizabeth and George.'

'No!'

'Yes!'

It seems like a sign, like fate. If they can make it, we surely can. It feels as though the hall has a magic about it, helping couples find each other despite the obstacles in their path. Helping people find what they most need in life, whether that's love, friendship or acceptance.

'I can't believe you collect stamps?!' Wait until I tell Maya! We laugh and I slip into his arms again. 'I'll show you mine if you show me yours?'

'Are we talking stamp collections …?' he asks.

'Let's see how the date goes, eh? And then I'll tell you.'

With that, he kisses me once more and makes me forget all about love stories from another time as he breathes life into me, and our real-life love story starts in earnest. I've got a feeling I won't need the paddles again, not for a long, long time. Until I feel a peck at my ankle and let out a scream loud enough to wake the dead.

'Mother *clucker!*' I spring into Leo's arms.

'I really love this chicken,' he says, grinning.

Acknowledgements

A huge thank you to my Filipino friends and family for your patience with all my Pinoy questions and helping me bring the colourful Esterlita to life. I've wanted to write a Filipino character ever since I was first invited to sing karaoke and share a table full of food with my new Filipino family and friends, who took me under their wing, even though I can't sing and really shouldn't attempt dancing either. To them, none of that mattered – it's all about enjoying the performance!

I wanted to showcase how joyful and fun-loving (and always cheeky!) big-hearted Filipino people are, so I hope I managed to convey that with tell-it-like-it-is Esterlita, who was so much fun to write.

Esterlita shares so many traits taken directly from friends, from her love of karaoke, doing the duck face, and all those wonderful superstitions that I am still obsessed with learning about today. (My personal favourite: Jump into the New Year so you grow taller).

Special thanks to:

Gina, Mazel, Sharmaine and JM. Thanks for giving me such detailed descriptions and making me laugh!

Thanks to Jovelyn Aum Cabriles for all those feasts and karaoke sessions!

291

And to Jhem Sinalan Raisin, for the many messages over my early drafts and checking I had my facts straight.

To Lily Marcon-Perez, I couldn't have written this without you! Thanks for sharing all your stories and those of your friends with me. For always being there when I needed to clarify, and for the amount of fun we've had doing it all! I am counting down the days until that hubby of yours can whip us up a Filipino feast and I can sink into a proper food coma, instead of dreaming it about it ogling all your foodie pics! Thanks for making Esterlita who she is and for giving me so much material to work with. You're the best!

Keep reading for an excerpt from
Rosie's Travelling Tea Shop …

Chapter 1

'You're just not spontaneous enough, Rosie ...'

I've misheard, surely. Fatigue sends my brain to mush at the best of times but after twenty hours on my feet, words sound fuzzy, and I struggle to untangle what he's getting at.

It's just gone 2 a.m. on Saturday 2nd February and that means I'm officially 32 years old. By my schedule I should be in the land of nod, but I'd stayed late at work to spontaneously bake a salted caramel tart to share with Callum, hoping he'd actually remember my birthday this year.

He's never been a details man – we're opposites in that respect – so I try not to take it to heart, but part of me hopes this is all a prelude to a fabulous birthday surprise and not the brewing of a row.

'Sorry, Callum, what did you say?' I try to keep my voice light and swig a little too heartily on the cheap red wine I found in the back of the cupboard after Callum told me we needed to have a chat. Surreptitiously, I glance to the table beside me hoping to see a prettily wrapped box but find it bare, bar a stack of cookbooks. Really, I don't need gifts, do I? Love can be shown in other ways, perhaps he'll make me a delicious breakfast when we wake up ...

My eyes slip closed. With midnight long gone, my feet ache, and I'm weary right down to my bones. Bed is calling to me in the most seductive way; *come hither and sleep, Rosie*, it says. Even the thought of a slice of luscious ooey-gooey birthday tart can't keep me awake and *compos mentis*. But I know I must focus, he's trying to tell me something …

'Are you asleep?' The whine in his voice startles me awake. 'Rosie, please, don't make this any harder than it has to be,' he says, as if I'm being deliberately obtuse.

Make what harder – what have I missed? I shake my head, hoping the fog will clear. 'How am I not spontaneous? What do you even *mean* by that?' Perhaps he's nervous because he's about to brandish two airline tickets to the Bahamas. *Happy Birthday, Rosie, time to pack your bags!*

He lets out a long, weary sigh like I'm dense and it strikes me as strange that he's speaking in riddles at this time of the morning when I have to be at the fishmonger in precisely five hours.

'Look …' He runs a hand through his thinning red hair. 'I think we both know it's over, don't we?'

'Over?' My mouth falls open. Just exactly how long did my power nap last for? 'What … *us*?' My incredulity thickens the air. This does not sound *anything* like a birthday celebration, not even close.

'Yes, us,' he confirms, averting his eyes.

'Over because I'm not—' I make air quotes with my fingers '—*spontaneous* enough?' Has he polished off the cooking sherry?

My husband still won't look at me.

'You're too staid. You plan your days with military precision from when you wake to when you sleep, and everything in between has a time limit attached to it. There's no room for fun or frivolity, or God forbid having sex on a day you haven't sched-uled it.'

So I'm a planner? It's essential in my line of work as a sous-chef in esteemed Michelin-starred London restaurant Époque, and he should know that, having the exact same position in another restaurant (one with no Michelin stars, sadly). If I didn't schedule our time together we'd never see each other! And I wouldn't get the multitude of things done that need doing every single hour of every day. High pressure is an understatement.

'I … I …' I don't know how to respond.

'See?' He stares me down as if I'm a recalcitrant child. 'You don't even care! I'd get more affection from a pot plant! You *can* be a bit of a cold fish, Rosie.'

His accusation makes me reel, as if I've been slapped. 'That's harsh, Callum, honestly, what a thing to say!' Truth be told I'm not one for big shows of affection. If you want my love, you'll get it when I serve you a plate of something I've laboured over. That's how I express myself, when I cook.

It dawns on me, thick and fast. 'There's someone else.'

He has the grace to blush.

A feeling of utter despair descends while my stomach churns. How *could* he?

'Well?' I urge him again. Since he's dropping truth bombs left, right and centre, he can at least admit his part in this … this break-up. Hurt crushes my heart. I hope I'm asleep and having a nightmare.

'Well, yes, there is, but it's not exactly a surprise, surely? We're like ships that pass in the night. If only you were more—'

'Don't you dare say spontaneous.'

'—if only you were *less* staid.' He manages a grin. A *grin*. Do I even know this man who thinks stomping over my heart is perfectly acceptable?

He continues reluctantly, his face reddening as if he's embarrassed. 'It's just … you're so predictable, Rosie. I can see into your future, *our* future because it's planned to the last microsecond! You'll *always* be a sous-chef, and you'll *always* schedule your days from sun up to sun down. You'll keep everyone at arm's length. Even when I leave, you'll continue on the exact same trajectory.'

He shakes his head as though he's disappointed in me but his voice softens. 'I'm sorry, Rosie, I really am, but I can see it playing out – you'll stay resolutely single and grow the most cost-effective herb garden this side of the Thames. I hope you don't, though. I truly hope you find someone who sets your world on fire. But it's not me, Rosie.'

What in the world? Not only is he dumping me, he's planning my spinsterhood too? Jinxing me to a lonely life where my only companion is my tarragon plant? Well, not on my watch! I might be sleep-deprived but I'm nobody's fool. The love I have for him pulses, but I remember the other woman and it firms my resolve.

He sighs and gives me a pitying smile. 'I hate to say it, Rosie. But you're turning into your dad. Not wanting to leave the …'

'Get out,' I say. He is a monster.

'What?'

Cold fish, eh? 'OUT!' I muster the loudest voice I can.

'But I thought we'd sort who gets what first?'

'Out and I mean it, Callum.' I will not give him the satisfaction of walking all over me just because he thinks he can.

'Fine, but I'm keeping this apartment. You can—'

'NOW!' The roar startles even me. *You want to see me warm up?* 'LEAVE!'

He jumps from the couch and dashes to the hallway, where I see a small bag he's left in readiness, knowing the outcome of our 'quick chat' long before I did. With one last guilty look over his shoulder, he leaves with a bang of the door. He's gone just like that.

As though I'm someone so easy to walk away from.

Laying down on the sofa, I clutch a cushion to my chest and wait for the pain to subside. How has it all gone so wrong? There's someone else in his life? When did he find time to romance anyone?

Sure, I don't go out much, other than for work purposes, but that's because there's no bloody time *to* go out! I'm not like my dad, am I? No, Callum is using that as ammunition, knowing how sensitive I am to such a comparison.

The sting of his words burns and doubt creeps in. Am I not spontaneous enough? Am I far too predictable?

Admittedly I'd been feeling hemmed in, ennui creeping into everything, even my menu. Each day bleeding into the next with no discernible change except the *plat de jour*. Sure, my professional life is on track but lately even my enthusiasm for that has waned. I've had enough of tweezing micro herbs to last a lifetime. Of plating minuscule food at macro prices. Of the constant bickering in the kitchen. The noise, the bluster, the backstabbing. Of never seeing blue skies or the sun setting. Of not being able to sit beside my husband on the couch at a reasonable hour and keep my eyes open at the same time.

Is this my fault? Am I a cold fish? I like routine and order so I know where I fit in the world. Everything is controlled and organised. There's no clutter, mess, or fuss, or any chance I'll lose control of any facet of my life. That need to keep life contained is a relic of my childhood. Is my marriage now a casualty of that?

But he'd promised he'd love me for better or worse.

Am I supposed to hope he comes to his senses or to beg him to come back?

Sighing, I place a hand on my heart, trying to ease the ache. I could never trust him again. I'm a stickler for rules, always have been, and cheating, well … I can't forgive that.

But bloody hell, our lives had been all mapped out. Our first child was scheduled for conception in 2021. The second in 2023. And he's just blithely walking away from his children like that! Didn't he understand I would have given up my career for our future family? The career I'd worked so hard for! And I would have done it gladly, too.

Now this?

The gossip will spread like wildfire around the foodie world. My name embroiled in a scandal not of my choosing. It's taken me fifteen years to get to where I am in my career, and that's meant sacrificing a few things along the way, like a social life, and free time, real friendships. But that was all part of the bigger picture, the tapestry of our lives.

It hurts behind my eyes just thinking about it all.

And I mean to cry and wail and torment myself about the 'other woman', or force myself up off the couch and throw my lovingly baked birthday tart at the wall, or eat it all in one go as tears stream down my face – something dramatic and movie-esque – but I don't. Instead, I fall into a deep sleep, only waking when my alarm shrills at stupid o'clock the next day, and with it comes the overwhelming knowledge that I must leave London. At 32, this could be my rebirth, couldn't it?

Not spontaneous enough? Cold fish? Spinster? Like my dad? *I'll show you.*

Chapter 2

At Billingsgate Market the briny smell of seafood hardly registers. I dash to the fishmonger, rattle off my order, too distracted to make the usual small talk. John, the guy with the freshest seafood this side of Cornwall, notices my jittery state.

'What's up, Rosie? There's something different about you today.' He gives me a once-over as if trying to pinpoint the change.

'Oh,' I say, mind scuttling. 'I haven't had any tea.' My other great love. Making hand-blended teas for various moods. Wake-me-ups. Wind-me-downs. And everything in between. If I ever leave my job, I have a backup plan at least ... tea merchant!

John cocks his head. 'You don't look like you need it though, Rosie. You look alive.' He shrugs. 'And utterly different from this fella.' He points to a dead flounder whose glassy eye stares up at me as John lets out his trademark haw, while I flinch slightly at being compared to deceased marine life. He bags my order, promising to courier it on ice to Époque immediately.

Do I look alive?

As I make my way to the butcher to confirm my weekly order, it occurs to me. Shouldn't I be puffy-faced, red-eyed, fuzzy-headed from tossing and turning all night? Instead, I feel this sort of frenetic energy because I realise that I'm about to do something very out of character, bold and brave, and completely unexpected – what that entails, I'm still not quite sure, but the desire is there and I'm about to implement a huge change. *Shriek.*

I'm steadfast Rosie, I don't *do* change.

I'm going to prove to the world that I'm not staid. Not stuck in a rut. I'm going to surprise even Callum, by doing the opposite of what he expects because I know if I don't move on fast, I never will.

Being predictable has its disadvantages, and it's time I shook things up a bit. Jumped, as it were, into a new reality.

What that is though exactly, remains to be seen ...

When I think of my once heart-melting, lovely, red-headed husband my lungs constrict, so I push him from my mind as quickly as possible. As I walk, I repeat the mantra *do not fall apart, hold yourself together,* and promise myself I can wail in privacy later.

I visit the butcher at Borough Market, then the French boulangerie, and finally our fresh produce supplier before all my jobs are done and I'm ready to prepare for lunch service.

When I arrive at Époque, I find the restaurant manager crunching numbers, a steaming espresso in front of her untouched. I've always liked Sally; she's a sassy, funny Glaswegian, who chain smokes and is fantastic at her job.

'Coffee?' she says absently, fiddling with paperwork.

'And a chat,' I say, dumping my bag on the bench and joining her at the table.

'That sounds ominous.' Her eyes dart to me before she bustles to the coffee machine, which spits and hisses under her hand.

A headache looms. Am I about to make a huge mistake? I've been yearning for change for such a long time, but it's hard to tell if it's a lie I'm selling myself. Callum might have pushed me to act, but I'm not being impetuous, am I?

As worry gnaws away at me, outwardly I remain calm and busy, unwinding my scarf and taking in the restaurant. It's not often that I'm front of house. When I first started at Époque the décor was art nouveau, then it went on to have various makeovers, and right now it's industrial chic. Any successful London establishment must move with the times, so the *in* crowd doesn't become the *out* crowd.

And the kitchen is no different. I'm always looking for the next foodie sensation, the dish that will blow patrons' minds, get us write-ups and reservations booked solid for the next six months.

You name it, I've tried it. Molecular gastronomy, sensory gastronomy, *multi*-sensory gastronomy. While it's all very theatrical, and a feast for mind, body and spirit, there's times I just want to cook up a big, hearty bowl of comfort food without any flourishes – real, honest meals that will fill your belly and warm your heart. Alas, that's never going to happen in a Michelin-starred establishment like Époque.

Sally returns and places my tiny cup down. 'So, talk,' she says, staring me down. It's her no-nonsense attitude I love. She doesn't mince words, and you always know where you stand with her. Do her right, and you'll have a friend for life. Cross her and forget working in London again. Sally's been around forever and knows everyone there is to know in the industry. We get on well because she accepts me for who I am, a cookery nerd. That, and she's partial to my twice-cooked fromage soufflé.

'I'm officially handing in my notice,' I say, surprised by the confidence in my tone. With that sort of voice, I could almost fool myself into believing I know what I'm doing! What the hell *am* I doing?

Handing in my notice?

I hope my brain will catch up with my mouth, sooner rather than later.

Sally purses her lips and nods. 'And you don't think this is a knee-jerk reaction to what that despicable excuse for a husband has done to you?'

'You've heard *already*?' That's got to be a record, even for the likes of the London cookery establishment.

With an airy shrug, she tries to downplay it. 'You know what it's like. There were whispers about him a while back, but I didn't think they had any substance, hence why I never said anything.'

Just how long has the affair been going on? Were they having mad, passionate, *unscheduled* sex, while I worked? My heart bongos painfully inside my chest as though it's preparing for an attack. I will myself not to give into it. He doesn't deserve that. The rat. The pig. The cheating no-good husband. But oh, how it hurts.

'So who is she?' I hate asking but I need to know who he's replaced me with.

Sally takes a cigarette from her purse and lights up, despite the restaurant being a strictly non-smoking venue and the fact there's enough smoke alarms installed to have half of the London Fire Brigade here within minutes if they're set off.

When she doesn't answer I urge her on. 'It's OK, Sally, honestly.'

With a tut, she says, 'I want to wring his scrawny neck! The things that guy has put you through.'

I'm not a fan of wandering down memory lane. What point does looking back serve? Sally's never been keen on Callum; she's of the opinion he rides on my coat-tails. And I suppose for a while he did. And once, early on before we were married, he did sort of try to steal my job from under me and Sally hasn't forgotten that. I had until this very moment. Clearly I've used poor judgement in the whole choosing my husband department. Back then I had love hearts for eyes, and the world was a wondrous place.

'Who is she?' I prod.

'Khloe,' she says, with a reluctant sigh.

I shake my head. 'Why is it *always* the chef de partie? What a cliché. And Khloe with a K, for God's sake.' I'd met the exotic-eyed vixen at an industry party, and she actually introduced herself as 'Khloe with a K'. Who does that? Kardashians and husband-stealers, that's who.

That means Khloe worked *under* him, literally and figuratively. The thought leaves a bad taste in my mouth so I sip the bitter coffee to wash it away.

Sally leans closer, surveying me, as if waiting for me to cry, for one solitary tear to fall, or my bottom lip to wobble, something – anything – that shows her I'm not a robot, but I use all my willpower to remain calm and keep telling myself he does not warrant such histrionics. I'm a professional, dammit, and I won't be a sobbing mess at work. I suppose this control is what makes people think I'm aloof, steely, strange, when in fact it's the opposite, it's purely a protective instinct.

Inside my heart twists and shrinks, this pain probably doing me lifelong damage. Will my heart shrivel up altogether, leaving me as predicted – a lonely old spinster? Is rebound sex the answer? No, I will fall in love, not lust.

Hearing about Khloe firms my resolve. London is too toxic for me right now. I need to put some space between me and the city I've loved for so long.

Sally rubs my arm affectionately. 'The whispers will die down, you just need to keep focused, keep working and ride out the storm. Don't give up your career because of that snake in the grass. Please. You've worked harder than anyone I know. Don't let that go to waste.'

I take a moment to decipher my feelings. Eventually I say, 'It's not just him, Sally. It's everything. I've had this nagging feeling life is passing me by for a while now. I've been slogging it out here since I was seventeen. I'm in the prime of my life, and if I don't look up, I'll miss it. What Callum did might have been the catalyst, but it's not the entire reason. I promise I'm not making this decision lightly or *just* because of him.' As the words rolls off my tongue, I feel the truth in them. I've been unhappy for such a long time but put it down to overwork, life fatigue, the daily grind.

'Listen, you're giving me four weeks' notice, right?'

I nod.

'Take that time to think it over. I mean, *really* consider it. Instead of interviewing for a replacement straight away, Jacques can hold the fort alone for a month while you decide.'

Jacques is the celebrity chef de cuisine and won't like having to wait in limbo for my decision. He's an ogre to work under. In actual fact, I do his job so he can sashay about front of house before returning to the line and barking orders and cursing. As his star rose, I worked my way up behind him, and we have a sort of grudging respect for one another. While he has an ego the size of the *Titanic*, he lets me control the menu and I have complete freedom in the kitchen, even if he does take the credit.

'Thanks, Sally. I appreciate that. But I'm quite sure, so you can start interviewing.' No point pretending. They'll need a sous-chef so things run smoothly, and while I'm not super friendly with Jacques, I do like the other staff and would hate for them to have to carry the extra weight of my absence.

After one of Sally's breath-stealing hugs, I leave her and go to the kitchen to shuffle the fresh produce around and prepare the day's menus, hoping the kitchen staff won't pry, even though I bet they've woken up to gossipy text messages about me and Callum.

That's the culinary scene for you.

Dear Reader,

Thank you for shutting out the real world and diving into the land of fiction for a while. I hope you've journeyed far and wide and had an incredible adventure from the comfort of your own home.

Without you I wouldn't be able to spend my days talking to my invisible friends who become so real to me I name-drop them in conversations with my family, who all think I'm a little batty at the best of times ... so thanks again!

My sincerest hope is that you connected with my characters and laughed and cried and cheered them on (even the baddies who I hope redeemed themselves in the end) and that they also became your friends too.

I'd love to connect with you! Find me on Facebook @RebeccaRaisinAuthor or on Twitter @Jaxandwillsmum. I'm a bibliophile from way back, so you'll find me chatting about books and romance but I'm also obsessed with travel, wine and food!

Reviews are worth their weight in gold to authors, so if the book touched you and left you feeling 'happy ever after', please consider sharing your thoughts and I'll send you cyber hugs in return!

Love,
Rebecca x

Dear Reader,

We hope you enjoyed reading this book. If you did, we'd be so appreciative if you left a review. It really helps us and the author to bring more books like this to you.

Here at HQ Digital we are dedicated to publishing fiction that will keep you turning the pages into the early hours. Don't want to miss a thing? To find out more about our books, promotions, discover exclusive content and enter competitions you can keep in touch in the following ways:

JOIN OUR COMMUNITY:
Sign up to our new email newsletter: hyperurl.co/hqnewsletter
Read our new blog www.hqstories.co.uk
🐦 : https://twitter.com/HQStories
📘 : www.facebook.com/HQStories

BUDDING WRITER?
We're also looking for authors to join the HQ Digital family!
Find out more here:
https://www.hqstories.co.uk/want-to-write-for-us/
Thanks for reading, from the HQ Digital team

ONE PLACE. MANY STORIES

HQ

If you enjoyed *Escape to Honeysuckle Hall*, then why not try another delightfully uplifting romance from HQ Digital?

Katie Ginger
The Secrets of Meadow Farmhouse

RACHEL DOVE
The Second Chance Hotel

Rosie Chambers
Katie's Cornish Kitchen
It takes a village to mend a broken heart...

Aria's Travelling Book Shop
REBECCA RAISIN

The Little Bookshop of Love Stories
JAIMIE ADMANS

The Forget-Me-Not Bakery
A Port Landon Novel
CAROLINE FLYNN